PLAYING FAITH

A Novel by

P.E. YoungLibby

First Edition

ATOMIC TYGER

ISBN: 978-1-79-501992-7

PARENTAL ADVISORY:
The main character in this book experiences some intense and adult situations, including graphic violence, attempted rape, sex between consenting adults, torture, and child abuse.
Also, a dog gets hurt (not intentionally, though).
It may not be suitable for all readers.

If you enjoy this book, please give it a good review!

Also, if by some strange quirk of the Universe I managed to
channel some weird state secrets that violate National Security, or
hidden crimes that hit too close to home for somebody in power,
please don't kill me.

I made it all up. Honest.

"Grief is an artist of powers as various as the instruments on which he plays his dirges for the dead."

AMBROSE BIERCE

DEDICATION:

To my grandparents, who taught me love endures,
To my parents, who taught me love creates,
To Reid, who taught me that love is vulnerable,
To Otter, who taught me that love is play,
And to Military Brats all over the world.

Thank you all for your sacrifices.

CHAPTER ONE

"It's not the fall," Papa used to say, "but the ground that kills you." According to the Navy, he died in a HALO accident when I was fourteen, so I guess he knew what he was talking about. Trouble was, I'd been free-falling for six months, and I hadn't hit ground yet.

It wasn't that I wanted to self-destruct. More like I'd been scrambling to hold my life together, to set a good example for Chris. Since I'd never really had that great of control, anyway, watching him blow his brains out while tripping on CYBL kinda made me lose my grip. He was my little brother. I should have been able to save him.

Jim kept telling me it hadn't been my fault. Deep down, I knew he was right. He was always right. Sometimes I hated him for it, but only sometimes. He smoked cigarettes and didn't care for Kabalevsky and looked ridiculous in a tux; but he was my best friend, so I put up with his shortcomings. Besides, he could cook as well as he played music, and he never complained when I owed him money.

But Chris' suicide had torn some deep hole inside me that even Jim couldn't fill. Maybe, if he hadn't been gay, or I hadn't had breasts, things might have been different. If he'd been more than just a friend, he might have kept me from sailing off the deep end. But I doubt it.

Even if I hadn't spent all of January spiraling down into a black pit of guilt and despair, I'd still have shattered my right hand against Pinky Webster's jaw in February. I can't abide bullies. Or bigots. Sometimes you have to draw the line, no matter the pain. No matter the risk.

I felt sorry for Jim, though. We'd been playing together for three-and-a-half years, building up a reputation, expanding our repertoire, and the week after we score our first recording deal, I break three metacarpals and get thrown out of school.

He could have gone solo. He was good enough. But, for some stupid reason he stuck by me. When the V.A. hospital revoked my privileges because I wasn't a student anymore, Jim got Vic, a top-flight orthopedic specialist, to take me on for a nominal fee.

Since I'd been expelled from the dorm for what I'd done to Webster, and all my excess cash had gone into medical bills because the University wouldn't refund my tuition, I'd ended up living in my car. But Jim wouldn't allow that during the worst of the surgeries. He made me sleep on his couch, even though we got on each other's nerves a lot of the time. He was like that. A sucker for lost causes. He kept throwing me parachutes, hoping to slow my descent.

Or maybe he just couldn't bear to let the music die. He kept trying to line up auditions, even when my medical bills had gone to collections. He just wouldn't give up on me. On us.

This was how it all started. This was how I wound up sitting at a concert grand piano on the stage of Scott Foster's renowned Concerto Club, wiping the sweat from my palms while Jim did a last minute check of his synth. His hair was combed back with too much gel, his pale stick of a neck bracketed by the crisp black of his tux. He looked like an oil-slicked stork.

I took a deep breath, listening to the muted walla-walla of the crowd behind the closed curtains, the clink of china and glass as the waiters cleared the tables in preparation for the show. In preparation for us.

I still couldn't believe we were there, really there. I mean, the Concerto. Movie stars, politicians, the financial elite; everybody wanted to be seen in this oasis of gourmet food and classical music. Crystal glassware, fine china, gold-plated flatware, sustainably sourced candles on the tables. It was one of only seven restaurants in Southern California with one of those neo-tech, holographic décor systems.

Four of the other six were also owned by Scotty. Jim told me that Scotty had gotten some kind of national environmental award for saving all those trees and gypsum bushes by making the walls out of Mylar baffles instead of employing carpenters and plasterers to build out each restaurant's theme. It was a big deal to be here.

Admittedly, we were only filling in for some chamber musicians who had missed their flight in Zurich, but still, with this on our résumé, we had a shot at breaking into the big time. Or as big a time as classical musicians get.

"Thirty seconds," Lonny, the stage manager whispered from the wings. He cast a questioning glance at Jim, who returned a thumbs up, then turned and smiled at me, his warm, honey-brown eyes shining with anticipation.

His eagerness infected me, and for the first time since Chris had died, I thought that maybe Jim had done it, after all. Maybe he had saved me from myself. After five months of casts and splints and surgeries; endless weeks of physical therapy, I had a hope of redemption. I would savor this glorious, golden second chance, tear it open like a warm loaf of sourdough and consume it utterly. I owed it to Jim.

The stage lights dimmed, the noise behind the curtain winding down to a low murmur, then slipping into silence. My heart rose up in the expectant gloom. Adrenaline pumped through me, making me feel every form-fitting curve of my black suede mini-dress, every minute imperfection in the cool ivories beneath my fingers.

God, I was so hungry for this.

Jim and I locked gazes, breathing in at the same moment, and then the notes sliced through the darkness, the warm, mournful, resonant tones only a grand piano could make. Only I could make, sitting in front of a roomful of strangers, begging them to share with me, to let me belong, if just for tonight. If just for right now...

And Jim as the orchestra, his playful-serious-shy-mysterious harmonies. The human drama on two keyboards.

The stage lights flared to life and the curtains crawled back. People peered up from their plates, awed faces lit by flickering candles. They surrendered to me, let me into that secret part of themselves that was too vital for words, too complex for anything short of eighty-eight keys.

I lost myself in the music, in the communion, until the end of the set loomed. Jim glanced up, eyes sparkling.

I grinned back, alive again, burning with the need to express it, to show these people what I could really do. I gave Jim the signal, darting my gaze around as if pestered by an annoying insect. His jaw dropped. He shook his head, brow furrowed with concern.

Nothing strenuous, Vic had said, when I'd told him about the upcoming gig. The tendons aren't fully healed yet. Take it easy. Play some slow pieces. Adagios.

But adagios couldn't contain the shouting, kicking rhapsody within me, the laugh-out-loud fire in my veins. I nodded once, to let Jim know I was going ahead anyway, and dove headfirst into his transcription of "Flight of the Bumblebee." He struggled a split-second over the transition, and then we bounded over the keyboards like puppies in a sunny field.

My hand ran out of strength just as Rimsky-Korsakov ran out of music. There was an intense, breathless moment of silence, and then the audience began to clap: big, thunderous applause, whistles and shouts, glasses clinking.

I walked front and center and stood, basking in the glow, as Jim disengaged from the cocoon of synthesizer keys and joined me. He twined his arm with mine and gently cradled my spasming right hand against the dark leg of his tux as we took our first bow. The applause surged, and we bowed again, my lungs so full of exhilaration I got dizzy on the way up. When we finally left the stage, I had to wipe the corners of my eyes.

"Jeez, Rad, the 'Bumblebee?'" Jim griped, as soon as we hit the wings. "What the Hell were you thinking? You're gonna—"

"They loved us!" I peered through the teaser curtains into the main house for another glimpse of the crowd, shifting from foot to foot with a joy too intense to remain in one part of my body. I was here. And I had rocked it to the foundations. Nothing else mattered. "We were great! Did you see that? We're gonna knock 'em dead with the next set! We're gonna—"

"Rad," Jim held up my right forearm, shaking my palm in front of my nose. "There won't be any next set."

I stared blankly at my wrist, amazed to see it had already swollen to the diameter of a coffee mug. My ring and pinky fingers had gnarled into a kind of convulsive claw, my adrenaline level still too high for me to actually feel it. "Oh. shit."

"What were you thinking? You know what the doctor said!"

"I'll ice it," I offered desperately. "It's forty minutes between sets, maybe the swelling will go down enough to—"

"Rad, there's no way you're playing again tonight."

"Sure I will. I'll ice it, take some anti-inflammatories, and if that doesn't work, we'll do the Left-Handed Concerto."

"I don't have music for the Left-Handed Concerto."

"Don't need it. I know it by heart. Been playing it for the last five months."

"You gonna play the orchestral sections, too?" He glared at me, frustrated, accusatory. "I don't have the chip for that arrangement. And there's no time to change all those settings manually."

"I can ice it," I repeated, the hope dying within me. There was no way Lonny would hire us back after giving him only half-a-show on our first night. Without the Concerto, there'd be no other offers. No gigs, no tours, no recording contracts. Not only had I dive-bombed myself into obscurity, I'd taken Jim with me. I sighed and looked away, wondering why he didn't just unload on me then and there. If I'd had to deal with me, I would have kicked my ass.

"You, uh..." I cleared my throat. "You have the chips for Scriaben, don't you? You could just set the synth on auto, do the piano without me."

His anger melted into that solemn look, the one with the brows arching melancholy over soulful brown eyes. If he grew a beard, he'd look just like those pictures of Jesus you see in mortuaries. "I'm going to have to."

Something lurched inside me and tore away from its moorings. I nodded, figuring it was just as well. Better I cut him loose now than drag him all the way to the impact zone.

"I'm sorry, Rad."

"It's okay. I mean, it's my screw up, right? It's okay."

We stood there, facing each other in miserable silence, and then Jim sighed and turned away. "I'll tell Lonny."

I watched him thread his way around the shadowy jumble of cables and curtains that made up the backstage, trying to work up enough courage to wade through the crowd out front to the bar and ask Tina for a rag filled with ice. How was I going to smile and talk happy with defeat burning through me like white phosphorus?

A hand fell heavily on my shoulder and I turned to find Sloan glaring at me. He worked the stage because Lonny said he was too ugly to work up front.

If you asked me, he was too ugly to work anywhere. Missing half an ear, with a scar on his chin that made him look like he had two sets of lips, and three little dots tattooed in the web of his hand. To top it all off, his greasy black hair was gathered up into a scraggly man bun. Plus, he dressed like he was some sort of a hard-core gangster, and not the backstage security man for the most prestigious piano bar in Beverly Hills.

Why Scotty would ruin the ambiance by hiring this guy, I didn't know. But he did. Probably his brother-in-law, or something. Which meant I shouldn't groin-kick the cockroach if Jim wanted to put this gig on his resume'.

"What?" I prodded, sloughing his hand away. I don't like people touching me. Especially not a gum-crust like Sloan.

"Scotty wants to see you."

"Scotty?"

"Scott Foster."

My breath caught. "*The* Scott Foster?"

"The boss himself."

I grinned, spinning away toward the stage manager's desk, where Jim and Lonny were speaking earnestly in low tones. "I'll get Jim."

"No." Sloan caught me by the elbow. "Just you. The fag stays here."

"Don't call him a fag," I warned, twisting out of his grasp. "And don't touch me again."

That axe-murderer smile must have crept across my face, because he stepped back, unsettled by the change in me. Most people didn't expect a mere pianist to radiate such seething violence. Then again, most people didn't know my father had been the commander of the most elite anti-terrorist task force in the U.S. Armed Forces. And from the moment of my birth, Papa had obsessed over the idea I might follow in his footsteps. I only got to play with Mozart when I'd finished my karate for the day.

"Mr. Foster wants you," Sloan repeated, leering at my cleavage, as if that would keep him from looking spooked. "Just you."

"Great," I mumbled, knowing what that meant. Scott Foster was a busy man. Influential. Owned an airline, five nightclubs, and half a recording studio. If the music had impressed him, he'd have wanted to meet us both. But if he wanted me alone, then the only thing which had impressed him was my smokin' hot Italian good looks and the way I filled out my dress.

Sloan raised an eyebrow. "You goin', or do I gotta escort you?"

"I'm going." I slipped by him, heading out the stage door toward the main house. This sucked. Even if my hand didn't hurt like Hell, I couldn't schmooze to save my life. Jim called it smart-asspergers.

The crowd slowed me as I reached the end of the corridor. The house was packed, every table full. And the décor...

The Concerto was the first venue on the West Coast to install holographic décor, but I'd never been in here with the projectors turned on. I gaped at the walls and ceiling, marveling at how the acoustically engineered Mylar baffles and deflectors were now rococo panels of naked, garlanded cherubs blowing horns and playing harps in an orgy of gilt and uvula pink, like someone had vomited Goldschlager and Pepto-Bismol all over the place. Lonny said the design was an exact replica of an eighteenth-century Belgian palace ballroom, but I took it as undisputed proof that you don't have to live in modern-day America to have more money than sense.

The crowd pressed around me, thick and happy. People glanced up, smiling in awe and appreciation as I passed their tables on my way to the office door. I smiled back, feeling incredibly out-of-place. I couldn't get used to the idea that they'd all paid a two hundred dollar cover charge to come here and listen to me, a scrappy, no-class, Navy brat who had the audacity to take Beethoven's music and make it her own.

And they had loved it. Hell, I had loved it, but now that my stage high had worn off, and I actually felt the sharp spike of pain shooting up my right arm from fingertips to elbow, I wondered if that little romp had caused any permanent damage. I hoped not. God knows, I didn't have enough money for another operation.

I made a detour to the bar, to see if I could get some ice, but before I made it to the rail a man's hand fell onto the epaulette of my suede matador jacket, partially trapping my shoulder-length hair.

"Well, Radiana Damiano!" a gruff baritone declared enthusiastically. "What a terrific performance!"

I turned to see who it was and straightened up, like a jarhead snapping to attention. Scotty Foster stood there, reaching out to me. He had blonde hair graying at the temples, deepening wrinkles in a yacht-tan face, and deep-set hazel eyes. He wore a dark blue Brooks Brothers suit that fit him like a sausage casing. He was exactly like his picture in the lobby, the one I was going to deface with a scar and moustache before Jim pulled the plug with a lecture about acting juvenile. Maybe I was, but at least I had a sense of humor.

"You're fantastic," Scotty continued, leaning toward me. The sour weight to his breath told me he'd been drinking. His gaze lingered just above the top button of my jacket. "Impressive."

I gave him a wooden smile, unbalanced by his enthusiasm. "Glad you liked it, Mr. Foster."

He rested his hand on my right forearm. "You've got a quick pair of hands there. Let me see them."

I stifled a cry, trying to jerk away as he squeezed my injured wrist, but he just dug his fingers in, an odd grin on his face, like he enjoyed my discomfort. He was surprisingly strong, even if he did wear suits that were too small for him.

"Can't let talent like yours get away." He winked, his grip twisting around into a veiled come-along. "Come in my office. We'll talk."

I suddenly found myself stumbling after him through the door to the club office, murmuring little "uh-uh-oh's" in time to the screaming in my muscles and tendons. I really should have thumped him, but he was Scott Foster. He could kill Jim's career with a single phone call. "Uh, Mr. Foster, I—"

"Shut up." He slammed the door behind him and shoved me toward an oxblood leather wingchair. "Sit."

I flopped into the chair, cradling my hand in my lap and making owie noises as I eased my fingers flat. I tried to rub the fire out of my palm. "What the Hell was that about?"

"You tell me." Scotty glared down at me. A row of flat screens on the wall behind him cast a flickering glow across his shoulders and threw demonic shadows across his face. "You know what I'd like to do to you? For all the shit you've put me through?"

"What shit?"

"You think you can change your hair and eyes, dump your Houston accent, and I'll stumble right by you? I'd recognize you anywhere, Faith."

"Who's Faith?"

He grabbed me by the hair and pulled my head back, his hazel gaze flaring with a savage, sadistic light. "You are. That bastard Dutchman sent you here to stab me in the back again."

"I don't stab people," I explained patiently, trying to weasel out of his grasp. "I'm Rad Damiano. A pianist. I play music."

He gripped me tighter. "That was all rigged. The only C-note a toneless whore like you could hit is the green kind."

Calling me toneless was like calling me a child molester. "Give me a piano and I'll hit your note, you psycho-ceramic sonuvabitch." I spit in his face and planted the heel of my pump in his stomach. My kick sent him staggering back into the desk.

He grunted and wiped the saliva from his cheek. An awareness dawned in his eyes that maybe I wasn't who he thought I was. "Anybody here see you play?"

"Sure. Lonny hired me. Jim and I both auditioned for him. Don't you know how your own club works?"

"And Tina? The bartender? She see you?"

"The whole rehearsal." I jutted my chin out. "Go ask her about me. 'As good as Ashkenazy,' she said. Ask her."

His face reddened. His lip lifted in a sneer. "I will." He looked over at a partially open connecting door behind the desk and shouted, "Villalobos! Come see what I've got!"

A Latino man appeared in the doorway, nursing a snifter of clear liquid. He was short, with broad cheekbones, a mahogany brown complexion, and wavy black hair streaked with gray. A large diamond stud earring graced his left ear, and he was dressed like an upscale mobster: black silk shirt, white silk tie, charcoal gray pants, and a black, preacher-cut leather jacket, even though it was the first day of July. Funny how styles never changed much for politicians and mobsters.

"This is Faith." Scotty gestured at me. "Watch her."

Villalobos grinned, the way a mortician grins at a page full of obituaries. "Sure."

"I'm not Faith," I said. As if anybody was listening.

Still grinning, Villalobos ghosted toward me with the same fluid self-assurance as the Spec-war assassins my father used to train. A string of be-carefuls scraped along my spine and drummed forebodings into my skull. This guy was dangerous. This guy was deadly.

Even wealthy, powerful Scotty moved away at the man's approach, like a rabbit dodging the shadow of an eagle circling overhead.

It cooled me down a bit. A high-caliber hardliner appearing in a place like this—as Scotty's guest, no less—meant that the Concerto was not all cherubs and harps. The way Villalobos looked at me told me I was way too close to falling into whatever dark fate he represented. This man, this moment would change my life.

"Don't let her leave," Scotty commanded. He spun around and stormed out into the hall, whumping the door so hard against its hinges that it slammed shut on its return.

The room grew quiet. The only sounds were the faint hum of the electronics and my leather skirt squeaking against the leather chair as I massaged my wrist. Villalobos regarded me with glistening, obsidian eyes. He sipped from his snifter, and then placed it on the mahogany end table.

"I'm not Faith," I told him, frightened at his interest in me. "I'm just a musician."

He nodded and eased his butt onto the arm of my chair. His legs stretched out in front of mine, blocking an escape. He smelled of tobacco and leather and expensive cologne. "You play extremely well," he said, with the silken hint of a Colombian accent. "That adagio, in particular, was very moving."

I blinked, surprised. Most gangsters think Albioni is a type of pasta. "Thanks."

He nodded again, then twisted his head to watch the screens. His jacket fell open just enough to reveal the butt of a pistol peeking out of a shoulder holster. On the monitor behind him, Scotty plowed through the crowd and slammed his hand on the bar, gesturing for Tina's attention.

Villalobos watched them speak for a while, pretending to be interested in what happened on the screen. I knew he was just baiting me, trying to sucker me into grabbing for his gun and bolting for freedom. It was in the blatant sprawl of his limbs, the subtle tensions of his body. His hands and arms were positioned for instant defense, his weight perfectly balanced for combat. This guy knew what he was doing.

But, then, so did I. Papa had made sure of that. And my fancy footwork may have put Webster and his cronies down for the count, but there was no way I'd be fool enough to take Villalobos on. All the karate chops in the world won't stop a bullet.

"Can I have some ice?" I asked softly. "My wrist hurts. See? It's swollen."

He regarded me for a long moment, then stepped away from my chair and pointed across the room, where a bar ran along the wall opposite the vid monitors. "There's a bucket over there."

I walked slowly to the bar, careful not to make any sudden moves. A mahogany bucket sat on the marble bar top next to the sink. I popped the lid up and found a mound of half-melted ice cubes. As I reached for a drawer handle, Villalobos cleared his throat.

I stopped short. "I'm looking for a towel," I explained to his hard stare. "To wrap the ice up."

"Just stick your hand in the bucket and bring it over here."

I did as he suggested, resuming my seat in the chair. The pain flared with a cold fire from the initial shock, then dulled slowly. "So," I said, a tad quavery, because Villalobos continued to stare at me. Didn't this guy ever blink? "Do you work for Scotty?"

He chuckled, without humor. "No. We're...acquaintances."

"What's he got against Faith?"

"She stole some money from him."

"A lot?"

"Not really. About forty million."

I coughed, astounded. How could anybody think I'd stolen that kind of money? Even if I had, why would I come back to the scene of the crime? "Guess I sort of look like her, huh?"

"Maybe." He shrugged, slipped a cigar out of the humidor on the desk, and lit it up. "I never met her."

The room filled with the heavy, sweetish scent of cigar smoke. Funny, how smoking laws never apply to rich club owners and their guests. He glanced up at the monitors, where Scotty was now elbowing his way through the crowd toward the lighting booth at the west end of the house. Which meant Tina had probably told him I was kosher, but he didn't believe her, so he was going to ask Lonny about me, too.

Villalobos took a few long puffs, then waved his cigar at the light booth door. "When Scotty returns, he'll kill you."

"I'm not Faith."

"Doesn't matter. He'll kill you just for looking like her." He grinned that mortician's grin and tapped his temple. "Love does that to a man. Scrambles his wetware."

"How would you know?"

He shrugged. "I'm married." I must have looked dubious, because he showed me the ring.

Scotty was out of the booth, now. He waved Nick, the head bouncer, toward him. They conferred for a few moments, and then Nick toggled his radio and spoke discreetly into the mic.

"Scotty won't kill me. I mean, look all at the money he's got. He's not dumb enough to leave a bloodstain on the carpet."

Villalobos nodded. "You're absolutely right. That's why he's massing all those bouncers and bodyguards out there." He gestured to the monitor, which showed at least five big, burly types congregating around Scotty. "He'll have them pin you down and choke you out. Then they'll toss you in a van and drag you to one of Scotty's warehouses. That way, he can kill you slow. He likes that, when they scream. I hear he even records it."

The skin along my spine goose-pimpled as I remembered the sadistic glint in Scotty's eyes. Some part of me was starting to believe this story. Not the killing part, of course, but what was to keep Scotty's bouncers from giving me the bum's rush?

My getting thrown out of a place like the Concerto in front of the nightly bigwigs was sure to kill Jim's career. After all, hadn't he recommended me? Even though I'd grown used to being coldcocked by the hand of Fate, there was no way Jim deserved such humiliation. He had talent. He had drive.

Villalobos saw the fear tighten my face and grinned, the hard lines of his cheeks softening as the smoke trailed out of his nostrils. "Looking for another line of work?"

I frowned, imagining all the humiliating things a man like him might ask for. "I'm not that kind of girl."

"It's not that kind of job." He reached into his breast pocket and held out what looked at first like a plastic bag of foil-wrapped chocolate coins.

He set them into my hand. Way too heavy for candy, I realized they were actually those new 5D data storage discs. Jim's boyfriend Richie had been going on about them, since he'd been working with them at the Computer Science Lab at the University. They could each store a petabyte, whatever that was.

I examined them, fumbling them around with my good hand. There were thirteen. They were solid glass, each slightly larger than a quarter and three times as thick. Twelve of the disks were shrink-wrapped in gold Mylar, like pirate doubloons. One was shrink-wrapped in silver Mylar, with a five-digit number written on it with black Sharpie. "Are they blank?"

"Doesn't matter. I'll pay you ten thousand dollars to walk out with them. Just leave. Right now. Before Scotty gets back. Bring them to the info booth at Union Station, at noon tomorrow, and I'll give you the money. Cash."

I gaped at him. Nobody gets ten grand for delivering blank 5D discs, no matter how cutting edge the tech might be. This had to be some sort of set up.

He took my silence for awe, and leaned in with a conspiratorial whisper: "You know who I am?"

"Sure. You're a music critic. For the Gangster Gazette."

He sniffed and regarded his cigar. The brown skin over his jaw pulsed with tension. "You always such a smart-ass?"

"Only when strange men proposition me."

"Do we have a deal?"

"I don't think so."

"It's easy money," he said, face going hard.

"That's the point." I held the baggie out to him.

He took it, and locked gazes with me for a long moment, gauging my resolve. Then he sighed and glanced over at the monitors, where Lonny was now gesturing to Scotty to calm down and disperse the bouncers. Scotty shook his head and pushed Lonny away.

The next thing I knew, my view was blocked by the gun Villalobos was holding to my forehead. "I think," he suggested pleasantly, "that you and those discs should leave now."

I nodded, too stunned to do anything but draw my hand out of the ice bucket and clutch the baggie against my belly with both my forearms. It was probably only a 9mm, but Christ, that pistol looked big, the end of the muzzle dark and cavernous.

"Union Station," Villalobos admonished me, tracking me with the pistol as I headed for the door. "Tomorrow. Don't forget. And don't lose them. I want all thirteen."

I nodded again, afraid to look behind me. He wouldn't shoot me in the back, would he? I didn't know.

Luckily, Scotty was nowhere in sight, so I made it safely down the corridor, through the stage door, and into the backstage gloom. I didn't see Jim anywhere, but the way my heart was pounding, I wasn't sure if I'd make any sense, anyway, so I just tucked the baggie into my purse, slung the strap over my shoulder, and hurried out of the dressing room.

Everybody was busy preparing for the next set, so nobody noticed me slinking toward the back door. Just walk out, get in my car, and drive away. Simple. Easy. Just leave.

Except, I stumbled headlong into Sloan as I rounded the last teaser. He made a grab for me. I ducked away instinctively and shuffled back into the curtain.

"What do you think you're doin'?" He slipped a double-edged knife out of his sleeve. "Boss don't want you goin' nowhere."

"Oh, Hell." I spun around and sprinted back through the curtains, hoping to find a broom handle to keep his dagger at bay. Sloan raced after me. He body slammed me into the door of an unused dressing room. The latch gave way, and we swung inside. I tried to dip down and let his momentum force him past me, but his fingers had hooked into the epaulette on my shoulder. He pulled me with him, yanking me off-balance as I side-stepped and planted my heel in his knee.

He yelped and let go of me, twisting around to jab the knife at my throat. I ducked under his striking arm and kicked an awkward sweep of his ankles. My foot glanced off his shin. He kept his balance, slicing the blade at me again. I jerked away, but my purse strap caught on the arm of a chair. I fell to one knee. He froze for a instant as he saw the discs in my purse. He grabbed the baggie. So did I. The plastic shredded between us.

The discs flew up and rained on my shoulders and chest before falling down to roll in circles on the hardwood floor. We both looked at them for a moment, then Sloan threw another stab at me. My right hand flew up to block.

A gun boomed behind me, close enough for me to feel the heat of the discharge, and a flower of blood and bone erupted out of my palm. The bullet had ripped through my knuckles on its way to Sloan's heart.

In the sudden, awful quiet, Sloan clutched the hole in his chest, whimpered once, and then crumpled to the floor. The knife dropped from his dead fingers. The blade teetered on the edge of the chair arm, then clunked through the rungs to the floor. I watched it, unwilling to look at the bloody slab of meat that had been my hand.

Oh, God, it was ice and fire. I couldn't think, couldn't move. I'd just gotten it fixed, and now—

Villalobos closed the door quickly, gun still smoking in his hand. He squatted next to Sloan's body and felt for a pulse.

Satisfied, he drew his fingers from Sloan's neck, then turned to me. His gleaming black gaze roamed over the blood spilling from my injured hand, lingered on my body, moved up to my face. "Sorry," he said, pointing his gun at me and tucking the scattered 5D discs back into my purse. "But I have to take you out."

He was gonna kill me.

I knocked his pistol away with my good forearm, flinging blood into his eyes as I scrambled past him towards the door. Blinded, Villalobos fell back with a curse. I rabbited through the wings towards the stage. My hand...

God, my hand was ablaze, the front of my skirt all hot with blood.

"Rad?" Jim smiled at me from within his shroud of synth keys. "Guess what? Lonny said that it was okay if you—" He broke off as his gaze fell on the butcher basket at the end of my arm. "Oh my God," he whispered, struggling to get free of the synth cables and come to me. "What happened to—?"

"Hide, Jim. *Hide.*" I bolted past him, through the darkness of the opposite wings and out the back door.

"Rad, wait!"

I tumbled out into the night, throwing myself into my car. I depressed the pedals with my feet and hit the start button with my left index finger, grateful to whoever had invented the keyless ignition. The Mazda roared to life. I slammed it into gear with my bloody wrist, ignoring the streamers of fire raging through my right arm. I pulled a partial J-turn out of the lot, smoking the tires as I accelerated up the alley.

As I blew through the red light at Camden and Wilshire, I wondered if Papa had felt this way when his parachute had failed and he saw the earth rushing up to meet him.

After six months of free-fall, I'd finally hit ground.

CHAPTER TWO

I wrapped an old Hollywood Bowl program around my hand to splint it and staggered woozily out of the Mazda. I fumbled for the keyfob in my purse, thinking to lock up, only to drop it in the footwell. Screw it. I'd get it later. The adrenaline rush had worn off, and now every little movement was another hammer blow.

I staggered along. The two hundred yards across the parking lot to the emergency entrance of County General seemed like an impossible distance. If I'd been thinking more clearly, I would have tried to get closer, but blood had made the shifter knob too slick and I'd stalled the Mazda coming into the lot. Rather than get her going again it had seemed easier just to coast into a parking slot. One of the few times I wished I'd gotten an automatic.

I tottered across the ominous blacktop, fueling myself with the knowledge that County General was in a particularly crime-infested area of town. Passing out here would be like anointing myself with chum and diving into a tank full of sharks.

My military dependent privileges had been revoked when I got kicked out of school, so the VA hospital was out. And Vic's hospital was in the Valley, way too far for me to drive in this condition. At least I'd be safe here. For a while, anyway. Villalobos wasn't stupid enough to be arrested for Sloan's murder, but even if the police did detain him, he was bound to have his gangster friends sweeping the hospitals, looking for me. My only hope was to get treatment and get out of here before his people found me.

When I reached the automatic doors, the security guard frowned at me. Her expression flashed with both suspicion and concern: Suspicion at the slick paper hiding my hand; concern at the blood dripping off the pages, splattering across my legs as I walked.

"Can I help you?" she said, peering carefully down the center of my makeshift splint, like I might be concealing some kind of weapon. "Whoof." She recoiled at the sight, shaking her head. "Through here."

She took hold of my good arm and steered me through a set of windowed double doors into the emergency room waiting area. She left me there, in front of a squat, washed-out woman with a recessed chin and a mole on her cheek. She wore pink scrubs dotted with teddy bears and eyed the blood trickling out of the magazine and dripping off my skirt and then stared at my face. "How long ago were you injured?"

I shrugged. "Fifteen, twenty minutes ago."

"And the bleeding hasn't stopped?"

I shook my head, then sighed and blinked hard, fighting to keep my head clear. I had a high pain threshold, but this thing was really starting to hurt.

She regarded the rows of seats which lined the wall behind me, her gaze traveling over the rag-tag collection of people awaiting treatment for broken arms and knocked-out teeth and various other injuries. A decision drove the sag from her shoulders. She stood up and buzzed me through into the emergency room area. "Follow me."

She guided me toward a Daliesque maze of green curtains. We moved through the wall of fabric and into a large room lined with draped cubicles. A chorus of disembodied screams and moans sounded all around me, punctuated by the cool, rational voices of various nurses and orderlies. She led me into a cubicle, patted the clean sheets of a gurney. "C'mon up here."

I clambered up with her help, feeling faint and queasy.

The nurse checked my pulse with her fingers over my good wrist. Her gloves felt warm on my skin, and, in an odd way, comforting. "How did you get hurt?

"Uhmmm..." I wasn't sure what to tell her. What was a good lie? By law, the police had to investigate all gunshot wounds. And I wasn't sure I wanted the cops to find me in possession of whatever contraband Villalobos had foisted off on me. For ten grand on delivery, these discs had to be mega-incriminating.

"Freak accident." My voice sounded a lot more unsure than I wanted it to. "Helium tank. I was at a birthday party and the top just blew off when I turned the crank."

The nurse nodded and tore a package of gauze open, packing it gently against the wound. I moaned anyway, gritting my teeth and closing my eyes until she finished.

When I opened them, I saw a sallow faced, stringy haired guy in green scrubs standing in front of me. He held a battered County issue tablet in front of him like a prayer book. "I need your ID."

I fished around in my purse. It took a while. After the Webster incident I had gotten very good at left-handing things, but the contents were sticky with blood, and the 5D discs got in the way of finding the money clip that held my driver's license, VA card and student ID. I dropped it on his tablet. He picked it up like it might contaminate him through his latex gloves, then swiped my driver's license through the reader attached to the edge of the tablet.

My name, image, birthdate, and former dorm address flashed on the screen. About ten seconds later, some proprietary hospital software dug into some electronic repository of creditworthiness, and all the numbers that made up my financial vital signs appeared. He stared at the numbers. "Damiano?"

"Yes," I said, as the nurse took my purse away and sliced my once gorgeous black suede Matador jacket from the injured wrist all the way up to the armpit. She peeled it back and shucked it off my good arm. I hated seeing that. It had been one of my favorite jackets. Cost a good three hundred dollars, too.

"Radiana Damiano?" the clerk asked.

"Yes," I said again. How hard could my name be?

"Who's your insurance with?"

"Nobody." Since the V.A. had canned me, I'd been denied by all the private policies I'd applied for, and I didn't qualify for the low-income policies because they said I had money in some bank account I never heard of, opened at a branch in a state I had never been in.

"What's your Medi-Cal number?"

"Don't have one. Not a California resident."

"But, this your correct address? In Westchester?"

"Yeah," I lied, not up to the whole sordid explanation as to why I was homeless.

He frowned at the readout on his tablet. "There's not enough money in your account to cover a major surgery. And your credit lines are tapped out."

I stared at him. Why was I sweating so bad when my body was a block of ice? "I don't want major surgery. Local anesthetic. No general. I just want the bleeding stopped."

He looked at me dubiously, then glanced toward the nurse. Her frown pulled her mole down with disapproval. "Miss," her voice was calm and measured, as if I were threatening suicide, "I really don't think you should be—"

"By law you have to treat me, even without insurance. I want the bleeding stopped, and then I want you to splint it. Just fix me up enough so I won't croak on my way to my own doctor."

"Who's your doctor?" the clerk asked, fingers poised over his virtual keypad.

"None of your business," I grouched. No way I wanted those gangsters tracing me to Vic. Bad enough I'd left Jim to fend for himself at the club.

"We can get your doctor to come here," the nurse offered. "You're in shock. If you move around right now, you could go into cardiac arrest. Give us your doctor's name and we'll—"

"No. I'm twenty-three years old. I don't have to stay here if I don't want to. You have to treat me, then let me go."

The nurse sighed, then nodded resignedly at the clerk. "Give her what she wants."

He digested this. Took him forever. Lobotomies must be a prerequisite for anybody who works hospital admissions. "Fine." He called a form up on his screen and handed me a stylus. "This is a Promise to Pay."

I signed it and pushed the thing back to him.

"And this one." He changed the screen and held it up for me to sign. "It's a release form, stating that you have specified minimum emergency treatment, only."

I signed that one, too, the effort making me dizzy. My ears rang. I felt cold.

The clerk checked over the forms, then wrapped a printed Tyvek bracelet around my good wrist and returned my driver's license to me. He disappeared behind the wall of curtains surrounding the cubicle.

"Could you hand me my purse?" I asked the nurse, gesturing to the bloody lump of black leather sitting next to my ruined jacket. She looked up from wrapping the blood pressure cuff around my good arm and caught the strap, slinging it over to drop in my lap.

"Thanks," I mumbled, tucking my license underneath all of the 5D discs. What was I going to do with them? And what about Scotty? Did he have anything to do with this? What if they were Scotty's to begin with? Is that why Villalobos wanted me to leave with them, he was stealing them from the club?

I moaned, feeling the noose tighten around my neck. Scotty was bound to be looking for me, if only because he was so convinced I was Faith. What if the 5D discs were his, and he found me before Villalobos did? Here I was, holding even more evidence to convince him I was Faith, out to stab him in the back.

Panic drew an icy blade down my spine. My fear dulled the pain throbbing up my arm. Once they got their contraband back, Scotty and Villalobos both had a vested interest in keeping me quiet.

Permanently.

If I hid the 5Ds, they would have to keep me alive to find out where they were. That might convince them to let me go.

"Hmmmn." The nurse slipped the blood pressure cuff from my good arm, then strapped it around the forearm above my injured hand, pumping it up until the pressure grew painfully uncomfortable. I realized belatedly that she was using it to restrict the blood flow to the wound. "Don't move. I'll be back with the doctor." She slipped past the wall of green curtains.

I sighed, glancing around for a likely place to stash the discs. Everything around me looked too obvious. Too easy to trace me to this cubicle. I tore the blood pressure cuff off and lurched away from the gurney. Unsteady but determined, I slipped my purse over my shoulder and pawed one-handed through the curtains into the center of the room.

An orderly looked up from his mop as I stumbled by. "Can I help you?" He was more surly than concerned. Even with the gauze, I'd dripped blood on his clean floor.

"Uhmm," I rearranged the program around my hand so that the blood dripped into my purse, instead. "Where's the bathroom?"

"Why don't you use a bedpan?"

"They're undignified. Where's the bathroom?"

"Over there." He pointed toward another double door. "Across the hall, second door on the left."

I moved carefully past him. Double automatic doors opened at my approach, revealing a corridor of linoleum leading past a series of numbered doors. I tottered down the line until I reached the ladies' restroom and ducked inside.

Faint and trembling, I leaned up against the white tile beside the door, concentrating on a single melodic line from Beethoven's *Appassionata*, filling my head with it to crowd out the relentless pain and the leaden fatigue which threatened to buckle my knees. It was a trick I'd learned early on, a way of removing myself from my mother's capricious rages. With the music, I could block out anything: her voice, the extension cord, even the cigarettes.

When the dizzy spell passed, I staggered to the nearest stall, closing the door behind me. I'd wanted to hide the 5Ds in the paper dispenser, but this one was broken open, barely clinging to the wall by half-a-hinge. But there, bolted on the wall behind the toilet, was a paper seat liner dispenser. Hurray for California OCD.

Relieved, I fished a few of the discs out of my purse. Using one of the seat liners, I wiped each Mylar wrapping free of blood, then dropped the disc between the painted rim of the dispenser and the cardboard package insert. Each one clunked lightly against the metal dispenser bottom after disappearing from sight.

Repeating the process, I emptied my purse of the rotten little things, then threw the bloody seat liner in the toilet and flushed it away. Feeling immensely unburdened, I started back. Had to return to the gurney before the nurse brought the doctor.

I made it all the way to the center of the cubicle room, but couldn't remember which had been mine. Bewildered, I stood there, with the smell of blood and hospital all around me, suddenly more frightened than I'd been all night. Throbbing spikes exploded up my arm and smacked starbursts against the backs of my eyes. A few of the patients waiting in the chairs along the wall stared at me. "Don't see why they took her before me," groused a red-faced man holding a bag of ice to his ankle. "She can still walk."

"Can I help you?" the orderly with the mop said, this time approaching me with concern.

I just stared at him, suddenly overwhelmed by all that had happened to me. I had no idea what to tell him, no idea what to do. In that one moment, it had all hit me. It had all become real: The gunshot. Sloan's murder. Villalobos.

Despair tumbled through me, hot tears welling up in my eyes.

"Miss..." The orderly dropped his mop. He put his hands on my shoulders and eased me towards a cubicle that looked like all the other cubicles. "I think you should lie down, now."

I nodded slowly, fighting the lump in my throat, the pain and exhaustion bleeding the strength from my limbs. My teeth chattered. My head buzzed. It seemed like I was looking at him through a long tunnel. No. Can't pass out. Hang on. Hang on. Can't afford to black out.

Papa could have made it through this. Papa could've made it through anything. Except, of course, whatever had really killed him.

But I wasn't Papa. Just as the orderly pulled the curtain back, a wall of red flared up inside my skull, a howling shower of sparks. My knees melted away, the orderly's hands dug into my biceps as I fell spinning into a warm, dark void.

Even unconscious, I hurt.

***

"Miss Damiano?" a man's voice inquired.

I opened my eyes, but nothing focused. A green blob wavered in front of me. It finally coalesced into a worried man in a medical smock. He was older. Dark eyes. Lots of chest. Hair on his face. Looked like my Uncle Fangio.

"I'm Dr. Rifkin."

I nodded like I understood what he'd just said, all the while trying to figure out what Uncle Fangio was doing wearing a doctor's uniform. Maybe it was just a new style of mechanic's coveralls. My hand hurt. Had I taken the Formula Ford for a joyride out at the track and crashed it somehow? No wonder Fangio looked so serious.

"Miss Damiano, you can wake up, now." The man's voice was different than my uncle's. The nightmare came flooding back. The Concerto. The murder. The gunshot.

I groaned. "What time is it?"

Dr. Rifkin's eyebrows arched, surprised by the question. He checked his tablet. "Nine-forty-three A.M."

"Crap." I closed my eyes, trying to adjust to the fact that I'd now been here more than ten hours. Plenty of time for Villalobos to have his gangsters canvass every single hospital in the Greater L.A. area. Even though I hurt, it wasn't anywhere near as bad as it had been before. They had probably shot me up with morphine.

"You've lost a lot of blood," the doctor continued, "but we've cauterized the arterial damage and pumped a couple pints in you. The fingers have been splinted in an electronic traction device. Just a temporary measure, until the swelling goes down enough for us to continue the surgery."

Villalobos was after me. I had to stay conscious, not doped up on some operating table. And no county butcher was going to touch my hand, not if I wanted to play again. "No," I gasped, opening my eyes to glower at him. "No surgery. Let me go."

"Miss, gunshot wounds are—"

"Gunshot? It was a..." I pawed through the black wool in my head to remember what lie I'd told the nurse. "Helium tank."

"Helium tanks do not leave gunshot residue on the skin around the wound. It was a gun. Small caliber, say thirty-two, maybe nine millimeter. Close range. Who did this to you?"

Oh, Hell. Now I was going to have to talk to the police. What would I tell them? Becoming a witness for the prosecution didn't seem like a job with much career potential. But what other options did I have? If I kept quiet, there was no guarantee that Villalobos wouldn't hunt me down anyway. He'd been awfully gung-ho about those 5D discs.

Dr. Rifkin's dark eyes narrowed with sympathy. "You're safe here, you know. Nobody's going to hurt you. You can tell me what really happened. Who shot you?"

"Don't remember," I mumbled, figuring that was safe. I could always remember later, if I needed to. "Don't remember anything. Just let me go."

I tried to sit up, only to stop mid-way through the motion when I saw the cheap metal and plastic traction splint around my hand. I'd had a much better one after the first Webster surgery, back when I could afford the latest recovery tech. This one was such a poor imitation of that one that I wondered if hospital sourced all of its devices from the Brothers Knockoff.

The formfitting hard plastic support was transparent, with a pink tint. It strapped on with Velcro ties, and had an electronic control board that adjusted the little gears along the back of the wrist to keep tension on the traction wires attached to the sleeves holding up my injured fingers. But what really floored me was the wound beneath all the tech.

My hand was as big as a softball. My fingers—what I could see of them through the reddish-black pudding of half-clotted blood—were gray and puffy, like rotting sausages. The two middle ones were supported by nothing but the wire-backed splint, the bones which anchored them either broken or nonexistent. The ivory ends of my metacarpals jutted through an angry red crater of torn flesh.

It hurt—God, it hurt so bad, but the pain was nothing compared to the bloody destruction of my future, the desecration of my music. Should've let Villalobos kill me.

"You're safe here," the doctor soothed. "You don't have to be afraid. I'm sure once you give a description of who did that to you, everything will work out fine."

Something in his manner put me off. Or maybe I was just angry about everything. Furious with the world for what had happened to my hand. I gave him my maniac glare, the one with my lip curled at one corner. "Let me the Hell out of here."

"You need surgery. The possibility of infection increases as you postpone treatment. You could lose the entire hand. As it is, you'll most likely lose a finger or two."

Lose a finger? Or two? Vic, where are you when I need you?

"Let me go," I growled through gritted teeth. "Got my own surgeon. Just let me go."

"Very well." He sighed and yanked the curtain back to reveal a white woman in a gray suit. She looked me up and down. Beside her stood a huge, older Samoan-looking fellow, also in a suit, although his was dark blue. The doctor shrugged at them, annoyed. "She's all yours."

The woman nodded, her blonde hair riffling from the movement. "We appreciate your help," she said to his back as he walked off toward another cubicle.

The big Samoan man gently tugged the curtain shut, while the petite woman flipped some sort of badge at me. "You Damiano? Radiana Damiano?"

I nodded. I had a bad feeling. They were detectives, not uniformed flunkies. Detectives only got involved when there was something heavy to investigate. Like murder.

The Samoan coughed once, then pulled up the doctor's stool and sat beside the bed. "You, ah," his voice sounded deep and muddy, like his throat was full of donut paste. "You cooperate with us, you can get up to fifty-thousand dollars towards your medical bills from the Victim's Assistance Fund." He pointed at my splint. "Might pay for that. All you got to do is tell the truth about this thing. The whole truth. You can trust us."

I chewed my lip, undecided. They must already know about Sloan, and now they were trying to tie me to the homicide. They needed a witness to put Villalobos away.

The lady cop moved to the head of the gurney and put a gentle hand on my shoulder. "You want to tell us what happened?"

I knew from the practiced way she touched me that her concern was nothing more than sugar-coating for her professional interest. I'd seen the same false sympathy in the investigators who had come to the base suspecting my mother of child abuse. I hadn't fallen for it then, either. With Mother in jail, Papa would have been forced to resign from the Navy.

"What happened?" the lady cop wheedled. "You can tell us. Who shot you?"

"Don't remember," I repeated, not trusting her. Not trusting either of them, because of how they'd had the doctor try to get me to talk.

The Samoan glared at me for a long time. I ignored him, having long ago become immune to the silent stare tactics used by authority figures. I could tell he thought I was lying. "What's the last thing you do remember?

"Dunno."

They stared at me some more. Skeptical. Expectant.

After a while, they realized it wasn't working. The Samoan cleared his throat. His gaze followed the spaghetti straps on my suede dress down to my cleavage. "You a whore? You're dressed awful nice."

"No." I glowered at him, my good hand curling into a fist. "I'm not like your mama."

His eyes narrowed. The muscles bunched in his thick jaw. "You watch your mouth or I'll take your ass in."

"Piss up a rope," I gruffed, too tired to be scared of him and too hurt to be tactful.

He stood up, probably to intimidate me, but the lady cop waved him to a seat, turning her phony smile on me. "Do you have any identification?"

"It's in my purse. Wherever that is."

The Samoan glanced around, then reached under the gurney. He produced an opaque plastic bag and pulled it open to reveal my purse and my ruined matador jacket. "This it?" he asked, holding it up. His anger had congealed into a distant apathy.

I nodded again, holding my good hand out to take it from him, but he scooted his stool back out of my reach, a smug grin on his wide face. He popped the clasps, pawed around in my purse and withdrew my license. Handing it to the lady cop, he continued poking around, opening my lipstick, taking apart my wallet, examining every item before laying it on the small metal table next to him.

"Don't you need a warrant, or something?" I asked.

"Dunno," he threw my own line back at me. He continued to systematically remove everything. When it was empty, he tipped it upside down, just to be sure.

Meanwhile, the lady cop had run my license. She read the screen thoughtfully, then looked over at me. "This your correct address?"

"No."

"Where do you live now?"

"Around."

"Around where?"

I shrugged, not mentioning my car. The Mazda was my home, the only hard asset left in my life; I couldn't afford to lose it to an impound, where a bunch of cop geeks would go through it the same way the Samoan was rifling through my purse. "Around."

"How'd you get here? Did you drive?"

"Dunno. Don't remember."

"Do you have a car?"

"No," I lied, noting that my key fob was missing from the array on the table. I'd probably left it in the foot well where I'd dropped it, too worried about my hand to remember such minor details. The prospect didn't brighten me much. Every thief in the neighborhood would drive off with a gimme like that. But, on the plus side, at least it made these jerk-off cops work at pinning me down. The lady cop sighed, glancing over at the Samoan.

He shook his head, frustration pulsing in the muscles of his jaw as he winnowed through my lipsticks and eyeshadows. "No keys in here. Check the database for vehicle registrations."

The lady cop plinked something into her device and waited for the readout. "No good. Nothing."

"You sure?" he asked, peering over her elbow to check the screen himself. He glared at me, like I was putting something over on him. Maybe I was. There was no way they'd trace the car to me, even through the database.

Although I held a California Driver's license, the Mazda was still registered and insured in Washington under Aunt Rosa's name, because I'd bought it from her when I was seventeen, before the money from Papa's trust had cleared the bank.

"Let's cut the bullshit." The Samoan leaned forward. His exhaled breath struck my face, making my eyelashes waver. "We know you were at the Concerto last night, when everything went down. What we want to know is, where are the data discs?"

My jaw dropped. I'd known this question was coming, but I hadn't expected it to be the first card on the table. No "Who killed Sloan?" or "Did the guy who shot you kill Sloan, too?"

It scared me, more than anything else about these two. Truth was, they didn't care about who killed Sloan, not as long as they found those discs. And detectives who didn't object to murder were like hand grenades without the pins.

"I don't know," I said, forcing my voice to stay even. "I don't know what you're talking about. I don't remember anything about last night, I mean."

He sighed deeply and drew his thick fingers along the stubble at the side of his neck. All at once, he hopped to his feet, towering over me like a terrier waiting for a rat to bolt the hole. "You 'remember' any more about this, make sure you contact us. Withholding evidence is a crime. Especially evidence relating to a homicide." He stuck a finger in my face. "Think about that, why don't you?" He spun on his heel, sweeping the curtains away with a broad, angry gesture.

The lady cop took a few steps after him, then paused and tucked a business card atop the collection of objects from my purse. "When you come to your senses," she admonished, "call."

I listened to her heels clack across the hard linoleum of the waiting area, and jabbed the nurse button on the bed railing with my good hand. I wanted out of here. And I wanted out now.

After a few minutes of arguing with the day nurse, she finally took the I.V.'s out of me and let me get to my feet. She handed me two prescription bottles, explaining one was a painkiller, and one an antibiotic. Because I'd specified minimum treatment, they hadn't bothered to undress me, so all I had to do was slip my shoes on, scrape my things back into my purse, and wait for them to issue me an invoice for services rendered.

The day nurse told me to wait for a wheelchair to take me outside. I told her I would, but as soon as the orderly left, and I was alone again, I pawed one-handed through the curtains into the adjacent cubicle, and kept pawing until I reached another corridor. Not only did the detectives have me spooked, but I had to get out of here before Villalobos and his gangsters found me.

Too late, I discovered when the corridor dumped me out in the hospital's central lobby. A big, burly man wearing a black silk shirt, a white tie, gray slacks, and a gray leather jacket stood beside the elevators, picking his back molars with an index finger the size of a .45 caliber gun barrel.

He had short brown hair and enormous ears sticking out at right angles above his five o'clock shadow. His lips were full, his brows like huge caterpillars across his Neanderthal forehead. If I hadn't been so scared to see a gangster here, I'd have handed him a cup and hummed hurdy-gurdy music.

He smiled at me—a smile of recognition—and removed his finger from his mouth as he sauntered toward me.

Panicked, I ducked back down the corridor, moving as fast as my thrashed anatomy would take me. Another automatic double-door opened up at the end of the corridor, and I hung a right into a hallway leading to a small foyer on the east side of the building.

From there, I trotted out into the parking lot, circling the hospital across a half-acre of shimmering blacktop to the spot where I'd left my car. A sigh of relief hit me when I rounded the corner and saw the little gray Mazda in the corner of the parking lot, right where I'd left it. I must have lost Neanderthal, because I didn't see or hear him behind me.

All the movement made me dizzy. My body didn't seem to want to listen to me, but I put my head down and slogged through, determined to get out of this mess alive. All I had to do was get to my car, and I'd be home free.

Way I drove, God couldn't keep up with me.

Except, when I got about twenty feet away, I realized somebody was standing next to the Mazda. Two somebodies, both wearing gray slacks and leather jackets, even though it was July. Neanderthal and Villalobos grinned and glided toward me.

"Shit." I backed away. "Your 5D discs are in the hospital. First floor, Ladies restroom, first stall."

"Don't care about the discs." Villalobos eyed me speculatively. "Lotta blood on your car. Lotta blood on you. Doesn't look good."

"I'm fine." I held up my splint in a placating gesture. "See? Fine. Go away."

"Relax." Villalobos put up his hand. "We just want to talk about last night."

"Nothing to say." The words tumbled out thin and quavering. "Didn't see anything. Nothing happened. Don't have anything to talk about." I bumped into the back of a Chrysler and sidled around it, keeping my gaze pinned on them.

No guns, so far. Might get out of this yet.

Villalobos stalked me between the cars. "It's not professional to leave you wounded like this."

"Might come back on us," Neanderthal added.

I glanced around to see which way to turn and my heart slammed into a brick wall. Well, actually, it was a chain link fence, and it was two feet behind me. The hood of the Chrysler was on my right, an electric Honda to my left. Shit, there was nowhere to go. Nowhere but ballistic. I kicked my shoes off, flipping one up into my left hand. Adrenaline surged through me, driving the pain and confusion away, until all that was left was the cold, focused clarity of the moment.

"Knew you'd see it my way." Villalobos grinned and reached inside his jacket.

I bellowed and twirled my shoe over my head, whipping it down and around to snap the heel into Villalobos' eye. He dodged enough to avoid being blinded, but I still carved a groove across bridge of his nose.

"Damn!" He stumbled backwards into Neanderthal, gun still under his jacket where it belonged.

I bellowed again, cross-stepped a sidekick into the two of them and whacked Villalobos in the neck with the shoe. He snatched it away, and I spun around, clambered up on the Honda and bolted across the hoods of the vehicles, heading for a gap in the fence about ten cars away. Set off three alarms along the way, but I made it a good twenty feet ahead of the gangsters. Wasn't much, but it was a start.

The sidewalk rasped against my stockinged feet, each footfall sending a searing jolt through my right arm. I heard their steps behind me, along with the soft swishing of their pants and the easy rush of air in their lungs. Twenty feet wasn't enough. Not nearly. The Metro entrance was still half-a-block away. I wasn't going to make it. No way I could make it. Why bother? Bastards had ruined me, anyway. Bastards had stolen my music.

Rage welled up inside me, hot and bitter. After Chris dying and the fight with Webster and getting kicked out of school. Months of surgery and casts and spending all my money to repair the broken hand, and just when things were looking up, the gunshot. After all that, I'd be damned if I gave them the satisfaction of killing me.

Fury fueled me those last fifty yards to the gloom of the station. I barreled through the sparse crowd near the ticket kiosk, heading for the trains. Our rapid footfalls echoed against the barren walls. God they were close. I could hear one of them cursing in my right ear.

Something cut into my shoulder and yanked me backwards. My purse. They'd grabbed my purse. Before I could shuck it off the strap snapped. I sailed sideways into the turnstiles, hugging my splint across my chest to keep from smashing it. My momentum spun me over the counter column, and, in some vague body memory from high school gymnastics, I kicked my heels over my head, twisting so I landed on my feet, legs still pumping.

Villalobos shouted a curse and I heard a crashing thump as one of them fell. I flew up the platform and dove into the open maw of a train right before the bell shrilled and the doors slammed shut. I hit hard on my good side. Something shifted in my bra, and the silver 5D data disc slipped out from between my cleavage and hit the floor under me. The world lurched forward.

"You all right, lady?" A teenager with purple hair and a chain that ran from his nose to his earlobe picked up the coin-like disc and examined it. "You dropped this."

I huffed there in a red haze, staring at the writing on that gleaming Mylar. Where had that come from? I'd gotten rid of them all. And how in the world had I run in so much pain?

"Lady, you okay?" The boy with the nose chain and the purple hair helped me up and sat next to me like he thought I might black out. He had a Boy Scout kerchief tattooed across his left bicep. Webelos, I think.

He pressed the silver disc into my good hand. "Here. You dropped that."

I nodded, still a bit breathless. "Thanks."

"No sweat." He gave me a warm smile, his cheek straining against the nose chain, pulling his nostril to one side.

I wondered if I was hallucinating.

He noticed me staring and scowled. "I didn't want this snotline. Or the hair, either. My mother made me get them."

"Mothers..." I nodded sympathetically, "...can be bitches."

CHAPTER THREE

Nobody followed me when I got off the train, although that didn't mean much. The gangsters would track me down eventually. Didn't pay to leave a murder witness on the loose. Either I blew town in the next couple days, or I ended up as spatter stains on those ugly silk ties. Always wanted to make a killer fashion statement.

I'd tucked the silver 5D disc under the control panel of the splint, keeping it hidden and out of the way. I wasn't sure it would be any use, but it might be enough to offer the cops if I decided to stick around and make a stand. Right now, the first priority was to get to Vic.

I crossed the street, my shoeless feet searing on the hot asphalt. My skirt was stiff with dried blood and I smelled like a piece of meat that had been left out in the sun. None of my body parts were happy with me, least of all my stomach. Hadn't eaten since lunch yesterday.

Have to wait. No purse meant no phone and no money. I'd have to call Jim from Carmen's. Jim would buy me lunch. He was a social crusader who felt sorry for everybody. Hell, shape I was in, Carmen might even feel sorry for me.

Carmen Black was a lean whip of a woman who owned a karate school near Franklin and Cahuenga. She knew her stuff—even took me down pretty regularly—but she didn't have an overly generous spirit. I used to teach some classes for her before Webster broke my hand, and damn if she didn't try to short me every chance she got. Other than the cash, we got along all right.

She used to let me rehearse with Jim at the dojo after closing. Even let me sleep there for the two months I was suspended from the dorm for riding Sue Epstein's motorcycle up and down the stairways of the Fine Arts Building. University police can be so humorless.

Since the Red Line ran north through Universal and Jim lived in Tarzana, the dojo was a good place to meet. At least there I could trade my blood encrusted skirt for a *gi* and stretch out on the mats while I waited for Jim to give me a ride to Vic's.

I scudded the door open and bowed inside. As I stepped onto the painted concrete floor an air-conditioned funk struck me, the humid stink of sweat, plastic mats, and mildewed ventilation shafts. In California, all dojos smelled this way. I think it comes in the leasing agreement.

"Hey, Rad." Eddie Moamar looked up from pounding the bag. His jaw dropped, eyes bugging. "What the Hell happened to you?"

"I had more than twelve items and paid by check."

A snort of amusement escaped him. He shook his head in disbelief. "You're crazy, you know that?"

"Thanks for the insight, Eddie. Carmen around?"

"Nope. Tournament in Long Beach."

Good. She'd never notice. I grabbed an over-sized *gi* off the shelf in the office and ducked into the bathroom. Stripped off and tossed my bloody clothes, and then washed up a little before slipping into the *gi*. Vic was gonna love seeing me in a karate uniform.

I stopped by the desk to call Jim from the dojo's landline, to ask him for a ride to Vic's. He sounded relieved to hear from me, and promised to pick me up at Carmen's. He'd be there within the hour. With that out of the way, I called Vic at his home number.

When his wife answered and explained he'd stepped out to buy lunch for the kids, I asked her to please, please tell him to meet me at his office in an hour or so. This was a major, major emergency. She promised to give him the message. I thanked her profusely.

Frazzled and fatigued and hurting all over, I sat down on the mats and watched Eddie pound the bag. He was overextending, but Carmen wasn't paying me to teach lessons anymore, so there was no point in getting up and showing him how to do it right. Besides, I hurt all over. But, I couldn't help feeling guilty about closing my eyes and keeping my mouth shut.

Papa would've shown him, no matter the money. No matter the pain. Papa would've made sure he learned correctly, because his life might depend on it. That's how Papa had always taught me.

In the beginning, I had hated karate. It took time away from my piano lessons. Later though, when I got older and understood what it meant when more servicewomen were sexually assaulted on their own military bases than were injured in combat, I was grateful for all those katas Papa taught me. For the precious leave time he spent with me in the basement, practicing kicks and blocks and punches until I could barely stand.

"No asshole is gonna touch my little girl," he'd say, and then he'd make me go through the whole drill all over again.

Mother would appear in the doorway, a scowl on her face, saying "Nico, don't teach her that. It's not ladylike."

They'd look hard at each other for a long time, like they always did when they disagreed. I'd get bored and scratch my nose and Papa's hand would flash out, quick and deadly. I'd be on my butt in an instant, cheek stinging, blinking back the tears.

"Radiana, you keep that guard up," he'd growl, still glaring at my mother. "I've seen what happens to women who can't defend themselves. They get raped."

Her eyelashes wavered every time he said that, like he'd hit her somehow. "The Lord knows the truth," she'd say, and spin around in a huff.

"So do I, Sophia," he'd say to her back. "So do I."

***

"Rad." Someone shook me awake.

I groaned against the effort of moving and looked up to see Jim squatting above me. Early afternoon sunlight slanted through the back window of the dojo, and the way the light hit his face accentuated the deep circles under his eyes. His hair was a straggly mess, slicked with sweat and old gel. A burning cigarette hung from his left hand.

"You look like Hell," I said, trying to lighten the mood.

He didn't respond, just stared at me with a weird, distant kind of intensity, his eyes filling up with tears.

"You okay?" I asked, struggling to sit up. I put my hand on his shoulder, suddenly worried about the deep weariness behind his eyes. "Did something happen?"

He shook his head, took a long drag on his smoke, regarding me with that half-cocked smirk that meant either he hated my guts or he could barely believe I was still alive. Probably both. "Couldn't find you all night. Thought you were dead."

Our gazes locked. His face hovered inches from mine, his gently intelligent eyes shiny with relief and concern, and I couldn't help wondering how glorious it would be if once—just once—he would kiss me. Wrap me in his arms and—

I glanced away quickly, ashamed of myself, ashamed of my need. He had made it clear—very clear—that our friendship wasn't that way. "Vic's waiting at his office," I mumbled, holding my splint up. "I called him after I talked to you."

His breath caught, his gaze drawn to the nightmare that was my hand, like it was some wild animal ready to pounce.

"Thought you quit smoking," I said, to stop him from fixating on the gore.

He broke away, snatching the Marlboro out of his mouth sheepishly. He threw it down on the strip of concrete by the door and ground it out. "That was when you still had a hand." He bent back down and caught me under the armpits with his strong, fine-boned fingers. "C'mon. Let's go."

I wobbled a little, but remained on my feet with his help. His eyebrows arched when he saw my toes. "No shoes?"

"Naw. I'm going Bohemian."

"Can't take you anywhere." He gave a melodramatic sigh and helped me out the back door into the alley. I squinted against the afternoon glare, feeling faint. Jim held me, kept me from melting to the gutter. The spell passed and we hobbled to where his beat-up old Dodge roasted patiently in the heat of the alley.

"Jeez," Jim leaned me against the car and opened the passenger door. "You are really fucked up."

"No f-words," I reminded him breathlessly. I hate f-words. Used to get the tar beat out of me for even hearing them.

"Sorry. I forgot." He laughed nervously, then eased me onto the seat. "Worried about you."

"I appreciate that," I mumbled, trying to focus on a simple Bach toccata, but my denial was running thin. My ribs ached from the landing on the train, my hand a bright supernova of pain.

Jim closed the door, strolled around to the driver's side and slipped behind the wheel. The engine caught on the third try and we cruised down the alley toward Cahuenga.

"You know," he began, "right after you left last night the cops closed the place down. Said a bomb had gone off in a dressing room." He chanced a look in my direction. "Is that what happened to you? A bomb?"

My mouth dropped open. "The cops said that?"

He nodded, gripping the wheel more tightly.

Why would the cops lie about the shooting? It didn't make sense, not unless—a flutter of panic rose in my gut. "What did they look like? The cops, I mean?"

"Like—cops." He shrugged, glanced at me as if he thought it was an odd question. "Detectives. A blonde woman, and a big dark-skinned guy. Kinda sexy, in a Dwayne Johnson way."

The lady cop and the Samoan. "Did they arrest anyone?"

Jim shook his head. "Not that I saw. They just wrote down everyone's name and address, then they cleared the place out. Said the first one already killed Sloan, and they couldn't take a chance on another bomb going off."

"But they didn't arrest anybody? You're sure?"

"I'm sure. They said it was a random bombing, they didn't have any suspects. The only person the cops brought out of there was the lump under the sheet."

I sighed and tried to think past the body-noise that was scrubbing my brain raw. So, they had known about Sloan, but they hadn't arrested anybody. And they'd lied about the murder, at least to the public. Which meant either Scotty or Villalobos had paid them off. Probably Scotty. From what I'd heard, he hated negative publicity. "Did you tell anybody about Vic? Did you say anything about me sometimes staying at your place?"

He shook his head. "They didn't ask, and I was too busy packing the synth up to volunteer anything. Although..." He wagged his index finger at me. "As I was loading up the car, Scotty said that there were some things missing from his office. He asked me if I'd seen you with anything that looked like gold coins."

Of course. The discs.

Villalobos must have pinned the whole thing on me. It was the only way he could have walked away from Scotty's place after the killing. He'd probably said that Sloan had tried to stop me, and that I'd shot myself during the scuffle. Scotty must have believed him and sent the dirty cops out to get the discs back without raising too many eyebrows. Damn that bastard Scotty, anyway. If he sicced those dirty cops on Jim...

I twisted in the seat to face him, my voice going deep and urgent. "Listen, Jim. If you see Scotty again, tell him I ditched town. Tell 'im the only place I can get med coverage is back in Tacoma, so I left this afternoon and you don't know what happened after that. If the cops ask, tell them the same thing."

"You want me to lie? To the cops? Why? Did you steal some gold last night? If you committed some kind of crime, I'm not gonna go to jail for you."

"No." I was a little hurt by his lack of faith. "No crime. I just—" How to explain it to a man whose biggest problem in life was spilling cappuccino on his sheet music? I sighed and covered my eyes with my good palm. "I saw something I shouldn't have seen."

"Like what?"

He could be so naive sometimes. "Like how the guy got under that sheet."

"You saw the bomb go off?"

"It wasn't a bomb."

"Then what happened to your hand?"

I thought about what to tell him, wondering if I hadn't already dragged him into the line of fire simply by asking for this ride. But the milk was spilt, and he'd find out from Vic what the damage was, anyway. "I got shot."

"Shot? You mean like by a gun? Who did that?"

"You don't want to know."

He laughed. He actually laughed. "Rad, you are so goddamned paranoid. 'Fraid the bogey man'll catch you?"

"No." I looked at him seriously. "'Fraid he'll catch you."

His eyes narrowed. He ran his hand through his hair. "You're serious."

I nodded, closed my eyes, suddenly tired and hurt and overwhelmed. All I wanted to do was stop aching.

"Are you—" Jim cleared his throat, voice muted, hesitant. "Are you saying you witnessed a murder?"

"Give the man a cee-gar."

"Where? In the club? Where?"

"Doesn't matter. What matters is I lay low until everybody forgets about me."

"You're not gonna report it? You'd let them get away with murder?"

"Jim," I intoned patiently, "these people don't play games. They'll delete me as soon as they find me—and you too, if you let on you know anything. I report this, I'll be dead by nightfall."

"But the police. They have to protect witnesses."

A bitter laugh escaped me. "This is Los Angeles. You know how many murders hit the courts every month? I'm really sure the LAPD can spare an officer to keep me from becoming fish bait."

He didn't argue. He knew I was right. We drove the rest of the way in silence.

When we parked, he helped me out of the car. I pushed the sleeves of my gi down so they covered my hands as we threaded our way through the nearly vacant halls of the medical building. Better not to upset Vic before it was absolutely necessary. Some of the best surgeons are temperamental about their work, and Victor Balcour was probably the most gifted, and temperamental, of the bunch. One of the things I liked about him.

The bell dinged as Jim eased the door open. The reception room smelled of lavender and disinfectant. I shuffled inside, Jim right behind me.

"What's the emergency?" Vic peered around the door to the inner office. He was tall and thin and had skin the color of burnt umber. His face was grooved with age and a white mustache graced his upper lip. Thick, white, bushy brows shaded his warm, intelligent eyes. He took one look at the karate uniform and went into a pout. "This better be good. I'm missing a Hell of a baseball game for you. Better not be some little scratch."

"Oh, it's good all right." Jim pawed his pockets, absently searching for a cigarette. Since I had tossed them out the window once he'd started driving, he didn't find one. So, he pulled his cellphone out, instead. "Rad got shot in the hand."

His jaw dropped. "When?"

"Last night," I responded. "About ten o'clock."

"Right, or left?"

"Right." Jim began to play one of those stupid freemium games. He must really be upset.

Vic arched his brows thoughtfully, then motioned us to follow. We walked to the back room, the one with the X-ray booth and the window that overlooked the hospital across the way. I sat in a chair next to the exam table. Jim sat by the door, still fiddling with the game. Vic pulled the computer cart out from behind the table and keyed my name in. "Gunshots have to be reported, you know."

"Already been." I shrugged because he looked at me funny. "I was bleeding a lot, so I went to County. Cops took a report."

"County? That graveyard?" He stuck the thermo-sensor in my ear, pulled the trigger. "Why didn't you call? I would have checked you in next door."

"Vic," I intoned, "I don't have any money left."

"Oh. Yeah." He issued a frustrated sigh. "I forgot." The sensor beeped. He checked the readout and frowned. "You feel a little feverish? Didn't those people at County give you antibiotics?"

"Yeah."

"Why didn't you use them?"

"They're in my purse."

"So, where's your purse?"

I shrugged. "Lost it."

Vic rolled his eyes. "Rad, I need a little help, here. If you can't keep track of a prescription for longer than four hours, how can I kiss everything and make it better?"

"I don't want you to kiss everything. Just this." I eased the splint out of its hiding place and rested it on the examining table. Vic didn't say a word for a good thirty seconds.

He stared, the veins in his temples pulsing as he gently lifted my hand and examined the palm through the clear plastic of the splint. The whites of his eyes went into saucer mode, his lips pressed so tight I thought his face might rupture.

"Good Lord," he finally said. He shook his head, eyes shiny, like he was going to cry. "Someone took your future and put a bullet through it."

"It can't be that bad, Vic."

"You're missing an entire joint! You'll need four, maybe five separate surgeries. And that's just to keep the fingers. If you want to use them, you're talking bone grafts, stem cells, and other experimental procedures. A rebuild like this is, at the very least, a three surgeon operation. This is major bucks, major pain."

I stared at him, not wanting hear what he said. Not wanting to believe it.

"You're looking at two-hundred thou, bare minimum. If I can convince the other surgeons to be like me and agree on a charity case. And there's still no guarantee you'll play again."

Jim snapped his head against the wall with a solid thump. "Shit, Rad. You don't have that kind of green."

I didn't say anything. Couldn't, really.

It was a joke. Had to be a joke. I knew the damage was bad, but Victor Balcour could fix anything. He was brilliant and committed and caring. He'd repaired everything from the fight with Webster. Vic wouldn't write me off, wouldn't let me down. He was only joking, getting back at me for making him miss his—

"Rad," Vic touched my shoulder.

I blinked, suddenly realizing he'd been talking. I hadn't heard a word he'd said.

"Rad," he laid his words out carefully, so that I wouldn't stumble over them. "We'll check you in right now, and I'll schedule the surgery for this evening. I think maybe we can get you in and out before they run a full financial."

I smiled. He had been joking, after all. Son-of-a-bitch really knew how to get to me.

"Shouldn't take too long to amputate the fingers," he continued. "Might even be able to—"

"Amputate?"

His turn to nod. "You can't afford to do anything else. Either you go full experimental, or you amputate. Anything in between has too high a risk of infection. Might lose the whole hand."

He hadn't been joking. I stared at him, my chest cavity slowly filling with ice, my jaw clamped so tight my teeth hurt. I couldn't lose the music. Please don't take away my music. Not forever.

He squatted down in front of me, searching my face with the gruff compassion that was his trademark. "Can't do this by myself, Rad. Too many factors involved. And if I admit you without financial backing, amputation is all we've got."

Jim thumped his head against the wall again. "Shit."

"No." My voice sounded far away, "I want to play."

Vic glanced up at Jim, then turned back to me. "Rad, you don't have the money."

"I'll get it." I snatched the phone out of Jim's hand and pecked the number out with my thumb before I lost my nerve. "Have to get it." I waited for her to pick up. "My mother's still got about three hundred grand from that money my father left."

"In your condition?" Jim grabbed for the phone. "She'll eat you alive. I'll call."

He kept trying to snatch the phone, but I held it away from him. "She won't talk to you. She thinks you're a deeve and a pervert." I heard it ring a few times.

I tried to force myself to relax. Maybe she'd be too drunk to answer. I heard the click of her picking up and turned my face to the wall so Jim and Vic wouldn't see the fear in my eyes. God, I was crazy for doing this.

"Hello?" Her voice was clear, unmistakable.

"Hello," I said in an even monotone.

She gasped, but recovered quickly. "May I ask who's calling?" She used the same affected tone she reserved for her bridge club.

She was baiting me already.

"It's me," I answered dutifully. "Your daughter."

"Radiana." Her voice grew cold. "You've got a lot of nerve calling here. Are you in jail again?"

"No." Why wouldn't she let that drop? Hadn't been locked up since I was fifteen. And that had been self defense. "I, uh, I got hurt. Need some money." Apparently she hadn't expected this, because the line went so quiet I thought it was dead. "Just an advance," I said to fill the space, "the rest of Papa's trust will come to me when I turn twenty-five."

"That's your brother's money." She sounded mad. "For Christopher to go to college. That was supposed to be for him."

"He's dead, Mother. His trust comes to me, now."

"You'll just fritter it away making music." She paused, smacking her lips as if a thought had just occurred to her. "No graduation announcement in my mailbox. You dropped out, didn't you?"

I ignored the barb. "I really need the money. If you want, I'll send you a promissory note."

After a long silence she asked: "You're really hurt?"

"If I don't get treatment, I'll lose some fingers. Maybe even the whole hand."

"How much do you need?"

Oh, boy. Something was up. This was too easy. "Two hundred thousand."

"Christopher's trust was two-fifty," she pointed out.

I knew what she was hinting at just by the way she said the words. "Fine, Mother. Whatever you want. I'll sign whatever's left over to you. Just please, send me the money."

She grew very quiet, surprised at my quick acquiescence. "That's not what I meant." Her voice was hard. It was exactly what she meant, but she didn't like the way I'd seen through her so quickly. "You have no faith, Radiana. A parent doesn't do these things for money. Did I feed you and clothe you for money? Did I take you back from that foster home for money? Not many mothers would want a child who went on trial for murder."

It was self defense, I reminded myself, biting my tongue. *The petition was dropped.* If I blew my top she'd have an excuse to turn me down.

"I warned Nico he was raising a killer."

"For crying out loud, Mother. The man tried to rape me."

"And the other crimes? Those burglaries when you ran away? You know how I feel about thieves. I let you come home anyway."

"I appreciate that," I said, because it was expected. If I'd spoken my true feelings she would've hung up in my ear.

"You have no sense of family, Radiana. You didn't even come to your brother's funeral. Rosa was there. And Fangio. And all your cousins. How do you think I felt? My own daughter not there to pay last respects."

Last respects? He died in my arms. I rested my forehead against the wall, gutted by the memory. Did grieving ever stop?

She heaved a long-suffering sigh and continued: "You were never an easy child, Radiana. Not like Christopher. It's such a shame you ruined him like that. Because of you, I had to take him along on all those trips to court and Juvenile Hall. That's why he started spending time with those drug addicts. Christopher was a good boy. You poisoned him. Put all those rebellious ideas in his head by getting arrested after his father died."

I stopped listening, struggling to control the firestorm seething inside me. 'His father,' she always said. Like I didn't count. Like I wasn't worth counting. We both knew that Chris was not Papa's biological son. Chris was born with the wrong blood type. He was the result of her affair with Mike.

God, I hated that woman.

"I should've left you in jail, where you belong," she continued. "You're nothing but a murderer. You know as well as I do that Christopher would be alive today if it wasn't for you."

I sighed, holding onto the phone so tightly my forearm spasmed. "You won't give me the money." A statement, no question about it.

"No." I could tell she enjoyed saying it. "I don't think so. A troublemaker like you doesn't deserve help. After all the time I spent, all that discipline, you still turned out bad. Don't know how I could have raised such an evil, selfish—"

I slammed the phone on the table top before Jim snatched it out of my hand. He hit the icon to hang up.

"Fuck you," I snarled at the screen.

I should have known she'd do it. Outmaneuver me. Make it morally right to shove my head under until I drowned in my own rage and despair.

"Fuck you," I repeated in a low whisper, sharking around in a compulsive circle, looking for some place to put all the fury spilling through me. My left hand cocked back to drive itself into the wall.

Jim lunged and grabbed my wrist. "Rad, no. Relax. Sit down."

I shook my fist, arm-wrestling with him. Too hyper to sit. Too mad to relax. "He was hallucinating. She wouldn't let me take him to the hospital."

He hung on desperately. "Relax, damn it! You want to break this one too? She'll win, just like she did before."

"She never won," I growled.

"Bullshit. She's turned you into a basket case. Got you so mental that you went and fought Webster."

"I did that for you. He was—"

"You did it for you. To let some of the pressure off. You've been spoiling for a fight ever since you came back from Christmas break. Blaming yourself for your brother's—"

"No!" I pressed him into the wall. "Shut up!"

"Rad, you knew what was at stake. You knew that if you took a swipe at Webster, his buddies would—"

"He was beating on you! How could I let him—?"

"So, I get a black eye! Maybe lose a tooth." His long fingers curled into fists, the corded muscles of his neck taut as catgut. "Better than being a one-handed pianist."

Hadn't seen that coming. Not from Jim. It hit me hard, knocked the fight out of me with a wound so deep, so raw all I could do was back away and gape at him.

But he wasn't finished. All the frustration, all the resentment he had built up over the past months tumbled out: "You," he pointed an accusing finger. "You had it all. Gigs. Recording contracts. What the fuck were you thinking of, jumping in like that? What the Hell was it supposed to prove? That a few pokes from a stupid-ass frat-brat was worth more than your music? Than our music?" He shook his head. "Now look. Goddamn losing your fingers."

"But the gunshot wasn't my fault."

"Like Hell. If you hadn't fought Webster, we would never have played the Concerto. We would have gone on that European tour."

He was right. I hated him for it. God, I hated him.

Hated me even more, because I'd let her win again.

Why couldn't I ever see it? Why was it that no matter what I did, she always managed to blindside me? I sank down onto the floor and hid my face in the crook of my good arm.

Had she known how crippled I'd become? How much she was forcing me to lose? All those nights filled with glory, when the winds wailed and the strings crooned and for one God-inspired moment I actually belonged somewhere. Nobody judging or criticizing or condemning, just the awful, electric joy of the music shared between us. She never knew how much misery was funneled through those sonatas, how much loneliness and grief I was able to express in spite of her...

Or maybe she did, and that's why I didn't get the money.

"Rad." Vic cleared his throat. "I'll start the paperwork, get you admitted. Hopefully we can get you into surgery tonight."

"No." I sighed, held my head up high, refusing to give in. "I'll get the cash. Give me a chance, Vic, just a couple days. I'll go to the bank, borrow against the trust."

"You need to be hospitalized. The longer you wait, the less chance you'll have for a full recovery."

"But without the loan I won't recover at all."

He stared at me for a long moment, then nodded solemnly. "All right. If you have the money, or at least the surgical part, I'll do the initial prep on Monday. Otherwise, we amputate." He forced a painkiller and an antibiotic into my palm. "Take these."

He glowered at me until I put them in my mouth and handed me a paper cup of water to wash them down. As I swallowed, he pulled a handful of drug sample packets from a drawer and handed them to Jim. "Have her take these antibiotics every six hours. Make her stay in bed. Don't let her move around." Jim nodded and put the packets in his pocket.

Vic turned back to me. "Keep the wound elevated, above your heart. I'll write you a prescription for opiates."

Right then, I didn't need any drugs. I was too scared to feel any pain.

***

"Where you going?" I asked, when Jim drove onto the wrong freeway to take me to the bank. My branch was in Westchester, all the way over by LAX. I'd opened an account there during my first week of school because it was near the campus.

"Home."

"Your house? What for?"

"You're wearing a gi, remember? You need to change into something decent and clean up a bit. What loan officer in his right mind is gonna give someone two-hundred-thou if they walk in barefoot, wearing black pajamas?"

He had point. Leave it to Jim to pick up on the social graces. I nodded and leaned back in the seat, waiting for the analgesic to shave the edge off the pain.

"You hungry?" he asked, as we cruised down Ventura Boulevard, approaching the fast food joint near his house. "Want me to buy you lunch, or something?"

"Naw." I didn't feel like eating, not when I looked down the side street and saw his front door wide open. I caught the wheel before he could make the turn. "You forget to lock up?"

He shook his head, eyes bugging a little.

Damn. I never should have asked Jim for help. I should have known his place would be the first spot they'd look.

"Go around the block." I motioned, and he pulled back into the flow of traffic, heading down Ventura to the next side street and back around, so we could come at his house from the south.

I studied the streets for anybody staking the place out. Didn't find much. No car in the driveway, none out front. Nobody sitting in a car at the corner, no one loitering along the sidewalk. Of course, there could be someone in the coffee shop behind his house, but no way to know that for sure. "Go down the alley."

Jim steered the Dodge down the narrow strip of pavement between the houses and the commercial buildings on Ventura. At least the alley was clear, too. Maybe they were gone.

Then again, maybe they were still in the house.

"Park over there," I waved toward the parking lot for the coffee shop at the end of the alley.

"Why?"

"Just do it."

He pulled in and stopped the car, face pale. "Should I call the police?"

"No," I said, a little too sharply. I slipped the seat belt off, reached for the door. "I'll be back."

"Where are you going? You're not going in there, are you?"

"Just to check it out. Make sure it's safe."

"Rad, you're hurt. We should call the cops."

"No. No cops. I don't want you dragged any further into this mess. You understand?" I glared at him. "Just stay here."

"But what if they're still in there? What if they catch you snooping around?"

"Nobody'll catch me. Just stay here," I repeated, stepping out of the car. "Don't panic. Don't do anything. Promise me."

Our gazes met for a long moment. I could tell he was scared, overwhelmed by the circumstances, but he knew I wasn't going to back down from this. Finally, he nodded.

I slammed the door and trudged across the hot asphalt of the boulevard. I reached the side street and walked down the alley. Sweat poured down my temples and pooled between my breasts before soaking the midriff of my gi. I told myself it was only the fever, or the heat of the day, but the knot in my gut and the goosebumps on the back of my neck exposed the lie. I was a lot more afraid than I'd let on, but there was no way I'd let Jim take point on this. He was a great musician, but he had the survival instincts of a lemming.

Bees droned among the bottlebrush trees marking the fence line of Jim's backyard. The house was a small two bedroom, one bath Craftsman-style. It had been built in 1948, when most of the San Fernando Valley was orange groves and dairy farms, before millionaires and celebrities decided Tarzana was the place to plunk down their mansions. Jim's grandparents had owned it since 1975. His mother inherited it, but since she had married rich and preferred living in New York and Colorado, she gave it to Jim when he turned twenty-one.

Must be nice.

I peered through the foliage, seeing past the gloom of the screened porch to find that the door to the service room was wide open, too. I studied the layout for a minute or so, seeing no evidence of movement inside. Silently, painstakingly, I eased the chain link gate open and ebbed through.

No shouts from the house, no bullets ripping through my flesh. Heartened, I eased my way along the side of the garage, keeping in the shadows of the fruitless mulberry tree dominating the small yard.

Heart pounding, I approached the back porch, and snatched a glimpse through the window of the den, which Jim had refurbished as a music studio. The place was fragged. Furniture ripped apart, recording equipment strewn all over the floor, photos knocked from the walls. The synth was smashed.

I eased into the house and found the kitchen in shambles and the new ultra high-def TV in pieces in the middle of the living room. There were no intruders, just a sadistic, methodical destruction that made me acutely aware of how stupid I'd been to ask Jim for help.

Villalobos must have done this to intimidate me, to remind me that if I was with Jim when the gangsters finally tracked me down, we'd both be dead. I had to disappear. And quick.

I picked my way across the debris on the floor, looking for the contents of my duffel. I borrowed a pair of Jim's jeans and a T-shirt from the ransacked pile of clothing, and slipped on an old pair of Reeboks I'd left around when Jim had kicked me out a few weeks ago. As I struggled to roll up the cuffs of the jeans with my good hand, I noticed Jim's desktop computer was on. I tapped the keyboard, and found it was open to the music department directory, highlighting my former address at the dorm.

I took one last look around, then returned to the car. Jim rolled down his window as I approached the Dodge, relief shining in his eyes that I was still in one piece. "So?"

"It's safe. No one's there."

He smiled. "Good. That's good."

Guilt stabbed through me. It'd cost a few grand just to replace the synth and TV. "Not really. They've trashed the place." I sucked in a deep breath, held it. This was going to be touchy. "You got any cash?"

"For what?"

"The bus. I'm taking off. Bad enough I brought you this far into it."

"Into what?"

"Just give me the money, okay?"

"Rad, no. Stay here. I'll call the cops."

"No cops." I leaned forward, drilled my gaze into his. "Promise me, Jim. No. Cops."

"Jeez, Rad, you don't think the police are involved?"

"They are. Up to their eyeballs. And if Scotty shows up here asking about me, lie to him. Tell him what I said. You let on you know what happened to me, you'll end up worse than I am."

His brow furrowed, eyes going dark and murky at the logic in my argument. He searched his pockets, found only a single, crumpled twenty and three fives. "Here." He pressed them into my palm, popping his door open. "And here, take my car. You'll need to—"

"No. I don't want anything that proves you helped me."

"But—"

"Jim."

He ran his hand through his hair, tears forming in his eyes. "It can't be that bad, Rad. It can't."

I turned, started walking away. Why did he have to get all sappy on me? "Goodbye, Jim."

"God damn you." He said to my back, a quaver in his voice. "God damn you."

"Hey," I croaked, trying to sound cheerful even though my throat was tight. I held the splint up. "Better me than you."

CHAPTER FOUR

I walked a few long blocks up the street before ducking into a convenience store to break the twenty, so I'd have the correct change for the next bus link to the Red Line. My plan was to check the parking lot at County. If my car was still there, at least I'd have transportation and a place to sleep.

As I sat down at the bus stop with a fountain drink, I realized I'd left the painkillers and antibiotics on the seat of Jim's car. Damn. Couldn't go back. How could I face him after he got a look at all the damage I'd caused? The synth, especially. I didn't have enough money to buy him another. Besides, I didn't think I could stand leaving him again. Why did he have to cry, anyway? Made me wish I hadn't forgotten how.

I hit the Mission Street station at about four-thirty. I trudged through the hospital parking lot twice, but I couldn't find the Mazda. Lightheaded, my body screaming at me, I sat down on a bus stop bench and fought back a wave of hysteria that threatened to crush me.

I needed that car, and not just for the safety and mobility it offered. Everything I owned was in there: my laptop with the demo of me and Jim, the letters and voice recordings of Papa, all the photos of us together, the drawings Papa and Chris had made for me, the silly little stuffed baby grand Chris had given me on my sixteenth birthday. All the things I had managed to hang on to, in spite of my mother. Now, even those were gone. Probably destroyed like Jim's synth. I grew so angry thinking about it, I kind of floated there, buoyed up by my own rage.

If I ever saw Villalobos again, I'd kill him. I'd rip his lungs out through his nose and garrote him with them, I'd scoop his heart out with his kneecaps, I'd—

I'd better get to the bank before it closed.

Had less than twenty-seven dollars left out of the thirty-five, and that wouldn't buy me five minutes in a roach motel. Had about a hundred left in the bank, but I couldn't get that without my ID unless I went to the account branch in person.

On the positive side, it was Friday, so they were open until six PM. I just might have enough time to catch the Flyaway bus from Union Station to LAX.

I started walking.

***

"Damiano?" The bank teller swept a wisp of auburn hair away from her mouth. Her attention was fixed on the two uniformed security guards who were locking the front door to keep late-coming customers away. I could tell she wished they'd gotten there in time to bar me.

"Yes," I responded, glad she'd heard me. Between the pain and the fever, it was getting hard to put words together in some semblance of order.

She held her hand out. "May I have your ID, please?"

"It was stolen."

"Oh." She pressed her magenta lips together, thinking hard. "I don't see how I can help you without any identification."

"What about the signature card? Don't you still have that?"

"Of course." She spun around curtly, more than likely miffed that I'd told her how to do her job. She came back and held up the card's photo ID, comparing it to my face. "Right thumbprint, please." She indicated the swipe screen on my side of the Plexiglas barrier.

"Can't." I held up the splint. "Can you use the left?"

"No. We don't store full print records in the computer. Only right thumbs and right indexes. We can't issue you a new debit card for your account without verifying your fingerprint information on file."

"I don't want a new card. I want to close my account."

"No need to get testy, Miss." She rolled her eyes and grudgingly scanned the bar code on the signature card. The monitor flickered, then glowed with my financial status. Or more accurately, the lack thereof. "You have no funds available."

"What? What are you talking about?"

"There's a hold on that account. L.A. County Health Services. See?" She swiveled the monitor toward me and jabbed a finger at the flashing prompt. "No funds until payment is made for services rendered."

"I have to pay off County before I can get my own cash?"

"Yes, that's what it looks like." She waved her hand as if to dismiss me and started counting a stack of receipts. I didn't budge. After about two minutes of my pointed presence, she sighed and looked up. "Can I help you with anything else?"

"I want a loan for two hundred thousand dollars."

She frowned at me as if I'd just suggested smearing her with tuna salad and dumping her into a lion's cage.

"I have a trust," I explained. "It's supposed to come to me when I turn twenty-five. I want to borrow against it."

"Do you have documentation?"

"Not on me. It was in my car, and that was stolen."

"We couldn't consider it without documentation."

"It's in a Seattle bank. Call 'em and have 'em verify it."

"We do not accept interstate phone calls as collateral. When you have the proper documentation, we'll be happy to discuss it. Right now, I'm afraid we can't help you." She offered a pre-formed smile and made a shooing motion toward the door. "Have a nice weekend."

"But I need the money by Monday." Panic had crept into my voice. I knew I was blowing this, knew I sounded like some refugee from a bad gambling debt, but most of my wits were occupied just keeping me on my feet.

"I really very sorry." Her voice grew stern. "I can't help you."

I gaped at her. *Oh, no, no no. This couldn't be happening. What was I going to tell Vic?*

"Miss, I'm sorry but you have to leave. The bank is closing." At her tone, the guards looked up. One of them edged toward me.

I couldn't move, just stood there gaping, waiting for a miracle I knew would never happen, but waiting just the same. If she just knew what was at stake she'd help me, wouldn't she?

Wouldn't she?

The other guard came around behind me, unsnapping the flap on his handcuff holster. The two sandwiched me between them and forcibly escorted me to the door.

If she knew, she'd help me. There had to be some mercy in the world. "They're gonna cut my fingers off!" I bellowed, and clawed at the jamb to get back inside.

They shoved me out onto the sidewalk, averting their eyes as they locked the door in my face.

***

I sat on the bus with my eyes closed, savoring those sweet moments between heartbeats when the blood paused and the pain eased, because that was the only thing left to look forward to. I couldn't survive on the streets one-handed, not in this shape. I knew that much from having been a runaway. Nothing left to do but check myself in and go under the knife.

Maybe I should go back to County General, let some stranger disfigure me. Seemed kind of cruel to make Vic destroy some of his best work. Either way, I'd have to take the Red Line when the bus got back to Union Station. Part of me hoped I had enough cash left for the fare. Part of me didn't care what happened. Once I checked into a hospital the gangsters were bound to track me down. Why bother having surgery when I wouldn't live past the recovery period? The weird part was, the idea of being murdered didn't bother me. So what if they killed me? It was a *coup-de-grace*, a deliverance from a life without music.

Or maybe it was just the pain talking. I wasn't sure.

I wasn't sure of anything anymore, except I wanted the goddamned Mazda back. Wanted to curl up in that steel cocoon with Jim and Papa and Chris and forget any of this had ever happened. With my laptop back, I could watch the video we'd made that Easter in Georgia, when Papa was teaching at Glynco and we saw him almost every night, and all day on Saturdays and Sundays.

He had promised me a piano, then. A shiny, black concert grand, with real ivory and ebony keys and a tone as mellow and bold and furious and pleading as I wanted it to be. As soon as

Papa was promoted to JSOC, we would buy a house in North Carolina, and *stay* there. Until then, a piano was too big to be moving across the country every year.

I had believed him, dreaming of the day when we'd have one in the parlor. We'd be a real family, like those smiling happys on the TV, where mothers didn't drink, and fathers came home every night, and kids didn't have to lie to their teachers about how they got the marks on their backs. It had been a stupid, hopeless fantasy, one that had died in the mission that killed Papa.

But right now, I needed something to cling to, so I crawled inside the flimsy cardboard walls of the daydream and lost myself in the ridiculous banality of a piano in the parlor. A piano. A concert grand.

The bus pulled into Union Station. Reality grabbed me as I disembarked, sinking its fingers into me like a vicious jailer, dragging me confused and beaten out into the dusk. I stood alone on the asphalt and stared at the red sunset bleeding all over the horizon and knew the brutal truth of my future: the Metro from here to the hospital, where they would cut my fingers off, because that's all they could do.

Or, maybe not. Maybe I could...

It might work. What did I have to lose? I looked for some bored traveler and asked to borrow their cellphone, coming up with some cockamamie story about leaving my phone at the hotel and getting separated from my tour group. A nice middle-aged Pakistani lady loaned me hers. I drew in a deep breath, then keyed in the landline for the club. Had to get this over with, before I lost my nerve.

"Concerto," A man who might have been Lonny answered on the third ring.

"Scott Foster, please."

"Who's calling?"

"Tell him it's...Faith."

I heard a click, then another, followed by the long, scuzzy pause of being put on hold. Suddenly, the earpiece exploded with the sound of a receiver clattering across a hard surface, and then a gruff, spiteful baritone filled my ear:

"Listen, cunt," Scotty growled. I imagined him pacing in his over-tight suit, the way he'd done at the club. "You give me everything you stole back, or I swear to God I'll—"

"I'm not Faith," I said, knowing he wouldn't listen. Counting on that fact. If I was to be of any use as a fall guy, Villalobos must have convinced Scotty that I was Faith, and that I had every one of those 5D discs. "But give me two-hundred-fifty thousand dollars, and I'll tell you where they are."

"Oh, you're extorting me, now? You think you can—"

"Technically, it's blackmail. Two-hundred-fifty thousand, sent to my email address. The one Lonny has on file."

"You can't email cash."

"What, you're too rich for Paypal? Figure it out. Tonight."

"Why should I give you anything after all you've—"

"I want printed proof of the payment in an envelope with my name on it. Leave it at the Lost and Found at Union Station by—" I checked the clock on the departure board. It was a little after eight, now, so ten would give him enough time to get the proof here without giving him much room to plan a double cross. "Ten o'clock tonight."

"Are you crazy? I can't get that kind of money in just a few hours."

"Sure you can. You're Scott Foster. You lost forty million without a peep."

"You fucking—" He broke off with a long, angry sigh, like he was trying to get ahold of himself. "Even if I do give you the money, how do I know you'll hold up your end?"

"You don't." I was starting to understand why Scotty hired people like Sloan to work for him. "But if I don't have that money by ten P.M. tonight, my next call is going to be to the cops. And I'll tell them everything. Ever'thee-in'." I added a bit of Texas twang to this last, remembering Scotty had said Faith was from Houston. Since I knew the accent from spending two very formative years on a Navy base in Corpus Christi, I might as well play the part.

Scotty sucked in a deep breath. "You say anything, Faith," he warned, his voice so full of venom that I shivered despite the heat. "You say one stinking word about what's gone on between us, and I promise you, you'll wish you had died the way Omar did."

I wanted to ask who Omar was, and how had he died, but it would have ruined the flow of the negotiations. "Two-hundred-fifty thousand," I admonished, copying Villalobos' style. "I'll check the account. If it's good, I'll call you Monday with the location of the discs. And don't bother calling back. This is a burner phone."

"Don't you tell me what to do, you little—"

I hung up in the middle of his reply, then handed the phone back to the lady with a grateful smile. She'd been busy watching her two grandkids, so I didn't think she'd overheard my conversation.

I wasn't sure if this blackmail thing would actually work, but it was the only chance left. Two-hundred-fifty thousand was cheap compared to what Scotty would lose if those 5D's were as incriminating as I suspected. Why else would everybody be so hot to get them? To get me?

Maybe I'd been stupid to call Scotty. Maybe he wouldn't show up with the money. Or worse, he'd send Nick and a few of the other bouncers down here to snatch me when I came looking for the envelope.

I'd have to stake out the Lost and Found and keep track of everyone who came and went to make sure no one was stalking me. If they were, I'd just lose them in the station and duck onto the Red Line. It might be hard to do, given my questionable physical condition, but if I could get away from Villalobos and Neanderthal, I was sure I could give Scotty's bouncers the slip. Nick didn't even carry a gun.

And if I couldn't shake them, well, the potential pay-off was worth the risk. I'd already lost Chris. And Papa. I couldn't let the music go without a fight.

I canvassed the waiting areas and found a good vantage point in a dark backwater of the waiting room that had both a clear view of the manned booth and easy access to the tunnel leading to the Red Line.

I bought a fare. According to the signs in the waiting area, I'd be rousted without one. I sat down to wait, only to be assaulted by the delicious scents wafting out from the small café nearby: coffee and broiling beef and the thick, greasy vapor of french fries.

My stomach leapt to the end of its chain like a starving sled dog, growling an urgent reminder that I hadn't eaten in—what? Twenty-nine hours? Thirty-two? No wonder I was so lightheaded. I spent my last few cents on a burger and a large drink. Fries were out of my budget. I headed back to my chair, sucking the soda dry before my butt even touched the seat.

Damn, I'd been thirsty. Must be the fever.

I took one bite out of the burger, then just stared at it, the smell of meat suddenly making me sick. All I could think about was last night and the blood coagulating in the gory mess that had been my hand. Suddenly, exhaustion hit me like a sledgehammer between the eyeballs. It all hurt so bad.

Humming Mozart, I rested the ice-filled cup on the arm of the chair and propped the splint against it, hoping the cold and elevation might cut the swelling down. Ten o'clock seemed awfully far away.

But I could do this. I had to do this. I'd let Jim down so many times before, couldn't I—just once—pull something miraculous off? Couldn't I keep my music?

I closed my eyes, took a few deep breaths to gather focus...

And passed out.

***

"Get up," a voice whispered, full of gravel and threat. I blinked, yawning groggily at the narrow, foxlike face hovering over the slab-sided arm of my chair. The man sneered, his starched white shirt buttoned up to his throat, the way Latino gangsters dressed in eighties movies. "Get up, bitch."

Damn, it was hot in here. I glanced around and found my corner of the waiting room empty, save for Fox-face and another, dough-faced guy dressed in gray pants and a leather jacket. Patches of moonlight spilled through the big arched windows and across the Southwest patterned floor. The clock on the departure board displayed 02:38.

Oh, Hell. I was supposed to be watching the Lost and Found counter. Now I didn't know who had left the envelope, or if it had been left. And this jerk kept standing in my line of sight. "Go away," I gruffed, motioning for him to move. "I can sleep here. I have a ticket."

"Shut up," Fox-face snarled, nodding to the doughy guy on the other side of my chair. Doughboy clamped his hand around my left arm and yanked me up, causing my right hand to knock the cup of melted ice to the floor and sending a cluster bomb of pain up my arm.

"You guys suck," I muttered.

Fox-face grabbed the back of my neck and pushed me ahead of him. Doughboy pressed the cold hard circle of a gun muzzle into my ribs, so it was hidden by my elbow as we walked towards the exit to the south patio. "Not another goddamn peep."

"What about a holy poop?" I probably should have been afraid, but being rousted always made me passive aggressive, and I had exhausted the last rat's ass I had to give on trying to keep my music. They shush-hissed me and steered me past a dozing Amtrak policeman sitting near the door. I thought about calling for help, but some part of me hoped they were just escorting me somewhere that they could turn over the money from Scotty.

Once outside, we headed past the low hedges towards the covered arcade tying the clock tower to the restaurant. The night air was warm and summery, but I shivered anyway. My fever had turned into chills.

We turned left, hugging the shadows of a tile-covered colonnade paralleling the parking lot on Alameda, until we reached the designated smoking area. It was a square, portico-like structure tiled in the Southwestern style of the rest of the main terminal. Built-in, concrete benches flanked the central openings of all four interior walls. They walked me through the archway facing the Metropolitan Water District building. The structures around us hid us from view of everything but the foot of the ramp that curved around towards Union Station East.

Fox-face spun me around and backed me against the rough stucco of the smoking area with one hand across my collarbone. He took the gun from Doughboy and stuck it in my face. "Where are Mr. Foster's discs?"

"Did he transfer my money?"

"Fuck your money. Where are those discs?"

No money, my hand was killing me, and I was still super annoyed with them for waking me up. "Uhmm..."

"Don't lie to me."

"How is uhm a lie?"

"You know what I mean."

"An uhm is an uhm. There's no truth or untruth to it. It's just, uhmmmm."

"I got a fucking gun on you, bitch."

"I fail to see how superior firepower affects the truth or untruth of an uhm."

Like a telemarketer forced to go off script, Fox-face was confounded by my utter lack of terror. He glanced over at Doughboy for help. That big lummox slapped me so hard across the face that my jaw clicked and my cheek stung from the blow.

It woke me up. Drove the fuzzy distance away. Fury surged through me, hot and vital, suppressing the pain with cold clarity. "Don't hit me again."

"We do what we want. You're ours, *comprendes?*" Fox-face pressed his hand across my throat, rubbing the gun barrel between my breasts. "We gonna find those discs."

Behind him, Doughboy laughed and dawdled a lean, double-edged knife from his fat fingers, grinning like a kid with a Christmas toy. He squatted down and cut the laces of my shoes. He pulled them off and turned them upside down before tossing them away.

I became acutely aware of Fox-face's positioning. Of his lax, almost bored grip on the gun and the exposed, heedless way he leaned his weight on me. Doughboy, too, didn't take me as a serious threat. Good. I'd use their complacency against them.

I started to wail and sob. Big, blubbering crocodile tears, bait to snooker them in.

Fox-face backed away as the larger man brandished the knife with his right hand and forced his left into my pockets, checking both front and back. He grabbed my T-shirt, yanked it up, and ran his sweaty palm along my torso, digging his fingers into the underside of my bra.

I bawled harder, twisting away, drawing him even more off-balance. My limbs shook from the adrenaline pumping through me. I felt wired, jangly, all crackling, fearless rage.

These guys should not be touching me.

Tires hissed on pavement as a white stretch limo rounded the corner, coming down the ramp towards the parking lot. Headlights flashed across us. Fox-face and Doughboy quickly lowered their weapons out of sight.

I seized the moment, moving with pre-programmed fluidity, echoes of my father's katas. My foot snapped into Fox-face's unprotected groin. As his body folded in on itself, he tried to raise his gun, but I slammed his elbow up with my knee and his wrist down with left forearm, turning his arm inside out. The gun went off as he screamed. It blasted out a cloud of stucco beside me, and painted my cheek with hot gas, deafening my ear on that side.

"Shit," Doughboy lunged at me, smack into the donkey kick I planted in his knee. He staggered back with a cry.

"You bitch!" Fox-face rushed me, swinging his good arm.

I stepped easily past his flailing left fist and slammed my skull into his nose. At the same time, I looped my good arm around his neck and used my hip as a fulcrum to hook his temple into the sharp, tiled edge of the archway. Something squelched when he hit. His body followed through with the with the full force of his momentum, swinging through the opening. I guess necks weren't supposed to bend that way, because there was a sickening *pop!* and he went limp. His head wasn't pointing the right direction when he hit the ground.

"You fucking bitch!" Doughboy attacked me from behind, but I was already ducking. I spun under his leading arm, blocking his knife hand with my splinted forearm and slammed my left fist just below his sternum to knock the wind out of him. He shifted his bulk to retreat, but overbalanced. I swept his feet out from under him with another kick, then stomped his windpipe when he hit the ground.

As soon as I realized they had stopped moving, the pain, fatigue and fever hit me like a sap. Blood throbbed in my ears, a shushing, roaring sound that drove a searing buzz saw through my arm with every beat.

I sank down to the curb and tugged the first shoe on, but then the dizziness overwhelmed me and I slumped back against the exterior wall of the smoking area. I closed my eyes, catching my breath, promising myself I'd put the other shoe on and run away as soon as my strength came back. After several minutes, I opened my eyes with great effort. As I reached for my other shoe, I found myself staring down the barrel of a big, black gun. The kind Feds use. Or Amtrak police.

"Freeze," the cop demanded. The nameplate over his badge said Uribe. "Hands up. Slowly." Behind him were two other train cops and a small crowd of people, mostly janitorial staff from the water district building.

A sorry sort of snicker escaped me. I pulled my shoe on. "Little late, don't you think?"

"I said get your hands up!"

He looked nervous, so I complied as best I could. The other two cops knelt down over Fox-face and Doughboy. "No pulse," said the one who had Fox-face. "This guy's dead."

Uribe gaped at me like I'd just sprouted tentacles from my eye sockets. "You killed him?"

I shrugged, slightly miffed that he hadn't noticed the loud report or the gun near Fox-face's cooling fingers. My ear was still ringing on that side. "He tried to shoot me."

"This one's still breathing." The other cop examined Doughboy. "I'll call for an ambulance." He snatched a radio off his belt and started speaking into it.

"You killed him," Uribe shook his head, incredulous. "What the Hell?" He captured my left wrist and brought out some handcuffs.

"Wait a sec, wait a sec." I tried to jerk my hand away, but the cuff had already clicked shut around my good wrist. "You can't arrest me. It was self defense."

"You just took out two armed men. One-handed. I'm not taking any chances." Uribe pulled my arms together in front, but couldn't get the other cuff around my splint. He settled for my upper arm, just above the elbow, then turned to the cop on the radio. "Call LAPD. Have 'em send a car for pickup."

I slumped wearily against the wall, too exhausted to fight. "He had a gun. It wasn't my fault."

"It wasn't her fault." A tall, muscular, regal-looking man pushed through the crowd, stepping up next to Uribe. He wore a sleek white suit, expensive cut. A shoulder-length mane of wavy black hair snaked wildly about a chiseled face, giving him a cultured, devilish look. Damn, he was hot. And a baritone. Was there such a thing as Lust at First Sight?

"Who asked you?" Fox-face's cop said, trying to push the man back into the crowd.

"I saw it while we were driving by." The tall man pointed at a silhouette behind the wheel of the white Mercedes limo parked crookedly in front of the clock tower. "My driver saw it, too. They attacked her. Held her at gunpoint."

"Tell it to the LAPD," the radio cop said. "They got a detective on the way."

The tall man stared at me, concern knotting his brow. I returned his gaze, until something about the compassion in his blue eyes made me turn away. Why would a guy like this stick his neck out for me? In the distance, sirens wailed, coming closer.

I sighed. Jail again. I was an adult this time, so things were bound to be worse, especially if Villalobos had friends on the inside. Maybe that's why I was sweating so much. I could feel it dripping down the small of my back.

Uribe toed me with his boot. "What's your name?"

I stared at the crowd, at the cops, at the good-looking stranger who was trying to save me.

"What's your name?" Uribe insisted.

"Trouble." I looked a veiled warning to Mr. Sexy. "As in 'Nothing But.'"

An ambulance squalled up, followed by a black-and-white and a sand-colored sedan with a dash cherry. They all parked with their headlights on, thrusting the area into a harsh, flat light that hurt my eyes. I scrunched lower, seeking refuge in the shadows cast by the bodies of the crowd.

The paramedics descended on Doughboy, checking vitals, asking questions of the train cop with the radio. The LAPD uniforms strolled from their black-and-white, pausing to let a wiry-haired detective catch up from the unmarked. The detective was a big, beefy man with a florid face and a nose the size most Brussels sprouts would envy. He peered down at Fox-face, at the gun, then flipped a badge at no one in particular and said: "Detective Hollis. What's the problem here?"

"She killed him." Uribe pointed at me, still bothered by the fact that I was capable of such a thing. Bothered me, too, but I'd still rather be alive.

"They attacked her." The tall stranger plowed past the train cop and tapped Hollis on the shoulder. "I saw it."

The detective turned to face the man, then looked away sharply, jaw clenching and unclenching. "What in the Hell are you doing here? Thought you only protected people from Bel Air, or Beverly Hills."

"Wanker, you can't arrest her. Those two attacked her. The fat one sliced her. All she did was fight back."

Hollis' eyes narrowed. "Don't call me Wanker, you oily son-of-a-bitch." He put his hands on his hips and jerked his chin at me. "Besides, where's the blood? Where's the knife?"

The paramedics loaded Doughboy onto a gurney and wheeled him past me. His eyes were open, and when he saw me, he made sucking sounds, like a boot being wrested from the mud. One of the paramedics peeled out of formation and headed toward me. His foot sent something skittering across the concrete. It came to rest between Detective Hollis and the tall stranger. Hollis picked it up gingerly, between thumb and forefinger, careful of the prints. It flashed metallic in the harsh, bright lights.

"See?" The stranger smiled, vindicated. "Told you there was a knife."

Hollis frowned. "Blood on it." He sauntered over and stared down at me curiously. "Somebody stick you?"

I shrugged, noncommittal.

The paramedic pushed Hollis away and squatted down in front of me. He was a small, sandy-haired guy, with constellations of dark, reddish freckles scattered haphazardly across his face. He set his kit down and popped it open. "You okay?"

I laughed at him. After everything that had happened to me, was I okay? It was like saying to Nagasaki: "Oops. We dropped one of those pesky atomic bombs and leveled your city. Are you okay?" What else was there to do but laugh?

I guess he took it as a "no," because he leaned over and wrapped a blood pressure sleeve around my good arm. He went to stick the thermo-sensor in my ear, then paused upon seeing the splint. "You on any drugs?"

"Antibiotics. Painkillers. Worn off, now."

He nodded and shoved the sensor in, frowning at the readout. "Your fever is pretty high. You should be in bed."

Hollis scowled, obviously irritated by the paramedic's interference. He hunkered down off to my left and glared at me. "What's your name?"

I thought about it. Decided on the truth. "Rad."

"Somebody stick you, Rad? One of those guys do you with this knife." He held it up.

"Tried to."

"But you stopped them?"

I nodded. My mouth was a lint ball.

Hollis grunted and steered a pensive glance at the tall stranger, then turned abruptly back to me. "You know Tovenaar here?" he asked in a low voice.

I shook my head. "Can I have some water?"

The detective scratched his bulbous nose and looked up at Uribe. "Get her something to drink." The Amtrak cop nodded and disappeared through the crowd. Hollis indicated Fox-face. "You put both those assholes down clean, Rad? Neither guy touched you?"

"Not that I know of," I said, trying to be equivocal.

"How can someone knife you, and you not know?" He stood up, rubbing a massive paw along his pink jowl, as he regarded Tovenaar. "She's not one of yours, is she? I would expect all this if she was one of yours."

Tovenaar didn't respond, just glanced at me with a look of somber apology, as if he somehow felt responsible for all the woe that had fallen upon my head. A strange sensation rolled over me as I met his gaze, totally at odds with the situation. It felt like we were exes who really wanted to get back together, even though I didn't recall ever seeing him before tonight.

The paramedic rocked back on his heels, keying something into the computer in his kit. "Everything else checks out okay. Do you hurt anywhere?"

"Here." I raised my splint.

He cradled it gently, grimacing at the blood and lymph oozing from a crack in the seam. "When did this happen?"

"Just now. It wasn't leaking before."

"No." He taped over the gap in the splint. "I meant when did the gunshot happen?"

"Yesterday," I replied without thinking.

"A gunshot wound? Yesterday?" Hollis spun around and stared at me, questions swimming in the murky depths of his eyes. "Day? Or night?"

Too late to take it back. Tell the truth. "Night."

Something happened in Hollis' face. A shift, a subtle hardening. He tapped the paramedic on the shoulder. "Is she good to go?"

The sandy-haired man shrugged. "I guess so."

Hollis turned to the uniforms. "Put her in my car."

They flanked me, reached under each armpit, and hoisted me up. I teetered, unsure of my legs, and one of the cops steadied me with a hand to my back.

"Shit!" He yanked his hand away. A red smear crossed the width of his palm.

It dawned on me slowly. Not sweat. Blood. Doughboy had cut me, and I'd been so adrenal I hadn't even felt it.

The paramedic moved to swab the cut, but Hollis pushed him away and peered at my back. He shook his head. "Not bad. Just a scratch. We'll treat it at the station."

Tovenaar caught him by the shoulder. "You can't arrest her. It was self defense. The D.A. will throw—"

"Who's arresting? Call it protective custody."

"Don't think I won't follow up, Wanker."

A snide cackle erupted from the detective's barrel chest. "Go right ahead, you slick bastard." He watched, grinning, as the uniforms stuffed me into the unmarked police car.

I never even got my water.

CHAPTER FIVE

Hollis called ahead and had two uniformed officers and a nurse waiting for me when we got to the station. The nurse swabbed my back with some antiseptic that stung, then taped gauze across it. When she was finished, Hollis said to the uniforms: "This is the APB from Beverly Hills that Rossi has been looking for. Take her to room seven. I'll put in a call."

They swept me away to a small room the size of a walk-in closet. They sat me down, still handcuffed, in a hard plastic chair in front of an electronic table, and left.

The table was fake wood, with dual touchpads and a bi-directional, pop-up viewing screen in the center. The tops of three chairs peeked over the opposite edge. The room itself was pretty bland. A mirrored observation window ran along one wall, with camera lenses poking out above the mirror. What must have been the floor was hard to distinguish from scuff marks, old grit, and crusted chewing gum.

Nobody came in for a quite a while, long enough for my heel to start aching from the shot to Doughboy's knee and my shoulders to cramp from the awkward position of my hands. Added to what was going on inside the splint, it topped out my pain scale.

I closed my eyes and hummed Chopin to distract myself. I started to nod off and almost fell from the chair, so I laid down on the floor along the wall under the mirror, just to drive them crazy. I woke up with a start when the door opened and two suits walked in.

I blinked, surprised. I'd expected Hollis.

"Ms. Damiano?" the smaller one said. It was a woman. Took me a second, but I finally recognized them. The Samoan and the lady cop. "Ms. Damiano," the lady cop said again as they lifted me back into the chair. "I'm Gloria Rossi. We'd like to ask you a few questions about yesterday night."

I cleared my throat, trying to figure out what their presence here meant to my continued-but-sorry existence. All my radar signals screamed "bogey." My body tensed with that same precognitive rush of dread and adrenaline I'd had when Villalobos first fixed his gaze on me. "Am I under arrest?"

The Samoan introduced himself as Manny Iso Iso. He shook his head. "We just want to ask a few questions."

"If I'm not under arrest, why am I still handcuffed?"

"Guess somebody forgot about you," the lady cop said, emphasizing 'forgot.' It wasn't clear whether she meant it to be coercive, or sarcastic. She unlocked me, putting the handcuffs on the table between us. I sighed and moved my arms and shoulders around to help circulation. The police officers sat down opposite me.

Rossi began: "Ms. Damiano, about the other night—"

"Can I have some water?" I said, still slogging through the fevered morass of my thoughts, trying to come up with some defense against these two.

They exchanged glances. Without a word, Iso Iso got up.

"Make it two," I said, as he headed for the door. "And put one of those little paper umbrellas in each of them."

"Ms. Damiano," the lady cop said again. "We have over a hundred witnesses who put you in a nightclub on Brighton Way forty minutes before you appeared at the hospital last Thursday night. You still want to claim you can't remember what happened?"

"Can I have a lawyer?"

"You're not being charged with anything. We merely want a statement."

"Just a statement? Is that all?" A chuckle burrowed up from deep in my chest. Of a sudden, everything seemed funny to me. My life had become so surreal.

"This is regarding a murder investigation," Rossi said sternly. "It shouldn't be taken lightly." She fingered a few keys on the touchpad. An image popped up on the view screen. A mug-shot showed a front and side view of Sloan.

"You recognize him, Ms. Damiano?" A subtle smile edged Rossi's lips. "His name is—was—Justin Sloan. He was shot yesterday night. In, by some strange coincidence, the same nightclub where you happened to be. Now, Mr. Foster, the owner of that nightclub, claims that Mr. Sloan was killed trying to stop you leaving after you burglarized the nightclub office. Would you care to elaborate on that scenario?"

"If I'm not under arrest, why are you trying to incriminate me?"

"I'm not. I'm merely—"

"You're saying I'm a thief and a murderer. That seems pretty incriminating to me."

"I'm merely presenting one person's hearsay explanation of yesterday night's events. If you have another version, I'll be more than happy to—" She broke off as the door opened. Iso Iso sauntered in and placed a foam cup and a liter of Evian next to my elbow.

The bottle was new and I had trouble unscrewing the cap one-handed, so he opened it for me and poured me a cupful. I sucked it down and poured another one. Sucked that one down too. After half the bottle found its way down my throat, and I thought I would throw up from so much water in my stomach, I turned my attention to the other side of the table.

There was a new mug-shot on the viewer: Fox-face's. The lady cop noted my reaction. "Mr. Gomez here is—was—an associate of Mr. Sloan's. As was Mr. Maitlin, the gentleman whose voice box you shattered this evening down at the train station. They are—were—allegedly working for some pretty nasty people. People with a lot of power. A lot of money. People who got that money by some very unsavory practices. You follow me, Ms. Damiano?"

I nodded, immediately regretting the act because it made me even more queasy.

"Excellent. Allow me to postulate a little theory of mine. You stumbled into some kind of business involving Mr. Sloan, during which he was killed and you were shot. In the hand. A traumatic experience for a pianist, wouldn't you say?"

"You ever think of selling used cars?" I said with wide-eyed innocence. "You have the voice for it."

"Almost as traumatic," she continued, "as having men like Mr. Gomez here," she pointed at Fox-face's image, "and his buddy Maitlin threaten you with bodily harm. Now, despite the fact they underestimated your body's ability to avoid harm, you are still in a very dangerous position. Not only do you know something you shouldn't know, and possibly have something you shouldn't have, but you've also killed or maimed a couple of well-connected gangsters. I imagine that some very ruthless people are extremely upset with you. Is that an accurate picture, Miss Damiano, or do you need something clarified?"

"Well," I sniffed and wiped my nose with the back of my good hand. "There is the matter of the electoral college. I mean, how can you justify—"

"Miss Damiano—" Iso Iso began.

"Call me Rad," I said. The redundancy was getting to me.

"Rad, then." He drew in a deep breath, trying another tack. "Why did you tell James Throckmorton you witnessed a murder?"

I sat up taller, on guard. How did they know about Jim?

Rossi grinned, and I realized I never should have shown an interest. To cops like these, any weakness was a paved road to the jugular.

Iso Iso nodded sagely. "Mr. Throckmorton reported a break-in at his house this afternoon. According to the report, he was pretty shaken up about the extent of the damage."

He touched a key and the text of an affidavit flashed on the screen, at the bottom was the familiar signature of James Philip Throckmorton. My queasiness returned full force. *God, Jim, why did you have to bring the cops into this? Of all the stupid—*

Iso Iso continued: "He also was quite concerned about a friend of his. He filed a missing person report, seeing as this friend told him she'd been shot the night before while witnessing a murder."

"I don't know any James Throckmorton," I said with a shrug.

Rossi chuckled. "Then why were your fingerprints all over his house?"

I didn't answer, not knowing what else to say.

"Look, Rad," Iso Iso leaned across the table toward me. "We both know you were there when Sloan got shot. All we want is for you to let justice be served. Tell the truth about it."

"And what happens if I do?"

"Well," he pointed toward my splint. "For one thing, you'll get that money we talked about. The Victim's Assistance Fund will pay up to fifty grand toward your medical expenses."

"What's the catch?"

"No catch. All we ask is that you cooperate with the investigation." He smiled and sat back in his chair, body language oozing victory.

I thought about it. Thought some more. I still didn't trust these two. But what could I do?

Iso Iso got tired of waiting. "You know, if you refuse to help us, Mr. Throckmorton is the only reliable witness we've got. And seeing as people like Gomez and Maitlin are involved, well..." He picked up the handcuffs from the tabletop between us. "We just might have to drag good ole Jim in here and slap him in protective custody." He shook the metal restraints daintily, the way a kid shakes a sparrow carcass to see if it's really dead. "Very protective custody."

"You wouldn't."

"Try me."

I glared at him, hating the corner he'd painted me into. I'd tell them anything they wanted to know. I'd have to tell them, to keep Jim out of it. "How do I know you haven't already locked him up?"

He unclipped a phone from his belt and offered it to me. "Why don't you call his house and find out?"

I grabbed the phone. Keyed it about five or six times, but couldn't get through. "This thing doesn't work."

"You need a special code." Rossi set her briefcase on the table and removed a tablet. She set a stylus on top, and pushed them across the table toward me. "As soon as you sign this, I'll give it to you."

I scanned the neat, black rows of print. A cold fist slowly squeezed the breath from me as my brain deciphered the meaning behind the paragraphs:

Villalobos owned these cops.

Why else would they have already prepared a statement saying the bastard was innocent? A statement explaining he'd shot Sloan in my defense, to save me from a killing blow from Sloan's knife. And it had my name typed under the dotted line, waiting for my signature.

"With that," Iso Iso indicated the affidavit in front of me, "we'll have all we need. We'll never have to bother you, or your buddy Jim again."

Our eyes locked. The phone burned a hole in my palm as I realized exactly what was left unsaid. Favor for a favor. Protection for protection.

I signed on the dotted line.

Rossi gave me the access code and I dialed Jim's cell.

The phone purred intermittently as it rang through the static. I heard a sharp click, the sound of random items knocking around the dresser top as a hand fumbled for the phone, and then Jim's sleep-muddied voice came on line: "'Lo?"

"Hey," I said, relieved to find the crooked cops hadn't lied to me. He was home, safe and sound. And with Villalobos off my tail, maybe things would turn out okay, after all. Or as okay as they could be once my fingers were gone.

Jim gasped, and things rustled around like he was sitting up in bed. "Rad is this you? Like really you?"

"It's me."

"Shit, it's four-thirty in the morning. Where have you been?"

"Thought we agreed, Jim. No cops."

"I've been worried sick about you. And besides, you saw the house. How could I file an insurance claim without a police report?" He breathed a long whoosh of relief. "Damn, it's good to hear from you. Where'd you go?"

"Auditioned for the Philharmonic."

"Don't be a smart-ass."

"Have to. It's in my job description."

He laughed that high, maniacal hyena laugh that always sent me up the wall. I loved it. When he settled down he said: "Where are you now? I'll come and get you."

"Downtown. At Central Jail."

He went quiet for a moment. "You didn't get arrested, did you?" he said, trying to be tactful and accusatory all at once.

Didn't work, but I forgave him under the circumstances. "No. Picked me up as a witness. Offered me money to help to fix my hand."

"That's great."

"Yeah," I said, noncommittal. Maybe I could use part of the pay-off to buy Jim a new synth. "Look, I need a ride to the hospital. Can you—?"

"Absolutely. I'll leave right now, but the drive will take almost an hour. Can you wait?"

"Sure," I said, grateful to have somebody else make the decisions for a while. "Oh, and Jim I, uh... " The words refused to come, hanging up at the base of my throat in a sticky, burning ball of sap. I finally choked them out. "Sorry to put you through all this."

He didn't respond right away. I didn't blame him. It sounded so inadequate. Eventually, his sigh broke the quiet. He chuckled wryly. "Rad, you're the sorriest person I ever met."

***

I sat on a wooden bench in the antiseptic station lobby and closed my eyes because I didn't want to look at the bulletin board that touted the dangers of CYBL, the new street drug that had killed my little brother. The flat, annoying hum of the fluorescent lights bothered me, and all I wanted was to doze off until Jim arrived to collect me. An hour wasn't long, but after all I'd been through, it was forever.

"You okay?" a vaguely familiar baritone boomed above me.

My eyelids parted. A paper cup steaming with coffee hovered in front of my face, held by a large, masculine hand with a gold nugget pinky ring the size of an asteroid. But nothing on the ring finger. I looked up into shining blue eyes and a smile charming enough to seduce the Mother Mary.

Tovenaar. The tall stranger, the one in the white suit and even whiter Mercedes limo who had tried to keep me from going to jail. He had been good-looking in the harsh light of the police cars. Right now, up close, where I could smell the smoky, spicy musk of his cologne, he was absolutely riveting. Tanned, rugged face. Laugh lines at the corners of a sensuous mouth. A mega-carat diamond stud in his left ear. "I'm Tony."

"I'm Rad," I chirped, so he wouldn't catch me drooling.

He pushed the cup toward my hand. "Here. Take it. You look like you could use a jolt."

I took it, careful not to spill the hot liquid on the expensive fabric of his suit cuff. The cup felt good in my hand. Warm. Comforting. I held it against my stomach, but didn't drink it. The coffee smelled wonderful, but I could tell by the color he'd ruined it with cream.

"Something wrong?" His eyebrows arched. "You don't like coffee?"

"No, no. Coffee's great." I took a quick sip. "I'm just tired." I smiled and sipped again, trying not to make a face at the odd taste. He'd loaded it with some kind of sweetener with a bitter aftertaste, but beggars can't be choosers. "It's great. Thanks."

"My pleasure." He sat down on the bench next to me. "I see Detective Hollis has finally decided to let you go."

"You been here all this time?"

He nodded. "Wanted to give a witness statement. Sort of felt responsible for you. Not every day something like this happens."

"Yeah. Not to most people, anyway."

His brows furrowed. "You in trouble?"

"Not really." I shrugged and took another sip of coffee. "No house. No hand. No money. Cops don't like me. People I don't know are trying to kill me. With stats like that, somebody's bound to send me a pre-approved palladium card."

Those eyes regarded me, searching, like he wasn't sure if I was serious or not. "You always so flip?"

I stared back at him, but couldn't hold his gaze. I looked at the floor instead. "Listen, Mr. Tovenaar, I, uh—"

"Call me Tony."

"Look, uh," I cleared my throat. "Tony. Thanks for sticking around. I appreciate that."

"Least I could do. My knight in shining armor act has gotten a little rusty. Where'd you learn all that ninja stuff?"

"My father was a TURTL."

One corner of his mouth hitched up, and I could tell he thought I was being flip again.

"Tactical Urban Reconnaissance and Terrorist Liquidation," I explained. "It was a semi-secret, multi-agency task force. Sort of like the SeALs. Papa saw some pretty gruesome stuff when he was in country. Civilians tortured, raped. He wanted to make sure I could take care of myself."

"Well, hooray for your father. More people like you around, violent crimes against women would be non-existent."

"You a lawyer?" I asked. Seemed a safe bet from the way Hollis had talked to him.

He chuckled. A deep, warm, rumbling sound, like logs shifting in a hearth fire. "When I have to be."

I didn't see what was so funny, so I gulped down the rest of the coffee to cover. God, he was handsome. I wondered if he was any good in bed. Guy like him would have to be. Damn.

Here I was, reeking of blood and sweat, shirt torn, hair matted, hand made of hamburger. Who would be interested in me? Life was so unfair.

He angled sideways across the bench to face me. "You need a ride? I'll drop you off wherever you need to go."

I shook my head. "Got somebody coming. Be here in about forty-five minutes."

He stared at me like he didn't believe me. "Well, then." He stood abruptly, patting his stomach. "I'm starving. There's this little falafel joint around the corner. Open all night. Want to come along? I'm buying."

I was so surprised I didn't say anything. Never tried for a 'pity pick-up' before.

His face clouded over at my hesitation. "I'll drop you off back here in plenty of time."

"Sure," I finally croaked.

He laughed and slipped a phone from his inside jacket pocket. A quick tapping on the touchscreen and a little chime sounded. "Percy, bring the limo around," he said into the phone, then slipped it back under his jacket and smiled at me. "All set."

I tried to stand up. Didn't work. Everything was catching up with me: the pain, the fever, no food for two days. Too much sitting after too much stress. I tried again.

Somber sympathy tugged at Tony's mouth. He helped me up and out to the street. My legs were rubbery, my arms like sandbags.

The word 'limo' reverberated around my skull. Handsome, generous, and rich. Maybe he'd fall in love with me and loan me the money to get my hand fixed. A stupid fantasy, but I needed a little hope. Just a little one. Reality was always so brutal.

We stood at the curb, Tony's strong arm cradling me. Headlights flashed down the street. The limo cruised towards us through the pools of light under the streetlamps and stopped at the curb with a soft growl. Tony opened the rear door, placed me gently on the seat facing the rear of the limo, and then climbed in and sat across from me.

I sank against the soft cushions as the limo pulled forward, the lights of the police station swimming into darkness. The movement stormed my senses with a wave of dizziness.

Tony leaned toward me, frowning. "You okay?"

I sucked in a deep breath, let it out. "Yeh. Be fine."

At the next intersection the limo slowed to a stop, idling patiently through what I figured was a red light, but since I was facing the back, all I saw was the empty street behind us. I breathed deep again and looked past Tony as the dark figure of a man detached from the shadows of an alley a few feet away. He glided toward us with the fluid menace of a predator. As he entered the red glare of the stoplight, I saw the bulge of a shoulder holster under his gray leather jacket:

Villalobos. He was going to kill me so I couldn't recant my affidavit. And Tony, too, just for being with me.

"Shit!" My heart clawed into my throat like a frightened cat. I tried to point but my arms wouldn't listen. My whole body was deadweight. "Shit!"

Tony looked at me like I was crazy, then craned his neck, following my gaze. "What's wrong?"

"That man!"

"What about him?"

Villalobos was close now. His hand reached for the door, a cold, bloodthirsty smile on his lips. I was frantic, unable to move, the urgency in my voice the only chance I had to save us both. "He's got a gun!"

"Of course he does." Tony grinned. "He works for me."

CHAPTER SIX

"So," Villalobos sat down beside Tony and assessed me with a casual sweep of his obsidian eyes. A jagged scab traversed his nose, and he had a scrape along the side of his neck. Reminders of what I'd done with the heel of my shoe. "You got her."

"Was there any doubt?" Tony knocked on the smoke-tinted Plexiglass divider behind my head, trailing a knuckle softly along my cheekbone as he drew his hand away. The limo lurched forward into the night.

"Bassard," I fumed, trying to keep my head from drooping. My vision kept going in and out of focus, and it was hard to form words correctly. At least the pain had drifted away, along with my ability to move. "Ya doped th' coffee."

"Smart girl." Tony nodded. "But not smart enough." He studied me intently, the idle speculation in his gaze hardening into something more hungry, more immediate. "Where's the silver disc?"

"Lost it."

Tony frowned, considering this. Abruptly, he turned to the bar, chunked some ice into a highball glass, and poured himself three fingers of Glenfiddich. He took a sip, studied me again, his eyes narrowed in thought. "You're lying."

"Eff yoo," I said, furious at being suckered so neatly. This S.O.B had kidnapped me right out of the police station, and I'd be damned if I made this part easy for him.

He sighed, gave a nod to Villalobos. "Search her."

Villalobos grabbed my shirt collar and yanked me forward, so that I fell to my knees on the floor, my face pressed into the velour seat between him and Tony. Oddly, the seat smelled like hyacinth.

I tried to resist, to recoil, but my body refused to act. I growled, cursing my helplessness, fury spiraling into panic as he peeled my shirt up over my head and threw it on the floor. He stripped off my bra, then gently lowered me onto my back on the carpet, my head a foot away from Tony's black leather Guccis. Surprisingly, he seemed to be very careful not to jar my splint during all of this.

Tony sipped his drink, gazing at my naked chest with a pensive, amused expression. It was weird. I couldn't move my limbs, but I could feel my skin goose-pimpling.

Villalobos removed my shoes, my socks, then deftly unzipped my jeans and tugged them off. I held my breath as his manicured fingers hooked under the waistband of my panties.

"No," Tony said.

Villalobos gave him a questioning look.

"No," Tony repeated. "Not yet."

Villalobos nodded, then sat back on his haunches, collecting my things and setting them on the seat I'd so recently vacated. He sat down next to them and tore the insoles out of my shoes.

As he methodically went through every seam and stitch of my clothing, Tony continued to study me, like an artist confronted with a blank canvas. He bent down to get a closer look, his tie falling across my left breast as his hand reached out to touch my—

Belly.

"Appendix?" he asked, brushing his fingers along the scar.

"Don' tush me," I snarled, helpless and hating it. They could do anything they wanted to me. Anything.

He turned his head to meet my gaze. His breath caught. He froze with a look of shocked recognition. His hand jerked away as if it had been burned.

"It's her," he murmured, gaping at me. "It's her."

Villalobos looked up from feeling the hem of my jeans, brows arching in surprise as he saw the look on Tony's face. "Who?"

Tony shook his head, eyes going vague and unfocused. He sat back, grabbed his glass without even looking at it, and drained it, still staring off into space like a man faced with a ghost.

Villalobos watched him for a moment, then glanced at me, dubious. "Her? You sure?"

"I think so."

Villalobos stared at me, his surprise turning to alarm. He regarded Tony seriously. "What do you want to do about it?"

"I don't know. I don't know. Do you feel it?" Tony asked, searching my gaze.

I felt naked, terrified, and absolutely fuming, but I knew from the fiery, almost manic light in his eyes he wasn't interested in any of that. He wanted to know if I felt I was her. Whoever that was.

"'M nod Fait'." It was the only person I could think he might mistake me for.

"I know." He grinned, a strange, mournful tenderness in his eyes. He slipped his suit coat off, draped it over my torso, covering me from shoulders to thighs, then sat back and poured himself another drink.

Villalobos stared at him a moment, the way a man stares at a friend who's just gone completely loopy, then shrugged and resumed examining my clothing.

Tony kept peering intently at my face, like he was trying to etch it into his brain. I stared back, feeling the warmth of his body lingering in the heavy, perfumed softness of his suitcoat, wondering what in the Hell his belated chivalry meant, and if there was any way I could use it to get out of this mess alive.

"Nothing," Villalobos announced, when he'd inspected the last seam in my jeans.

"Where's the disc?" Tony asked me, expression hardening into a sizzling, predatory alertness that took my breath away.

"Wish one? Derteen..."

"Yes, I know. We recovered the twelve you left at the hospital. There's only one left. The silver one. Where is it?"

"I tellya 'boud th' dis', yoo gon' kill me."

"You're no good to me dead."

"Don' bl'eef you."

He leaned forward, cupping my chin, forcing me to look at him. "We don't have time for this," he said voice going soft and gentle, eyes swimming in sincerity. "I give you my word. I won't kill you."

That instant kindness, the way he could switch the charm on and off, scared me more than anything. I couldn't trust him. No way I could trust him. "V'lobos kill me."

"No. None of my people will kill you. Just tell me where it is."

"Don' haff id."

Tony scowled, glancing over at Villalobos. "Have Ravi check her car again. And get a second sweep of that hospital."

My car? These bastards had my car?

Of course they did. I'd left the key fob in it. What a dumbass. "Wan' muh car bag. An' two-hunner-fifdy thou."

"And you'll turn over the 5D?"

I nodded. It was worth a shot.

"Done."

I blinked, surprised it could be that easy. I dipped my chin towards the splint. "In dere."

A little smile tugged at one corner of Tony's mouth. He leaned over, fingering the little bulge under the control board where I'd stashed the disc. "Clever."

Despite the drugged coffee, I gasped and writhed as he turned the splint off. He flipped the panel open, withdrew the silver disc, and carefully turned the splint back on. I squeezed the tears from my eyes as the tension returned and the pain spiked all over again. Luckily—or unluckily—the drug reasserted itself, sweeping me along in a slow, floaty slide into semi-consciousness.

As Tony examined the silver disc in the light from the bar, Villalobos slipped a phone from inside his jacket and keyed a number.

"That's it." Tony slid the disc in his inside coat pocket.

At this, a weight seemed to lift from Villalobos. He grinned, his fierce, dour face transformed with victory.

"Slager," a woman's voice said over the phone.

Tony snatched it, held it to his ear. "We've got her. Grab Lelani and meet us at the boneyard."

Boneyard? Oh, Hell.

They weren't going to follow through with the deal. They were going to kill me, now. I wondered if I'd see Chris. Or Papa. Or if death was just absence, cold and eternal.

***

Head swimming. Lights. Faces crashed over me in waves. Tony smiled down at me, a ragged red sun dawning over his shoulder as he and Villalobos lugged me—where?

An expensive tract house?

A dog barked from inside the house. I closed my eyes, but couldn't get them open again. Door hinges groaned. Words echoed, garbled and urgent. Someone lifted my limp body, stretched me out on a hard bed and then the hands were all over me, wrapping cold, rough fabric over my wrist and ankles, pulling me spread-eagled. Cold metal skimmed my belly, my skin recoiling from its touch as somebody cut my panties away. Distant fingers pulled my thighs apart, stroked my pubic hair. I tried to fight, but nothing worked.

Somebody threw a sheet over me, and I panicked. What if I was in a morgue? What if I was already dead?

I'm sorry, Papa, I prayed silently, because he'd kill me all over again if he ever found out I'd gone down without a fight. He'd raised me to take care of myself, not to—

I felt a pinch in the crook of my arm. An odd warmth squeezed into my vein. It spread up to my bicep and shoulder, spilled into my chest with a delicious speed that made me sigh. My limbs began to tingle, and all at once, a floodlight went off in my brain, chasing away the woolly darkness that had swamped me.

I gasped and opened my eyes, crashing back into awareness. I was suddenly, acutely aware of how much my hand hurt. I lifted my head past the sheet and glanced clumsily down at it, my head swaying drunkenly from side to side. I was strapped to an operating table in an oversized tile bathroom. To my left, Tony peered down at me, a syringe in his hand. "You awake?"

I knew I should be mad at him. Or at least scared. But all I could feel was a kind of pleasant, bubbly attentiveness. That, and the throbbing agony in my right hand. "Yeah."

He set the syringe down on a small metal table and leaned over me, eyes brimming with sincerity and concern. "I'm going to ask you some questions. I want you to answer them completely and truthfully. Okay?"

"Okay," I said, smiling back at him.

"Good." He gave me the most dazzling, most sexy smile any man had ever given me, and I knew I'd tell him anything. Because he wanted me to. Or, because he wanted me, too. I wasn't sure of the distinction. "What's seven plus eight?"

"Fifteen."

"Who was the first President of the United States?"

"George Washington."

"Good." He gave me that mega-candle watt smile again. "Very good. Now, what's your full name?"

"Radiana Damiano."

"No middle name?"

"Papa said middle names are pretentious bullshit."

"Your mother's maiden name?"

"Bergamo."

"Your social security number?"

I told him that, and my date of birth, and my password for my bank account, and all the other things he asked me. When he finished with those questions, he asked: "Anything else you think I should know?"

"I think you're an asshole. Even though you're sexy as Hell. And Villalobos is a shithead for shooting me. And I am pretty sure you gave me some kind of truth serum. Which is a very dick move. Which kind of goes back to you being an asshole. Even though you are sexy as Hell. And if I was functional I would kick your ass."

"Duly noted. Anything else?"

"My hand hurts."

"I know. I'm sorry about that. Now, can you tell me a secret? Something you've never told anybody else?"

I tried really hard not to let it slip, but in the end I blabbed: "I'm in love with Jim."

"Is he in love with you?"

I shook my head, swallowing past the tightness in my throat. "He's gay. He doesn't like me that way."

"Do you have any other secrets, Rad? Anything that might get you in trouble if you told it? Like, maybe, how you got those scars?"

I stared at him, alarm bells going off in my head. This was wrong, all wrong. I should be fuming at him. I should be tearing his heart out and making his entrails into violin strings.

"Rad..." He caressed my cheek with his knuckles. "You know I won't tell anybody. You know your secrets are safe with me."

"No." I closed my eyes, trying to block out the mesmerizing blue of his gaze. "Nothing's safe."

But closing my eyes couldn't block out the soothing warmth of his fingers on my face, the compassion in his voice. "Come on, Rad. Tell me. You know you want to. A secret like that, it burns. It hurts. Tell it to me. Get it out. Where'd you get those scars?"

"Appendix," I said, hoping to pacify him. I didn't want to say this. I didn't. I hated to admit it to anyone, even myself.

"No, not that. The other ones. On your back. Whip marks. Cigarette burns. Who did that to you?"

"Can't tell you."

"Do you like that kind of stuff?"

"No. *No.*" I looked at him, pleading, afraid it would come flooding back, surge up from that deep, dark hole I stuffed it all into. "I don't wanna do this anymore."

"Was it Foster? Did Scott Foster do that to you? Mess with your mind? Make you work for him?"

"No!"

"Then who did it?"

"Fuck you!" I screamed at him. "Just fuck you!" I lunged against the restraints, thrashing my splint around, trying to break free so I could smash his face in and wipe away that smug compassion that even now tugged at me like a riptide. Had I just used the F-word? I must really be pissed off at him. Funny how it seemed so distant.

Why wasn't he pissed off back?

"Relax!" He grabbed my shoulders, pressed me down on the table, pinning my elbows with his forearms. "Relax, relax, you're going to hurt yourself. You're okay. You don't have to answer that. You don't have to answer, right now."

I stopped fighting and glared, panting into his face. My breath bounced off his chin, my gaze locked with his.

A tenderness shone in his eyes that confused me. His empathy resonated with a forgotten hunger deep inside me. Despite everything he had done, all the tricks and shenanigans, for some reason, this one thing felt real. He folded an arm behind me, drew me into a gentle embrace.

I drove my face into his neck, drinking in his touch, his closeness, the clean, manly scent of his cologne. I knew he didn't really care, knew he was just trying to mess with me, to show me the power he had over me, but it had been so long since anybody had hugged me like this. Since anybody had wanted to hug me that way.

"Relax," he murmured. His fingers brushed a few stray hairs away from my mouth. "Get some rest, now." He started to pull away, but I resisted, pressing harder against him, suddenly, desperately afraid of being alone.

I closed my eyes, hating myself, hating my weakness. Because I'd say anything, just to have him hug me again. Except the truth.

He slipped his arm out and lowered me toward the bed.

"You gonna kill me now?" I asked him, because, quite frankly, I wouldn't have minded it. I didn't want any more questions. I didn't want any more truth.

"I told you. You're no good to me dead."

"What do you want with me, then?"

"I want you to work for me."

"Doing what?"

"Playing Faith."

"Scotty's Faith?"

He nodded. "You be Faith Hopkins, and I'll fly the top five surgeons in the world here to rebuild your hand. Pay all the regeneration costs. Everything."

"Re-gen's not real. That's like, sci-fi bullshit."

"It's real," he assured me. "Very expensive and still highly experimental, but it's real. We can fix your hand. Rebuild it. Plus, I'll give you the two-hundred-fifty thousand dollars, payable two weeks after the completion of the job."

"This the job Villalobos was trying to offer me?"

Tony nodded. "We been waiting over a year for someone like you. Same facial features, same body type, same bone structure. That's why I'm willing to pay you so much."

I scowled. "I turned him down. He shot me for it."

"He saved your life. Sloan had a second knife."

My eyes narrowed. "There was no second knife."

"Then tell me what his other hand was doing," he challenged.

I couldn't remember. Racked my brain, squeezed it dry, but I couldn't remember. "There was no other knife."

He withdrew his phone from his pocket, keyed up something and turned the screen toward me.

A fish-eyed view of Sloan and I appeared on the screen, framed by the doorway of the dressing room. Villalobos must have had a body cam. I had just fallen down to one knee, purse strap caught on the arm of the chair. Sloan was stepping in, his right hand arcing down at me, drawing my block, opening my defenses up for a killing blow: A six inch stiletto was in his left hand as it plunged towards my heart. And then that fateful second unfolded, the muzzle flash of Villalobos' gun turning half the screen white for an instant before Tony froze the image and regarded me expectantly.

"No." I shook my head. "You faked that. For the cops. So Villalobos wouldn't get arrested."

He showed me the time-date stamp code on the image, then pulled the camera card out of the phone and showed me the holographic geo-sat authentication stripe. A single-use security encrypted camera card, one designed specifically for evidence cams. Very hard to fake. I gaped at it, at the implications of it. "What are you guys, cops or something?"

"Or something," Tony answered cryptically, popping the card back in and stowing the phone. "Do you want to work for me, or not?"

"What would I have to do? As Faith?"

"There are risks involved. You could get hurt. Killed. But my people will protect you. As long as you stick with the program, you'll be reasonably safe. And if you are injured during the mission, I'll pay those medical bills, of course."

"Of course," I said, oozing sarcasm. "What if I say no?"

"You'll wake up about eight hours from now in a motel room somewhere in Southern California with a thousand dollars and a set of new clothes. The rest is up to you."

"The rest of what?"

"Fixing your hand. Staying clear of Scotty. He thinks you stole some very confidential data. Yes," he nodded to my look. "That's what was on the discs. Plus, Scotty's quite upset about what you did to Gomez and Maitlin. They were two of his favorite thugs. Word is, he's offered half-a-mil to whoever brings you in. Plus, he knows you've been shot. He'll be watching the hospitals."

"I could just stay away from hospitals for a while."

"You could. But the longer you wait, the more likely you'll lose the hand. You've already got an infection."

I sighed. "Do I get my car back?"

"I'll go you one better: I'll buy you a new car."

"I want that one. And everything that was in it. Everything. Plus, you pay for what happened to Jim. Pay for trashing his house."

"Scotty trashed his house."

"Because Villalobos made me leave with those 5D's."

"Fine. He'll be reimbursed for his losses."

"And I want my own doctor to be part of the team. Vic Balcour. I want him."

"Why? I told you I'd get you the best."

"He is the best. I can trust him. He won't let you shoot any more of that happy juice into me." I tilted my chin at the syringe.

Guilt furrowed his brow and tugged the corners of his mouth flat. "I'm sorry about that. I know it's unpleasant, but I had to be sure you weren't a plant. Scotty would murder his own mother to get close to me."

"Why?"

"You don't need to know. Now, do we have a deal?"

I thought about it, surprised he was giving me a choice. Or at least going through the motions. But, I wasn't sure I liked what I was agreeing to. "You're going to use me as bait. To get to Scotty."

"Yes," he conceded, after a long pause.

"You want him to capture me?"

"Yes. But you'll have an implant. We'll know exactly where you are at all times."

"And if you don't get to me in time?"

"We'll get to you. Scotty likes to take his time. And after what Faith did to him, he's bound to take a long time."

A cold fist grabbed my heart as the sadistic glint in Scotty's eyes came back to haunt me. I blew out a long breath, considering my options. Not many. "All right. I'll do it."

Tony considered this. "Good. But I have some demands of my own. Number one: you do what I tell you, when I tell you, for the duration of your employment. Number two: in the event you betray me or any of my people, this contract is null and void. You turn on me, you'd better run as fast and as far as you can, because what'll happen once I catch you will make Scotty's little games look like a three-day vacation in Maui." He held his hand out just above my left one. "Agreed?"

I hesitated. Lifted my hand to the limits of the restraint. "Agreed."

As his fingers curled around mine in a token handshake, I looked up, meeting his gaze. Before I knew it, I was falling again, sucked into the black void of pupil at the center of those blue irises. I held my breath, cursing myself, my need. I shouldn't like this guy. I shouldn't *want* to like this guy. Deep down, I sensed he was more dangerous than Villalobos or Papa could ever be.

The weird thing was, he seemed to feel it, too. That strange, pulsing attraction. His eyes wavered, and he looked away, breaking the spell.

"Who is she?" I asked, in the uncomfortable silence.

"Who is who?"

"She. Her. In the limo, you said I was her. Who is she?"

He paled beneath his tan, jaw pulsing. A flicker of real fear flashed behind his eyes before he slammed that icy control down. "You don't need to know that right now."

I stared at him, disturbed. I'd heard those words, or variations thereof, more times than I could count. Every time I asked Papa about his missions, about what he did when he was gone all those months. I was about to argue that I very much needed to know when the door behind him opened.

A tall, thin, wheat-blonde woman stepped into the room, moving with the determined, steel-jawed avarice of a moray eel. I thought it might be Rossi, but then I realized the body type was too different. This woman was much too tall, too lean, and too athletic. Like an Olympic sprinter wearing an eleven-hundred-dollar, shell-pink linen suit and carrying a large, black gator skin briefcase.

Her cheeks were the delicate pink of alabaster, her eyes the same color as my Mother's: the deep, greenish-yellow of pond scum. She'd made herself up so that she wouldn't appear made up, but she still looked to be about thirty-five. I disliked her immediately.

The feeling, apparently, was mutual.

"Tony." Her voice was clipped, authoritative. "It's not too late to cut our losses. Everyone already thinks she's dead, so we can still purge her from the program. Nobody would be the wiser. As it is, she's an unnecessary risk. A wild card like her could—"

"I know the risks. Just do what I pay you for." Tony turned to me. "This is Jana Slager. She's my attorney."

"Among other things," Jana added, drawing an ultrathin tablet from the briefcase. She stepped beside Tony, her body language possessive, protective.

I got the message.

She looked me over, lips pursing with disdain. "If she breaks during stasis, she'll be useless to us. I really can't advise—"

"Then don't," Tony interrupted her. She glanced at him in supplication, but he was staring at me again, thoughtful, absorbed.

I tensed, feeling like a lamb being examined by a butcher.

"We'll see," Tony pronounced, "how she makes it through the lag. If she breaks, well, then..." He shrugged, shook his head, not bothering to finish the thought.

A superior little smile tugged at Jana's mouth. She held the tablet screen up to me. It was a Memorandum of Understanding. For my services. She pointed at the red X. "Sign here. Left thumbprint here."

I shook my head and read the damn thing. Fool me twice...

She must have been watching, or listening in, as all the terms I had just discussed with Tony were there. Something about the language reminded me of the two jokers from the CIA who had tried to recruit me during my freshman year of college. As if spycraft could ever be more interesting than a grand piano.

I looked up from the tablet, first at her, then at him. Tony turned the charm back on, his smile mild and reassuring. "As soon as you sign, I'm going to send some people in, and they're going to put you under, to make you look like Faith. You'll wake up in the hospital. Mando will be your bodyguard until you've—"

"Mando?"

"Villalobos. Since he started this mess, he gets to teach you how to act like Faith. You'll be alone with him until I'm sure you can pull it off. Then, I'll assign more bodyguards to you. They'll take shifts until your surgeries are over."

Suddenly, it all made sense: Tony's suave, chameleon qualities. Villalobos' deadly, war-trained mannerisms. And Jana, the tight-ass legal eagle ice queen. Of course. What else could they be?

"You used to work for the government." I accused. "Now you're one of those private sector Spec-Int teams, and you contract out to Uncle Spam, or the State, or something."

He shook his head, his face going hard. "I can't tell you."

"Can't? Or won't?"

He shook his head and strode wordlessly out into a darkened hallway, answering me with eloquent silence.

I stared after him, my heart in my throat, unsure whether to laugh, or cry. What in the Hell had I gotten into? I mean, sure, Papa had always harbored this fervent hope that I would follow in his footsteps. Become the first female TURTL, and command the unit he'd founded.

Because he was Papa, and I was so glad that he was spending time with me, I'd tell him, "Yeah, sure, that's what I want, too," all the while wondering if getting waterlogged during Hell Week would make my fingers too wrinkled for the piano. But Papa's hope, and my obligation to fulfill it, had died nine years ago, in a tearful salute to his empty, flag-draped coffin. Hadn't it?

Jana stared down at me, waiting.

Either I signed, or got hunted down by Scotty and tortured to death. Or worse, I lost my hand. I signed with my left index finger, then held my left thumb to the corner of the screen outlined by a red box. It bleated an acceptance. She snatched the device away.

From the way she stalked out, I guessed that she hated my joining the team even more than I did.

CHAPTER SEVEN

After Tony and Jana left, three people in doctor's smocks and surgery masks came in. They put an anesthesiology mask over my nose and mouth, and the next thing I knew, I woke up in the hospital, just as Tony had promised.

What he hadn't warned me about was the pain: A throbbing, tooth-pulling torment that felt like someone was reading my palm with a blowtorch. I groaned, clutched the sheets, fingers of my good hand white-knuckled and aching from the force of my agony. That ominous bull terrier Villalobos watched me from a chair near the door, polite concern rounding the almond-shape of his eyes. "You okay?" He rose and approached the bed.

I licked my lips, trying to coax my heart rate from wild rabbit down to human again. Damn, that man had me spooked. The only other person I'd ever known to radiate that kind of lethal grace was my father, Nico "The Demon" Damiano, battle-hardened commander of the most deadly anti-terrorist team in Spec-war history. And Papa had never shot me.

Villalobos pressed a button to raise the head of the bed. "You okay?"

"Hand hurts," I mumbled, realizing belatedly that it was buried up to the elbow in a white, bread-box sized contraption that made an intermittent humming noise like a paper shredder.

Felt like it was shredding me. I tried to pull my arm out, but a padded metal hoop secured me to the machine, snugging a clear plastic bio-seal just below my bicep, encircling the bruise left by the Amtrak cop's handcuff. "It hurts."

He nodded. "I paged your doctor. He should arrive shortly. But if you want, I can adjust the incubating unit for you." He pressed a few strip switches on the side of the box.

"Ho!" I arched back, tried to squirm away from the white-hot spike flashing up my arm.

"Sorry." He quickly pressed another button, twirled his finger across the touchboard, and thankfully, blissfully, the pain dulled to muscle-ache status. "Better?"

"Yeah," I gasped, blinking at the peach and forest green walls around us. My eyes were sore and scratchy, like they'd been packed with cement mix.

"You want a drink?" He poured some water from a pitcher into a plastic cup and held it out.

I just stared at him, not knowing what to say.

"You're safe, you know. I'll protect you."

"From you?"

His cheeks twitched. His face hardened. His shoulders dipped, just a little, as if he was trying to hide the fact that I'd wounded him somehow.

Good. About time somebody else suffered around here. I was tired of having the monopoly.

Villalobos continued to hold the cup, waiting patiently for me to take it. I let him wait, peering around the room, trying to get my bearings. I was in a large, homey suite, complete with upholstered armchairs, a video fireplace, and a virtual fish tank. Smelled like a hospital, looked like a bed and breakfast. Made me think of mortuaries. But, I didn't like where that was going, so I took the water from Villalobos and sipped it tentatively, finding refuge in its cool, neutral taste. "How long have I been here?"

"About twelve hours. They've got you on antibiotics, trying to knock that infection down. They can't start on the re-gen until it's taken care of and the drugs clear your system."

"Why not?"

"Drugs interfere with the process. That's why they had to invent stasis."

"What the Hell is stasis?"

"It's an acronym for Short Term Anabiosis, Systemically Induced State. Your blood is replaced by a chilled solution of saline and protein peptides designed to suppress all bodily functions, and then you're put into a biostatic field. Heart stops beating, lungs stop breathing, everything but your brain shuts down. Even that is paused during critical points in the surgery."

"So...I'll be temporarily dead?"

"Kind of, but not really. The process prevents cell death. Think of it more as severe hibernation."

"How long does it last?"

He shrugged. "Depends on what the surgeons need to accomplish. Anywhere from fifteen minutes to four hours per session. In severe trauma cases, they can stretch it to eight, but the longer it goes, the worse the prognosis and the more potential for side effects."

"Such as?"

"Hallucinations. Mental disorders. Sleep walking. Memory loss. Coma. Death."

"None of those sound good."

He shrugged. "Can't do re-gen without stasis. The conditions required are very precise. Even your heartbeat could interfere with the process. Stasis avoids those complications."

"Great," I mumbled, rolling my eyes. "I'm hating this already."

"Could be worse. You could be with Scotty."

Point taken. "Does Scotty really torture people?"

He nodded. "I've seen his work. Not pretty."

"Wonderful." I set the cup down on a tray beside the bed.

"Look, uh..." Villalobos cleared his throat. "I know this has been an ordeal for you. But there are some things we need to go over before the doctor gets here. First off, you are now Faith Hopkins, and you will refer to yourself as such. You will respond to that name, and that name only. Do not endanger your life, the lives of the medical personnel, or that of anyone assigned to protect you, by referring to yourself as Radiana Damiano. Understood?"

"Fine, but—"

"Good. Now, until you learn how to be Faith, do not speak to anyone but me unless I authorize you to. If you need to say something beyond nodding 'yes' or 'no' to the doctors or nurses, you let me know when we're alone, and I'll pass on the information. Don't worry if you screw up, at first. I've got—"

He paused and touched the diamond stud in his left ear. He seemed to be listening intently for a few seconds. The muscles in his jaw pulsed, his ebony eyes flashing with concentration. He looked over at me. "The doctor just left the hotel. He'll be here shortly."

"Doctor?"

"Balcour. You insisted on him, if I recall."

"Sure. But..." I shook my head, confused. I hadn't expected them to actually honor my wishes in that regard. And now that I suspected Tony and Villalobos of being covert operatives, I regretted involving Vic in all of this. "Vic will know I'm not Faith. He saw my hand."

Villalobos nodded. "He did. But the marshals paid him a visit last night, so he thinks you're with WitSec, now." He grinned, a hint of playfulness in his eyes. "Do not dissuade him from that idea, Miss Hopkins, because as far as he and everyone else is concerned, Radiana Damiano is dead. Her torn, bloody clothing was discovered in a storm drain in the L.A. River basin this morning. Preliminary tests prove the blood a match, and there was enough tissue to make a DNA match. It will, of course, be positive. Damiano will be officially dead, a victim of foul play."

"That's a leap. The cops find some bloody clothes, and 'poof!' I'm dead?"

"The burned-out hulk of Damiano's vehicle was discovered a few hundred yards away, along with more DNA evidence."

A wrecking ball tore through my chest. "You torched my car?!"

"The fire was so hot, the interior—and everything in it—was reduced to ashes. Traces of Damiano's blood and hair were found around the car, and the composition of the ashes is consistent with cremated human remains."

"But that wasn't the deal! Tony agreed—"

"Tony did what was necessary to protect your friends and family. Or would you rather your Aunt and Uncle and your buddy Jim are all terrorized by Foster's thugs until they come up with Rad?"

"No, but—" I clamped my eyes shut and covered them with my good hand. My throat closed. To lose everything...every photo, every letter, every memento I had left of Papa and Chris...

Villalobos kept talking, but I had stopped listening. There was just the roaring in my ears, and a seething red that bubbled up in the blackness behind my closed lids. Knowing that Chris and Papa had been in my life had been the only thing that had kept me going in spite of everything. Without them, without Jim, I never would have survived this long.

"Do you understand?" Villalobos said very close to my ear, an edge of annoyance to his voice. His fingers wrapped around my elbow and tugged my hand away from my face. "Are you listening?"

I opened my eyes to see him leaning over the bedrail with a stern, expectant look, his nose inches from mine. Rage flooded me, buoyed by a tidal wave of grief. Violence crackled wild along my limbs and exploded through my knee and good elbow as they snapped up to pincer his temples. I would kill him. I would kill everyone and everything, smash it all in an attack so blinding, so brutal, there would be no time to grieve for any of it.

"*Dios!*" Villalobos ducked back, narrowly escaping my attack. He followed through, wrapping his fingers around my wrist, twisting my good arm back and up. I fought him, thrashing against the restraints, trying to savage him anyway I could, but he had already circled to the head of the bed, out of reach.

"Relax!" he scolded. "Relax, or you'll hurt yourself!"

Some part of me knew he was right, but I couldn't stop. My body had taken off without me, caught up in this compulsive frenzy, and even the tortuous hammer blows that bit into me as I struggled to get my hand free of the box seemed somehow distant and irrelevant. Like I was a kid again, a tiny little person hiding off in a corner of myself, watching my life explode.

Still holding my wrist, Villalobos circled the head of the bed, crossing my arm over my chest and pulling me up over the incubating unit. He pinned me there, with my torso curled around the contraption, my face mashed up against the stippled plastic. I howled. I kept howling as I struggled to break free, but he had all the leverage. My rage eventually bled away, crowded out by the needle-toothed dragon devouring my right hand.

I sagged down, exhausted, sweat bursting from my pores, in so much pain I thought I might puke. The walls echoed with an intermittent bleat, like a wounded saxophone. After a while, I realized it was me, and I shut my mouth, embarrassed.

"You okay?" Villalobos asked. "You calm now?"

"Huh," I said, not sure which question I was answering.

"*Dios.*" He released me, mumbling a short, frustrated stream of Spanish that ended with "*Pinche loca.*" He watched as I fell back against the pillows, then shook his head and stepped around the incubating unit to re-adjust the settings.

The pain in my arm eased and became a dull, burning ache. But inside, next to my heart, where it all really mattered, I couldn't feel anything. Nothing, at all. It worried me.

Villalobos backed away and sat heavily in one of the upholstered armchairs, still shaking his head.

Neither of us spoke for a while.

In the stillness I heard faint hospital sounds leaking through the walls: muffled voices, the fuzzy yodel of water moving through pipes, a phone ringing. Around us, the machines hummed, the readouts ticking off their flashing numbers. A busy contrast to the nothing inside me.

I cast about, searching for something, anything to fill up that cold and hollow void, but even the music eluded me. The laughter of Mozart, the fire of Beethoven...I couldn't feel any of it. Couldn't feel a thing. I closed my eyes, suddenly weary, so weary. "I quit."

His jacket squeaked as he shifted in the chair. When he spoke, his voice was softer, more gentle than I'd ever heard it before: "It'll get easier."

"No. I mean I quit. I'm not being Faith."

"You do that, you'll lose your hand."

"Cut it off. Cut 'em both off. I don't give a rat's ass what you do to me."

"Ms. Hopkins, I—"

"I'm not Faith. I won't be Faith. Not in a million years."

"Thought you were a fighter."

"Nothing left to fight for. You assholes torched my car."

"It's only a car. It can be replaced."

"No." I glared at him. "You and Tony have taken everything from me. *Everything*. So. As far as I'm concerned, you can go to Hell. Because I'm there already. And nothing, *nothing*, you or Scotty or anybody else does to me could be worse than what you've already done."

He leaned forward, studying my expression. Amazingly, I found his fierce black eyes brimming with something I'd never expected: Compassion. "I'm sorry," he said, gaze locked with mine. "For all the grief I've brought you. It was never my intention to hurt you. But the moment you got Scott's attention, you became a target."

"Because I look like Faith?"

He nodded. "I tried to get you out. It almost worked." He sighed and looked down at his own hands, as if he didn't want to believe they were attached to his arms. "I didn't want you involved. You're an amateur. A wildcard. To throw you into a black cover op like this is a disaster waiting to happen. But Tony is—" He sighed, shook his head. "He's committed. The window is closing, and you're the only girl we've found that even comes close to a physical match. So, the only way out is through."

He kept his gaze locked with mine, earnest and urgent. "You've got to be Faith. You've got to play along, until you're out of the hospital. That's the only way to get the re-gen done on your hand. But once that's over, I promise you, you can walk away from this job. No strings. No obligations. You won't have to go up against Scotty. And I'll make it so he won't come after you, even if I have to kill the son-of-a-bitch myself."

"What about Tony? You know he's going to hunt me down for checking out of this thing."

"He'll be upset. He may even cancel my contract. But it'll be me he's angry with. By the time he's forced to abort, your hand will be back in working order, and you can go back to your life."

"Why? Why would you go up against your own boss for me?"

"I've been in this business for twenty-three years. You're the only civilian I've ever shot. I had to make things right. Especially after I saw your performance at the club. I wouldn't be able to live with myself, knowing I'd killed that talent." He turned and regarded me, his feral, jaguar face full of somber truth. "I make good on my mistakes."

I stared at him, distrustful at first. He sounded good, but he was probably just jerking my chain, throwing out all this noble, because-you're-worth-it crap so that I'd keep to my part of the bargain. But his gaze caught mine again, and for one, brief moment it was like seeing my father buried under all those layers of gangster chic. Villalobos blazed with an absolute commitment, an unequivocal sense of duty. Of honor. I knew, beyond all reason, that whatever happened, this man was on my side. This man would see me through.

I glanced at the lumps my feet made under the covers, not knowing what to say. So what if he could get me out of this? He was stupid for trying to save me. My own mother hadn't cared enough to help me keep my fingers.

"Will you do it? Play Faith until I can get you clear?"

I sighed. Why not? It didn't really matter what I did, anymore. At least this way, I could get back at Tony for torching my car. "All right."

"Good." He grinned, warm and empathetic in a subversive spec-war kind of way. He moved back to his chair and picked up the gator skin briefcase. He popped it open and removed a very high tech virtual reality set up, showing it to me. "This will help you learn her speech, her mannerisms. It's preloaded with surveillance vids."

"Did you know my father?" I blurted out, not sure where the question came from, but wanting an answer once I had voiced it. If he and Tony were spooks from the Agency, then there was a good chance Papa had trained at least one, if not both of them.

His eyes narrowed. He pulled back a bit, body language going defensive, guarded. "I can't tell you that."

"Can't? Or won't?"

"Both."

I looked away from him with a fey grin, amazed at the weird little twists and turns of life. Although the official story was that he had died in a HALO accident, we all knew that Papa had been K.I.A., his body lost in a mission so secret, I'd never to this day found out how he'd really died. He had known the risks. He'd braved them anyway, because he had believed in the cause, and believed in his unit. And his men had believed in him.

I had always been jealous of that, never quite understanding how those raucous, wild-eyed men who got shitfaced every time they visited the house could mean more to him than Chris and I. If he really loved us, why did he go and get killed, so we were stuck with her?

But then there were those times when he saw himself in me, and he would laugh that deep, resonant belly laugh, the sweat trickling down through the dark hairs on his tanned, bare chest; the bright sunny open of the shooting range smelling of cordite as I pulled off another perfect grouping.

"Hot damn, kiddo, you're gonna do it," he'd say, giving me a hug as I tipped the spent cartridges out of my gun. "You keep this up, you'll be the first female TURTL."

Since Chris wasn't his biological son, Papa had pinned all his hopes on me. So, of course, I'd shrug and mumble something vaguely agreeable, very proud that he wanted to share his world of covert warfare with me. From Villalobos' evasive answer, I suspected Papa had shared that world with him, too.

"Not telling me means you did know him," I surmised. "Did you work together? Or did he train you?"

"I can't tell you," he repeated, an edge to his voice. Something else swam around in his eyes, but I couldn't figure out what it meant. I found myself wishing that I could be scared of him again.

At least that way, I'd be able to feel something.

CHAPTER EIGHT

I wasn't ready for what happened next, although Villalobos seemed to have been expecting the knock at the door. He stowed the VR rig in the briefcase, and then drew a pistol from under his jacket in a single fluid motion, as deadly and as graceful as the jaguar he resembled. "Come in."

The handle turned slowly, hinges squealing as the door swung open. A white-haired black man poked his head into the room.

Vic. God, it was so unfair. They go to all the trouble and obvious security risk to bring me Vic, but they take my car away from me. What kind of sadistic bastard was this Tony, anyway?

Vic seemed a little intimidated by Villalobos. Or maybe it was just the gun. He drew in a deep breath, gave a brief nod. "I'm Dr. Victor Balcour. You must be Mr. Villalobos."

"Mando. I prefer Mando."

"Mando, then." Vic cleared his throat. "Can I see the patient?"

Villalobos nodded, lips twisting in a polite grin as he slipped the pistol back under his jacket and stepped aside. "All yours."

Vic paused for a moment, unsure, then walked over to the bed. He stared, brows furrowing the longer he looked at me. "So, you're Faith Hopkins, huh?"

I stared back, not knowing what to say. Was I even allowed to say anything? Part of me was really glad to see him. He was more than the best doctor I'd ever had. He was a good friend, and arguably the kindest human being I'd ever met. Except for maybe Jim and that priest who'd helped me off the streets when I was fifteen. But another part of me hated that he was here, as if his presence was a direct result of the sacrifice of my car.

I knew, of course, that it wasn't his fault. He'd had no clue about Tony's plans. He'd come here just to help me. But if I could have traded his care for just one of the keepsakes I'd lost, I would have done it in a heartbeat.

"Did you bring the forms?" Villalobos asked him.

Vic nodded and handed over the tablet he'd had tucked under one arm. "Sorry it's taken so long. You know the paperwork involved when someone gets shot, even accidentally." He chuckled, gave me a sly wink. "You should be more careful about which end of the barrel you pick up at the shooting range."

Villalobos checked the readout, then grunted approval, holding the tablet out for me. "Sign on the pad, Faith."

I fumbled the stylus into my left hand and did as I was told.

Villalobos gave the board back to Vic, who shook his head, still staring at me. "Wow." He shone a light into my right eye, then checked the left. "That's amazing. I mean...wow. They don't look like contacts."

"They're not," Villalobos volunteered. "There's a treatment that diffuses the melanin content of the iris, lightens the color of the pupils. For a bluer green they can—"

"But look at her. I mean..." He fluffed his hand through my hair, which was a lot shorter than I remembered it, brushing away bangs I didn't even know I had. "What happens when this grows out? It'll be brown."

"It'll grow in red, same as that. We've installed an implant to make sure of that. It also alters the melanin content of her skin. As far as her body knows, she was born looking that way."

"That can't be healthy..."

"Healthier than dying of lead poisoning."

Vic frowned, regarding me dubiously. "Is it really you?"

I gave a vague nod, sliding my glance away to stare at the illusory flames under the mock mantel. So what if I looked like Faith? My hand ached fiercely. My eyes still hurt.

"You can talk to him," Villalobos told me. "He's aware of your...situation, Ms. Hopkins."

I shrugged, wondering what to say. "Have they paid you?" I finally ventured, because it seemed important to make sure somebody got something out of all this misery and loss.

Vic nodded. "In full. In advance, including the hotel and a bonus fee for inconveniencing all the patients I rescheduled so I could be here." He chuckled. His chestnut eyes sparkled with relief. "Have to admit, I'm impressed. I didn't think you'd be able to scare up the money for an amputation, let alone Experimental Regeneration. How long you been dating Mr. Tovenaar?"

"What's today?"

He chuckled, shaking his head. "Always the smart ass. But seriously, this is a dream team. Dr. Maserly, Dr. Kalisat, Dr. Wachtel, not to mention the others. The best on the planet. If anybody can rebuild that mess you call a hand, they can."

"You're not doing the surgery?"

"I'll be observing, mostly. I don't have any training for something this experimental. I've never actually seen human regeneration in action."

"So it's really real? It's not just a movie thing?"

"Apparently the technology has been around for quite some time. It was developed by DARPA over a decade ago. But it's still very costly and very..." He glanced towards Villalobos and then at me, his voice hushing as he added: "Secret."

He slid a touch board out from the side of the box my hand was trapped in and keyed a few strokes. The virtual fish tank along one wall winked out, replaced by skeletal image of my mangled hand. The undamaged bones were represented in light green. The broken bits were represented by an angry red. But it was the blank areas that really froze my blood. An entire joint, completely missing. I knew it was bad, but I hadn't wanted to believe how bad it really was.

"Here's what we're going to do." He fiddled with the touch board and the red areas dissolved, rearranging into a solid, healthy-looking series of joints. "It should take a week to ten days to clear your body of infection. Once you're ready, Dr. Wachtel will be sculpting a fine titanium alloy honeycomb for the bone cores, coating them with a blastematized calcium sheath. Then, you'll undergo the Maserly-Kalisat regeneration field." He tapped the box encasing my hand, "For three hours on, three hours off, four times a day. That should take about a week." He punched few more keystrokes and a latticed network of glowing colors overlaid the basic yellow pattern. "Once the skeletal reconstruction is in place, we repeat the process for the deep tissue regeneration phase, and then the surface tissue phase. After three weeks of regeneration procedures, you'll have a fully functioning hand again."

"Really?" I felt a tiny stir of hope among the ashes. "Like, 'poof,' I'm playing the Hollywood Bowl with Jim?"

His mouth pinched down, his lips pressed into that same sad line of compassion he'd had when he argued for amputation. "The limb itself will be complete—you'll even have limited use a few hours after the final process. But all that regenerated tissue will be virgin. Clumsy, just like a baby's. The muscles and neural pathways have to develop. Even with the most aggressive physiotherapy, you won't regain concert quality for at least a year. It's more likely to take two or three."

"A year..." The words still didn't make any sense. What good was a hand without music to move through it? The piano had been my salvation. The voice of things I had never been able to say. More eloquent than words, more passionate than any mere sentiment. With the ivories under my fingertips, I never had to feel. The piano did it for me. How could I stand to be silenced for a whole year?

"Don't worry. You'll get it back. You just have to keep working at it. You can even start practicing a week or two after the surgery's complete."

Vic put the touch board back in its slot. The image on the wall flickered and returned to the virtual fish tank. He placed a phone sized, hospital-issue tablet in my hand, and pointed to an icon on the screen. "Those are your instructions on how to care for that hand when this is all over. Study them. Know them. When we finish with all the surgery, I'm going to quiz you, and if you fail even one question, I will personally hack off both of your hands at your ungrateful wrists. Is that understood?"

I cleared my throat. Nodded solemnly.

"Good," he beamed, satisfied, but then his smile melted away, disquiet clouding his eyes as he studied my expression. "You sure you're okay?"

"I'm fine. I'm just—" I sighed, shook my head, not knowing how else to express it. "I'm dead, that's all."

He sighed, glanced at Villalobos, then back at me. He leaned forward and patted my hand conspiratorially. "For what it's worth, Jim's taking it pretty hard, too. He's been planning the memorial."

"Jim?" I echoed, amazed I could have forgotten about what he must be going through.

"He called me from the police station, to see if you'd decided to leave without him. And then when it turned out you'd been kidnapped..." Vic broke off with a grim sigh. "He thinks it's his fault. Thinks if he'd been able to pick you up sooner, you'd still be alive. I've tried to talk him out of it, but..." He shrugged, one corner of his mouth twisting up wryly, pulling his mustache out of shape. "Look, I've got a meeting with the other doctors to coordinate your surgeries. I'll be back to check in on you in a few hours."

I nodded vaguely, not really paying attention to him.

Jim. It figured that he'd be beating himself up over my death. He'd always looked out for me, even when I didn't look out for myself. And now I was gone, nothing but ash, like the rest of my life, leaving him to mourn and pick up the pieces. And I couldn't even feel guilty about it.

I told myself that was okay, it was better this way. Jim had talent. He had drive. He didn't need to pour all his money down a rat hole like me. And even if Tony reimbursed him for the damage to his place, there was still all the mooching I'd done since I'd gotten kicked out of school, not to mention the stupid, sappy way he'd catch me looking at him when we played duets. He was better off without me, that was for sure.

"I'll see you, Faith." Vic patted my shoulder warmly, then turned away from the bed, flashing a courteous smile as he side-stepped Villalobos on his way to the door.

After he left, Villalobos slipped a small black box from his pocket and circled the room with it. I realized he must be checking for bugs. Like Vic was a spy, or something. But the box beeped and flashed a little green light, and he slipped it back into his pocket and settled back into his chair.

That morose silence filled the room again, a heavy, oppressive hush leaking from the walls. I couldn't stand him looking at me that way, like I was so pathetic I need an almost total stranger to feel sorry for me, so I asked him if he had a secret decoder ring to go with his jammer.

"I hear the CIA has a special Sponge Bob model," I added. "But it can only be operated by agents with crabs."

He snickered, shaking his head. "What'd I do to deserve you?"

"That's what happens when you try to pick up strange women in piano bars."

"Only strange woman I ever picked up was my wife."

My mouth fell open. I'd forgotten he was married.

He held up the ring. "A wife, two kids—and another one due this month," he said to my disbelieving look.

"You have kids?" I squinted at him, trying to picture the deadly Villalobos as a smiling icon of family. Didn't work.

My reaction amused him. He nodded, spreading his hands in an expansive gesture. "And a mortgage. And a dog. And three hamsters, a parrot, a tank of fish, and a racer snake. A regular American Dream."

"Then why are you working for Tony?"

"Somebody's got to feed the snake."

"No, I mean, why aren't you...? Why not do something legal?"

All at once his look was guarded, like a castle gate slamming down. "Tony is not a crook."

"Then why do you dress like a gangster?"

He looked away. "I can't tell you. But he's not a crook."

"He has to be. Look at the money he's throwing at me just to pretend I'm someone else. And what about the cops, the way they had my affidavit all prepared for me to sign? You can't say that was exactly legitimate."

"Look," he sighed. "I can't tell you how we operate, and I wouldn't expect you to understand even if I could. After what I did to you, I don't expect you to like me. I don't even expect you to be civil. But don't talk shit about Tony."

Such a rabid outburst of unexpected solidarity surprised me. I remembered that I was flat on my back, and he was the one with the gun. I shut up.

When it was clear my lips were staying zipped, Mando continued: "That man went through Hell to cover my ass. When you've been through half of what he's been through, then you can talk."

"Fine," I conceded. After a long stare down, that I let him win, Mando returned to his seat. I could tell by his stiff posture and the measured pulsing of his jaw muscles that he wasn't continuing the conversation. So much for small talk.

After several minutes of uncomfortable silence, I scooched to the side of the bed and fumbled with the rail. "Hey, Villalobos, can I—?"

"Mando. Call me Mando, Faith."

"Mando then. Can I get up? I have to pee."

"Sure." He rose, popped the rail down, lending me a hand as I swung my legs over the edge. "Just don't pull against the unit or tangle the cables up, and you'll be fine." He released the stays on the incubator box, then wrapped one arm across my shoulders and helped me off the bed.

I settled my feet on the floor. An odd roaring accompanied a tickly, light-headed feeling of sand rushing down my neck into my limbs.

"Easy." Mando held me against him, steadying me. We stayed like that for a few moments. He waited with patient, professional courtesy while I blinked and caught my breath.

The leather of his jacket pressed cool against the bare skin at my back where the gown didn't close. The bulge of his holstered pistol dug into my shoulder blade. He smelled like leather, and cigars, with a whisper of citrusy fern wafting up from his slicked back hair. I realized with surprise that I was actually a few inches taller than him. Guess when you're afraid of someone, you make them bigger than they are.

After my head cleared a little, I tottered forward, allowing him to bolster me while I got the hang of rolling the incubator box ahead of me. It was like having a mail cart welded to my forearm.

My muscles ached in odd places. My joints were stiff and uncooperative. My body felt heavy, sodden with inactivity. My feet fell in ponderous slaps on the floor. The tile was freezing, slick as wet ice, but it soothed the sharp pain in my heel where I'd bruised my foot with that kick to Doughboy's knee.

When we reached the bathroom I sloughed his hand away, thinking he'd allow me some privacy, but he just stood there in the doorway, watching me inch my way toward the toilet.

"You gonna be okay?"

"I can do it," I nodded, and then promptly caught the wheels of the box in a seam between tiles and fell against the sink.

He lunged in and caught the device before it toppled, saving me from another searing bout of pain. I was about to bat him away, to regain a modicum of dignity, but then I caught my image in the mirror and froze, dumbfounded.

Gone was my wavy, shoulder-length, chestnut brown hair, my olive skin, my elegant dark eyebrows, and my burnt sienna irises with a hint of topaz around the center.

While still possessing the same basic facial dimensions, the woman who stared back at me had ivory, freckled skin and apple-green eyes. Coppery blond hair, straightened and hacked short, with eyebrows and lashes to match. My lips were fuller, a different shape, somehow, and I had a mole on my temple, one I'd never seen before. One that hurt when I tried to flick it off.

No wonder Vic had been so impressed. Even I barely recognized me.

CHAPTER NINE

After all that had happened, it was a relief to be Faith. Just put on the face, adjust the vocal cords, and *voilà*, I was one of the opportunistic, carefree rich. Not a problem in the world I couldn't handle with money.

Mando briefed me on her, showing me surveillance videos of her on what I discovered was a biometric VR rig encoded to my retinas. For anybody else, it showed nothing but crappy reality TV shows, but for me, it displayed hours and hours of footage that cemented my suspicion about Mando and Tony being some sort of Spec Int operatives with connections to at least one Federal agency.

I spent the afternoon playing Faith, trying to crawl so deeply inside another woman's skin that I didn't feel the icy emptiness beneath my own. Better to be a swill-brained dilettante named Faith Hopkins than to live with the emptiness inside. And Faith was a wetbrain. A scotch-swilling lush, just like my mother. She was drunk in every vid Mando showed me. She chattered, giggled, swished around like a social butterfly. Her voice was thick and muddy, her sentences disjointed.

The sad part was, I could do her so well. Match her timbre and pitch, her facial gestures, mimic her absurd running commentary the same way I'd been able to imitate my mother as a kid, contemptuously ridiculing her alcohol-steeped mannerisms for the entertainment of my fellow schoolmates.

"You're good," Mando commented after I'd been practicing for an hour or so. "You've got the voice down pat." The look on his face reminded me of the way Papa used to smile when I'd hit a bullseye at the range. A little flame of pride warmed me.

After a time, we took a break. A nurse brought in a meal, some kind of vegan sandwich wrap that resembled lawn trimmings wrapped in beige construction paper and drizzled with balsamic vinegar.

During the time it took for the infection to clear my system, I dozed off and on when I wasn't eating vegetable crap or practicing Faith, plagued by a strange jumble of dreams that always ended with me in Scott Foster's office, sneaking up to garrote a grotesque, blood-soaked humanoid dodo bird as it watched videos of a little boy being tortured on the security monitors.

"You okay?" Mando poured me a glass of water after I woke in a cold sweat for the third time in as many hours.

I grunted and took the glass from him, sipping it as I tried to make sense of the dreams. They had a different quality from normal dreams. Somehow more real, despite the strange logic and the fantastical appearance of the bird man. "Weird dreams."

"Want to tell me about them?"

I did, because it was nice to hear my own voice, rather than Faith's. I described being chased through a landscape of palm trees and volcanoes by shadowy men carrying automatic rifles. Watching a man I didn't know, but somehow felt was my best friend, as he was crushed by a car compactor, his skull exploding like a grape. Suspended by my wrists in a dim, cavernous space, the taste of my own blood in my mouth as someone pounded my torso with a galvanized pipe. And throughout it all, the dry, strident cackle of the dodo man.

As he listened, Mando's body language became more and more alarmed. When I finished with the incident in Scotty's office, he stood up, dark brow furrowed with both unease and puzzlement. "But you haven't even had stasis, yet."

"What does that have to do with anything?"

He shook his head and just stared at the flames in the virtual fireplace, as if trying to make sense of the impossible. The silence stretched out into an uncomfortable, awkward roadblock.

At first, I thought I'd offended him somehow, but then I realized he was exhausted. A sparse, black smear of stubble peppered his jaw and upper lip. His eyes held the stubborn alertness of a Marine on guard duty after two days of forty-mile forced marches.

"How long you been here?" I asked him.

"Since you were admitted." He checked his watch. "About forty-six hours."

"Without sleep?"

"I've dozed a bit." He drew in a deep breath and exhaled in a long, resigned sigh. "Time to get Tony in here."

He pulled his phone out and left the room without a word, leaving me to wonder why my dreams had affected him that way. As I waited for him to return, I discovered the virtual fish tank doubled as a TV. It was the typical hospital cable feed, with no internet access, but at least it gave me a distraction from the sensation that the dreams had somehow driven a wedge between Mando and me.

About a half hour later, the door opened, and Tony stepped inside, although not the Tony I was used to.

Gone was the pristine, white-knight suit and the gold nugget pinky ring. His devilish black mane of hair was pulled up into a samurai bun. His chin and upper lip were dark with stubble. He wore leather sandals, blue jeans, and a T-shirt with "Haji Sukti's Gamelan and Grill" stretching across his magnificent chest. A large, purpling bruise traversed his left cheek. Other bruises circled his wrists and dotted his arms.

He shut the door quickly and moved over to the bed, leaning down to study my face intently, as if next week's Lotto numbers were printed on my eyeballs. He gently cupped my chin. For one singular, giddy moment, I thought he might kiss me, but he just tipped my head from side to side, inspecting my every pore.

"It's good," he finally said, smiling. "Damn good." He met my gaze, seeing me, behind all the things that made me look like Faith. It creeped me out, that he grasped the distinction between the two so clearly. That he could make me feel the difference with a mere glance.

The door opened, and Mando began to enter, but Tony held up his hand. "Go home. Get some sleep. If she," Tony indicated me, "makes it through the first bout of stasis okay, I'm putting you in charge of her security. I've already got Glen and Kam lined up as your relief."

Mando glanced at me, a kind of wistful disquiet in his eyes. I could tell he felt responsible for what had happened to me. He didn't want to leave until the damage had been repaired. But fatigue pulled on him, dulling his features, glazing his eyes. He sighed and nodded wearily. "Fine."

"You have a back-up piece?"

"Yes..."

Tony held his hand out expectantly. "Give me your rig, then. That wanker Hollis confiscated mine."

"You never learn." Mando removed his coat and laid it across the bedrail, then unhitched his shoulder harness and holster, handing them gingerly to Tony. "You wouldn't bait him so much, you wouldn't have so many problems with the man."

"I want advice, I'll ask a bartender. Now, go home, kiss your wife, and sack out for a day or two. If I need you, I'll need you fresh."

Mando pursed his lips, looking me, then Tony over. He nodded and stepped out into the hall. "Take care."

I watched him leave, not sure if I wanted to be left alone with Tony. Dressed that way, with his hair slicked back and the dark stubble dusting his chin, he appeared both more genuine and more crafty. The bruises didn't help. Neither did the way the heat ran up my spine as he brushed by the head of my bed and my nostrils filled with the spicy musk of his cologne. The way the muscles of his back rippled through the thin fabric of his shirt made it hard to remember how much I wanted to kick his ass for torching my car.

He made sure the door was latched shut, then set the briefcase on the floor beside the chair and sat down, regarding me.

I looked away quickly, hoping he hadn't caught my covert stare of appreciation. I could still hate his guts and think he was sexy, couldn't I? Hormones have no loyalty.

"Tell me about the dreams." His tone held an odd gentleness.

It made me uncomfortable, so I changed the subject: "What happened to you? Who roughed you up?"

"Hollis arrested me for Damiano's murder."

"Did you resist?"

"No. He just likes to rough me up, because he knows I'll skate." He shrugged, unconcerned. "I always skate from these kinds of things." He winked conspiratorially. "It's what makes Hollis so mad. That, and he hates me. Blames me for—" he broke off, cleared his throat. "Something from a long time ago..."

"Is he right? To blame you, I mean."

He rose, his face hard and serious, and stalked silently to the bedside, leaning over the rail to stare me down. "That wanker doesn't know the whole story. Not then, not now. And he's never been one to let the truth destroy a good case. I mean, look at you. He thinks Damiano's dead."

"Will I be?"

He chuckled. "We all die, sooner or later. You, I think, will be a later. Much later."

"What makes you say that?"

He smiled, leaning closer, so that I could feel his breath soft and warm on my cheek. "I have a feel for these things."

Time seemed to twist and distort as I fell into those eyes, making me feel as if I was some other where. Some other when. My lips parted, my own breath coming a bit harder than I wanted it to, but maybe that was just because I was furious with my body for trying to knee-jerk me into kissing him when I was still super mad at him. "What about you?"

"Me?"

I nodded. "You a sooner? Or a later?"

His smile faded, and he slipped back behind that inscrutable mask. "Tell me about the dreams."

"Why? They're only dreams. Probably from the fever."

"Tell me," he repeated, this time with an edge to his voice.

I did.

A weird, dark heat seemed to build around Tony as I described what I had seen. He sighed and retreated to his chair. He leaned back, gaze searching the ceiling. "The worst ones are always true," he whispered, so faintly I had to strain to hear him.

"What's that supposed to mean?"

He studied the ceiling for a long time, private thoughts simmering in the guarded depths of his eyes. When he finally spoke, his voice was distant, faraway: "About seven years ago, Scotty was in charge of an import-export business for a few select 'investors.' They made a chunk of money, until rumors spread that they were transporting more than clay pots and circuit boards made in Malaysia."

"Drugs?"

"People. Slaves."

I laughed at him. It seemed so ludicrous. "That stuff doesn't happen anymore. Human trafficking has been outlawed since—"

"Outlawed, yes. Doesn't mean you can't be kidnapped and fed drugs until you're addicted, then trafficked off to another state to work as a prostitute, or shipped off to slave away in a mine or factory somewhere your rights are below those of a pig or cow."

"Something like what Brighton Leigh did?" Brighton Leigh had been the overseer of a massive international human trafficking ring. I remembered the stories of his capture years ago, sensational accounts splashed all over the vid. Women and children chained to beds, forced into prostitution. Tortured to death by a bunch of rich deviants at certain "resorts" where local law enforcement was so well greased the "fun" houses could operate with impunity.

If even half the allegations were true, he was the Josef Mengele of organized crime. Especially since he escaped a year after his forced extradition from Indonesia.

Tony nodded. "Exactly like Brighton Leigh. As a matter of fact, Scotty works for him."

"Used to work for him," I corrected.

"No. Works. Present tense."

"That's impossible. Leigh's a fugitive. How can Scotty—?"

"Watch." He synched his phone with the flat screen on the wall. "This is how the Concerto really makes its money. Laundering the cash that Scotty makes smuggling people and streaming videos like this." He held his breath for an instant, then pressed his phone screen. The room darkened and the speakers crackled to life. A technicolor blur leached into focus on the screen.

As soon as I realized what it was, my gut twisted, my intestines crawling all over each other to be the first in my mouth. It was the exact same thing the dodo-man had been watching in my dream: A high-def video image of a child, six, maybe seven years old, being tortured by a man in a full-face Halloween mask. The boy was covered with welts and burns. Chunks of ripped flesh still clung to the pliers in the man's left hand. The soundtrack was one long, low wail, the cry of a child who had long ago abandoned tears.

"Turn it off," I pushed the words past gritted teeth.

Tony didn't respond, his entire attention focused on the scene before him. It frightened me, that he could stand to watch this. That he wanted to watch it, because it fed some deep, seething fury inside him. Hatred shone in his face. Hatred, and a vengeful hunger that devoured him, transformed him into something only vaguely human.

"Turn it off!" I shouted, throwing my glass of water at him.

It hit him in the chest, splattering ice and water across his neck and face before bouncing off and clattering to the floor. Even then, he didn't react immediately, but tore his gaze from the screen slowly, as if waking from some horrible dream. He touched his phone and the image died. The lights surged up to normal, the speakers blissfully silent.

"Brighton," Tony said, hoarse and trembling. "Brighton's work." He looked at me, but didn't see me, senses still turned inward on some seething inner landscape. "He, uh, he never lets his men touch their faces. Wants to catch every twitch, every nuance of their pain. Considers himself a connoisseur."

"How do you know?"

He returned his phone to his pocket with exaggerated care, as if it might somehow contaminate him. "I used to work for him."

I recoiled. Disgust, revulsion swept over me like a horde of cockroaches. "You were a slaver?"

"I was a slave." He cleared his throat, dropped his gaze. "Back in the old days, when I was young and foolish." His voice was distant, matter-of-fact. "Three of us went undercover to bust the ring. And we had him. Almost had Scotty, too, but a simple thing, a tiny little oversight gave us away. One got out in time, but the other two..." He sighed, shook his head. "The first was handcuffed to the steering wheel of a car and put in a crusher. His coffin was a three foot cube."

I winced, remembering how that skull had popped in the dream, but Tony continued despite my horror: "Scotty's 'investors' decided to have fun with the other one. They strung the bastard from the ceiling of a warehouse and hung weights from his feet until his shoulders separated. Beat him with pipes. Broke his ribs. Cracked his skull. Then, they rolled him up in a carpet and dumped him down a mineshaft."

I chewed my lip, believing him, and yet not believing him. Especially not wanting to believe that the dream had somehow shown me a truth I had no way of knowing before now. "If you got out, how do you know Scotty crushed one of your partners and tossed the other one down a mineshaft?"

"Mando got out." He leaned forward, pulled a slick mass of hair away to reveal a wicked, jagged scar that traversed his skull just above his left ear. "The mineshaft one was me."

He waited for his words to sink in, until my eyes grew nice and round, my throat dry enough to plant cactus in. And then he grinned, lips stretched back cruelly, a strange, dark light in his eyes. "It was Brighton's money that Faith stole. That's why Scotty wants her so badly. To give her to Brighton, so he can avenge himself on her. And that's how I'll find the vulture. That's how I'll end him."

"You want them to snatch me?"

He nodded. "Once your hand is fixed. Not before. But don't worry. The implant is also a transponder. We'll nail them before they do anything to you."

I gaped at him, speechless. To be the bait in a trap for Brighton Leigh...

I was in so deep, the Titanic was an airplane.

CHAPTER TEN

I wasn't sure how to respond to Tony's revelation. I wanted to help, to be Faith, if that's what it took to bring a man like Leigh to justice. Yet, Tony had explicitly stated the dangers involved, and his description of the tortures he'd survived stirred up a fear in me that went arm in arm with fascination.

If I had been faced with the things Scotty had done to him, the threads of denial that held me together would have frayed and snapped, and I'd be left holding the ragged pieces that were the true measure of who I was. But not Tony. He had taken the broken beast Leigh and Scotty had made of him, and forged it into this quietly laughing man of silk and iron.

I wanted to find the same strength he had, wanted to discover the mysterious property that had allowed Tony to re-make himself into something so focused. So self-assured. So deadly.

Yet, maybe that transformation called for more than I was willing to give. I didn't want to become like this spooky Tovenaar sonovabitch, who sat there watching me, drinking in my pain, feeding off my fear the same way he had with that little kid on the chip.

I hated him for that. For making me watch that thing. Even now I saw them. The welts, the burns, the torn flesh and the degradation. The desperate, pleading gaze and the endless, hopeless wail. He was just a kid. Just a little kid. Why would anyone want to do that? Why would anyone want to watch someone do that? What pleasure is there in an innocent child's pain? And to think Scotty was making money off of it...

It disgusted me, made me ashamed to be human. Ashamed to share a species with men capable of enjoying that. And shame awakened a dragon in me, a savage monster fueled by rage and retribution. Hot and fierce, it lurked, coiling along my spine, waiting for the right moment to strike, to avenge all the dark, aching nights of my own childhood. If I ever met Brighton Leigh, I'd rip his heart out and shove it down his throat.

Nobody should hurt a helpless little kid. Nobody.

"You okay?" Tony asked. He waited for me to say something, and when I didn't, he crossed over to my bedside. The wet fabric of his T-shirt had turned transparent, a dark mass of chest hair visible beneath the soaked cotton. The air conditioning vent blew down over him, and his nipples had hardened from the cold—or was there another reason? I couldn't tell.

"You okay?" he pressed. He rested his forearms on the railing, leaning in to study my face.

I nodded, swallowing hard, trying to figure out why the tender concern in his eyes made me feel so trapped. It was an act. Had to be an act. It didn't matter how good looking he was. Or how good he smelled. He was going to get me killed. Slowly. Painfully.

"I'm...fine." I hated the way my body itched to embrace him. Funny, how your libido tries so thoroughly to destroy you despite the alarm bells clanging in your brain.

"You're afraid of me," he observed.

I opened my mouth to deny it, then nodded with a sigh.

"I thought so." He chuckled without humor, stepping away from the bed to sit in the chair by the door. The one that wasn't wet. "That better?"

I nodded again. A prickly silence reigned. I watched the fish tank for a while. He stared at the ceiling. Eventually, the two nurses came in again. Just like Mando, Tony greeted them with the gun drawn. Ignoring him, the nurses set a tray of food down in front of me, then busied themselves checking the fluids on the incubator machine and printing out a new status report.

I lifted my fork, poked at the mass of greenery before me. All manner of strange leafy things, pale, greenish stick things, coin-sized slivers of carrot and radish—topped with the final insult: purple cabbage. Could have been edible. I wasn't sure. Might be someone's landscaping. I opened my mouth to complain, but a wave and a glower from Tony warned me to keep quiet.

Belatedly, I realized that I was supposed to be Faith. I never saw her eat this kind of crap on the vids, so I figured Tony didn't want me talking until he was satisfied with my east Texas accent. He was the type who had to approve everything before putting it into effect.

After the nurses left, he withdrew a black box just like Mando's, and swept the room. I took the plastic carafe of salad dressing and sniffed. Vinegar, mustard, various spices. Might deaden the taste of vegetation. I slopped some indiscriminately over the mess and started to eat. Growing up the way I had, you cleared everything from your plate, even if it was green.

Considering how nice the room was, the food certainly sucked. You'd think they could afford a steak or two, at least. A big, juicy rare one, with the steam rising off and the blood running down, a little horseradish on the side. Maybe some mashed potatoes with gravy, some steamed broccoli in cheddar sauce, a few sautéed mushrooms. Something like Jim used to make.

Jim. God, I missed him. Had my death hit him hard? Or was he relieved to see me gone? Probably relieved. After Chris had died, keeping me out of trouble had been a full time job.

I finished with the salad and pushed the tray and table away. My eyes still hurt from whatever they'd done to change the color. They burned with fatigue, watering slightly. Every time I blinked, it became harder to open them again. I didn't want to sleep, to dream around Tony, but I was losing the battle.

He watched me, searching. The light reflecting off the dark sheen of his bruise made him seem lost, somehow. Vulnerable.

So, I took a shot: "Why do you have that vid on your phone? Hollis could throw you in jail for pedophilia if he found that on you."

"It's encrypted. Hollis plays it without the proper keys, he'll see legally duplicated Bollywood movies."

"Like the VR rig?"

He nodded. "How else do you think Scotty can distribute this crap with impunity? Without the encryption keys, there's no way to prove what he's up to."

A thought struck me. "Is that what I smuggled out of the club? The keys?"

He raised a brow, assessing me with a look that was both wary and appreciative. "More than that. The encryption software. The specialized algorithms that create both the locks and the keys."

"That explains why Scotty was so hot to get them back. But it still doesn't explain why you carry that with you."

"To remember," he said evenly, although the leather arms of the chair dimpled under his fingers.

"Remember what? How can you forget being tortured?"

His eyes flashed with sudden heat. His upper lip curled, his face going slack as his fingers dug deeper into the arms of the chair, his knuckles ridged with white. Abruptly he stood, pacing away as if he could leave his thoughts behind. Brow furrowed, he circled the bed, stopping beside the med monitors. He traced the readout with his finger, a sad, hollow look in his eyes.

"He was my son," he admitted softly.

"Your son?" I echoed, surprised.

He nodded, face impassive, a slight sheen to his eyes. "Brighton had him kidnapped three years ago. He made that video and sent it to me. To get back at me for extraditing him."

"You did the extradition?"

He nodded. "My team did. Back when Hollis and I worked for the Government. It's how I ended up in the mineshaft. Scotty did what he did to me because my people had already nabbed Brighton." He chuckled bitterly. "And then, after all we'd done, all we'd gone through to nail that sonuvabitch, those assholes in the States let him escape."

His face contorted. He turned away from me, covering his eyes. After a few brief moments, he was looking at me, his proud, sculpted features a mask of inscrutability. "I can't forget what horrible things they did to my boy. I can't let myself forget."

I realized then that the video was his cross to bear, his penance for failing to save his child. "I'm sorry," I said, knowing how inadequate it sounded.

He frowned at me, likely unsure of my sincerity. Our gazes met, locked in a brief moment of recognition, then slid past each other in that awkward, uncomfortable way of people who have seen too much of themselves in one another.

"You, uh," he cleared his throat. "You should get some rest. You need to get past this fever. You've got a long stretch of surgery ahead of you."

"Yeah," I said, continuing to stare at him, unsure what I was feeling, or why. The world seemed out of sync, and Tony's face kept wavering in and out of focus.

His eyes burned like twin gas flames, that flickering, demonic blue. Anger smoldered behind his pleasant facade. Anger, and a strange echoing pain, as if he were an instrument resonating with my misery. Or was I resonating to him? The physical attraction still pulsed between us, but now another, deeper current had opened up. A dark, lethal energy, sizzling with vengeance and bloodlust. He was every murderous impulse I'd ever had. Every moment of helpless rage at the brutal injustices of life.

"You okay?" he asked, approaching me cautiously.

"Yeah," I said, still fascinated by the fury buried so deep within him. It crackled, shot black, arcing plumes into the air around him like a dark sun, broiling his flesh away, blackening his bones. "You're burning up," I told him, in case he didn't already know. "From inside. You're burning."

"You're hallucinating," he replied, matter-of-fact. As he said it his charred skeleton crumbled into dust, replaced by a perfect, if wary image of Tony, standard issue. Minute lines pulled the corners of his mouth into a somber, weary look, but the rage was still there, a hard black kernel, a cancer waiting for the right moment to bloom.

"It'll kill you." I reached out, touched the spot on his chest over his heart. "It wants to kill you."

"What?"

"I don't know," I whispered, suddenly unsure if the rage I had seen was his, or just mine reflecting in his eyes. "I don't know anything anymore."

"It's okay," he murmured, stroking the side of my face. "Stay calm. Breathe steady. It'll pass."

I closed my eyes and drew in a long breath, following his advice. Let it go in a slow, measured sigh. I still felt the heat burning within him, heard the low, faint cries of anguish buried deep beneath his tanned, butter-smooth skin.

"Go to sleep," he scolded gently, tucking the blanket up under my chin.

"How come," I said with a yawn, "you have that scar? Didn't re-gen get rid of it?"

"Can't re-gen head tissue. It's where the stasis machine goes."

Right. I should have thought of that. I hated being this tired. It seemed rude to fall asleep after Tony had confessed such intimate truths about himself. "Did you—you know, when you were in stasis, did you dream about that stuff? What Scotty did to you?"

"Not at first. But as the procedures wore on, I started to. The lag only affects long-term memory. You usually don't dream about anything that happened in the three to five months immediately preceding the re-gen process."

"Months?"

"Re-gen used to take a lot longer. I was Maserly and Kalisat's guinea pig for almost a year, but the technology is far more advanced, now."

"Good." I nodded, taking another deep breath. Maybe I wouldn't dream about Chris. I might actually survive the rest, as long as I didn't have to see him die again. It had been six months, but the memories still seemed so fresh. That would count as short term, wouldn't it? Wouldn't it?

"I don't know." Tony shrugged, folding my hand between his two, and I realized I'd just said all of that out loud.

God, I was losing it.

"Who's Chris?" he asked.

"My little brother. He, uhm..." I closed my eyes, not wanting to say it. Not wanting to really think about it, because that might trigger the nightmares. "He had patched some CYBL and he, uhhhmmm..." The words seemed too heavy to carry. "Shot himself," I managed at last. "In the head."

"CYBL..." Tony let out a low whistle. "That's dangerous stuff when not handled properly. Especially for Y-types."

I nodded, swallowing hard. I didn't know what a Y-type was, but clearly, I hadn't handled Chris properly.

"I'm sorry," Tony said, squeezing my hand. I squeezed back, clinging desperately to his warmth. To his presence. Wanting my touch to ease some of his pain, the way his did for me.

He could understand my rage and loss, better than anybody. Better, especially, than Jim, who had only ever offered sympathy, never commiseration. Tony knew. He had lived all of it. The grief. The pain. The terror. The shame. A different instrument, perhaps, but the melodies were the same.

For one brief second, he looked to me like Chris. A grown up, blue-eyed Chris. And then sleep sucked me down a long tunnel into darkness.

***

When I woke up, they started the surgeries. Vic held my good hand while two nurses wheeled my gurney out into a corridor. Tony followed along, dressed in surgical gear, just like the others, except his gown had a bulge underneath it where the shoulder holster poked up underneath the fabric.

They took me into a complex surgical chamber which seemed somehow vaguely familiar. The other doctors were there, waiting. They all greeted Tony like old drinking buddies who hadn't seen each other for years.

The nurses applied the stasis and monitor pads all over my body. Vic whispered a few consoling words and settled the stasis machine over my forehead. I heard a peculiar ultra-low hum, and then a zillion tiny little bursts of light exploded my skull...

And I descended into Hell.

A weird feeling of living death consumed me. Trapped in a body that wouldn't move—not even to breathe—vaguely aware of an itchy, painful tickle in my right arm. Disembodied voices I heard but couldn't comprehend. And cold, so cold.

After that, the frozen purgatory of stasis thawed into a restless sleep, and I relived moments of stark terror and quiet anguish even I'd forgotten about. And not just the night I'd killed Mike. There was Papa's destructive fury in Corpus Christi, when he found out Chris had been born with the wrong blood type. The constant moves and the fights to protect Chris from the bullying cliques of enlisted brats, and Mother especially vicious, because she hated moving, too.

I relived the night I snuck into Badger Carlisle's house and hid in his closet and recorded the things his father had been doing to him. The night Aunt Rosa told me that I could come live with her, but Mother refused to give up Chris. And that day in Juvey, when those gang girls tried to jump me in the bathroom and I accidentally took out Luisa Gonzales' eye with a toothbrush.

Sometimes, there were dreams that didn't make sense, but felt incredibly real. Like the one where I was garroting a dodo bird in the back room behind Scott Foster's office at the Concerto Club, and I could somehow see images of tortured men, women, and children dancing through the holographic décor in the main house.

Or the one where I walked through my mother's house, hands wet with blood. Blood on the walls, on the counters, on the floors and the furniture. Panicked that everyone would think I had killed her.

Or the one where I was dragging a deathly pale, dark-haired little boy with blue-lips out of a swimming pool and giving him CPR. I could feel his ribs cracking under my desperate compressions. A jackal licked the tears off my face, and when the little boy finally spasmed and coughed and opened his eyes, he turned into Tony, and the swimming pool turned into a brewery.

Awake, I had to endure Tony's sympathy. Wriggle under his kindly, probing interest, frantically avoiding the conversations that would allow him to strip away those ancient scabs and expose the festering wounds underneath.

I hated him for being there, for caring about me. For making me care about him. He would leave me. They all had. Papa. Chris. Every teacher I ever believed in. Every friend I ever knew. Gone. Why should Tony be any different? He'd hired me to play the cheese in a rat trap. And every kid in nursery school knows what happens to the cheese.

My hand ached fiercely and relentlessly, no matter what setting Vic put the box on. A kettle drum resounding through every cell, resisting every effort to ignore. Mozart, Chopin—even Beethoven couldn't tame it. And so, I just lay there, staring at the fish tank, my mind shearing into smaller and smaller islands of lucidity. For long stretches I gave up all dignity and just howled, keening like a wolf with its foot in a trap, wild and hurting and alone.

Unbearably, the cycle repeated, and I was back in surgery again, stuck in the icy, living grave of stasis. Then came the thaw, and sleep. And the dreams, jumbled and compressed. All the broken shards of my life come to cut open my veins.

I was alone in the kitchen with my mother the night the men had come to tell her Papa had died. Furious, she body slammed me into the corner of the counter as a sudden hard squall thrummed on the roof over head. And more rain, in the cemetery, with Chris' warm, tear-sticky hand in mine as we trudged through the cold Seattle mud toward an empty grave that was all we had left of our father. And then the world shifted again, and I was driving, hurtling south through a thick and murky Oregon downpour toward the blue skies of California. Chris' blood had caked under my fingernails, rusty-red smears of it painting my sodden shirt and jeans, and I knew.

He was dead. Chris was dead.

A chill ran through me. I was in the dream, and not in the dream, and both parts of me rebelled against what I started to flash to next.

I couldn't stand in the flowerbed amid Mother's purple irises and watch him on the roof. I couldn't see his brains fountaining out his temple, or watch him fall, or hold his body in my lap as the steam of him danced away through the freezing December rain.

So, I retreated into myself, searching for some dark, forgotten tunnel where I could hide, willing myself not to feel, not to think, not to care.

"Rad," a voice said, thin and ragged from the distance. I recognized it vaguely as Vic's. Strong hands lifted me under the armpits, shook me hard. "Rad, open your eyes."

I ignored him, burrowed deeper. There had to be somewhere away from all this. There had to be.

"C'mon, Rad, open 'em," Vic insisted urgently. And then: "Oh, God, we're losing her."

I drifted down to a place where there was no light. No pain. A tiny place, where Mother would never find me, and the walls hugged me as tight and solid as Papa's arms. Sealed in this dark silence, nothing could touch me. Nothing could hurt me ever again.

And then I heard it: A tinny, music box rendition of the Moonlight Sonata. Papa's voice telling me to "hang in there, kiddo. I'll be home soon, and—"

Like a rubber band, I snapped back into the thing that was my body. Vic and Tony peered down at me with worn, pleading faces. Vic held the stuffed wind-up baby grand Chris had given me for my sixteenth birthday. Tony held the ancient portable DVD player

I kept in my car. It played the CD Papa had sent to me when I was five and he was off killing people in some foreign country somewhere.

I howled with indignation, thrashing my head from side to side. I tugged despairingly against the restraints. They had tricked me, suckered me back into facing this misery with the promise of finding Chris and Papa alive again.

"Lemme go, lemme go. I can't do this, anymore."

"Rad," Vic soothed. "I know it hurts. I know it does. But stay with us for while. Just a little while. You can do it."

"Don't give in," Tony commanded, setting the DVD player on my chest. He held my head, forcing me to lock gazes with him. "Don't give up."

"I can't do this," I whispered, ashamed.

"...all this sand really sucks," Papa was saying. It was an early one, from when he'd been in Kuwait, his voice distorted as a truck rumbled by in the background. "And you wouldn't believe the beetles they've got here. One of the jarhead M.P.'s hit one the other day, busted out the whole front end of his jeep." He laughed, cocksure and exuberant, and I missed him so ferociously my throat hurt. "No." I let my eyes roll shut, breaking away to look for that dark, abandoned place again.

"No!" Tony shouted, thumbing my eyelids open. A strand of his hair, black as a raven's wing, had worked loose from the bun and now hung across his face. His eyes were red-rimmed with fatigue, the blue of his irises encircled by a thin ring of dark gray. His fingers mashed my ears against my skull, dug into the soft flesh under my jaw.

"Rad," he pleaded. "Stay here. Don't go catatonic on me."

A violent shudder racked me, my skin suddenly burning under his touch. I gasped. The world seemed to shift around me, splitting into a strange, dual landscape. Everything—the bed, the machines, the men, myself—was somehow there, and not there. Like I had one foot in a place outside myself.

"You here, Rad?" Tony asked. "You staying here?"

"Yeah," a stranger inside me said, recoiling at what I saw in him. Or of him, I wasn't sure. The room seemed filled with ghosts. Thirty or forty of them, at the very least. Gaunt, hollow-faced men and women with broken necks and bullet-ridden chests, struggling fruitlessly to escape a shimmering, transparent web. A web with Tony at its center.

Tony, but not Tony. Older, with chestnut brown hair and lion-gold eyes and a ragged, ruddy beard streaked with gray.

"Radiana," a man whispered at my elbow.

I cranked my eyes as far left as they'd go, and a low moan erupted from me. Mike. Oh, sweet Jesus, it was my mother's boyfriend, Mike, coming to punish me for killing him.

"Radiana," he repeated, reaching his skeletal, half-rotting fingers toward my shoulder. Behind him were the two men who'd attacked me at the train station, Fox-face and Doughboy.

I arched against the restraints with a hopeless, desperate shriek. "He's dead, he's dead, make him go away!"

"She's hallucinating again," Vic said, moving in to help the present day Tony hold me down. The older Tony just stood there shaking his head, a sad, wistful look in his leonine eyes.

"Relax," the now Tony soothed, struggling to keep my head still. "Don't pull against the machine. You'll hurt yourself."

Mike reached into me, his bony, ice-cold fingers sweeping through my flesh. I felt a wrenching, queasy sensation as his hand closed around something at my core, and then he was stepping back, a shimmering, transparent strand in his fist. Fox-face and Doughboy did the same.

"They're touching me!" I shouted, straining furiously. I shuddered again, a sudden, electric cold slamming into me as the golden-eyed, bearded Tony grabbed a strand of his own. At that moment I became the center of a web, and I knew who all the ghosts were. I knew they were real, because this wistful, phantom Tony who reached into me was from the future.

And all the ghosts were there because I had killed them.

I searched for Chris among the crowd, finding solace in the fact that he wasn't there. I'd only been a witness. Not the agent of his death.

"Radiana?" Papa's unmistakable voice sounded behind me. "What are you doing here?"

I whirled around to see him standing alone on a flat, featureless plain of dead, ice-frosted Bermuda grass. Behind him, a glistening black river snaked across the horizon, the far bank lost in the mists. Papa, like the yellow-eyed Tony, was decades older than I remembered him in life, his hair grizzled and shaggy. A jagged scar bisected his right eyebrow, his right eye socket a pink mass of scar tissue. He wasn't in uniform, but barefoot in jeans and a T-shirt. He seemed surprised to see me.

"Papa!" I rushed towards him, my feet moving noiselessly on the brittle grass.

He held his palm up, shaking his head. "Go back. You shouldn't be here."

"Papa!" I kept heading towards him, although my progress slowed, as if he could stop my approach by the sheer force of his will. "Chris is dead!"

"I know. Go back. You won't find him here."

I halted, bewildered by his demeanor. He seemed alarmed by my presence. Not happy to see me, at all. "But, Papa. There's nothing to go back to."

"You don't want to be where I am." There was an urgency to his voice that I recognized as an order. "Go back. Now."

Bewildered and hurt by his unwelcoming attitude, I glanced at the web of ghosts behind me, and then back at him. A faint, translucent strand extended from him, but it wasn't attached to me. I turned to follow it, and saw it was in the fist of yet another Tony. This one was about my age. Beardless and yellow-eyed, much younger than the blue-eyed one I knew.

"Did you kill my father?" I asked him, becoming more and more confused. "Are you going to kill my father?"

This Tony grimaced at me, and looked down at the single strand in his fist. I wondered where all the other ghosts had gone, and what had happened to the web. He looked around the icy plain, at the river, and then back at me.

"I think I'm dreaming," he said, and faded into mist. I rushed towards him, lunging for Papa's strand, not wanting to give up. I tried to snatch it away before he dissolved completely, but my hand passed through the glowing thread, jolting me with an electric shock that snapped me back into my body.

I was in the hospital bed. The ghosts were gone. Vic and the normal, blue-eyed, samurai-bunned, super-sexy Tony peered down at me with concern.

"You here, now?" Tony asked, still clutching my head in his hands. "You going to stay here with us?"

I stared at him, blinking several times as I tried to make sense of what had just happened. My breathing evened out into a steady rhythm. I knew I'd been hallucinating. It had felt like something more. Something weird and powerful and otherworldly. Something I never, ever wanted to experience again.

The pain had become tolerable. My body was not a bad place to be any more. I took a few more deep breaths, and finally nodded. I felt exhausted. "I'm here."

"What happened?" Tony searched my gaze. "What'd you see?"

"I think Papa's in Purgatory," I murmured, and drifted off to sleep.

CHAPTER ELEVEN

When I came to, my arm ached with a slow, relentless throbbing. My throat was sore, and a strange, sulfurous taste coated the back of my mouth. Around me, the room was dim, both the virtual hearth and the fish tank screens were off. I sat up—still a bit woozy—and reached for the pitcher of water on the bedside table, only to have Tony lift it from my grasp.

"How are you feeling?" He smiled and poured me a cup, holding it until I could get my fingers to wrap around it. His man bun was gone and his long mane of hair framed his face. "Still hearing things?"

I shook my head, and glanced around the room. We were alone.

"The first stasis series is always the worst. Once you make it through that, you'll be all right." He placed his palm to my forehead, as if testing for a fever. Then he leaned over the mattress and leveled his gaze with mine. "I need to leave. I have some business that can't wait. I won't see you again until after you're discharged. But, before I go, we need to talk."

"About what?"

He didn't answer, just stared into my eyes, searching. I set the cup down on the table, fighting back a moment's panic. What in that intense blue gaze made me feel so trapped?

"You're still afraid of me," he observed.

I opened my mouth to deny it, then nodded with a sigh.

"I thought so." He chuckled without humor, stepping away from the bed to sit in the chair by the door. "That better?"

I nodded again, raising the glass. I swallowed a mouthful of water, and then another, while he looked on. I couldn't get the taste of sulfur out of my mouth. Like Satan had been French kissing me in my sleep, or something.

"I know what stasis can do to a person," Tony began, his voice solemn. "I had seven months of it, off and on." He paused to let that sink in.

"Seven months?" I gaped at him.

"I was the fourth person to ever undergo these procedures, and survive. So, I know what I'm talking about. What you dreamed..."

"They were just hallucinations," I interrupted, before he could continue. I had a sneaking suspicion I knew where this was going, and I didn't want to talk about any of it. "Flashbacks. They didn't mean anything. The past is the past. It's over and done."

"But it's not." He pursed his lips, trailing a finger along the arm of the chair, a strange sadness in his eyes. "You saw things that haven't happened yet. People you haven't met yet."

"No," I lied.

"You saw your father."

"And my mother. And my brother. And other people. So?"

He stared at me, inscrutable, then looked across the room. "Temporal displacement is a side effect nobody talks about. The theory is that the stasis field creates some kind of quantum entanglement."

"You're saying that it makes you see the future?"

"And the past. And sometimes, it entangles you with other people who have also had stasis. That's why this tech is still Top Secret. Why it has never been commercialized."

"Why do I need to know this?" I asked, throwing that cloak and dagger trope back at him, trying to get him to stop talking.

"I dreamed you. When I was in stasis. Seven years ago. Back before I looked like this."

I swallowed hard, remembering the young, yellow-eyed Tony. This was really creeping me out.

"Whatever you saw," he continued earnestly, "Whoever you saw, I need you to keep quiet about it. Don't mention it to a soul. Except me. Can you do that?" He searched my face.

"I don't want to talk about it to anybody. Especially you."

He sighed and dragged his gaze away.

The silence stretched out between us, crowding against me, making me feel itchy and hungry and, despite everything, intrigued. I couldn't help asking: "What did you dream about me?"

"Most of it hasn't happened yet."

"But I'm 'her'? That's what you were talking about in the limo?"

He nodded. "I'm sure of it, now."

I digested this, unsettled by the entire concept. I had never believed in clairvoyance or psychic phenomena. Such things were fantasies, like unicorns, free lunches and honest politicians. "Do they all come true? Have any come true? I mean, other than you meeting me? And if you had really dreamed me, how come you didn't know it was me until now?"

"They're generated in the right brain, so they tend to be symbolic. Sometimes you don't realize what they're about until something triggers comprehension."

"So...there's this Top Secret procedure that induces a form of precognition that's only useful in hindsight? That's the government, for you."

He drew in a deep breath, exhaling slowly as he combed his fingers through his hair. "No one understands why I trust you enough to have you on the team. Not even Mando. They all think I've gone off the deep end. But you know. I could see it in your eyes the moment I first met you. You know we're entangled."

"That was just lust," I blurted out, immediately regretting it when he sat up in his chair and stared intently at me. "I mean, look at you. You're so smokin' hot, you're atomic."

He snickered, rising to his feet. "You're not bad, yourself." He moved over to the bed, leaned over, and kissed me on the forehead. "But I like you better Italian."

The touch of his lips against my skin sent strange tingles throughout my body. His scent filled my nostrils, and I drew in a deep breath, trying to hold on to him as he walked towards the door. As strange and uncomfortable as this conversation had been, I didn't want him to leave. "You and Faith are supposed to be dating, right? Does that mean we're going to shag?"

He paused at the door, glancing back at me with a speculative look. "Only if you want to."

A broad grin broke over my face. Finally, something to look forward to. "Hot damn."

***

Aside from the eerie, unrelenting barrage of stasis dreams, the rest of my hospital stay went reasonably well. When Mando was there, I studied the surveillance vids and practiced being Faith, so that when Glen and Kam, the other two bodyguards, took their turns watching me, there was no doubt in their minds I was a rich little Daddy's girl from Houston.

Glen, the thin, well-manicured, dark-complexioned African-American man, had none of the gruff congeniality of Mando, just a cool competence, a professional alertness that had nothing to do with the fact I was a living, breathing human being. He'd probably look the same way if he were guarding a pocketbook.

Kam, on the other hand, had a style all his own. A muscular but chubby-cheeked Pakistani with a California accent, he always entered the room with an expansive smile and a relaxed kind of intensity that put me at ease. Glen, on the other hand, often greeted him with a scowl, ignoring the piece of sugarless gum Kam invariably offered from the pack in his pants pocket. The typical exchange went as follows:

"You're late," Glen would say, heading for the hall as soon as Kam stepped into the room.

"Two minutes." Kam twitched his broad shoulders, like a duck shaking water off its back. "I'll make it up to you."

"You owe me ten, now."

"So sue me."

"I'll do more than that," Glen said, slamming the door.

"Ah, lick my fucking dick," Kam grumbled after him, and then turned to offer me a piece of gum. I shook my head. Kam pulled a foil-wrapped stick out with his incisors, skinned it, and shoved it between his teeth. His mouth didn't close all the way when he chewed.

I was surprised by his language. The Pakistanis I knew were devout Muslims and didn't curse at all. Of course, maybe he was Muslim the way I was Catholic. Or maybe he wasn't Pakistani. He certainly sounded like the end product of the great Los Angeles melting pot. And, unlike Glen, the fact that he truly enjoyed his work made him a much better conversationalist.

Even so, Tony's absence frustrated me. I didn't love him. Wasn't in love with him, not like with Jim. But I still needed him, somehow. I craved him like an anemic craves red meat. Yet, at the same time, it was a relief not to feel that pulsing electrical connection whenever he was near. It was too primal, too out of control.

I suspected that stasis had something to do with it, but not in that spooky, action-at-a-distance way he had explained. I had always believed that ESP was an acronym for Extra Stupid People. It was more likely that waking up to him while in such a fragile, defenseless state had imprinted him on my brain, the way a newly hatched duckling makes the first thing it sees into its mother.

Oddly enough, I found comfort in that thought. If Tony turned out to be my father's killer, I wouldn't feel so bad about killing him. Not that I actually believed in the dream, or anything. But it was comforting, in a freakish, twisted sort of way, that in doing the wrong thing, I might be doing the right one.

The days stretched on, each one running into the other, and with Mando's gentle, persistent molding I became so quintessentially Faith that I actually found myself craving a drink or two.

***

The day I left the hospital, I woke up in a small enclave swathed with white curtains. Masked, blue-clad people smiled at me, asking me questions that didn't seem relevant. I must have given them the right answers because they disconnected me from the monitors and wheeled me through the halls. I was both nauseous and incredibly thirsty. My mouth tasted like I'd been sucking on a rotten Easter egg, but my hand had stopped hurting. A man I eventually identified as Vic held my good hand as we moved. He seemed concerned when I told him the world kept approaching and receding, like waves plying a beach. I couldn't get that sulfur smell out of my nose.

They brought me into a room with pink walls, where someone handed me a plastic cup full of water. Magic, focusing water, because after a few swallows the sulfur smell went away and the world seemed a much more substantial and recognizable place. I blinked hard, sucked in a breath or two, and guzzled half the pitcher.

"How do you feel?" Vic asked.

Mando stood beside him, half-moons of fatigue under his dark eyes. He stepped back to make room for a nurse to checklist what Vic told me was a magnetic field generation splint strapped onto my right arm. A chuckle escaped me as I stared at the splint, relief overwhelming me as I realized what it meant: No more surgery. It was finally over.

Vic leaned over the gurney, fear lingering in his dark eyes. "Miss Hopkins? How do you feel?"

I laughed some more, spilling half the remaining water down my front. "Okay," I said, finally remembering Vic had asked me a question. "I feel okay. Can I have some more water?"

He gestured to a nurse to refill the glass, then checked over the monitor mounted at the foot of the gurney. "No headache? Double vision? Tinnitus?"

I shook my head, preoccupied with examining the splint. Unlike anything I'd ever seen before, it had all the latest high-tech. If I could find the right button, it would probably write my autobiography. Damn thing must have cost at least a hundred grand.

Vic wasn't convinced. "You sure you're all right?"

I shrugged. The hospital smells made me a little queasy. "Stomach hurts a little," I drawled, careful to sound like Faith.

He relaxed slightly and dismissed the nurses standing by with instructions to bring a wheelchair. He turned back to me. "Normally we don't wake you up this soon after the surgery, but Tony insisted we get you out of here today. Can you sit up?"

I complied awkwardly, because my sense of equilibrium was off, but I eventually managed to swing my legs over the side and hold myself upright.

Vic held me steady, his white mustache covering a pensive frown. "You really should stay here for another night or two." He grabbed my left wrist, checking for a pulse. We both knew the machine could do it better, but neither of us cared. "You read those instructions I gave you? Gradual strengthening. No sudden impacts, no sustained, intricate maneuvers, nothing that will strain those tendons. The splint can withstand almost anything, but your tissue is still quite fragile."

"I know, I know." I adopted Faith's annoyed librarian voice. "Paragraph one: 'A total re-build of the metacarpophalangeal region will return eighty to eighty-five percent usage of the injured area within a four week period following the procedure." Vic waved me to stop, but I was on a roll: "Remaining recovery depends on proper use of the Maserly-Kalisat electromagnetic field generation splint and physio-therapy to fully develop the regenerated tissues.' Paragraph two—"

"Fine," he cut in. "You read it." He dropped my wrist and pointed at the splint. "You can move around like normal—even your normal—as long as you wear that. Twenty hours a day for the first three days. Then, gradually wean yourself down from all night and four-hours in the middle of the day to nothing."

I nodded, having read all this stuff, but he wasn't finished: "Don't forget to do the exercises—at least twice a day, no matter what. And don't get overly dependent on the splint. To really get full recovery, you need to use that hand as much as you can. Especially after the first ten days. But don't overdo it, either."

"When can I play?" I whispered, hoping he could answer before the nurses returned. It was my last chance to be Rad.

Vic glanced at Mando, who gave a curt nod, saying, "Be quick about it."

"Okay," Vic spoke rapidly. "You can start that hand on the keyboard in a week. Beginning stuff. Easy-easy-easy stuff— fifteen minutes, no more than four times a day for the first ten days. After that a half-hour, maybe forty-five minutes. Don't push things. It'll take at least a month or two for everything to settle in right. Even then, I expect you'll have mild swelling and stiffness for another year or so."

A year.

I'd forgotten it would take that long to recover. Twelve endless months. And with the five-and-a-half Webster had cost me, I'd have to go back to school. Jim had already graduated, and without him to coach me on who to schmooze, it would all be a wasted effort. I could never get a gig or make the contacts on my own. Probably couldn't even get a diploma.

Vic nudged me, to shake the frown off my face. "Relax. These things take time. Here, let me show you how to remove the splint."

He stepped in and cradled my arm close, using his body to screen the splint from public view. Then, after a furtive glance at Mando to ensure he wasn't paying attention to us, Vic killed the power. I gritted my teeth. I'd expected it to hurt when the splint was down, but not quite this much.

"This is how you take it off," he said as he peeled back the seal. "Now, you have to be very careful not to bend or tweak the electrodes, see those there?" He cracked the case and pointed out where the pads rested against my skin. "Clean them twice a day." And be careful of this, too." He lifted the foam padding slightly and pointed out a folded rectangle of notebook paper. It had my name on it, in Jim's handwriting.

"He left it for you at the memorial," he whispered. "I picked it up. Thought you might want it." We exchanged conspiratorial grins, like two kids passing notes under the nose of a despotic teacher. Vic closed the splint up and resumed his instructional monotone. "And when you put it together, make sure your casing connectors are fully seated. Like so." He snapped the connectors together, then turned the splint back on.

The pain disappeared immediately. I sighed with relief.

"Ready to go?" Glen and Kam appeared at the doorway, flanking a nurse with a wheelchair.

Vic didn't look up at them, just kept staring into my face like he was trying to memorize it. He folded my good hand between his, gripping it warmly. Abruptly, he stepped away, face blank, like he was trying not to cry. "See you later, Miss Hopkins."

"Thanks, doc. Thanks for, uh, ever'thin'."

He signed the release forms with a grim-mouthed flourish, handed the paperwork to Mando, and left. I swallowed the lump in my throat, wondering exactly what that long stare had meant.

"Let's go." Mando handed me a wad of Faith clothes and motioned for me to get dressed. When I was ready they plopped me in the wheelchair, whisked me down the surgical elevator, and slipped me out the ambulance entrance. We approached a cobalt-blue BMW M5, so new it still had sticker marks on the window.

My jaw dropped when I saw Neanderthal behind the wheel. I started to bolt, but Mando snapped me out of it by shoving me into the back seat. He sat next to me, while Glen and Kam remained at the curb.

"Let's go, Percy." Mando tapped the back of the driver's seat. The M5 shot out into traffic. Percy? Neanderthal's real name was Percy? I started to laugh, which made me dizzy, so I leaned back against the headrest, breathing deeply.

"You okay?" Mando said. He seemed preoccupied. Probably worried I wouldn't be able to keep in character.

"Hunky-dory, darlin'." I gasped and chuckled and breathed some more.

Percy gassed the M5 through a yellowing intersection and up a freeway on-ramp. We zipped along in the fast lane, then shot across four lanes to catch the 405 at the last possible moment. Every once in a while Percy shot down an off-ramp and whipped the car around a few blocks before climbing back on the freeway again. Sometimes he'd get on the same direction, sometimes he'd go back the way we came. Played Hell with my stomach, with all that water sloshing around.

Then, without warning, the car skidded into a lot below a high-rise in Westwood and pulled up next to the elevator. Mando checked his watch. "Right on time."

The two men bustled me out of the M5 and into the elevator. The floor lurched beneath our feet, then settled into a steady, humming rhythm. My insides lurched as well, but couldn't settle on anything.

The elevator doors lisped open to where a four-bladed helicopter idled on the rooftop helipad, blowing dust and debris into our faces. Tony sat in the front seat, riding shotgun. He wore a black leather jacket, and smiled at me through the bubble glass.

A weird feeling of *déjà vu* struck me as I locked gazes with him, and I knew.

I knew.

This moment would determine the whole rest of my future. Getting in that copter would put me at the center of the web. Draw all those ghosts to me. All those people I'd never met would be dead because of me. Because of my relationship to Tony.

I pulled back and tried to bury my spine in the elevator's paneled wall, but Mando and Percy clamped firmly onto my biceps and forced me onto the rooftop. I squirmed, shoes scuffing a

108

pathetic tattoo against the painted concrete, drowned out by the loud, mechanical whine of the waiting bird.

Mando opened the door. Percy slipped his hands under my armpits, and hoisted me up. My left hand latched onto his ear. My fingers dug in with the desperate tenacity of a drowning pit bull.

"Owww," Percy complained, but didn't put me down.

"Why don't you fellas just leave me here?" I shouted over the noise of the chopper. "I'll be just fine without you. Really, I will." I twisted around and tried to crawl over poor Percy without giving up the death grip I had on his ear.

"OWWWW!"

Mando chuckled. "She's afraid. Miss Pucker-up-to-the-Devil is afraid of flying."

"No, I ain't." It was true. I wasn't afraid of flying.

I was afraid of the future that would come into being the moment I climbed into that chopper.

"Relax." Mando shouted as he tried to pry my fingers loose. "These are the safest flying machines in the world. More people die by slipping in their bathtubs than are killed in these puppies. You don't have to be scared."

"Not scared." My fingernails dug in so deeply that blood trickled down the side of Percy's neck.

He groaned. "Oh, man, get her off me."

Together, they forced my fingers from his ear and muscled me inside the bird with a maneuver that resembled stuffing a terrified weasel down a drainpipe. They strapped me, panting, into the seat, then strapped themselves in.

With the doors shut, the cabin was surprisingly quiet, but then, I'd only ever been in military transports before. Tony peered warily over his shoulder at me. The pilot too, seemed curious, his bushy eyebrows crawling toward his hairline. "Trouble?"

"She's afraid of flying," Mando explained.

"Gotcha." The pilot nodded understanding and turned back to his controls. The bird lifted up and the rooftops shrunk away, sliding along beneath us like surrealistic postage stamps. I gritted my teeth, hoping my innards would kindly remain where they were and not creep any farther up my throat.

Tony continued to regard me, face softening with compassion. "You're perfectly safe. Flying is nothing to be afraid of."

"Not scared."

He twisted his torso to lean over the back of his seat and tipped my chin up to meet his gaze. "Then why is your face so white?"

I screwed my eyes shut to block out the piercing blueness of his gaze, but it was too late. Something shifted inside my head. My blood became a glowing neon plasma beneath my skin. My whole body itched with the strange restless energy his presence woke in me. For no reason at all, I let out a low, keening moan so filled with loss and frustration, it scarcely sounded human.

"Hey," Tony said, as I felt his fingers brush my cheek. "You okay?" I opened my eyes, saw both Mando and Tony peering at me with gentle concern. "You okay?"

The sudden anguish faded as quickly as it had come, leaving me stained with embarrassment. I nodded, looked away quickly. "Fine," I drawled. "I'm fine."

"You know," Percy said to me as he rubbed his ear. "You are one phobic chick to have a name like Faith."

***

We were in the air a good hour—over water, no less.

I managed not to puke.

We approached a stretch of coastline that boasted a small, private cove. A few small craft were moored here, along with one of those sleek modern mega yachts with a helipad on the top deck towards the stern.

I thought we might be landing there, but the pilot kept going inland, over some low grassy hills and up over a chaparral and sage-covered mountaintop. We dropped down into a valley between two breadloaf hills. I saw coyotes with black heads and fawn-colored bodies running in packs across the chaparral-covered terrain. Or were they jackals? As we drew nearer I saw their collars and realized they looked like fast and sleek German shepherds, without that lowrider back end.

Dogs and I didn't get along.

Mother had seen to that when I was five. Aching with loneliness after we moved to Corpus Christi, I had brought a stray puppy home. She made me watch while she drowned it in the bathtub, and made sure I knew it was my fault. Ever since then, I'd never been able to shake the idea that they somehow knew what had happened. How I had killed one of their own. They were all out to avenge that senseless murder.

"What kinda dogs are those?" I asked, feeling the tension ramp up in me.

"Tovenaars," Tony replied.

"Tony, hon, just cuz you own a dog don't mean you name the breed after yourself."

"It does when I bred them myself. They're a mix of Belgian Malinois and Border Collie. With a little Dutch Sheperd."

"So...they're Malincollies?"

"I prefer Borgian Colinois," Mando smirked.

Percy snickered. Tony threw a mock glower at Mando.

Below us, the trees and brush stopped abruptly at a swatch of palm-lined grassy lawn, and then an enormous black-bottomed swimming pool glistened below. We flew over a massive adobe-style mansion bordered by a cobbled, crescent-shaped courtyard. An asphalt road led across more lawn to a red brick helipad, about three hundred yards from the main house. The bird hovered, then gently lowered itself onto the pad.

"Welcome to the Ranch," Tony announced.

As soon as the runners touched ground, and Mando opened the door, I flung the seat belt off and scrabbled crosswise across his lap. In my haste to get away from Tony before those weird glowy sensations started up again, I propelled myself out the door, thinking to tuck and roll and land on my feet. Except, I got a little dizzy along the way and wound up slithering down to smack my head on the bricks. Ended up flat on my back, wondering why there were so many stars in that cloudless turquoise sky.

Things got fuzzy, then. I blinked hard, my muddled view suddenly ringed by an impressive show of fangs, guaranteed to win the Gold Medal at any Transylvanian County fair:

Dogs. Angry, well-trained guard dogs.

I didn't move.

The helicopter rotors slowed, their thunderous chuff-chuff losing steam. In the relative quiet, the growling black faced beasts above me took on an even more sinister appearance.

"You okay?" Tony's human face appeared amidst the sea of Hell hounds. He looked mildly concerned and thoroughly amused.

"Wish you'd quit sayin' that," I drawled, closing my eyes against the stinking puffs of dog breath assaulting my face. Percy's big hands hooked under my armpits, and drew me to my feet. A bright light flashed across my closed lids, and I opened them, blinking painfully against the glare of sunlight reflecting off the windshield of a richly appointed, industrial-sized golf cart. The front had a single vinyl bench seat. In the rear, under a hard plastic canopy, two padded benches faced each other down the length of the vehicle.

Jana set the brake and exited the cart. "This package giving you trouble already, Tony?"

"She's afraid of flying," Percy explained, because Tony was busy patting various dog bodies and shooing the animals away.

She stepped up to scrutinize me, the glare making a sort of halo around her blonde hair and long, lithe body in its perfect sheath of tennis whites. I blinked at her, but didn't say anything. The light was hurting my eyes. The butterflies in my stomach milled around like crazed hooligans at a soccer match, and my head buzzed like a hive of goosed bees.

She sniffed in disapproval, then turned away from me to regard Tony, who was still busy with the dogs. The size of the pack hadn't dwindled any, despite his attentions. It surprised me, that he couldn't control a bunch of dumb beasts.

But then, I saw the cheery smile on his face and realized he hadn't meant to shoo them away. He was playing with the damn things, chasing them a few steps, then retreating with a laugh as they lunged snapping toward him, false growls in their throats.

We all stood there watching, waiting for him to finish. From the hesitant way they exchanged glances, neither Jana, nor Mando, nor Percy wanted to interrupt him. Finally, Mando cleared his throat and stepped toward him. "Uh, Tony, is it all right if I take the helicopter back? I promised I'd get there ASAP."

Tony stiffened, the easy laughter draining out of him, replaced by an iron distance. He nodded, but didn't turn to face us, remaining in profile. "Go ahead."

"You're not staying?" Jana glanced at Mando.

"Can't. Ruby called. Emma's dilated two centimeters. And I promised I'd be there for this one."

Jana sniffed again, disapproval showing plainly on her features as she pointed to me. "But she's your package."

"She's mine, now," Tony said, still staring at the milling, furry canines around him. "Put her in the blue room," he said to Mando. "Then take the bird back."

At this, Percy's thick fingers dug into my arms, and he guided me gingerly toward the cart. Mando moved with us, carrying the gator skin briefcase.

"Tony," Jana tried to get his attention, but he continued to play with the dogs. "The Trubys are squawking. They want Kam back."

"What's the problem with Boris?"

"They say he's not fun enough."

"He's not. But he's the best programmer on my payroll."

"They're on the board. We need to keep them happy."

Tony rolled his eyes with a long suffering sigh. He shouted something at the dogs, and they dispersed, loping off across the grass to disappear into the brush beyond a row of palms. Percy helped me into the cart. Mando sat beside me, propping me up a bit with his shoulder. Jana climbed in and sat on the bench opposite me, her pond-scum eyes regarding me with contempt.

My head was starting to hurt from the bounce it took off the helipad. I met Jana's gaze anyway, not wanting her to think I was afraid of her, even though I was. I was afraid of everything here in this strange bright world of luxury and sunshine. Afraid, especially, of Tony, and the sudden cool indifference that went up between us as he sandwiched me on the bench with Mando.

Percy sat behind the wheel and started the cart, whisking us across the vast green curve of the lawn toward the barrel tile-roofed mansion atop the hill. The knots in my stomach gave another turn.

Jana continued to stare at me, her displeasure growing at my refusal to lower my gaze. "Tony," she said, in a precise, autocratic voice. "I really don't think—"

"I know what you think," he warned, the smile on his face never reaching his eyes. "I had to bring her here."

"She's trouble, Tony," Jana grumbled. She tossed her hair back, then leaned forward to glare at me again. "You'll see. Nothing but trouble."

Overwhelmed by this hugely warm welcome, I threw up all over her skirt.

CHAPTER TWELVE

When we reached the house, Mando guided me up a broad wooden staircase to a landing, then opened a set of double doors and escorted me down a wide hallway of Mexican tile.

"Didn't know you were afraid to fly," he said, breaking the silence between us.

"I'm not," I snapped. The sour taste of bile still hung in my mouth, doing nothing to lighten my sullen mood. "It's just—" I growled deep in my throat, unable to explain it all.

"I don't mean anything by it." He shrugged, looking vaguely uncomfortable at my scowl. "It just puzzles me. You're not the type to scare easy." He fell silent for a while. We turned a corner and headed down yet another broad hallway.

This place was huge. The corridors alone could sleep half the homeless in Santa Monica.

"Don't worry," he murmured. "You'll have your old life back in a week or two. I've fixed it. You won't have to go up against Scotty."

"I want to."

He stopped short, blinking at me. "What? Why?"

"I want to help Tony catch Brighton Leigh."

"He told you about Brighton?"

I nodded, jaw setting, lip curling a bit as I recalled what was on that vid Tony had shown me. "And his son."

He stared at me for a very long moment, subtle changes happening in his face that I couldn't read, but knew were indications of him reformulating some plan or another. "It doesn't matter," he finally said, resuming his walk with a shrug. "He'll be forced to abort all this madness, soon. Until then, just keep playing along."

We continued on, our footsteps echoing off the stark adobe. Up ahead, I heard voices, two men speaking in a language I didn't recognize. We turned a corner, came upon two workmen dressed in gray jumpsuits.

Their skin was the rich reddish-brown of lightly roasted coffee beans, and they spoke in hushed, pleasant tones to each other as they re-stuccoed a hole in the plaster the size of a man's torso. They grinned as we walked past, calling out some greeting while bowing their heads deferentially. Mando nodded back, echoing a reply.

"Javanese," he explained to my questioning look. "Most of the staff here are from the same area of East Java."

"Why?"

"Tony grew up there. They're all related to his step father. Makes them incredibly loyal."

"What happened to the wall?"

"Hollis did that. When Damiano disappeared he showed up here with a search warrant. His team was here for sixteen hours. Knocked holes all over the place." He scowled, shaking his head. "Pain in the ass."

"What was he looking for?"

"False walls. Secret passages. This place was built by a major drug smuggler back in the 1980's. Rumor has it there's a network of bolt holes and secret tunnels running all over the property."

"Did Hollis find anything?"

"Of course not. Even if Tony had killed Damiano, there's no way he'd be stupid enough to dispose of the body back in L.A. The ocean's only a mile away. He would have taken the helicopter and dumped her out to sea, and nobody would have found a trace of that corpse."

The off-hand way he discussed my murder sent a shiver through me.

We stopped in front of a very solid-looking door, and he tapped a card key against what looked like a decorative panel. A series of sighs sounded as several bolts around the perimeter of the door clicked free.

Mando pushed it open to reveal a large, well appointed room with a queen-size, satin-sheeted bed and a down comforter with little blue blossoms embroidered along the edges. Two slate-blue, highbacked chairs guarded big picture windows. A white lacquer dresser lined one wall, complete with a lacquer framed mirror, filigreed in gold. Vases of flowers crowned the matching end tables. I gaped at the homey opulence, thinking that somehow a mistake had been made. Real people didn't live this way.

"See you later," Mando said. He tossed the briefcase on one of the chairs and turned to leave.

"Ummm," I blurted out, catching his arm before he could start down the hall. He was the closest thing I had to a friend in this alien world. "Ummm..."

"What?" he inquired. His eyes met mine.

I couldn't bring myself to ask him to stay. He had his own life, his own problems. "Good luck with the baby," I finished lamely.

He blinked in surprise, then grinned. "Thanks. See you later." He nudged me inside and closed the door.

It chirped as each bolt latched, and refused to open again. I pecked a sequence or two into the keypad next to the jamb, but all I got were error signals. I tried the other two doors and found an empty, cedar-lined walk-in closet behind one, and an enormous bathroom of polished stone behind the other.

The floor, the walls, the counter tops, the towel racks, even the shelf above the ultra-modern Japanese style toilet was carved out of marble or granite or some such thing. There was a step down marble shower stall you could hide a horse in, and the towels were thicker than a vain man's hairpiece. The soap was some shrink-wrapped handmade stuff chock full of organic rosemary, lavender and goat milk. But there were no windows in here.

I returned to the bedroom, coming to the slow realization that there was no TV. No laptop, no tablet, no game console, no electronics of any kind, aside from the high-tech toilet and the lock panel beside the door. Not even a port to charge a cellphone.

I was trapped. Isolated. Jailed. A literal prisoner of luxury.

In a sudden claustrophobic impulse, I tried the windows. Nothing budged the two-inch thick Plex. I sat on the bed, fighting something akin to panic. After a few deep breaths I composed myself enough to realize I was being silly. It was just the paranoia left over from stasis that was making me feel this way. I needed to calm down, to wash away the memory of the gunshot and the hospital and just pretend nothing had ever happened.

I needed a shower.

I pulled my shoes and socks off and plodded into the bathroom, shivering involuntarily when my bare soles touched the cold tile. I ignored the discomfort and flipped on the light, only to be half-blinded by the sparkle of polished stone.

I turned the water on in the shower to let it warm up and peeled my clothes off, noting with distaste the ragged smear of grease from the helipad across the back of my blouse. As I tossed the shirt away a movement caught my eye, and I looked up to find the ivory torso of a topless stranger moving in the mirror. I stared.

Green eyes. Short, coppery blonde hair.

I'd forgotten they'd made me Irish.

It rankled me, but then I wriggled my underwear off and discovered the final insult: my pubic hair was the same coppery blonde. The rush of anger, the feeling of violation hit me so hard I felt lightheaded. I'd seen it before. I knew in the hospital they'd done this, but this was the first time it had really registered. Goddamn them. Goddamn them all.

They had taken me away from myself when I'd been powerless to stop them, and the only recourse I had was to live long enough to become Italian again.

The air grew hot and hard to breathe, and the mirror began to fog from the steam billowing from the depths of the shower stall.

I readied myself for the inevitable ache, then turned the splint off and unzipped the plastic seal. I lifted the strip of foam padding off and carefully withdrew the note Vic had hidden underneath.

I don't know what I had expected, since according to both Mando and Vic, Jim thought I was dead. What I found was a letter of apology. Something he'd written after he'd kicked me out, but had never given to me.

He was always doing stuff like that. Writing letters to people who upset him, and then just filing them away. It was supposed to be psychologically freeing, or something. What a waste of paper. When I was upset with someone, I didn't need to write it down. I told them to their face. Usually with my fist.

Since Jim had nothing to apologize for, I didn't read past the first two sentences. He'd never meant for me to read it, anyway.

Still, it was comforting to see his handwriting, and to know Vic cared enough to salvage this letter from the memorial and give me a little piece of Jim to call my own. It made me feel less alone.

I searched the bathroom for a place to hide the letter, and discovered the high-tech, Japanese style toilet had a removable panel for access to the bidet mechanism. I stowed the letter in there, and then rested my arm on the vanity and resumed the process of removing the splint.

The stiff support lifted off, but the little electrodes of the built-in stim unit stuck to the skin of my palm, wrist and forearm. I peeled them away carefully and eased my fingers free from the sheaths around the curved splines—and time stopped.

My hand was back. Swollen. Yellow and green and purple, but it was there, and it was whole. I could move the knuckles and feel the cold marble beneath my fingertips.

"Yes." Laughter bubbled up from deep within me, relief and gratitude and soul-high exhilaration. "Yes!"

I whooped and hollered and tore around in circles like a dog crazy for a bone. After a while, I got dizzy and sat down on the toilet, breathless and giddy and naked as a swindler's lie. Being a nudist at heart, that didn't bother me so much.

What bothered me was Tony standing in the doorway, his handsome, chiseled face contorted in silent amusement.

"I see you're feeling better," he said pleasantly, stepping into the room. He had changed into a dove-gray linen suit that turned his strangely changeable eyes the color of storm clouds, and the pall of steam hanging from the ceiling made his loose black curls glisten. His steely gaze ran over me, resting briefly on my chest, and then again just below my waist.

I wasn't sure how to react. If I covered myself up I'd look embarrassed. And even though I was, I didn't want him to know that. Bad enough he'd caught me dancing around like a complete fool. No need to make him feel even more superior by scrambling for a towel like a helpless virgin.

Damn, he was good-looking. Should I invite him into the shower with me? No. He'd probably think I was a slut if I did that. Or Faith. "How old are you?" I asked bluntly. "Thirty-two? Thirty-three?"

"About that," he admitted.

I googled my eyes in mock surprise. "And your mother still dresses you?"

His mouth drew into a hard line. "What do you mean?"

"Well," I waved at the open door. "You obviously didn't master the simple art of knockin'. I just assumed you'd need help with the complicated things. Like that neck tie."

His hand covered his tie. He looked down at it, then back at me. "I don't have to knock. This is my house."

The logic of that escaped me, so I turned my back on him and entered the shower. If he was going to break rules, so would I.

"Get out," he called after me. "Get dressed."

I closed my eyes and let the warm torrent rush over me. Tight knots in my back and shoulders melted slowly under the onslaught, and a little hiccup of elation ran through me: I could feel water dripping off the tips of my fingers.

The water stopped abruptly. I opened my eyes and looked around to see him tapping out something on his phone. Did he really just turn off the spigots that way?

"Dude. Are you that much of a control freak?" I asked, unable to keep Rad from spilling through.

"Get dressed, Faith." He used that voice parents reserve for recalcitrant children. "Dave Seward and Randall Cortelaine are here for our meeting."

I sifted through my Faith files for anyone matching those monikers. Scored with the first. Dave Seward was Faith's accountant and financial advisor.

"It's all arranged," Tony continued. "Cortelaine is Scotty's lawyer. He's bringing the agreement for you and Seward to go over. Didn't Mando brief you?"

"Nobody told me about this meetin'," I complained. "And ain't none of my clothes in the closet." I flourished my hands along my naked torso to emphasize the lack. "I'll just go like this."

A low growl of frustration sounded deep in his throat. "The truck with your things must have been delayed. I'll go borrow something from Jana."

"You're shackin' up with your lawyer?"

"It's complicated." He turned to leave.

"Wait a sec," I said quickly.

"What?" He half-turned toward me, his body profiled in the glow of lights over the vanity.

I hesitated, then waved him off. "Never mind."

Men are so easy to read.

He disappeared with a puzzled frown. I waited for the door to latch before I turned the water back on and let the smile loose on my face. I'd seen what I'd wanted to see: Either his pants were too tight or somebody was holding a tent convention in his underwear.

Damiano one, Tovenaar nothing.

I finished my shower and toweled off, pacing naked around the bedroom while I waited for his return. For a time, I stood at the window and looked out. I had a magnificent view of that huge black-bottomed pool, with a vine-crusted arbor at one end and a tiki bar, barbeque and cabanas on the far side. An adobe wall separated the pool area from the vast, green lawn. Another putty-colored wall separated the lawn from the heart-shaped, chaparral-crusted hills beyond. Two armed, uniformed security types were up on the hillside, patrolling the fire road in a souped-up off-road golf cart. They carried themselves like knights sworn to fealty, not dudes pulling a paycheck. I wondered how many guarded the estate, and if any of them spoke English. In the cleavage between the hills was a slice of ultramarine. Must be the ocean Mando had referred to.

I shuddered involuntarily.

I hated being locked up. Felt like I was back in juvenile hall. I tried to burn my frustration away by practicing katas, but Tony arrived before I worked up a sweat. He frowned and closed the door.

"None of that," he chided. "Faith doesn't know that."

An itchy feeling of rebellion skulked up my spine. "What else am I s'posed to do? Ain't got a TV or a game console in here. Not even a laptop for streamin'."

"None of that for you, right now. I don't want any signals going in or out of here that are not strictly monitored."

"Then give me a keyboard."

"No keyboards for you, either. Faith doesn't play."

I gave him an imploring look. "I have to have somethin', or I'll go stark, ravin' bugshit."

Unswayed, he motioned to the gator skin briefcase. "You have the Faith vids. Study them. Do what I'm paying you for, and be happy you're not homeless without a hand." He handed me a hangar draped with a two piece outfit of purple silk embroidered with stylized flowers in gold thread. "Get dressed."

"I'm not wearin' that. It's purple."

"So?"

"I don't like purple."

"Faith does. Now stop wasting time."

"I'm not wearin' that."

"You don't have a choice. We had an agreement." The look on his face said I'd better fall into line. Or else.

I sighed and reluctantly donned the hideous thing. "What's this meetin' about, anyway?"

"You're buying out Gower Dillington's share of Foster's recording studio."

"Gower Dillington? The action hero?" I'd seen several of the guy's movies. He was a good-looking Welshman who'd made a career out of playing African Americans in smart, sexy shoot-em-ups. There had been talk about making him into the first black James Bond.

"Yes. He recently discovered that Scott Foster is not a good person to be associated with. He wants to divest himself of any association with Foster, especially since he's planning to make a bid in the next gubernatorial election."

"Gower Dillington wants to be governor of California?"

He nodded. "He's got a shot, if he gets his ducks in a row."

I thought about that as I forced myself to slide my feet in to the matching purple shoes. It was like stepping into barf.

Tony shot me a warning look at the face I made. "What's your deal with purple, anyway?"

"It reminds me of rain."

"What's wrong with rain?"

"Everything," I said in my Rad voice, giving him a look that told him to drop it.

He got the message. I stood up, smoothed the silk out, and took a deep breath to steady myself, trying to get back into character. He held his hand out. "Come on. It's show time."

The door opened and Tony hugged me close as we stepped into the hall. He kissed me lightly on each cheek, then on the forehead, staring into my face like it was the most precious thing he'd ever had between his palms. "You know I've missed you, baby."

Adrenaline surged through me, the same eager rush I always got when I was about to take the stage. This was it. Really it. Not eight hours out of the hospital, and I was supposed to perform as if I'd been Faith all my life.

He led me down the stairs. We stopped at the bottom landing and he pulled me close again, tipping my chin up, and brushing his lips against mine in a soft, seductive caress.

Wow, he knew how to kiss.

I gave him some tongue. He gripped me tighter and somehow, my hands found their way to his butt. His palms slid down my ribcage, drew my hips against him.

A cough sounded in my ear.

We both looked up reluctantly.

"Welcome to the real world." Jana stood at Tony's elbow, her long feline body posed ruthlessly in a clingy red dress. In her eyes floated a question to him. A challenge to me. You could play hockey on her smile.

Tony glanced back at me, then met her gaze with an insular chuckle. "Give it up, Jana." He guided me through the door and down the tiled hallway. "I'm not going to change my mind."

"Too late for that, anyway," she mumbled behind us, then stepped up to flank Tony.

We hooked left into a cozy, pine-paneled living room with a wet bar, ultra-modern style furniture, and a quadrophonic, infra-bass sound system with three pairs of speakers. Two men sat on a black leather couch, their backs to a floor-to-ceiling picture window made from tinted-plex.

The one on the left I recognized from the vids Mando had force-fed me. Dave Seward, Faith's financial advisor, was a nervous, brown-haired fellow with a mustache and pattern baldness. The fat, sallow-skinned, bug-eyed man on the right I figured was Randall Cortelaine. Scotty's lawyer.

"I'll get you a drink," Tony said, and headed for the bar.

"Not just yet, thanks." I patted my belly. "I've been feeling a little poorly. Stomach trouble. Jana can tell you."

Jana scowled as she settled into a chair, but Tony suppressed a grin. He poured two drinks, took a sip of one, and brought them both over. "C'mon," he chided. "It'll cool you off."

He rubbed the icy glass against the silk fabric covering my nipple, the seduction in his eyes straining my self-control. My breath caught, and then I was kissing him, his arms slipping over my shoulders to keep from spilling the scotch.

"You gonna quit fucking around, Tovenaar?" Cortelaine interrupted.

Dave and Jana craned looks at him, surprised by his breach of etiquette. He spread his doughy hands defensively. "I'm getting tired of waiting for them to get their shit together."

Tony glared at Cortelaine, his hand drawing back so that the highball glass was suspended in front of my face. I took it, because otherwise I couldn't see much.

During the long, heavy silence that followed, Tony moved around to sit in a chair. I didn't like the idea of sitting close to any of the others, so I sat on the arm of Tony's chair. The sun dipped behind the ridge. A mechanical hum started up outside the window, and a series of thin stalks rose about a foot above the fern-laden planter surrounding the pool. Little, lens-like hoods popped out from their tips, and the perimeter was suddenly illuminated in the soft glow of high-tech lamps.

It amazed me. I tried hard not to look impressed. Faith would have been used to all this billionaire gadgetry.

"Miss Hopkins," Seward glanced at me nervously, and the tip of his tongue ran along his lips. "We do need your attention. At least for a few minutes." He popped the clasps on his briefcase and laid it open-faced on the table. After a few minutes of finagling with his tablet, he handed it to me and circled the edge of the table to peer over my shoulder.

"I've gone over everything." He pointed to the form displayed in backlit legalese. "And, I'm convinced that this investment is sound. Mr. Dillington has made a full disclosure of the assets and liabilities attributed to the partnership, and Mr. Foster has approved your inclusion as his new partner in this enterprise. Put your signature here, here, and here, and we can all go home." Seward tapped the screen where the 'X' marked the spot and held a stylus out to me.

Uh-oh. How could I forge her signature, especially with all these people watching? It would be suicide, a dead-giveaway. Why hadn't Mando prepared me for something like this? I'd never practiced the handwriting—never even seen a left-handed example. I stole a glance at Tony.

He nodded, hint of a smile on his lips. "Go ahead. Sign."

I sniffed and set my untouched scotch on the coffee table. "I changed my mind." I batted the proffered stylus away with my splint and stood up, heading for the door. God knows where I was going, but I wasn't going to blow this Faith thing the first night out, even if it wasn't my fault.

"Oh, Jesus," Cortelaine spat out. "Faith you are such a greedy bitch!"

I spun on my heel and gawked at him, surprised at his vehemence.

"We can't go any lower," Cortelaine whined. "We're giving you the best deal we can."

"I know." I twined my fingers along a seam in the sofa. "It's just..." I searched for something that would fit.

"Faith," Tony warned, "you've already agreed to the terms." His solemn face confused me. It was as if he wanted me to sign.

No. He was playing the game, same as I was. Just trying to make things look good.

"I don't care. I'm not signin' that piece of cow pie." I stuck my lip out and crossed my arms in a pout. "I don't like Scotty anymore. He's too old."

There it was. Simple. Direct. So logically Faith.

And they swallowed it, the whole inelegant mess. A little thrill ran through me when I realized how much they believed I wasn't me. How much they knew I was Faith.

Dave sighed, shook his head. Cortelaine groaned.

"Perhaps..." Jana coughed politely. The men looked at her. "Perhaps Mr. Tovenaar can solve the situation. If Mr. Foster would offer him the same terms..."

Tony smiled. "I'd be happy to. If he'll have me as a partner."

Cortelaine cocked his head, then nodded. "Worth a shot. But if he doesn't, I'm keeping my commission."

Tony drained his glass, reached for the stylus, and signed. He handed the notebook over to Seward, who checked over the documents, then printed out copies for everyone.

Cortelaine tossed the papers in his briefcase with a relieved sigh. He stood as abruptly as a man of his bulk could stand, and headed for the door. "I'll contact you if Scotty rejects this. He may ask for a disclosure from you."

Tony nodded, shooting a glower at me before rising to accompany him into the hall. Jana followed after them. Seward cleared his throat and held his hand out to me.

"Faith," he murmured unenthusiastically. "Pleasure seeing you again."

I gave him a cutesy social wave, ignoring his outstretched hand. "Pleasure's all mine."

He nodded, glancing furtively toward the hall. He leaned in, voice dropping to a whisper. "You do realize what you're getting into with him, don't you?" He jerked his head toward the hallway. "I mean, Tovenaar's not known for his—"

"Isn't he somethin'? Don't know what I'd do without him."

"Faith, I'm just warning you to be careful. There are some risks I'm not sure you're aware of."

"Dave, honey, that man's hotter than Tabasco on a flamin' griddle. I'm not givin' him up."

He sighed, exasperated, and picked up his briefcase. He glanced up, stiffening with fear as Tony appeared in the doorway.

"Mr. Seward," Tony said pleasantly, although his eyes were cold and angry. "Is there something else we need to talk about?"

"No," the smaller man mumbled, rushing in awkward strides toward the door. "I was just telling Faith what a nice couple you make."

Tony nodded, clearing the doorway for him. "Your car's out front. Thanks for coming." He watched Seward walk down the hall, a grim little smile on his face. I heard Jana's voice, and then a door closed on Seward's footsteps. Tony turned to glare at me. "What did he say to you?"

I shrugged. "Nothin'. Just warned me to look out for you."

Tony crossed wordlessly to the bar, the muscles of his jaw bunching tightly. The silence badgered me, screaming insults and accusations. I'd screwed up, somehow.

"I'm getting tired of this," he said, chunking ice into his glass on the 'this.' He scrutinized me, expression souring when he saw the bewilderment on my face. "This contrary shit needs to stop. You do what I tell you to, when I tell you to, understand? I say sign something, you sign it."

"Didn't know the handwriting. Didn't think you—"

"You're not paid to think. You're here to do a job. To do what I tell you to do. Always. You got that?"

My face burned. I nodded, swallowing my frustration. It was almost like he wanted me to be discovered, despite the lecture he'd given me in the hospital. But why pour all this money into me, make me look so much like her if he wanted people to know I wasn't Faith? That was stupid. And whatever else he might have done, Tony hadn't amassed all this wealth with a potato IQ.

He'd probably technoed something. Hacking things to insert Faith's signature for my own wouldn't be hard, considering he'd there was enough gadgetry around this place to subsidize DARPA.

And I had blown it, thinking I knew more than he did. No wonder he was so pissed.

"And that." He pointed at the highball glass sweating on the coffee table. "Don't let that happen again. You swallow anything I put in front of you."

"I don't like alcohol."

"Faith is a lush. You won't smell like her if you don't touch your drink."

"Fine." I dunked my fingers up and down in the icy barf. "I touched it."

His mouth dropped open, like he couldn't believe I'd blown him off. His upper lip curled. His eyes flashed with eerie menace. "You signed a contract. Now, drink it."

How could I? It was scotch. "No."

He bent behind the bar, and I heard the soft scudding of a drawer being opened. His hand came up, a small, stainless steel pistol nestled in his palm. He pointed it at the ceiling as he checked the magazine. His steely gaze found me again. "I don't care how much you hate authority. Or alcohol. Or purple. This contrary shit stops now. Drink it."

I hefted the glass, swallowed a quick gulp, trying not to let the liquid touch my tastebuds. Tony smiled approval, tucking the pistol into his waistband. And then it hit me.

A line of fire snaked down my throat. My eyes watered. The smoky-sour burn at the back of my mouth smacked of all the dark, aching nights of my childhood, when Mother was so drunk I could literally taste it in the air around her.

Panic rippled through me, a dire fear the stasis lag would overcome me and I'd feel it all again and this spooky sonofabitch Tony would witness it.

"You hungry?" he asked, as if there was nothing wrong.

I shook my head.

"You know how to shoot?"

I nodded, blinking the moisture away. "My father taught me."

"Good. Faith loves target shooting." He smoothed his jacket down over the bulge and held a hand out to me. "I'll take you to the range."

"Can I go back to my room for a while? I don't feel well."

"I said, 'I'll take you to the range.'"

There have been few people in my life who could actually intimidate me into cooperation.

Tony Tovenaar was one of them.

CHAPTER THIRTEEN

Tony led me out into a cobbled courtyard and motioned for me to get into a small, roofless electric cart. He steered us briskly across the expansive lawn, through a break in the eucalyptus trees, and down a winding asphalt path.

Trees, shrubs whizzed by, looking twisted and ghostly in their fiber optic lamplight. Occasional four-footed dog shapes lurked in the foliage, eyes glowing green in the cart's yellow headlight. The sun was still setting, the horizon tinged with pink, but maybe Tony was the kind of guy who lit candles rather than curse. Either that, or he was afraid of the dark.

Neither of us spoke and the ride seemed interminable, especially sitting beside this silent, brooding Tony. I was rapidly starting to hate his guts. Well, not all his guts. He had saved my hand and swept me off the streets. And the compassion he'd shown in the hospital had seemed genuine. I decided I'd hate the first few feet of his colon. That way, if he kept acting like an asshole I had somewhere to go, and if he mellowed out I could pretend I'd liked him all along.

The cart bumped over a lip in the asphalt, then crunched onto a narrow gravel road. Up ahead a squat, adobe building rested on a plateau scooped out of the hillside, like a giant bread loaf set on a window sill to cool. As we approached the building a floodlight popped on from the rooftop and drenched us in a pool of light.

We rolled to a stop in front of a massive, mission style door. The door chirped and snapped open as soon as Tony left the cart. I wondered if it opened for just anyone, or if it had some kind of recog circuit, like the door to my room.

We walked through a cool, dimly lit hallway into a bright, low-ceilinged room. A long bench lined the wall to our left. To the right was a series of cubicles like voting booths, but open at either end. The range side of the booths had a broad wooden rail, almost a shelf. Controls for the target cables stuck out of the cubicle walls.

We passed seven of the boxy structures on our way to the far wall. Tony stopped in front of a six-foot high steel cabinet and striped a card key through the monstrous lock. Guy must be pretty paranoid the way he kept everything battened down. The lock tweedled and relinquished its hold.

Tony eased the door open to reveal a row of guns. Not many I recognized. A few shotguns, a twenty-two rifle. There was a revolver that looked pretty grizzled and an assault pistol that looked more like a squirt gun than a real firearm. He lifted a small wooden box from the drawer at the bottom of the cabinet, tucked it under his arm, and walked to the nearest cubicle. He motioned for me to put on a pair of safety glasses from the selection case on the wall, then donned a pair.

He removed the pistol from his waistband and tipped it toward me. "You familiar with this?"

I shook my head.

His eyes narrowed. "Thought your father taught you how to shoot."

"Revolvers. He didn't like picking up brass. Only time I ever fired an automatic was when Larry McGinley got a new Smith and Wesson and made everybody in the range try it." The memory made me homesick for the times when Papa had leave and Mother sobered up and we were almost a family. I had been so stupid, then, thinking it would last. Thinking Papa would live forever, because I needed him to.

Tony opened the wooden box and withdrew a metal cylinder about the size of a shot glass. He screwed the cylinder onto the muzzle of the gun, then clipped a silhouette target to the cable and ran it back to the fifty foot mark.

"Thought that was illegal," I said.

He raised the gun to shoot one-handed, his arm steady, relaxed. "What?"

"Silencers."

He grinned over his shoulder at me. "So, turn me in." He aimed and pulled the trigger. The target twitched once, twice, three times. Head. Stomach. Heart. The report was scarcely louder than a stifled cough.

Tony pushed the cable button with his elbow and the silhouette glided back to the very end of the range. He took the gun in his left hand. The pistol whispered, the target jumped again. All perfect shots.

I wondered if he was showing off, trying to demonstrate his lethality, his power, in order to intimidate me into obeying him. Or did he see this whole shooting thing as a bonding exercise. Something he and Faith had in common?

"Faith likes to target shoot," he said, as if reading my mind. Spooky. "This is hers." He set the pistol on the shelf in front of me. "Let's see you try."

I looked at the weapon, intensely aware of the raw, pungent scent of cordite. My insides churned. I hadn't fired a gun since the night Mike died. "I'd rather not."

"You don't have a choice."

His words echoed strangely in my head. I picked up the weapon, the cold metal heavy in my palm. Something told me this wasn't such a good idea. The blood hammered in my ears, a roaring accusatory rush. I held the grip tighter.

You're a pretty little thing, Mike's whisper echoed inside my skull, his ghost arm pressing on my throat.

I held my breath, not wanting to close my eyes. Not wanting to go back to that time, that place. I concentrated on the target, a man's silhouette, and I thought of the bastard in the vid Tony had shown me. The one in the Halloween mask. My finger squeezed the trigger.

Head.

Bet you're better than your mama.

Another squeeze, smooth as silk. Stomach.

Why don't we find out?

I gritted my teeth and squeezed again and again and again, until the chamber racked dry and there was a jagged, fist-sized hole over the target's heart.

Tony didn't say anything.

I stared at the target and felt Mike's blood spilling over me and my hatred deserted me, left me wallowing in guilt. How much blood was on my hands? Chris. Mike. Fox-face and Doughboy.

Too much.

I wavered and started to shake. The pistol tumbled from my fingers, landing with a clatter on the sturdy wooden shelf. I staggered back, sat on the bench, and leaned my head against the wall with a ragged sigh. *Too much.*

Tony broke the silence by clearing his throat. "You a lefty?"

"No."

He picked up the gun, ejected the spent magazine, and slammed a fresh one home, eyeing me with suspicion. "I don't see how you could maintain that level of accuracy without constant practice. Especially with your off hand."

He seemed to be accusing me of something, so I defended myself: "I'm a pianist. We have excellent hand-eye coordination. And I have good muscle memory. Used to practice all the time, with my dad. Like, six hours a week. Per hand."

"That ninja shit wasn't enough?"

"All the karate in the world won't stop a bullet."

He thought about that for a moment. "You ever shoot anyone?"

I leaned forward, ducked my head between my knees, breathing hard. "Mike Boniface. Shot him in the chest."

"Why?"

"He didn't give me a choice. I had to do it. Even the judge said it was self-defense."

"Judge? You were arrested for it?"

"He was my mother's boyfriend." And Chris' real father, but he didn't need to know that. "She told the police I'd murdered him."

"Did you?"

I bared my teeth at him, a wolf exhausted in a trap. "My mother's a drunken bitch. She wouldn't know a rapist if he rammed a fireplug up her ass."

"He was trying to—?" His breath stopped for a split-second. Clearly rape wasn't the answer he'd expected. "I'm sorry," he murmured. His face said he meant it.

I sighed and leaned back against the wall, wishing the smell of gunpowder would go away. All I wanted was to lie down somewhere, forget about everything.

A strange, rhythmic bumping sounded. Tony looked up, frowned, and started for the corridor, gun still in hand. I realized belatedly the noise meant someone was knocking on the door. I heard the lock chirp, then hushed voices and footsteps echoing against the stark walls.

A tenor. A soprano. And Tony's baritone. "Faith," he called. "Come here a minute."

I dragged myself dutifully off the bench and trudged past the row of cubicles to the mouth of the corridor, where Tony stood next to a big Samoan man in a tailored gray suit and a petite, frosted-blonde woman in a blue linen dress: Detectives Iso Iso and Rossi.

Tony cleared his throat, placed his palm on my back. "This is Faith Hopkins."

I wiggled my fingers, too tired to offer anything but stereotype. "Tickled to meet you."

Rossi nodded a reserved greeting. Iso Iso just looked at me, like he was trying to peel my skin off with his eyeballs. He grinned abruptly and glanced at Tony. "Good work. I can't tell she was ever Italian."

It wasn't fair. It wasn't. How come everybody knew what was going on but me? I offered Iso Iso a saccharine smile. "It's so nice to know how easily local law enforcement can be bought."

"We're Federal marshals," Rossi said flatly. "And we're not dirty."

I put my hand to my throat in mock embarrassment. "Oh, I'm sorry. I thought you were Tony's pet police 'defectives.' I feel ever so much better, now I know you're workin' for Uncle Spam." I expected them to get mad, but they both chuckled instead.

Rossi shook her head. "God, she's just like Faith."

Tony nodded benignly, jaw tensing just enough to tell me I'd better watch my mouth. He arched his brows at the marshals. "What brings you two here this evening? I didn't expect you until the end of the week."

"Hollis," Rossi replied.

"What about him?"

Iso Iso folded his arms across his chest and glared a challenge at Tony. "You won't be much good to us in prison."

"I'm not going to prison."

Rossi cleared her throat. "You might be a lot closer than you think," she said softly. "Hollis has built quite a case."

Tony was unperturbed. "All circumstantial. The D.A. will throw it out in a hot second."

"Gordo. Rolo. And now Sloan—not to mention the two Miss Karate Kid here—" Rossi indicated me "—took out at the train station. If I didn't know better, I'd say it was a systematic attack on Foster's organization.   You're not thinking of a hostile takeover, now, are you?"

Tony stared at her, a look of surprise mixed with contempt. "You backing out of our deal?"

Rossi laughed, a high musical sound.   "No. Of course not. I was just inquiring about your motives."

"My motives are my own."

"Then what about her?" Rossi pointed at me.

"What about her?"

"You guaranteed us she'd be perfect."

"She is. You just said so yourself."

"I said she's just like Faith. Meaning she has a record, too." She paused to let Tony digest that. "We have to abort."

"No."

Iso Iso shrugged. "You know we can't pass her without a clean set of prints."

"Let me try."

Rossi shook her head. "Not acceptable. The risks are—"

"I'll chance it."

"You don't have a choice."

A snort of amusement left me.   Funny to see those words thrown back in Tony's face. Iso Iso glowered at me, but Rossi and Tony continued to stare at each other like gunslingers, each waiting for the other to make the first move.

"I can call Paul," Tony's cool voice broke the stalemate. "And then we'll see who's choice it is."

Rossi twitched her shoulders. "I already have.   It's my ballgame. You want to pick up your glove and your bat and go home, that's on you. But until you do, I make the rules."

Tony's face showed no expression. His gaze darted from Rossi, to Iso Iso, to me. He sniffed, indifferent, and regarded Rossi. "And if I can pass the prints?"

She snickered, unimpressed. "You can't."

"But if I could? Would you make it a go?"

Her gaze fell on me, ideas, decisions filtering through the polite mask of her features. "Yes." She nodded a curt farewell. "Thanks for your time."

Iso Iso took one last look at me, at Tony, and turned to follow Rossi. He paused a few steps away and pointed to the silenced gun in Tony's hand. "By the way, those are illegal in this state."

Tony shrugged, disdain leaking through the stiff detachment in his face. "So, turn me in."

***

When we got back to the house I started for my room, but Tony grabbed me and steered me down a hallway. His explanation was brief and to the point: "Dinner."

As soon as the word left his mouth, mine started to water.

What I wouldn't give for a steak. A big, juicy, rare steak, with the steam rising off and the blood running down, a little horseradish on the side. Maybe some mashed potatoes with gravy, some steamed broccoli in cheddar sauce, a few sautéed mushrooms. Something like Jim used to make.

Jim. The guilt stabbed through me again, but I shoved it away, focusing my attention on Tony's measured footsteps, the taut, catlike way he stalked through the halls, the black fury coiled beneath his perfect musculature.

We arrived at a rustic-looking dining room, with six rough-hewn chairs set around a massive planked table. A chandelier of wrought iron flickered above us. The walls were rough stucco, stark white against the floor of blood-red Mexican tile. Service for three was set around one end of the table: placemats of coarsely woven linen, artfully decorated with thick, cut crystal goblets and slab-sided silverware. The plates were sandstone colored octagons. I wondered when *Lifestyles of the Rich and Famous* was coming to make the video shoot.

An old woman in a white apron appeared in the arched doorway to what I assumed was the kitchen. She had skin of red ochre and almond-shaped eyes set far apart in her head. She spoke to Tony not in Javanese, but in a language that sounded like German, but wasn't. He answered back in the same language. She nodded, offered me a smile, and disappeared through the archway.

"What language is that?"

"Dutch. Have a seat." Tony gestured to the chair on his right.

I sat, giving a Faith eye roll. "We're in Amurrica, Tony. Speak English."

"My step-grandmother doesn't speak English." He shot a glower at me. I shut up.

As he settled himself in the chair next to mine, a faint, persistent beeping began. Tony slid his phone out and held it to his ear. "Tovenaar." His eyes looked down as he listened, then off to the left. His lips pursed. "Yeah. Fine. Whatever." He listened some more. "Just do it, okay? Quit dicking around." He chuckled without humor. "Let the bitch try it." He flipped the phone shut with a scowl and stuck it back in his pocket.

Tony's step-grandmother reappeared carrying a tumbler of clear liquid in one hand and a highball glass with what looked like scotch on the rocks in the other. She set the tumbler in front of me, the scotch in front of Tony. He drained half the glass. I picked up my tumbler, held it to my nose, and sniffed.

"Go ahead," Tony sulked. "It's water." He sucked down the rest of his drink and murmured to the old woman, who he called Gwenda. An aura of sullen heat surrounded him, a threatening cloud of anger.

I wasn't sure if it was the marshals, or his finding out I had killed Mike that set him off. At any rate, I wasn't up to confronting that wall of fire. Best to tiptoe through this minefield, disturb as little as possible. I drank my water.

"Are we ready to eat?" Jana glided in from the hallway behind us and sat across the table from Tony. She wore that slinky red dress and smelled like those ladies who stumble out of department stores after trying all the ritzy perfumes at once. Her blonde hair was perfectly coiffed, alabaster skin accented by too-red lips.

Tony stared at her, vaguely suspicious, no greeting in his face. "Where are the backgrounds on Damiano?"

She hesitated, brow furrowed in thought. "Filed."

His jaw pulsed. He stared at his empty plate. "Bring them to me. ASAP."

She sighed, nodded, scudding her chair back.

"Who did them?" he asked, not looking up.

"Mando."

"Not you?"

She shook her head. "He insisted."

Ice tinkled as Tony regarded his empty glass. "Call him."

"Emma might still be in labor. You know he won't—"

"Call him in. He missed something." Tony flicked his fingers at me. "She was arrested for murder."

"You think he's—?"

"Might be an oversight."

She was dubious. "Might not."

"Just get him here by twelve-hundred tomorrow."

"Won't be easy."

"Jana, what the fuck do I pay you for?" He didn't raise his voice. Didn't have to. His Hellfire gaze said it all.

Before she could answer the old lady came out, whisked away the empty drink and put another scotch in its place. Tony gave it a healthy sip. Jana watched him closely, her cheeks twitching like a tigress on the scent. "Ruiz called, didn't he?"

"Fuck Ruiz. I asked you about Mando."

She gave a little sniff. Her body tensed as if expecting him to explode, although her face remained a mask of civility. "Fine." She stood up. "Excuse me."

"Twelve. No later."

She nodded and disappeared into the hallway. Tony stared after her for a moment, then shouted something into the kitchen. I heard a muffled reply, but no one appeared. I fidgeted, tapping my teaspoon against my plate, glass and goblet in an attempt to eke out a tune. Got through the first few bars of Ravel's "Bolero" when Tony grabbed my hand, squeezing it so hard I felt my knuckles grinding together.

"Ow."

"Stop that." He glared at me until I folded my hands meekly into my lap. The ice clinked as he drained his glass. He shouted to the kitchen again.

The old lady returned with a large tray. She set a carafe of dressing in the center of the table, placed a full salad plate at each setting, and scuttled off back to the kitchen.

She return with some plates piled with tofu and more vegetables in some kind of peanut-curry sauce and set them down in front of us. My heart sank. This was the main course. I'd endured all the vegetables I could take in the hospital, yearning for the day I could sink my teeth into something substantial. I knew Faith wasn't a vegetarian. At least she hadn't been on the videos. So why did I have to keep eating this crap?

Halfway through the meal, Jana reappeared. She mumbled some polite niceties and resumed her seat next to Tony, snapping her napkin out and settling it across her lap.

He fixed the weight of his attention on her, his knife and fork suspended in mid-air above his plate. "Well?"

"He'll be here."

"What took so long?"

She shrugged. "He didn't respond right away."

He accepted the excuse with reserve, like he really didn't believe her. "You bring the file?"

Jana placed a flash drive solemnly at his elbow. "I reviewed it. She's dirty. We have to abort."

Tony shook his head. "I'll pass the prints."

"How?"

He didn't answer. Jana shook her head. "She's a wild card, Tony. She could bolt, spill everything to—"

"She won't."

"How do you know?"

"She won't."

"That's what you said about Ilsa, remember? And how long has she been—?"

"That's over," he snapped.

"Is it?" She sniffed, ran her finger around the rim of her glass. Their gazes clashed, and then she gave a dainty little cough and wiped her mouth with the corner of her napkin. "Faith looks tired," she said pleasantly, turning her attention toward me. "Maybe she needs to go to her room."

Tony chewed for a moment, then nodded. "Take her up." He wouldn't look at me.

I got the message. If I couldn't be Faith, I didn't exist.

I threw my napkin on the plate and scudded my chair back, making as much noise as possible. Jana smiled a mouthful of daggers at me, but I followed her out the door, anyway.

CHAPTER FOURTEEN

When I returned to the room, I found the bed turned back and the walk-in closet door open, displaying the racks full of blousey silk pantsuits and black suede dresses. Shoes, too. Tons of mules and pumps, of every color imaginable. And the dressers had all manner of Faith clothes, all with faint signs of wear that would indicate I'd existed before today.

I put my splint back on and toured the room, uneasy with the idea someone—or several someones, judging from the sheer mass of items now pleasantly in their niches—had been here since I'd been gone. The note was safe in its hiding place, and the gator skin briefcase was still in the closet where I'd stowed it, so I relaxed a bit and stripped for bed. In every vid Mando had shown me, Faith had gone to bed naked. Admittedly, she was with Scotty, but from the licentious way she cavorted around, I figured sleeping in the buff was the status quo.

Not that I cared. I was a nudist at heart.

I turned out the lights, and crawled beneath the sheets. Despite a monumental fatigue that blurred my vision and made my ears ring, I found myself watching the pool lights dance in refracted ribbons across the flat white ceiling. Time crawled by, hours passing.

I couldn't stop thinking about Tony. About how I'd ceased to exist for him the moment the marshals told him they couldn't clear my prints. I guessed that meant that, because of my arrest record, they couldn't get judicial consent to provide me with a fake I.D. and credit cards under Faith's name.

Which explained why Tony was so upset. He'd invested a lot of time and money in making me Faith, but despite my uncanny resemblance to her, the only sure-fire way to make people believe I was the real McCoy was with a government backed credential. Without that, I was worthless. So much for being 'her'.

This was how Mando could guarantee I wouldn't have to face Scotty. How he'd ensured I'd get my hand fixed on Tony's dime. He'd withheld the sordid details of my past, knowing I would never pass the background. What that meant for Mando, I wasn't sure. I hoped it didn't mean his wife would become a widow, and his kids would grow up without a father, but Tony didn't seem the type to forgive and forget.

But would Tony really do it? I didn't know. By all accounts, he was a ruthless, manipulative bastard, one who turned tenderness and rage on and off like a faucet. There was nothing genuine about him. Nothing honest. Even his eyes were lies, that distant blue somehow masking the beastly yellow-gold of his true nature.

A guy like him could never really fall for me. The only thing he cared about was exacting vengeance on Brighton Leigh. I knew this. Logically, I knew this. But some part of me still held this fevered, desperate hope that his concern had been genuine.

Why did I do this to myself? Why did I hope, the same way I'd hoped that Mother would care when I'd called her about the money? The same way I'd hoped Papa would come walking through the door someday, because they'd never brought home his body? The same way I pined for Jim, hoping against hope that he would one day return my desire?

It was madness. Tony would never really care about me, any more than my mother would ever stop drinking, or the dream I'd had of a future Papa was anything more than a projection of my own desperate need to deny my failure with Chris. I knew this, but still, I hoped.

There was this part of me living under Tony's skin.

I got up and paced around in the darkness, trying to find a way to deny this obsessive fascination with him. Eventually, I found myself sitting on the toilet, staring at the folded note, running my fingertips over my name in Jim's handwriting.

He'd been right. If I hadn't broken my hand on Webster's jaw, we wouldn't have even been at the Concerto that night. We would have gotten that gig at the Disney Concert Hall, or gone to Europe on tour. Maybe even had a recording contract by now. I never would have been shot, or have met Tony, or ended up here in this strange, sinister world of mystery and extravagance, while Jim was left with nothing but a trashed house and a police report that said I was dead and gone.

He was a sensitive guy. Losing a friend, even a lame ass friend like me, had to be rough on him. With all those spooky, transcendental dreams I'd had in the hospital, couldn't I at least have gotten one through to Jim? Given him some hope that I might come back some day? Apologize for all the shit I'd put him through?

Not that I believed in those dreams.

I didn't, not really. The stasis had magnified my own fears, raked all the shame and loneliness out of the dark, putrid corners of my mind and molded them into some stupid fantasy of guilt and redemption. From the moment he first stuck up for me at the train station, I had wanted Tony to save me. This "entanglement" I had with him was just the projection of that hopeless infatuation, another way of denying the mess I'd made of my life. Another way of pretending I wasn't really a loser.

I could love Beethoven all I wanted, but I'd never be more than an angry, self-destructive impostor, always trying to make people believe there was something fine and noble if not in me, at least in my intentions. Whatever natural talents I'd been born with, I never had the *savoir-faire* to make it as a musician, any more than

I had the self-control to make it as a SeAL. I was what Mother had always said I would be: Shiftless. Defiant. Incorrigible.

It was hard, being naked like that. Knowing the truth about myself. But in some weird, ironic way, it felt comfortable, too. Like putting on your own clothes after spending days under the weight of someone else's itchy, beaded ballroom gown. There were worse things to be than perpetually delinquent. Like dead, for instance.

"What's that?" Tony asked from the open bathroom doorway.

"Whoa!" I snapped the note behind my back and jumped to my feet, ready to fight my way out of this, or die trying. "Where'd you come from?"

He wore no shoes, no shirt, just a pair of black sweats, the bruises from Hollis now faint yellow smears across his statuesque torso. The silenced pistol peeked out of his right hand, pointing at the floor. His steely gaze ran over me, resting briefly on my chest, and then again just below my waist. His handsome, chiseled face was as somber and threatening as the troubled storm clouds that were his eyes. "Who sent you here?"

I refuse to cringe under the dull heat of his gaze. "What kind of question is that?"

"Who sent you?"

"You did. You told Vic to cut me loose this morning."

"No." He advanced, near enough for me to smell the musky intensity of his cologne, the sour bite of exhaled alcohol. Even if he was drunk, it wouldn't help me. We both knew he could shoot before I could close the distance. "Somebody put you up to this," he accused, gun still pointed at the floor. "Somebody sent you after me. Coached you on what to say about those dreams. I want to know who."

"Nobody sent me. Mando shot me, remember? You kidnapped me out of the police station. How could anybody send me?"

"Mando," he murmured, his gaze turning inward. He twitched, his face contorting with sudden pain. And then his expression blanked, the pain pooling in his eyes. "He told you what to say, didn't he? In the hospital. He told you."

I shook my head, not sure what to make of this. "No. I—It was dream. A hallucination."

His eyes narrowed. He studied me for what seemed like forever, until the smell of him permeated the enclosed space, that sweet muskiness laced with the dark undercurrent of scotch. And still he stared.

"I know it's hard to believe, but it's true. Maybe..." I cast about for another explanation, one that might diffuse this standoff. "Maybe you talked about it when I was passed out in the limo. Maybe that's why I dreamed it."

"I don't talk about that. Only the doctors and Mando know about that." The pain flickered over his face again, but his eyes never wavered, still studying me, searching for some sign of my guilt or innocence. The silence stretched out into minutes. It felt like hours.

"Are you going to try and kill me?" I finally asked, tired of the waiting. Even adrenaline rushes can get old.

He shook his head. "Need to question Mando before I decide."

I sighed, relieved, and tried to sidle past him. The bathroom was becoming claustrophobic. I was almost clear when he snatched the note out of my hand, looking it over. "What's this?"

I grimaced, my good hand curling into a fist. "An apology."

He gave me a dubious look and opened up the folded paper.

As he read it, I growled and moved to the window, looking out at the moon-silvered hills with the hope of discovering some way out of all of this.

I heard the paper rustling. "Who's Richie," he asked. "And why is he moving in with your buddy Jim?"

I snapped my head around, opening my mouth to object, but nothing came out. There was nothing to say.

That's why Jim had kicked me out. So his boyfriend could move in with him. I sighed and rubbed my eyes with the heel of my good hand, turning back to rest my forehead against the window. Should have known Richie'd win out in the end.

"Tony," I tried to keep the quaver out of my voice. "Either kill me, or leave."

I heard more rustling as he set the note on the dresser, and then a pattern of beeps as he did something over at the keypad beside the door. There was no fizzing scream, no bullet ripping through my flesh, but I also didn't hear the door open.

Just as I turned my head to see what he was doing, a granite forearm slammed into my back as Tony pinned me against the window. He held me there, with my cheek and ear shoved hard against the unforgiving Plexiglass. His legs splayed mine apart, his forearm crammed solidly against the base of my neck, so that the slightest increase in pressure would snap the vertebrae. "Scott Foster sent you, didn't he?"

"No," I gasped, panic flooding me, my heart exploding in my chest as he raised the pistol and touched it gently to my temple. The cold metal burned like ice against my skin.

"Scotty programmed you to obey him. Planted you in his own fucking club, tricked Mando into saving your ass."

"No!" I tried to meet his gaze, to convince him I was telling the truth, but the only thing in my field of view was the arm that held the gun. "I never met Scotty before that night. I swear. Never met him, or Mando, or those marshals until after I got shot. Swear to God!"

"Then who did this to you?"

"Who did what?"

"This," he snarled, the contempt in his voice hurting more than the weight pinning me. "The whip marks. Cigarette burns. How'd you get these scars if Scotty didn't brainwash you?"

I opened my mouth, but the lies caught in my throat, stories to match each injury, a camouflage of wounding. Who was left to protect? Chris was dead, buried in the Seattle mud next to Papa's empty grave. I was in California, out of the rain, out of her reach, as long as I didn't need—

"Who did this?" he asked again, jamming the pistol harder, his whole body taut with fury.

My jaw worked soundlessly. I'd kept the silence for so long that now, even now, I couldn't bring myself to say it. I tried desperately to turn my head enough so that I could focus on his face, thinking that if he could just see the fear in my eyes, he'd believe me. He'd know I was telling the truth. But as I swiveled my head, I saw his finger tensing, the cold implacability in the eye above the gunsight, and the confession tumbled out in that one blind, hopeless moment: "My mother."

He froze, the words working their way through his rage, until they reached that part of him that could still hold back. He paled. "Your mother did that to you?"

I twitched my head up and down in a rapid nod, shame burning in my ears. Except for Chris, I'd never admitted the whole truth to anyone. Not the Feds, not the social workers. Not even Jim.

The pressure on my neck eased. He withdrew the pistol and stepped away. I spun around and hid my back against the window. Where could I go? This place was too small to hold the self-disgust I felt.

"Your mother?" he repeated. "That's what you were dreaming, in the hospital? Those were the flashbacks?"

I nodded, still too ashamed to speak.

He dropped his gaze. Shaking his head, lost in thought, he backed away. In the sudden quiet, the tiny metallic chink! as he flipped the pistol's safety back on sounded like a church bell. Without another word, he stalked into the bathroom. And I was alone in the terrible silence of that space.

All my hopeful delusions had evaporated, consumed by that white hot shame still burning within me. She had been right. She had been right, all along. I deserved every whipping, every raging night of fear and loneliness and pain. I hadn't saved Chris. Hadn't saved Papa. Hadn't even saved myself from one shitfaced, Spec-war widow.

Yet, some part of me refused to crumble into a fetal ball of despair. So, I just stood there, eyes closed, alone and defiant and aching.

"Hey," Tony murmured. Something warm and rough wrapped around my shoulders. I opened my eyes to see him gently guiding my splinted hand through one of the armholes of a thick, white terrycloth robe. "You okay?" He looked genuinely concerned.

"Yeah," a stranger inside me said, feeling him guide my other arm into the robe and snug it around me. He knotted the belt loosely.

"I'm sorry," he said, his mouth a thin, remorseful line. He tugged me away from the window and sat me on the edge of the bed, squatting down so that his face was even with mine. "This thing with Mando..." He shrugged. "I had to be sure about you."

All at once, a dry, gasping sob erupted from me, and I began to tremble uncontrollably. All the strength drained out of my limbs and I fell forward against him.

"Jesus." Tony caught me. He lifted me gently back onto the bed.

I clung to him, my teeth chattering, my breath coming in short, strangled gulps. I couldn't stop shaking.

"It's okay," he murmured. "It's all right. I'm not gonna hurt you. I won't hurt you."

"N-not s-cared," I managed, wondering at the way my body seemed to be doing all this without me.

"It's okay," he assured me. "You're okay. Sometimes, when they jolt you out of stasis prematurely, it overloads the central nervous system. You need to sleep, that's all."

I gasped a few more lungsful of air and nodded sheepishly. The trembling had subsided, replaced by an exhaustion so overwhelming, I couldn't hold on to Tony and sunk limply down across the bed.

"How old were you?" he ventured, when my trembling subsided. "When she did that?"

"Six. Eight. Ten. Twelve. Take your pick."

He grimaced, a sullen, vengeful heat in his eyes. "Why didn't you kill her? My mother did that shit to me, I'd kill her."

I gaped at him, thinking he was pulling my leg, knowing from the expression on his face he wasn't.

"You had the skill," he prodded. "You could have broken her neck, made it look like an accident. Why didn't you kill her?"

"She's my mother. I couldn't just—It's not right."

"Faith would have killed her. Or had her killed."

"I'm not Faith," I said, wondering why I felt so defensive.

"No," he conceded with the hint of a smile. "You're Rad. But still, you could have stopped her. You could have told someone. Had her ass thrown in jail."

"I'm not a snitch. Besides, the Navy doesn't allow single parents. If she'd been arrested, Papa would have had to resign."

He muttered something that sounded like: "Might have been for the best," as he draped the comforter around me, then admonished, louder: "Get some sleep. We'll talk more in the morning."

He leaned in to kiss my lips, but I drew back.

His gaze met mine, questioning, bewildered. And then he saw the fear in my eyes, and a tiny, rueful smile tugged at the corners of his mouth. "You can trust me, you know. I'll never lie to you. I swear it. I might omit. I might manipulate. I might obfuscate. But I'll never lie to you."

"Why?"

"Because." He pulled back, grinning. There was a brightness, a sheen to him, as if the electricity between us had caused his skin to fluoresce. "You're her. You're the one. With you in my life, no one can kill me."

"No one?"

"No one except you," he conceded.

"In that case," I said, uncomfortable with the weird turn things had taken. "You ever put a gun to my head again, I'll kick your ass from here to Tuesday."

He chuckled and patted my thigh, then headed for the door. As he stepped out into the hall, I heard the tik-tik of dog claws on the tile outside. "Hey, Zef," he said, patting the eager animal like it was an old army buddy he hadn't seen in years.

I watched them for a moment, before he closed the door and the bolts slid shut, blocking out the rectangle of light that silhouetted them. I waited for a while, to make sure he was really gone, then sat up and peeled the robe off, because it was too hard to sleep in. I laid back against the pillows, closing my eyes. I told myself not to believe him, not to believe anything, but as I drifted off to sleep to the faint, lingering scent of him, I realized that for the first time in my life, I didn't hate the smell of scotch.

CHAPTER FIFTEEN

In the morning, I was awakened by a a congenial, middle-aged woman who identified herself as "Kelani Lelani, M.D."

Her hair was pulled back in a bun, silver threads accenting the dusky brown. She wore a loose-fitting, oxblood leather jacket over her ample frame, and baggy black slacks. The jacket had a shell pattern imprinted in the leather, the bottom gathered in between her hips and knees. She looked like a polka-dotted baked bean. "Rise and shine," she chided, taking absolutely no notice of my nudity. "We've got work to do."

Before I knew it, she had the splint turned off, my arm stretched across her lap. The position sent throbbing hammer blows all the way up to my scapula. I groaned and gritted my teeth.

"That hurts?" she asked, apparently oblivious to the obvious. I grunted an affirmative, scraping the robe over with my toe.

"Hmmn." As I donned the robe, she rooted around in a little gear bag she'd brought with her. She slapped a patch on my arm, and another at the base of my skull. We waited for the drugs to take effect, and then the real agony began.

The regimen was pretty familiar: stretches, modalities, strengthening—the kind of things I'd done to recover from the Webster debacle. Simple, but by the time the splint went back on and the electrodes worked their analgesic magic, I lay sweating on the bed, dizzy with the effort of denying so much pain.

"Better get dressed," she goaded. "Your loverboy wants to see you downstairs."

I yawned, eyeing the bright, saffron orange outfit laid out for me with distaste. It was a two-piece affair, silk, cut along the same lines of a gi. At least it felt nice on the skin and it wasn't purple. When I finished dressing, she escorted me out the door and down the hall to an elevator.

My stomach growled just as the doors opened, but I didn't hold out much hope. If we were having vegetables for breakfast, I didn't want any. We went down, underground. The doors opened onto a short, stark hallway with steel doors at either end. Another door faced the elevator.

"Down there," Lelani waved toward the left. She smiled and punched the elevator controls as I stepped out. "See ya tomorrow."

The doors slid shut, left me completely alone on a thin, woven carpet that ran the length of the corridor. I wondered about this as I walked to the left. It was the first time I'd been in this house unescorted. Outside my room, of course. Maybe Tony really was starting to trust me. Either that, or I wasn't as alone as it seemed. Probably that.

The steel door clicked open at my approach. I knew by the smell what lay on the other side: A dojo. Same funk of sweat and plastic, same thickness to the air.

I pushed the door wide, found a long, rectangular, windowless room. On the entire wall opposite the steel door ran a seven-foot tall expanse of mirrors, reaching three-quarters of the way to the high ceiling. Thin, high-tech mats covered most of the floor, all except for a four foot strip of painted concrete near the door. At the right end of the room was a weapons rack. On the left was a series of punching bags and sparring gear.

Tony danced bare-chested in front of the mirrors, a heavy, sickle-type blade in each hand. He dipped and slashed and blocked an imaginary foe as he moved through a predetermined pattern of attacks and counterattacks known to me as a kata. Sweat matted his long hair, streamed down his chin to his chest. It made dark stains in the thin fabric of his drawstring pants. From the size of the stains, he'd been at this for a few hours, at least, but his face never lost its look of brutal concentration.

I waited for him to finish. The mirrored wall reflected his torso in all its sinewy glory, giving me a spectacular view of the eccentricities of his martial art. Never seen a footwork sequence like that. Couldn't be Okinawan or Korean. Lima Lama, maybe? Pencak Silat? Of course. Silat. Indonesian.

Each time he finished a kata, he started another, longer one. After about ten minutes, I became so intrigued by the Silat I found myself mimicking him, copying his every move by watching him in the mirror. No blades in my hands, of course, but after all those years of practice with my father I didn't need any weapons—Just ask Fox-face and Doughboy.

I coaxed my muscles through the first sequence, a complicated series of slashes and parries peppered with a number of low, sweeping kicks. I was a little weak from the weeks of forced bedrest, stiff and slow, but once I pushed myself past the inertia, I found my old endurance. My heart rate bumped up, my joints loosened, and my breathing fell into a steady rhythm.

Felt good to be physical again, to abandon myself to thoughtless action. Pure motion, no guessing or second-guessing, just the absolute childish pleasure of being. Senses alive, blood dancing in the veins, every limb an effortless extension of the whole. Like sex, or playing the piano. I finished a few seconds behind Tony, a glimmering smile on my lips.

Our gazes crossed in the mirror. Respect seeped past the guarded concentration in his eyes, a subtle appreciation spiced with challenge. He arched an inquiring eyebrow. "Think you can keep up?"

I nodded, jaw set. A dare, an acceptance. The game was on.

We bowed at the same moment, each focused on the other's reflection. Tony zoomed back into that crazy footwork pattern, twirling his blades in a circle block. I matched him step for step, twirl for twirl, mirroring his every move. Dip, spin around, up-slice while blocking with the other blade, shuffle back into the footwork again. Double fan block to the parries and slashes, faster this time, and then a sudden squat exploding into a flying scissors. Hit the ground in a crouch, monkey up to a spinning back kick, follow with the relentless flashing blades and that awesome footwork—

And do it all again. Even faster.

We moved in blurs, sweat streaming, muscles screaming for air and rest. On landing one of the kicks, Tony faltered. Not much, just a little slip, but enough to give me the lead.

I grabbed it and launched into an empty-handed Bo-staff kata, because it would be harder for him to match my moves with the encumbrance of two blades. He stumbled over the transition, but managed to keep up. The second time around he got it perfect and I was nearing exhaustion. I switched to a modified Five Animals, so he wouldn't pass me up and start calling the shots.

The snake form tripped him up a little, but the tiger style didn't phase him at all. When I got to the crane, I realized I was too tired to do it right, so I substituted the bear because at least I'd have both feet on the ground most of the time. My breath came in searing gasps, my thighs and calves and shoulders ablaze with the effort of staying ahead.

He was going to win, I knew. Only a matter of time before my body betrayed me. An easy combo: punch, block, kick, but I stuck my foot in the air...

And crumpled to the mat.

No strength left. No energy. Damn vegetables. If we'd had steak last night, I wouldn't be in this mess.

I rolled over on my back, panting like a steam train. I'd done all right. Gave him a run for his money, anyway. I looked over, expecting him to twirl his sickles in a flourish of victory. Be just like him to rub it in.

He wasn't even standing. Flat on his back, huffing and puffing, just like me. I found it hilarious. He glared at me, which made me giggle even harder, and then that deep, booming chuckle rumbled up from inside him. We laughed, long and hard, until even that became too much effort.

"Damn," he said when he caught his breath.

"Damn," I agreed, closing my eyes. We engaged in a long, comfortable silence, remarkable in its familiarity. Like I'd known him forever.

"What do you want?" he asked suddenly. "More than anything? You want it so bad you can taste it, swim in the wanting of it?"

"I'm not sure," I said, knowing it was a lie.

"My guess? I think you want your brother back. Maybe your father, too."

I shook my head, as if denying the hunger could erase the need, the burning ache to have them alive again. "Chris is dead. They're both dead."

"Well, then, what do you want?"

"A piano," I murmured, knowing as I said it I'd never get that, either. I'd be lucky to play somebody else's. "A concert grand. No, an imperial grand. What do you want?"

He didn't answer. After a while, I asked again.

"Closure," he said.

"What?"

"Closure. To bury things. Put them to rest."

I rolled onto my side and propped my head up on one elbow to regard him. "Your son?"

"Among other things."

"What other things?"

He sighed and fixed his gaze on the ceiling, a grim cloud of resignation surrounding him. "Do you want to back out?"

"No."

"Why not?"

I shrugged, unsure how to put what I felt into words. "I just don't."

"You could get killed, you know. You'll get hurt, for sure."

"I know."

Minutes passed as he stared at the ceiling with unfocused eyes, his fingers drumming idly on the mat. I studied him, both bewildered and intrigued by this strangely circular conversation.

"What happens to me," I murmured, "if you can't clear my prints? What happens if I can't be Faith?"

He sighed, regarding me wistfully. "You'll stay here until the implant wears off. Then, as long as you give me your word to keep quiet about this whole charade, you can go back to your old life."

"Really? You trust me?"

"Yes. You didn't snitch on your mother. You're not going to snitch on me."

I nodded, knowing what he said was true.

"Do you forgive her?" he said abruptly.

"Who, my mother?"

"Yes."

"No. Never."

He pondered this, chewing his lower lip. He nodded slowly, gaze far off, fiercely numb. "That's why."

"Why what?"

"Why you're the one. The only one who can help me do this."

"I don't understand."

"It's very simple." He sighed and rolled onto his side to face me. His fingers traced a seam in the mat, his eyes following them. "I can't forgive, either."

"I know."

He lifted his gaze to look at me. "You really want to do this? Be Faith?"

"Yes." My voice was a bit more husky than I'd expected. It was hard to meet his gaze and not remember the way he'd kissed me last night in front of Jana. My breathing quickened. My pulse stutter-stepped as his eyes roamed over my chest, where my erect nipples jostled under the sweat-soaked blouse.

Self-conscious, I unglued the shirt from my skin by tenting the fabric. He watched. Slowly, deliberately, he crawled toward me, looking the question that hung in the air between us.

I kissed him. He wrapped an arm around me and pulled me close as I forced my tongue halfway to his tonsils. Our bodies twined around each other, hands probing, pawing in a clinch so hot it neared meltdown. My fingers ran down the hard, slick forest of his chest to his navel, tugged on his drawstring. His hands peeled my blouse up and away.

"A-hem," somebody said. Not Tony. Not me. "A-A-A-hem."

We looked up to see Mando standing over us. Bemused, self-satisfied, and slightly disapproving, he held a pink-banded cigar over us like a hose over a pair of rutting dogs. "In case you're wondering," he said with a grin, "it's a girl."

Tony moaned deep in his throat and rolled onto his back. The truly magnificent rise in his drawers sent the hormones stampeding through my bloodstream all over again, and I turned my face toward the mat with a groan, tugging my shirt back down to give my hands something to do.

"C'mon," Mando waved the cigar in Tony's face. "Can't you say congratulations or something? It's the least you could do after calling me back when Emma's been in labor half the night. I mean, after all, you promised me—"

"Mando," Tony rolled to his knees. "Shut up."

"Oh," Mando's brows arched in mock surprise, "I was interrupting something?"

Tony didn't dignify that with an answer. He just stalked back to his blades. I sighed, finally under control. As I started to drag myself to my knees, Mando offered a hand.

I regarded it warily. He shrugged, a sly, fatherly smile on his lips that seemed to say "you'll thank me later." I slid my palm into his, feeling somehow both sheepish and accepted. His touch was cool compared to Tony's.

There was a loud thok! as Tony racked the sickles. He snatched a towel from an overhead shelf and wiped it across his chin and forehead. "You're early," he growled, not bothering to look up. The muscles of his back tensed as he spoke. "You weren't supposed to be here until twelve."

Mando sniffed, indifferent. "Jana said to come quick."

"She say why?"

"No. But the only way you hit the dojo this early is when you've been working out all night. Must mean—" A subtle twitch crossed Mando's cheeks. He stuck the cigar between his teeth and bit the end off, then slid a lighter out, and fired up. The smoke snaked into a blue-gray wreath around his head, then climbed upward. He drew in a hefty puff, held it for a moment, then released a single smoke ring toward the ceiling. "Bad news about Ilsa, huh?"

"Fuck Ilsa. Why do you think I called you in?"

"You tell me."

"Don't give me that shit." Tony spun around and stalked up to me. He stopped in front of me, all desire buried under a rigid facade of polite interest. "What's your name?"

I hesitated, unsure if he meant me me, or Irish me.

"Your real name?" he clarified.

"Rad."

"Radiana Damiano?"

I nodded.

"Born in Rochester, New York. Parents Nico Fausto Damiano and Sophia Bergamo Damiano. Father was a Navy man, now deceased. Mother resides in Tacoma, Washington. One sibling, Christopher. Also deceased. Drug-related suicide." He stared pointedly at me. "You do drugs, too?"

"No."

"What happened to all the money your father left you? Two-hundred fifty grand at the age of eighteen, and five years later you're living on the streets?"

"I went to school. College. Tuition alone is sixty grand a year, and—"

"You got yourself three counts of malicious mischief in your last two semesters alone. If you weren't on drugs, what in the Hell made you buzz the Alumni banquet with a model airplane stenciled 'Beethoven rules'?"

"That was a stunt," I countered, defensive. "Like the motorcycle thing. Sue Epstein dared me and I—"

"Like trashing three aisles of the library? Putting three guys out and almost killing another was a 'stunt?'"

"That was—Webster and those frat boys had it coming. He—"

"And that shit when you were fourteen? How many burglaries did you commit?"

My face burned. Why did this shit keep coming up? I'd been a runaway, for crying out loud. Not like I was proud of it. "Seventy. Eighty. Somewhere around there. Only got caught for three."

"And then there's the murder rap."

"It was dismissed," Mando interjected. "Self-defense."

Tony grabbed Mando's lapel, his other fist cocked back to strike. "I should waste your turncoat ass right now."

I eased toward the door. I really didn't want to be around for any of this. "I'm going back to my room now, okay?"

"No." Tony pointed me back to my spot. "You stay here."

I hesitated, unsure what to do.

"Let her go," Mando admonished. "She's a wildcard. She's not cleared for—"

"She's staying. I want her to see what a traitorous son-of-a-bitch you really are."

"Tony, I'm the most loyal man you've got. Cancel me without due cause, your whole corporation will turn to shit."

"Due cause. You talked me into her. Now, I find out she's got three arrests in California. Five in Washington State. You knew all this. You knew my linchpin would be sacked on a dirty background, but you didn't bother to tell me. Sounds like damn good cause."

Mando shrugged, waving his cigar at me. "She's the only civilian I've ever shot. I couldn't just leave her like that."

"You don't think I would have made it good?"

"Not if you thought her prints wouldn't clear."

"Mando, you know me. How can you think I'd do that?"

"I used to know you. Now, it's getting so I almost think I'm working for Brighton Leigh."

All the color left Tony's face. He tensed, tilted his head, like Mando was some kind of mesmerizing horror he couldn't bear to look at with both eyes. "I'm not like that." He faltered, relinquished his grip. "You know I'm not like that."

"How many times did we get wet in the past year? You don't think there's a pattern, there?"

"Those were all sanctioned."

"Because you fought to get them sanctioned. How many times do we have to jump in before you're satisfied? How long do we keep this going? You know they won't sanction Foster, any more than they'll sanction Leigh. Even you can't get away with drawing outside the lines. You try it, you'll crash and burn. Take us all down with you."

"I'll do what I have to do. I'll make it work."

"No. You won't. You can't. Jana's right. We've got to walk away. You jump in on this, you'll drown all of us."

"I'll do what I have to."

"God, Tony, listen to yourself! You're not even human anymore. Just a machine feeding off your own hate. You think getting yourself killed is going to put Stefan to rest?"

Tony's hands curled into fists, his arms rippling with tension. "Don't talk to me about Stefan. And don't tell me that a hard-core professional like you risked his neck for some lame-ass musician."

"Seem to remember," Mando puffed a drag, sent a circle skyward, "a hard core professional like me who risked his ass for some arrogant bastard down a mineshaft."

"That was different."

"Was it? Killed my career over you. I'll kill this one for her if I have to. I make good on my mistakes."

They stared at each other, power shifting in the thick atmosphere between them. Tony sighed and took a step back, looking at his reflection in the mirror.

"Damn." He ran his hand through his sweat-damp hair. "You sabotaged me. You knew Paul would never clear this."

Mando shrugged, staring up at the smoke curling up from his stogie. "Yeah. I knew. But there's too much between us for me to let you throw your life away on this."

"That's not your decision, is it?"

"Why not? Somebody's got to watch your back. Especially when you're too obsessed to watch your own."

But Tony wasn't listening, his gaze far-off, calculating. "Fuck it. I'll clear it myself. I'll talk to Flip. Faith can still fly." He drove his fist into his palm, nodding fiercely. "I'll make this work." He spun toward the door and stamped out.

Mando stared after him with a sad, weary look, then sighed and looked at me. I sniffed, scratching my nose in the awkward silence. I was grateful, even a little awestruck that Mando had risked so much to make up for shooting me. Problem was, I didn't know how to say it. What wouldn't sound stupid? Or sappy?

"What's her name?" I finally tried. "The baby?"

His face lit up with a proud father grin. "Espie. Esperanza, really. Seven pounds, nine ounces of pure love. God, is she cute." He fished another cigar out of his pocket and offered it to me. "I even got to hold her."

I shook my head. "Don't smoke."

"Here. Take it." He stuck it in my palm. "For luck."

For some reason, I felt honored. My fingers closed around the cigar. I held it tightly. "Thanks."

"Don't mention it." He chuckled as he guided me to the door. "With your background, you need all the luck you can get."

***

When we arrived back at my room, we found a mahogany serving cart loaded with breakfast parked by the window. Fresh fruit, oatmeal, coffee, croissants, rolls. No bacon. No ham. No eggs.

Mando broke off his enthusiastic blow-by-blow description of his wife's labor, dunked a wheat roll into a crock filled with frothy white stuff and shoved it in his mouth.

"Starving," he explained around bits of chewed roll. "Haven't eaten since breakfast yesterday."

I watched him for a while, then placed the cigar on top of the dresser and flopped down on the bed. I was tired, exhausted from Tony's katas, and from the tension of watching him and Mando butt heads. Be nice to go back to sleep.

"You want some?" Mando held out a croissant.

"Only if it comes with steak and eggs."

"I can call for some eggs, but no steak."

"Why not?"

He laughed, shaking his head. "Closest thing to red meat around here is dog kibble."

"Why?"

"Tony's sort of a vegetarian. He won't eat mammals."

"He wears leather shoes," I pointed out. "A leather jacket. Cattle are mammals."

"Leather's okay. He just doesn't like the smell of meat. Cooked or raw. Won't have it in his house."

"That's the stupidest thing I've ever heard."

"Yeah, well. That's Tony."

I shook my head and stared at the ceiling, wondering how a tough guy like Tony could be so squeamish. Or maybe he was squeamish because he was a tough guy. Smelling your own blood for three days probably did a number on him. "What did you mean by 'jumping in?'"

Mando acted like he hadn't heard me, although the slight pause he made before pouring a cup of coffee was a dead giveaway.

"What's 'getting wet?' You and Tony kill people, right?"

He tipped a teaspoon of sugar into his cup, followed by a short glunk of cream from the miniature silver pitcher. After a long moment in which the only sound was the tinkle of his spoon against ceramic, he sipped his coffee, pausing to stare at me over the rim of his cup. "So do you."

"That's different. Self-defense. What you guys do is—"

"Not any worse than what your father did as a TURTL."

"How do you know what he—?"

"What do you think 'Terrorist Liquidation' means? You infiltrate. You liquidate the targets, meaning you kill people, and you exfiltrate."

He was right. If Tony was a murderer, then Papa had been one, too. I turned it over in my mind, wondering how I felt about it. Decided that if all Tony's victims were like that asshole in the Halloween mask, Tony deserved a medal. "Who sanctioned these wet jobs? The marshals don't do that sort of thing, do they?"

"You don't need to know." He gave me a forbidding glower that told me this line of questioning was out-of-bounds.

"Then why were you talking about it in front of me?"

"Because I thought you should know the kind of man you were wrestling tonsils with."

"An assassin?"

"An executioner. And with Tony, the job comes first."

"Who sanctions you guys to do executions?"

"You don't need to know."

Stymied, I tried another tack. "So, why are you going after Brighton Leigh for the marshals? I thought the FBI did that stuff."

"They do. Usually. But Brighton's a fugitive, so it's under the marshals' jurisdiction. And if the marshals make a high-profile collar soon, they'll grandstand their way to a bigger slice of the budget. Rossi can't go to Quantico directly. The Feds would sabotage her because they think she's bucking for their PR."

"Rossi is working with you guys because the Feds don't want her agency to get any media attention for recapturing Brighton Leigh? That's like..." I trailed off, looking for a word to express the disgust I felt.

He read my face and nodded in agreement. "Shitty. I know."

"That's why they won't sanction Leigh. Or Scott Foster. Because they want them alive and kicking when they bring them to trial, right? That's the way to get the big media sweep. Except, Tony wants them dead. So, if they show up dead, Tony, and anybody else that the marshals know is on this job, are gonna get hung out to dry."

A glimmer of anger—or fear, maybe—washed across his face. He looked up at me, at my splint, then went back to his breakfast. "Anybody ever tell you that you're too smart for your own good?"

"Yeah. My mother, usually. She learned it from my probation officer." I sighed and scraped short, sweat-crusted bangs off my forehead. Who does bangs, anymore? Stupid Faith. "You think Tony can clear the prints?"

"We'll see." He pasted a generous dollop of strawberry jam on a fresh croissant, brow furrowed pensively. "If he does, I'll try to find you another way to get out of it."

"I don't want to get out of it."

"Why not? Thought you didn't want to be Faith."

"Changed my mind."

He gaped at me, amazed. "Why?"

"I just did."

He stared at me a long moment, jaw hardening as the thoughts in his eyes put themselves together. "How much has Tony told you about this job?"

"He said I could get killed. That I would get hurt."

"And you're okay with that?"

I shrugged, unsure how to explain what I felt. About the job. About Tony. "I guess so. But don't worry, though. Tony won't let that happen."

He chuckled, shaking his head in disbelief. "Tony's lucky he can wipe his own ass, right now. This thing with Ilsa has strung him to the edge."

"Who's Ilsa?"

"He didn't tell you?"

"No."

Mando scowled, shoving his half-eaten croissant back onto the plate. He stared at it, shaking his head. "He's a real shit, sometimes."

"Who is she?"

He picked up a napkin and wiped the red smear of jam off his fingers. "If he didn't tell you, I can't." He rose from the chair, tossing the napkin away. "Best I can do is go talk to him about it." He leaned over the cart, took one last draught from his coffee, then regarded me with a stern, fatherly glare. "Don't encourage him with this Faith thing. He'll get you both killed. Or worse."

"Thought you said you'd protect me."

"I will." He paced to the door, giving me a bleak, tired look as he waited for the lock to open automatically. "But if he starts drawing outside the lines, God couldn't protect you."

CHAPTER SIXTEEN

After Mando left, I fell into a heavy slumber as black and suffocating as a bath of hot tar. Smothered by a claustrophobic feeling that if I didn't get up and walk around, I'd be buried alive, I kept clawing my way back to consciousness to gasp a few times and then fall back to sleep.

I vaguely remembered Jana and the kitchen lady wheeling a cart laden with some kind of steaming peanut/tofu thing into the room, but it was vegetables, so I hadn't bothered opening more than one eye before nodding off again.

I finally awoke completely sometime after dark, judging from the way the pool lights danced in their refracted waves across the ceiling. I sighed and stretched and watched them for a while, enjoying the luxury of being alone in the silent gloom, untethered by medical devices, and unthreatened by imminent mayhem and violent death.

The long, embattled sleep had left me with a remarkable calm. I felt more composed and clear-headed than I had in all the time since I'd been shot. Remembering Vic's admonitions, I removed the splint and cleaned the electrodes with the contact cleaner Lelani had left on the dresser for me.

The cart of food sat near the door, everything artfully arranged, but stone cold, with a little crust of coagulated coconut oil on top. I eyed it as I slogged my way through the exercises, promising my unruly stomach that I'd eat as soon as the splint was back on. The pain wasn't as bad, this time. Or maybe I was just in a mood to appreciate it. Amazing, that what had been an insensate lump of meat and shattered bone was now capable not only of soreness, but of articulated movement.

Medical science, I decided, was a wonderful thing.

After I finished the exercises and put the splint back on, I pulled the cart over to one of the wing chairs and began to eat. The food was cold, as was the tea, but my stomach didn't care, gurgling thankfully as I filled it with salad and rice and chopped, spiced vegetables. About half-way through the meal, the lock chirped, and the door eased open, spilling a bar of muted light across the blue carpet.

I watched, curious, as Jana stepped quietly into the room, a long, flat cardboard box tucked under one arm. As she moved to close the door, her gaze fell across the bed, a frown twisting her alabaster features as she saw it was empty. Instantly on guard, she glanced around intently, her free hand reaching for the small bulge under her pink linen suitcoat. She relaxed a bit when she saw me, although her mouth still twisted in a suspicious sneer. "What are you doing over there?"

I shrugged, thinking the answer obvious. "Eating."

"In the dark?"

"Sure. So I don't have to look at the crap you're feeding me."

"There's nothing wrong with that food."

"Face it, honey," I said in my best Faith Hopkins drawl. "If God intended for Americans to eat rice, we wouldn't have so much land dedicated to grazing beef cattle."

"Listen, you neophyte little shit. Don't mistake the fact that I tolerate you for anything akin to goodwill. You don't belong here, and you don't belong with Tony. Eventually he'll see that."

"Aw, you're just jealous because you don't get to go tonsil wrestlin' with him, like I do."

She gripped the door handle tighter. Her stare was one of those you needed chains and snow tires to cross. She tossed the box on the foot of the bed and pointed a manicured finger at me. "You don't understand what you're diving into, little girl. But when you do..." She bared her teeth. "It'll be fun to watch you drown."

She tried to stare me down, not knowing that after decades of practice with my mother, as well as the various agencies investigating her for child abuse, she'd have better luck staring down the Lincoln monument.

After about thirty seconds, she slapped the box with her hand. "This doesn't leave your room." She spun on her heel and stalked towards the door, shaking her head in disgust. "Don't know what the Hell he thinks he's doing. Hundred-proof fantasyland, letting a wildcard like you run the field. Get us all killed."

She slammed the door on her way out. I listened to her receding footsteps, brightened by the knowledge that she'd never forgiven me for puking all over her.

Some things in life just can't be improved on.

When she was well and truly gone, I turned the lights on and picked up the box. It was about thirteen inches wide, four inches thick, and almost as long as the bed. No ticking. Relatively light. I was no bomb expert, but I figured those were good signs, considering the source of the package.

I worked the reinforced paper tape loose from one end and peered inside. Foam blocks secured a thin, flat object wrapped in sheet foam. I pulled it out carefully, until my eyes made sense of the sleek, black-and-white shape beneath my fingertips.

My heart tripped up in surprise. A portable keyboard. Full-size, with one-hundred-and-forty-four velocity-sensitive keys, AC back-up, recording and playback functions, and a screen for displaying sheet music. It even had a set of headphones. A sleeve of 5D discs pre-loaded with sheet music was taped to the controller pad, along with a typed note. It read, simply:

Here's to avoiding bugshit.

A.T.

Food now forgotten, I turned the unit on and plugged the headphones in. I plinked around for a while, until the agony of stretching my right fingers across the keys wasn't worth the strangled, pathetic noise I managed to eke out with it, so I put the splint back on and tried it that way. No good. Too awkward.

So, I concentrated on the left. It was fine. A little stiff, a little slow. Nothing a half-hour of practice couldn't erase. I limbered up a bit, but before I could play anything meaningful, the lock chirped. Thinking it might be Tony, I shoved the keyboard under the comforter and sat on the edge of the bed. But Jana held the door wide, glowering at me, while the kitchen lady scurried in, grabbed the cart, and wheeled it into the hall.

I smiled innocently at them both. Jana, however, wasn't having any of it. She glanced at the open box on the floor beside my bed, the sleeve of 5Ds I'd left on the end table, and scowled. "Absolutely worthless," she mumbled under her breath. "Should have purged you when we had the chance."

I was about to zing a snappy comeback at her, but she flipped the lights off, tossed a disagreeably sweet, "Good night, Miss Hopkins," over her shoulder, and slammed the door. Again.

Catching the hint, I grudgingly shoved the box under the bed with my toe, then scooped the sleeve of 5Ds off the end table and shoved them in the drawer. Not wanting to give her complete satisfaction by getting up to turn the light back on, I flipped the blanket back up and settled the synth across my knees in the gloom. I donned the headphones, adjusted the volume, allowing my fingers to move over the keys, drinking in their cool solidity. But the music wouldn't come.

Frustrated, I tried to force it out, anyway. Launched into Liszt's Left-Handed Concerto, only to stop a few bars later, disgusted with the performance.

What was technique without soul?

I pulled the headphones off, unplugged them, and let the sound waves crash against me and resonate with the hollowness beneath my skin, hoping to touch something warm and vital beyond the void I'd become since the hospital. I drove myself into the music, breathing in the passion the way a spaniel scents game on the wind, almost, but never quite, grasping the truth that somehow always eluded me.

I attacked it, pursued it with every note, each keystroke a prayer, an desperate invocation: please, please let me find it again. The music had been in me for so long...

Just as I finished the piece, a movement from the window caught my eye. I looked over, saw an outline of a man sitting in one of the slate blue chairs. "Tony?" I ventured over the fading echoes of the music, thinking that no one else could have slipped in so completely undetected. I was beginning to wonder if he had a secret passage into the room or something.

"Yeah." His voice was hoarse. I heard the unmistakable glunk of a bottle being tipped. "Mando said you were good. But I didn't realize how well you actually played."

Part of me was glad to see him. Part of me was creeped out by this weird night time visit. "What are you doing here?"

"I just...wanted to...see you. Wanted to—" He cleared his throat. The smell of scotch clung to him like a vengeful ghost. "You're very pretty when you play, you know? You look intense. But innocent. Passionate."

"Tony, maybe Mando's right. Maybe we shouldn't try to—"

"Fuck Mando. Goddamn choirboy." Liquid sloshed as he tipped the bottle to his lips. "Doesn't know shit."

I listened to him swallow, heat rising to my cheeks. "Do you have to drink that stuff around me?"

There was a long silence, and then the noise of a cork being tapped into the bottle. He leaned forward and pulled something from under his shirt. As he stood, the pool lights illuminated his face and torso. His eyes were red-rimmed, his cheeks wet and shiny above the dark stubble of a day-old beard.

He crossed over to me, his movements suddenly fluid and precise, all hint of sloppiness gone. In his fist was a wicked-looking, wavy-bladed dagger. He held it up in the light. "You know what this is?"

I studied it. The blade was a seven-inch, honed silver ribbon, double-edged and undulate, as if water itself had become a weapon. The carved, teakwood pommel was capped with a single, walnut-sized black opal that glittered in the undulating light. "It's a dagger."

"It's a *kris*. For the Silat." He held it out to me, pommel first.

Something about the offer made me recoil, as if the blade was white hot, radiating with some dark future I didn't want to go near. He hissed when I didn't take it, and then launched into that same fluid dance I'd seen in the dojo.

The *kris* flashed hypnotically, glinting here and there in the ribbons of light from the pool like a quicksilver eel. Without seeming to, he drew closer, until suddenly he was all around me, blade flickering less than a foot from my nose, my throat, my gut.

I didn't move, didn't react to his ritualized threat, recognizing in his movements a controlled release of emotion, a compulsive discharge of rage and grief. I'd done the same thing with both katas and keyboard, more nights than I could count.

But then, the *kris* sliced by my ear, so near I could feel the air of its passing ruffle my short Irish hair. *Too close.* "Stop it, Tony."

He kept going, obsession glinting in his eyes. His scent held no sweetness to it, only the smoky, bitter edge of whisky and spent cartridges. He brought the dagger around, passing it a few inches from from my right flank. "It's shaped like that to slip between the ribs better."

"Have to borrow it next time I eat Mongolian barbecue."

He halted in mid-kata, blinking at me like I'd just slapped him. And then he was laughing. Big, nervous guffaws of relief, of surrender. He sank down on the bed beside me and wiped his eyes with the back of his forearm.

I was relieved that he had stopped with the Silat, but unsettled by his proximity, and his strange behavior. Both Mando and Jana had hinted that his mental state was not the best. I was starting to see what they meant.

He fingered the *kris*, turning it over and over in his hand. "A *kris* holds a man's soul. It's how he knows he's a man, ready for a man's battles. Some are hundreds of years old, handed down from father to son. This is Stefan's."

"Your little boy's?"

He nodded. I felt his ribcage expand as he drew in a deep breath, and then contract with a long, measured exhale. "This used to be mine. It's why I didn't die, you know? In the mineshaft. Doctors, medics all said I shoulda died. What Foster did to me shoulda killed me. But it didn't. Because my soul was safe in here." He tapped the blade. "In my *kris*."

I glanced sidelong at him. Of all the things I dreamed might fall out of his mouth, I'd never imagined something that stupid. "You really believe that?"

He nodded earnestly. "I know it. Soul for a soul. A spirit can't leave the weapon without one to replace it."

I stared at him, not trusting myself to open my mouth, because if I did, I'd burst out laughing. This, combined with Tony's crazy entanglement theory, had topped out my nonsense meter.

"It's true," he insisted. "You know it is. The snake, the bear, the monkey...you feel them. The animal spirits there in the karate. How do you think they got there? The masters. The masters gave up their spirits, stepped into the animals. Brought life to the form. They give you the power to move. To kill."

He raised the dagger up and offered it to me, hilt first.

I took it, this time, figuring it was better to be armed when he was acting so loopty. I ran my fingers along the satin finish of rippling steel, surprised at the warmth I felt in the metal. The polished teak fit nicely in my palm. The blade was simply forged, oddly balanced. And the opal...it was like somebody had crushed a rainbow and scattered the dust across a flawless night sky. Beautiful. Mysterious. Deadly. Just like Tony.

I tried to return it.

"No." He shook his head, waved the *kris* away. "I want you to keep it for me."

"Why?"

The room grew still. The only sounds were our breathing and the electronic hum of the keyboard. When his answer came, it was a whisper: "I want to be your piano."

"My what?"

"Your symbol. The thing that keeps you going no matter what. The thing you believe in."

A cold fist grabbed my heart. I eyed him, the *kris* suddenly heavy in my palm. "You're drunk. You don't know what you're saying. You barely even know me."

"I know. More 'n you. I saw it. All those months of re-gen. I saw." He took the dagger from me. "Scotty couldn't kill me, 'cause my soul was fixed in here."

"Was?"

He nodded grimly. "It's not, anymore. When Scotty's men broke in to kidnap Stefan, they took my *kris*, too." He slogged his way over to the chair, sank heavily into it, resting the blade across his knees. He reached down, uncorked the bottle, and slugged back a swallow. "They killed him with it. Trapped his soul. Released mine."

He sat there, staring at me for so long, I wondered if he'd passed out with his eyes open. Suddenly, he stirred. "She told me, you know? Ilsa. Even before they took Stefan, she warned me something like this would happen."

"Who's Ilsa?"

He coughed. Cleared his throat. "My wife."

To his credit, he looked me in the eye when he said it.

"Your wife," I repeated stupidly.

He nodded. "Been married for twelve years. Separated for the last three. She says what happened to Stefan was my fault."

He rose and paced off across the room, bottle in one hand, blade in the other. "She used to beg me to leave it alone. Let Foster, and Leigh, and all those other sick fucks get away with what they'd done. What they were doing. 'Think about the children,' she'd say. And I did."

He took another swig, pausing to stare out the window, teeth bared. "Every night. Every time I tried to sleep, I'd see those kids in that whorehouse, that sonuvabitch Brighton Leigh gettin' rich off their misery. How could I turn my back on that? How could I let 'em get away with it? 'They're not yours,' she'd say. 'Stay home. Your own children need a father.'" His lips formed a hard line. "She didn't understand. I had to stop 'em. Had to stop that asshole, or what kind of father would I be?"

I wondered if Papa's reasons for being absent echoed Tony's, not sure how I felt about that. I could see Tony's commitment, his resolve mirrored in Papa's fierce devotion to his team. In some ways, I shared it. Nobody should hurt little kids. Nobody.

But, having grown up with an absentee father, I kinda sided with Tony's wife. I was pretty sure that if Papa hadn't died in some world-saving mission, Chris wouldn't be dead, either.

He sucked in a deep breath, then let it loose in one long, bone-weary sigh. "Brighton killed my son. Stabbed him with my own *kris*."

He leaned his head back to stare at the ceiling. Water spilled down his cheeks, glistening through the rough stubble of his beard, forming droplets on his jaw. He blinked, and blinked again, but the tears kept coming. He didn't wipe them away, didn't even seem to be aware of their presence. "I can't keep livin' this way."

I stood up and eased toward him. "You shouldn't have to."

He nodded. "Gotta bury him. Put him to rest."

"That's a good idea." I worked the bottle out of his grasp, recorked it, and shoved it under the bed. "You should rest, too."

He turned abruptly and searched my face, eyes wild and pleading. "No. Don't you see?"

"See what?"

"Soul for a soul. Stefan's in that *kris*. I gotta kill Brighton Leigh with it to set him free."

"You're not going to kill anyone, Tony. Even if we do find Leigh, you know they're not going to sanction him."

"No. You dreamed me. I dreamed you. Together, we can do anythin' if the spirits are with us."

"Tony—"

"It's true. Seen a man turn into a clouded leopard, once. In Sarawak." His head bobbed up and down. "You know it's true. A tiger's in the Silat. Soul for a soul."

"Tony, things like that don't happen. People don't turn into animals. Or daggers, for that matter. There are no spirits."

I wasn't sure about the soul part. I was ninety percent atheist. But every time I played with an orchestra, I couldn't help feeling that there was something inside me that lived beyond the meatsack I had been trapped in all my life. Something grand and glorious, ineffable and eternal. Maybe souls existed. Maybe they didn't, and it was just the music moving through me.

Either way, the stuff Tony was talking about was just, to put it kindly, wishful thinking. I got it. I really did. I didn't want to say goodbye to Chris. Didn't want to lose him forever. I knew Tony's grief, his pain. But this obsession wasn't helping anybody.

I stroked his shoulder, trying to put into my touch what I couldn't say with words. "Stefan is dead. Let him go."

"No!" He shrugged me off, stepping away as if I'd just tried to stab him. "He's not. He's in the opal. A little rainbow in the darkness. Just like your brother."

"Tony, you're full of shit," I snarled, fed up with this stupid, yearning babble. How could I have put my life in the hands of this drunken wretch? "My brother's in a cemetery plot in Seattle."

"No. I heard you. *I heard you.* He's not dead. He's in your goddamned music."

I opened my mouth to argue, only to close it again, amazed. He was right. I didn't know what to say.

He stalked away, the lock tripping silently at his approach. He threw the door wide, stepped through, halting in mid-stride. A shadow moved around his legs, the brittle clicking of dog claws echoing off the Mexican tile as Zef hedged nervously around him. He patted the animal, reassuring it, then spun around to glare at me, his impressive bulk silhouetted by the light in the hall.

"Jana was right." His voice was heavy, but emotionless. Like the fall of an axe. "You're just like Ilsa. A selfish, short-sighted bitch."

"I am not," I called after him, but he was already slamming the door, leaving me in gloomy, foreboding silence.

"I am not," I said again, to deny the coldness that covered me, the cavernous reverberation in that hollow place that had been my heart. I heard the rain, that steady shushing roar in my ears, and it all came rushing back:

It had been three weeks after we'd found out about Papa's death. A week after they'd held the service. Mother had broken my rib the night the men came to tell us. I'd been out of the hospital for three days, and Chris had been jabbering relentlessly every single one. He wouldn't shut up about how Papa would come back and take care of us and make us a family again. Because despite what the Navy said, Papa wasn't really dead. Not to Chris.

Papa would come back, when things settled down. When the mix-up was straightened out. Just stroll down the gangplank and step into our lives like nothing had happened, the way he always did. People did that all the time in the movies. Or on YouTube. So, why not Papa? And Chris told everyone this.

All his school friends. All his teachers. Even Mother. Who, of course, beat the snot out of me for filling his head with such nonsense. And still, he kept up this insane, hopeless fantasy.

Was it any wonder I'd snapped? I'd punched him right there in the rec-center parking lot while we were waiting for the school bus. The blood from his nose painted my right fist, mingling with the rain. All the other kids gaped wide-eyed as Seaman Ortiz pulled me off of him.

It had shamed me, to see the hurt in Chris' eyes. The bewildered realization that the big sister he'd depended on for comfort and protection was no better than the merciless bitch of a mother they both shared like a humiliating secret.

It was the only time I'd ever hit him in anger. The only time I'd ever let her violence spill over onto him. I'd been glad that Seaman Ortiz put one arm around my throat, his other pinning my elbows to my body, because seeing the truth in my brother's face had filled me with a savage, uncontrollable need to erase that knowledge from him, even if it meant beating him unconscious. Even if it meant beating him to death.

It had been that moment, I knew, when the seed had been planted. That incident which had driven Chris inside himself. So, when puberty struck, and he found himself alone and unreachable inside the dark warrens of despair, he had turned to drugs to forget how he had come to that place. Then, he'd patched that CBYL, started hallucinating, and fired a bullet through his brain, just to let the voices out.

Now, I'd done the same thing to Tony. He had offered his most precious secret to me, his most private self. I had known, at some level, that he wasn't talking about the *kris*, at all.

He was talking about his willingness to share with me, to find comfort in the fact that I understood his pain. Maybe even to seek some sort of proxy absolution. But, when the time came to accept the gift, and provide some succor in the process, I'd scoffed at him instead. Ridiculed and denied the deepest part of him, because I couldn't face that part of myself. Or, more accurately, I didn't have that part of myself.

It was, I realized, what I had been doing with the music all along. Trying to touch others, tap into their souls, because somehow, I'd lost mine. Or, as Mother was always so fond of saying, I'd never had one. I was, simply, a parasite, feeding off other people's passions, unable to produce any of my own.

I'd lived through Chris. Through Papa. And, to a certain extent, I'd lived through Jim. Deep down, I knew this was the real reason why I'd never make it alone as a pianist. I could play almost any keyboard piece anybody had ever written, but I'd never been able to compose. It's why I hated myself so much.

Disgusted, I picked up the keyboard and yanked the plug from the socket. I couldn't bring myself to smash it, like I wanted to, so I just shoved it roughly back into the box and jammed it in the darkest recess of the closet I could find, burying it under a mound of Faith shoes and Faith clothes.

I couldn't stop moving, after that, launching into the same type of compulsive frenzy Tony had performed earlier. Kata after kata, repeating over and over everything that Papa had ever shown me. Pushing myself until exhaustion left me panting on the bed, facing the window as dawn splashed the long gray shadow of the house out across the rocky, rust-colored hillside.

Sunlight bullied its way around the edges of things, thrust the world into brilliant definition. I stared out at the silent reflection of blue sky rippling on the dark surface of the pool, and wondered if Tony would keep his promises now that he knew who and what I really was.

CHAPTER SEVENTEEN

Over the next week or so, I remained cooped up in my room. Tony didn't visit. Neither did Mando. Jana and her 9mm Smith and Wesson made sure I didn't sneak out during mealtimes. The lock was too complex to pick, and I couldn't bear to even look at the keyboard again, so there wasn't much else to do but practice katas, review the Faith vids, and stare out the window.

The highlight of my days became the regular morning therapy visits by the cheerfully sarcastic Dr. Lelani. I tried to sneak out with her, once, but Jana was always waiting in the hall. The fact that she was armed made getting a clean kick on the supercilious bitch difficult. Plus, Faith wasn't supposed to know any martial arts, and I didn't want to give Jana any more ammunition for her "Prove Rad Incompetent" campaign.

As the week progressed, so did my hand. Most of the swelling went down, and the pain decreased to the point I didn't need the splint except to sleep and for the few hours directly after the therapy. The bruises had mellowed into greenish-yellow smears across my knuckles and the insides of my fingers. Even though the muscles themselves were weak, my fine motor control had improved tremendously. That was the good news.

The bad news was, with every twenty-four hours of enforced isolation, my claustrophobia quotient doubled. By the end of the week, even working through as much of the Silat as I remembered couldn't keep me from bouncing off the walls.

I paced around, itching to demolish all the polished marble plumbing fixtures and flush the stupid embroidered bedspreads down the toilet—not to mention the crap that rolled in at lunch time with the white-haired kitchen lady and her mahogany serving cart.

Jana guarded the hall. She still had a gun in her hand, even though she wore a bikini and high heels.

In a whisper, I asked the old woman to send Tony up, or Mando, if he was available. She smiled at me with a vague, placating nod that told me she had no idea what I was saying. She left me with a mound of rice, a bowl of chopped vegetables, and some soup made out of seaweed and tofu. Jana smirked at me as the door shut, sealing me in with yet another meal of lawn clippings and toe jam.

As I ate, I heard voices outside, so I looked out the window, and saw Jana moving out to the tiki bar on the opposite side of the pool, chattering away with a tanned, middle-aged couple wearing Eurostyle bathing suits. The man looked trim and fit, although balding with a comb over, and the woman had proportions that could only come from copious amounts of plastic surgery. Mando, wearing a Hawaiian shirt and cargo shorts, served drinks from the bar. Tony swam laps in the black-bottomed pool, wearing a tight-fitting pair of Speedos. Zef the dog lounged in the shade of the arbor, tongue lolling.

No fair. Everybody was at the party but me.

The view grew more interesting when Tony left the pool to soak up the sun from a chaise lounge just east of my room. I hammered on the Plex with heel of my shoe. Zef cocked his ears and looked up. Tony snapped his head up in alarm, following the animal's gaze. He relaxed a bit when he realized it was only me.

I pounded the Plexiglas again, and motioned for him to let me out. His smile fled. He shook his head. I raised my palms and shrugged "why not?" He faced the pool, deliberately ignoring me. When he didn't respond to any further attempts at communication, I threw one of the blue chairs at him. It bounced harmlessly off the thick Plex, but left a satisfying, inch-wide scrape across half the window.

At the sound of the impact, Jana and the couple she was talking with looked up at me. I flipped her off. She scowled and excused herself, heading into the house. The couple drifted over to sit on the chaise lounges flanking Tony. The woman laughed at something and put a hand on Tony's thigh. He put a T-shirt and some cargo shorts on.

Even so, I growled under my breath, wet a bar of goat milk soap and wrote a mirror image of "ATTICA!" on the window. Right about then, the door flew open and Jana steamed through.

"What in the Hell do you think you're doing?" she shrilled.

I didn't think. I just reacted. Threw the bar of soap at her eyes. While she dodged, I ran across the bed and out the door.

"Liberty or Death!" I shouted as I bolted barefoot down the hall, Jana's heels clacking a rapid tattoo behind me.

"Remember the Alamo!" I rabbited down the stairs. I hung a left at the landing, shot past the dining room, through the foyer, and rammed open two double, bronze-banded oak doors.

I found myself in the cobbled courtyard, where two of those off road security golf carts basked in the bright sun next to the cobalt blue BMW M5 we had used when I left the hospital. A shiny red Jaguar and a metallic green, late model Ford Mustang were parked nearby.

Breathless, and entirely caught up in the spirit of the moment, I sprinted to one of the carts, fired it up, and pointed it down a small asphalt road. My getaway was screened from the house by a row of cypress trees. No idea where I was going, but that didn't matter. I was outside. Free at last.

The breezy tang of eucalyptus tickled my nostrils as the cart whirred down the hill and along a tree-lined gully. The hot August morning massaged my lungs with the summery scent of liberty. I grinned so hard my cheeks hurt. I started to hum Beethoven's

Ninth. Gave up on self-restraint completely, and sang the damn thing.

I don't have that great of a voice, and my German sort of sucks, but what I lack in polish I make up for in enthusiasm. At least that's what I tell myself. What other people tell me is usually along the lines of put a sock in it. Which is exactly what I did when I saw the sleek, tawny shapes loping through the underbrush like masked outlaws flanking a stagecoach.

I had forgotten about the dogs.

Flat out on the cart was about twenty-five miles-per. I couldn't shake them, but as long as I kept moving they couldn't surround me, either. Could've held them off indefinitely if the tires hadn't suddenly crunched on gravel. I looked up from badmouthing my fur-bearing hecklers to find a squat, adobe building looming up with the demonic accuracy of the Titanic's iceberg. Shooting range, dead ahead.

I stood on the brake. The cart skidded broadside as I cranked a hard right. The tires dug into the gravel. The whole thing flipped up on the two outside wheels in a delicate, slow-motion arc, lifting my side up into the air. As the cart teetered at the apex, I made a valiant attempt to bail out.

My feet sent up roostertails of gravel as soon as they touched ground. Unfortunately, the panicked fingers of my left hand refused to release the steering wheel. My legs pumped furiously and overcame the added resistance of a half-ton machine welded to my palm.

The message "LET GO YOU IDIOT!" finally got through to my hand about the time I realized that off road golf carts make a Hellish amount of noise when they slam onto their sides.

I let go.

My legs continued their frantic gallop and propelled me nose-first into the hard cinderblock of the shooting range. My fingers had been right all along. Should've held on.

I peeled myself off the wall and spun around. The dogs were scattered in a dazed half-circle around me, disoriented from the noise and the cloud of settling dust.

I edged towards a ladder running up the side of the building. I scrambled upwards as the beasts lunged. One caught the hem of my shirt and tore through. Another took a solid kick to the ribs. My fingers touched asphalt and gravel as fangs grazed my heels.

I flung myself over the lip and kicked my legs up, scrambling away from the edge toward a skeet launcher bolted onto the roof. It was computerized, a sleek aluminum job with an auto-load chute stacked with about twenty clay pigeons. Next to it was a cardboard box half-full of the fluorescent orange pancakes.

A noise sounded from the ladder behind me. A clinking, clanging, rustling noise. I looked over the edge into a flashy white smile just as two forepaws hooked over the top ladder rung. The damn dog had climbed up.

I chucked a clay pigeon at it. Missed, but then my accuracy sucked when throwing left-handed. The dog hooked up with one back paw and pulled itself farther onto the roof. I threw another pigeon in its face. It yelped, then lost balance and fell, scraping another dog off the ladder on the way to the ground. The whole pack of them milled around like a 'B' movie lynch mob, and another one started up the ladder.

I ran back, dragged the box over, and fired at anything that approached. Seven misses. Two direct hits, one of which sent a mutt yelping blindly into the cart, which in turn teetered precariously before slamming back down on its rugged wheels with a bouncy crunch.

Right about then, I decided this was fun. Lots of it. Almost as much fun as that time Johnny Westlake and I bombarded the Navy luncheon with water balloons filled with Easter egg dye.

"Don't fire 'til you see the whites of their eyes!" I bellowed, in keeping with the patriotic theme, and lobbed pigeons as fast as I could. "Don't tread on me! I have not yet begun to fight!" At this last, I reached down for something else to throw, but the box was empty.

I ran over to the auto-loader to swipe some of those pigeons and managed to trip something accidentally, because the damn thing started up this piercing, intermittent beep, like the noise a truck makes when it backs up. I couldn't find the shut-off, so I gave up, scraped a bunch of clay pancakes into my arms, and scurried back into position. With my ammo running low, I had to make every shot count, so I hunkered down out of sight and waited for the telltale noise of fleabags climbing.

About half a minute later, I heard a clangety-clang and the tips of the ladder twitched. I popped up, hollering "Death before dishonor! No taxation without representation!" and flung the pigeon with wild, left-handed abandon.

Then, I saw what was on the ladder.

Luckily, I did not send a clay pigeon hurtling through Mando's forehead. Unfortunately, my stray projectile bounced off the hood of a golf cart driven by Jana and shattered against the magnificent chest of Anthony Tovenaar, who was sitting beside her. The pigeon shrapnel rained down on the couple sitting on the rear bench in a spectacular cloud of red clay and neon.

I froze. Tony froze.

There was a long, uncomfortable interlude where the only sounds were the couple clapping, the measured squalling of the launcher and Mando laughing so hard he fell off the ladder.

"Tony, hon," I said in loud, lubricated Texan. "Cain't you find a shirt that ain't got a big red smear acrost it?"

CHAPTER EIGHTEEN

While Mando caught his breath between guffaws, Tony glared at me, at the damaged cart, at the dogs, and shouted a command that sounded like "Caw-weg, Alla-mall."

The dogs scurried meekly into the underbrush.

The balding man on the rear bench of Jana's cart fished a few red clay chunks out of his margarita, and took a sip, and looking me over appreciatively. "Why, Tony," he said in an upper crust New England accent, "You didn't tell us you had a new lady friend..."

"Faith Hopkins, meet Charles and Nina Truby," Tony said dutifully as he crossed over to stand at the foot of the ladder.

I gave them a broad smile and a cutesy wave. "Pleasure to meet y'all," I drawled, trying to ignore the launcher still bleating behind me. "What brings you here?"

"Board meeting," Charles said. "Then perhaps some tennis?" He looked a question at Jana, who continued to excoriate me with her eyeballs. While Tony and Jana glowered at me, Mando climbed up. I stepped back to allow him onto the roof and he silenced the launcher, then helped me onto the ladder.

"Perhaps we should join Faith," Nina suggested. Her accent was British. Her eyes sparkled with glee. "That looked like a smashing load of fun."

"It was." I clambered down with the calculated, chaotic motions of a true drunk. As my feet reached the gravel, I winked at the Trubys. "I'm so parched, can I have a sip of your margarita?"

Tony grabbed me, his fingers digging painfully into my bicep. He steered me towards the cart I had crashed. "You're drunk. I'll take you back to your room."

"Oh, Tony, honey." I cooed, rubbing my body against him lasciviously. "Don't start fussin'. You know what they say: Reality is for them that cain't handle alcohol."

The Trubys burst into a grotesque, silent laughter, like a couple of cats coughing hairballs. When they finished, Nina waved us towards her and patted the bench. "You are so funny. Come with us. We're having drinks by the pool."

"I don't think that's a good idea," Jana said through gritted teeth. "She's not on the board. And it's a private meeting."

Charles gave a disappointed sigh, apparently seeing the logic in Jana's argument. "I'm afraid she's right, my dear," he said, patting Nina's arm.

Nina pouted, then brightened. "You are absolutely coming to our party," she told me. "Tony, you must bring her."

"I'd be delighted," I agreed, as Tony helped me into the crashed golf cart. "'Bout time I started rubbin' shoulders with folks like you. Tony's a hottie, but he's kind of revelry-challenged, if you know what I mean? I'm as bored as an oil well around here. And not in the good way," I added, groping Tony while giving the Truby's a meaningful look.

They did that cat barfing laugh again, and waved to me as Jana drove them away.

Mando got behind the wheel of our cart, sandwiching me between him and Tony. He glanced sidelong at my hand, which was still resting on Tony's sizeable package. His gaze lifted to Tony's face, his cheeks twitching, lips pursed like he was trying not to laugh.

"Drive," Tony growled, moving my hand away.

Mando concentrated on steering the gravel-scarred cart up the hill, keeping the wheel a little cranksided because the alignment was off. Every once in a while, he'd glance at me and smirk.

Tony ignored him, sitting stiffly with his arms folded across his chest, jaw clenched so tight I thought his blood might squirt out his ears. Pigeon dust coated his hair, which was still wet from the pool. It went well with the rusty-red smudge on his T-shirt.

Wedged between them on the hard vinyl seat, I remained unrepentant, despite the five-minute lecture I received from Tony on the proper treatment of his dogs.

Everything I'd done was well within proper Faith parameters, right down to the chair I'd thrown at the window. Faith didn't like being ignored any more than I did.

Mando eased the limping cart into a dimly lit garage bay, parking next to a row of cars that stretched out into the gloom. A four-by-four Lamborghini, an old Jag E-type, a late model BMW, the newest Japanese sports car, and, way at the end, a gunmetal gray Mazda, just like mine.

Bouyed by the sight, I headed that way.

"In the house, Faith," Tony commanded, yanking me toward a small cubicle housing a service elevator. We stepped out onto a hallway I didn't recognize. Pine paneled walls, more Mexican tile. Bronzes of cowboys on broncs stood guard in the center of the wide passage, walls hung with psuedo-Native American crap. Didn't seem like Tony, but, then again, the man had more faces than a Hindu god in a blender.

The hall made a ninety degree turn about ten yards down. We rounded the corner and headed up the stairs, navigating hallways until we once again arrived back at my room. The lock opened silently at our approach. Tony nudged the door wide and pushed me inside.

"Sit," Tony said.

I sat on the bed. Mando settled himself into the chair on my right. Tony remained standing, his blue gaze riveted on me.

I stared placidly back, secure in the knowledge that Faith was an even bigger screw-up than I was. For once, I had a legitimate excuse. As things stretched on, I played a minuet in my head.

"I thought we agreed that this contrary shit was going to stop," Tony said, when it sunk in that the stare-down wasn't working.

"It has."

"Then why the Hell did you break out? I made it clear you were to stay in your room."

"You made it clear you were ignoring me.   That's not something Faith takes lightly. I was being Faith. A spoiled, crazy, rich opportunist. It's what you wanted, right? What you're paying me for?

"You were being Rad."

"No. Rad would have busted the lock in the middle of the night and stolen the Mustang. Faith's much too lazy for that."

Mando nodded with a shrug. "She's got you there, Tony."

Tony sighed and ran a hand through his hair. The movement sent a vague smell of salt water from the pool wafting through the air.

"Is that my car down there?" I asked, since that question was burning a hole in my throat.

"Yes," Tony said curtly.

"Really? You didn't torch it?"

"Swapped the VIN plates," Mando confirmed.

I searched Tony's face. He nodded. "A deal is a deal."

"We should get back to the meeting," Mando reminded him, but I had already launched myself off the bed and wrapped my arms around the big guy, hugging him fiercely.

"Thank you," I murmured, face buried against the valley between his hard pecs. "Thank you."

I could feel the tension, the anger drain away from Tony. His arms slid around me, returning the embrace. I clung to him, drinking in his presence, soaking in every bit of empathy he could offer. He was the only man who had held me that way since Papa had died. As if I was important. As if someone cared. The warmth of him broke something loose inside me. It felt like I was flooding into him, and he was flooding into me.

In that moment, that brief flash of oneness, I finally understood what he had been trying to say about souls, and *krisses* and pianos. I pulled away and glanced up to meet his gaze before releasing him completely. I could see that he had felt it, too.

We both opened our mouths to speak, but couldn't find any words. Finally, Tony said: "Don't hurt my dogs."

I nodded. "It won't happen again."

***

After they left, I pulled out the keyboard, put on the headphones, and played. Whatever had happened between Tony and I had opened up the floodgates, and the music surged through me like a river overrunning its banks. I played easy pieces, mostly Kabalevsky and Khatchaturian and Grieg, losing myself in the simple, upbeat melodies. I made some mistakes because my right hand was slow and uncoordinated but all the basic pieces were in place. I tried not to push things, but the music fed me. And after being starved for so long, it was hard to avoid gluttony.

Sometime in the late afternoon, Tony once again appeared out of nowhere. Because of the headphones, I hadn't heard him come in, but the movement of his approach to the bed caught the corner of my eye. I glanced up, making a little murr of appreciation at the sight of him. He wore a plain tunic and drawstring pants made of thin white linen. I could see his sculpted musculature and black Speedos beneath the sheer fabric.

"Hi." I pushed the headphones off my ears.

He looked at the keyboard and smiled at me, but there was a sadness in the corners of his eyes. "How's it going?"

"Good." I didn't know if it was a lingering effect of our earlier embrace, or the simple pull of lust, but I couldn't stop staring at him. A wavering halo danced on the ceiling behind his head, painted there by the golden hour sunlight reflected from the pool outside. Fine, dark nubs of stubble dusted his jaw, surrounded his lips. The pool water had washed his cologne away and he had a wild, musky scent tempered by the sweetness of civilization. I leaned towards him to savor it, gripped by a sudden desire to kiss him. Among other things.

An echoing lust drove the sadness from his eyes, replacing it with a lively heat. His smile broadened, and he reached a hand out to me. "Not here. Not now."

"Where, then?"

"Come with me."

I stowed the keyboard and headphones. He took my hand and pulled me toward the door, pausing to slip a memory card into the lock. He keyed a sequence into the pad. When the door opened, he tugged me into the hall.

Zef rose from the tiles and danced around us, making enthusiastic little hops. Tony smiled at him, patting him on the head with his free hand. "Good boy, Zef."

The animal fell into step on the opposite side of him, the tikking of his claws a *presstismo* counterpoint to our stately footfalls. We headed down the hall and into the elevator. Tony glanced at me as we lurched downward, a strange, bright intensity to his gaze. "Promise me, you won't reveal this to anybody."

I raised a brow, but nodded. "I promise."

A tiny grin softened his features, and the tension in him faded, swamped by a deepening emotion I couldn't fathom. He squeezed my hand, and I felt the calluses along his thumb and index finger. The same calluses Papa used to get from spending all day at the firing range.

The elevator door opened onto the dojo floor, but instead of turning left we headed down the short, narrow hall to the steel door on the right. Tony used his chip to open this door, Zef surging ahead as we passed into a stairwell.

Tony started down after the dog, each step thunging on the metal stairs as the steel door clanged shut behind us. It spooked me a bit, since it reminded me of lock up.

We stopped at a landing, where Tony opened an access door to a small switch room and backed me inside, until I was pinned against a power meter bolted to the far wall as he and the dog crowded into the tiny room. Tony closed the door.

A thrill surged through me as his bulk pressed against my silk-clad body. His hot breath seared my cheek. I thought he was going to kiss me, but he reached past me to slot the memory card into a tiny gap in the cinderblock just above the power meter.

The wall to my right slid back to reveal a biometric steel door. He pressed his thumb against the glow pad and the latch released. He clutched the handle and pushed the door wide. The lights turned on automatically to reveal a large rectangular room.

Zef bounded ahead, grabbing a toy skunk and leaping onto a dog bed. He bit down on the skunk's tail over and over, making squeaky sounds as Tony took my hand and led me across the threshold. I looked around as he closed the door behind us. I could hear bolts sliding shut around the door's perimeter.

The ceiling was low, made of textured cellulose and painted black. One entire wall was nothing but flat screens. Zef's dog bed was beside a black leather sofa on the far wall, next to a closed door. A kitchenette took up the wall opposite the video display.

I was mesmerized by the images swimming before me. Each of the flat screens displayed different camera views of the estate, as well as night vision views of some underground tunnels. I recognized the pool, the helipad, the range, the courtyard, but there were many structures and buildings I didn't remember seeing. At the bottom of each screen was a five digit code. "What is this place?"

"My bedroom."

"Your bedroom? Where do you sleep?"

He jerked a thumb at the closed door beside the dog bed, then sat in a wheeled swivel chair at the console beneath the flat screens. His fingers flew across the keyboard, and the screens switched to various interior views of the house. He seemed to be cycling through the camera stations, looking for a particular one.

"Where do all those tunnels go?"

"Different parts of the property. I've even got a bolt hole to the yacht."

"That was your yacht we flew over?"

He nodded. "I own the cove. You've got to promise me you won't reveal any of this to anyone."

"You mean nobody knows about this but you?"

"They suspect. But none of them know the exact details of this location, or how to access the tunnels."

"Seriously? You can't be that paranoid."

"Rather be a live paranoid than a dead complacent."

"But how'd you get all this down here? Somebody had to build it all. They must know."

"The original house was built back during the Prohibition era. Used the tunnel to the cove to smuggle booze in from Mexico. Then in the 1980's it was owned by a druglord who expanded the tunnel system and put all the electrics in. Not like anybody pulled permits for any of that."

"But, who takes care of it? You must have somebody. Mando—or Jana—maybe? You couldn't do it alone."

"Mando and Jana are good people. But you can never be a hundred-percent sure of anybody."

"Then why tell me?"

"You're different. With you I can—" He broke off as an image came up of Tony and I, standing in my room. We were engaged in a liplock so steamy, I'm surprised the monitor didn't melt. I stared at us, wondering how the vid could show us doing something we'd never done, in a spot where we weren't anywhere near.

"I had the AI create a virtual image," Tony explained, reading my expression. "But it can only replace fifteen minutes of actual footage before the system resets on another, random frequency."

We watched as the virtual Tony stepped away from me and exited my room, leaving the virtual Faith to huff and storm into the bathroom. The virtual Tony walked through various screens until he disappeared out of view of any of the camera feeds.

I wondered about this, uncomfortable with it. "So, you've been watching me all naked and sleeping and whatever? Without my knowledge or consent? That's not skeevy at all."

"You consented. Didn't you read your contract? The only way to ensure your safety is to keep you under constant supervision."

"You make me sound like a delinquent."

"If the handcuffs fit..."

I scowled and motioned to the fake images of us on the screen. "So that's because you don't want anybody to know I'm sleeping with you?"

"No one's business but ours," he said spinning his chair around to face me. "I mean, if you still want to? Now that you know I'm married."

I thought about this. Concluded that all the feints and smokescreens served some purpose—to protect me, protect him, distract his enemies, something. After seeing my car in his garage, I knew he was, at his core, an ethical man. A noble, tragic fool who had martyred his honor, his very name to the unyielding pursuit of that scumbag Brighton Leigh.

It made him even more sexy to me.

I grinned and straddled his lap, resting my arms on his shoulders as I leaned in to kiss him. Our tongues entwined. A shiver tickled my spine as his hands moved up under my shirt, his callused fingers trailing up my ribs. His touch set my blood tingling and I could feel the heat of him swelling beneath the fabric of our clothes. His teeth caught my bottom lip for a moment as I drew back to push his linen tunic up. Our gazes met, his breath caressing my lips.

"I'm so in love with you, Rad," he murmured. "Been waiting for this for seven years."

Panic stabbed me and I recoiled, stepping off of him. I paced away. Sex was one thing, but this was too deep, too out of control. Like I was drowning.

A low groan escaped him. He searched my face with a bewildered look. "What's wrong?"

"I don't know you," I said lamely, not sure what I was feeling, or why. "I don't know anything about you."

"What do you need to know?"

What didn't I? Where did I start? "Where'd you get all this money? All this tech?"

"Cannabis, mostly."

"You're a drug dealer?" I gaped at him in disgust.

He bristled. "It's legal in Canada. And California. And my investments were in ancillary businesses, anyway. Security and tracking systems, biotech, software solutions, bioactive growing media. Got in on the ground floor. Made a killing."

"How much are you worth now?"

"Personally? On paper? A hundred and two million."

"And in reality?"

"Just shy of a billion."

"And where'd you get the money to invest?"

He sniffed and studied me. He seemed to be thinking, weighing his options. "I'm a bastard," he said quietly, a glimmer of a snarl edging his mouth.

"You stole it?"

"I said I was a bastard, not an asshole."

"What's the difference?"

"You ever hear of Willem DeKuyper?"

"The Dutch billionaire? The one with all the yachts and everything? Owns half the European Union?"

"Yeah. He vacationed in Bali a lot. My mother used to operate an airline there. He, uh, made her pregnant."

"Mama saw dollars signs and slapped him with a paternity suit?"

"No."

"But that's what you're getting at, right? He sent money off to his bastard son."

"Yeah."

"How much?"

"Seventeen million."

"Lotta money," I observed, not really sure if I believed him or not. "He must've liked you a lot."

He bit back a chuckle. "Not hardly."

"Then how'd you get it?"

"Blackmail," he confessed softly.

I couldn't keep the revulsion off my face. "What kind of scum blackmails his own father?"

"A bastard." His lips peeled away from his teeth in an angry grimace. "One whose mother was raped."

It stunned me. The confession was so indifferent, the lack of emotion so practiced, I knew his claim must be true. That was how I always talked about my mother. "I'm sorry," I said.

"Don't be. He's paying for it. For all the shit he put her through."

"What about your shit? What you've been through?"

"That's the least of it." For a moment that black rage flickered in him, but Zef jumped up and buried Tony's face under flurry of tongue swipes. Tony thumped the animal's side, his fury fading. "Who's my good boy?"

A sudden, inexplicable stab of jealousy ran through me at the easy intimacy between them. I knew it was ridiculous, to envy an animal, but it gnawed at me, just the same. It should be me in Tony's lap, not some halitosis-ridden furball.

I sighed and backed away to slump on the couch, defeated. Why did Tony have to go and use the L-word, anyway? Things had been going so well, before that.

He pushed the dog's front paws off his thigh and wiped away a glistening smear of slobber that stretched from his cheek to his earring. "Do you want to go back to your room?"

"No. Do you want me to go?"

"I want you to spend the night with me."

I met his gaze, and that electricity flared up between us, a blue-white arc of lust and longing. "Okay," I said, voice husky.

His breath caught for a moment, and he rose from his chair. I launched myself off the couch and then we were tearing each other's clothes off, burying one another in a flurry of kisses and caresses as the heat between us melted our knees and tangled us together on the floor.

He smelled of desire and immediacy; an honest, animal scent that set my skin ablaze, every nerve, every pore craving his touch. He slipped inside me slowly, every ridge, every ripple of his flesh sending shivers through me. His hands molded my breasts as I moved above him.

He played me even as I played him: layering the meanings, unearthing the fervor in the soft, tender movements of our bodies, like an adagio on a concert grand.

We pushed each other farther, stretching thought, stretching time, discovering the subtle rhythms and harmonies that made up our duet. My spasms triggered his; his, mine; smashing us against the limits of our bodies, reducing us to quivering, exhausted ecstasy.

Even the Bumblebee could never be this good.

***

All that time in the hospital must have played Hell with my endurance, because after that monumental romp with Tony, I passed out naked on the couch. I was awakened by an insistent, electronic tweet.

I rolled to my feet, ready to slam the snooze button for fifteen extra minutes. My hand was in mid-swipe before I realized I'd been kicked out six months ago and I didn't have a clock anymore, let alone a dorm room to be late to school from.

"Whoa!" Tony raised his palm in a stand down gesture. He'd put his pants back on, but left his shirt off. It was an excellent view to wake up to. "It's my phone." He pointed at the smartphone beeping on the console. "Just the phone."

I looked at the monitors to see that the only outside light coming into the house was from the telescoping floods around the pool. "What time is it?"

"After midnight."

"Why didn't you wake me up?"

He grinned, a little sheepish as he reached for the phone. "I like having you near. Hearing you breathe." He shrugged, not able to articulate further. "I like having you with me."

It embarrassed me, yet at the same time it sent a warm thrill through me. I wasn't used to people liking me do anything but drive a race car or play the piano. It felt good.

He thumbed the phone's touchscreen and held it up to his ear. "Tovenaar," he said, with quiet authority. He listened, his mouth pinching into a grim line. "Shit." He listened some more, then sighed and rubbed his forehead. "It has to be done tonight?"

The answer was long, and from the expression on his face, not one Tony cared much for. "Shit. All right. I'll be there. I'll take the helicopter." He disconnected, scowling, and moved across the room to open the door beside the couch. He left the door open, so I caught a glimpse into the room beyond.

In the center of the room was a bed with a headboard made from what looked like clear Plexiglas. The cream colored bed sheets were rumpled, and the bed itself was encircled by small satellites of dirty clothes. Along the far wall were a chair, an armoire, a bookcase, and two doors, both open. One led to a bathroom, which Tony disappeared into, and the other led to a walk-in closet. A woven jute fiber mat covered the floor. The air wafting in from the bedroom had the heavy, bittersweet tang of burned incense.

"Bad news?" I asked, taking his cue and reaching for my own clothes, only to find myself face to face with the dog. Black, glistening, beasty eyes studied me, ears erect, nose twitching.

Zef placed his head on my lap, the little whisker tufts on his eyebrows darting up and down as visions of Rad-burgers danced in his head.

"Tony?" I called out, hating the tremolo of panic in my voice. "Tony?!"

He sauntered back into the room, wearing only a towel around his waist. "What's wrong?"

I jerked my chin at the dog. "He's looking at me."

"So?"

"What does he want?"

Tony's gaze crawled from the dog to me, and a look of sincere puzzlement washed over him. "He likes you."

"Likes me? Like how does he like me? Is it a 'munch on my desiccated carcass' kind of like, or what?"

Tony stared at me some more, puzzlement developing into full-blown pity. "You don't know much about dogs, do you?"

The way he said it made me feel utterly lacking, as if he'd accused me of still being a virgin. "My mother didn't like them," I countered, more defensive than I wanted to be.

His jaw tightened, brow falling in heated disdain. "Your mother didn't deserve them."

"What do you mean by that?"

"Dogs are—" He broke off, searching for the words. There was suddenly an energy to him, a vitality shining through the taut fibers of his muscles, the golden tan of his skin. "They're like little kids. They don't care where you live, or how much money you have, or who your father is. They love you anyway. They'll fight for you. Die for you. Because they know what's really important is in here." He touched his chest. "And if you screw up, no matter how bad, they forget about it the next day, and go on loving you."

As he spoke our gazes locked, and I had the strangest feeling that the subject wasn't how he felt about dogs, but how he felt about me. How he wanted me to feel about him.

My mouth opened, but I couldn't think of anything to say.

He chuckled and moved around to squat in front of me. His broad hand rested on top of Zef's head, palm sliding across the glossy black face in a slow, sensuous caress. The animal made a contented snuffle and leaned more heavily against me. Funny how Zef's eyes narrowed into slits each time Tony scratched behind his ears. I felt the rhythm in my thigh, the steady, even pulsing as Tony petted the animal, and wondered why this all seemed so right, like the notes in a flawless concerto, the subtle magnificence of an orchestra in full crescendo.

It was only a dog, for God's sake.

And Tony, with his naked, washboard belly pressed against my knees. I studied the quiet power in his pectorals, the perfect interplay of his sinews with each movement of his arm.

"You want to try?" he asked.

There was just enough challenge in his voice to spur me into action. My hand moved out tentatively, found the bony ridge at the top of the Zef's head. I smoothed the black triangle ears back, amazed at how soft they were, such a contrast to the rougher tawny fur across his neck and shoulders. I did it again, bolder this time, and a nervous chuckle cut loose from wherever it was I'd been holding my breath. "He didn't bite me."

"No," Tony agreed. He stroked his fingers along my knuckles like a man soothing a wild bird. "He won't."

"I—" I wasn't sure what I wanted to say. Everything was tumbling around inside me: happy and sad and astonished and at peace all at once. "I'm not very good at this."

He smiled, a subtle, secret little smile that said he understood. "You don't have to be." He lifted my hand and kissed the back of my fingertips. "You just have to accept it."

"Okay." I nodded, trusting him.

He smiled and kissed my hand again, but then his expression grew serious. "I hate to do this to you, but I have to leave. Ruiz needs me up in Pebble Beach by oh-nine-hundred."

"Who's Ruiz?"

"My divorce lawyer. I have to go. Ilsa's finally willing to discuss visitation. I haven't seen my two little girls for almost three years."

"If it's been that long, how come you're not divorced by now?"

"I want visitation. She wants half of everything."

"Why don't you give it to her? Community property, right?"

"A deal is a deal. She signed a prenup. She's due half of what I owned when I married her. But she knows I've made more, a lot more, since then. So, she's holding my kids hostage for it."

"That's pretty shitty."

He nodded. "Her lawyers have never been able to figure out where the bulk of my money was."

"And now they have?"

"They think they have." He gave me a mischievous grin. He stepped over and sat at the console, tapping away at the keyboard. A panel slid back, revealing a cubby hole with a strange, blocky looking terminal, complete with full palmar biometric glow pad. Tony inserted another chip in the terminal's slot and resumed typing into the keyboard. "Put your right hand on it," Tony instructed me, motioning toward the glow pad. "Keep it still."

I complied, holding it there for almost a minute, until a beep sounded, and Tony keyed in another barrage of information. "Now your left hand."

I followed his instructions, wondering what this was all about. He couldn't actually be hooked into the Federal database, could he? No way a civilian like Tony could gain access to one of the most well-protected, hack-proof systems in the free world. Maybe he was just sending my prints to the marshals, so that they could process me through.

"Okay," he said.

I removed my hand. The progress bar twirled across the screen, and then the terminal beeped. It spit out a U.S. Passport card with Faith Hopkins' name and image. Tony handed it to me.

I looked it over, impressed. "This is a really good forgery."

"It's not a forgery."

I gave him a dubious look. "But these come from the State Department."

He shrugged, toggling a switch that closed the panel over the cubby. "Get dressed." He rose and went back into the other room, Zef padding along beside him. This time, he closed the door.

I pulled my clothes on, then sat on the couch and examined the card in my hand. The little holographic seal glinted in the light of the monitors as I turned it over and over. If it was real, then Tony must have passed my prints, somehow.

I was now officially Faith.

He re-emerged from the bedroom wearing a charcoal gray suit with a cobalt blue tie that made his eyes seem incredibly blue. He wore sapphire cufflinks to match the sapphire stud in his ear. His black mane had been tamed into a samurai bun. He held the *kris* in one hand, and a small, gray metallic rectangle in the other. He held the rectangle out to me.

I took it, surprised by the weight. It was the size of a credit card, but far too heavy. Must have been at least an ounce. The surface was cool, like actual metal. I held it up to the light and saw the security chip embedded next to the credit card numbers engraved in it.

Stupefied, I just stared at it for a moment before turning it over to find the Visa holograph next to a statement informing me: 'Your card is made of palladium.' Engraved beneath that was the left-handed Faith signature I'd used to sign the hospital discharge papers.

No way. An actual, honest to God, in the flesh palladium card. The kind gamblers dream of and movie stars use to buy entire islands.

"How did you get this?" I asked Tony. "These are invitation, only. You have to have like, twenty million dollars in a private investment account with them before they'll even consider you."

"Oh, Faith's got a lot more than that." He smirked at me. "She's got everything Ilsa's lawyers have been looking for."

My jaw dropped. My heart caught in my throat. "How much?"

"Eight hundred ninety-three million, five hundred seventy-one thousand, two hundred and six dollars. And forty-two cents."

I just stared at him, mind boggled. It was a fake. A mock-up. Had to be. Nobody would trust me with that kind of green. Bet the first time I tried to buy anything the card would freeze out.

He studied my reaction, bemused. "Scotty gets his hands on that, he'll know you've got a tap into my assets. He's going to try to make you bleed me. Are you okay with that?"

"I'd rather have the *kris*," I said, balking at the idea of carrying either.

"All right." He smiled and held it out to me, pommel first. I took it, still too stunned to do otherwise.

"Come on," he headed for the door. "Let's get you back to your room."

"You hand me a knife and then turn your back on me after giving me so much money? What happened to being paranoid?"

"You're different," he said pulling me against him as we crowded into the small switch room, leaving Zef behind with his toy skunk. He kissed me, smiling down to meet my gaze. "You're Rad."

I smiled at his use of my real name. I couldn't help it.

He was about to close the door when Zef ran out and wriggled between us, his tail sweeping from side to side so enthusiastically, it whumped against the walls.

"Nay, Zef," Tony pointed him back into the room and said something that sounded like: "Slap kah-mer. New."

Zef rolled his eyes, like a kid whose candy has just been taken away, then skulked back towards his dog bed. Tony closed the biometric door, then pulled me forward as the false wall slid shut.

We headed back up the stairs to the hallway leading to the dojo. Tony kissed me and motioned me towards the elevator. "I'll be back as soon as I can. Go on up. I'll send some food up, if you're hungry?"

"Is it vegetables?"

"What?"

"Never mind." I kissed him. "I'm not hungry. I just want to go back to sleep."

"Go on, then."

"How am I going to get in without you?"

"You're in the database, now. You can go anywhere in the house that will open to your print. Dojo, pool, game room, sauna, wherever you want."

"So, I've been promoted."

"Yeah." He stared at me, eyes smiling. "Big time."

CHAPTER NINETEEN

When I got back to my room, I stashed the *kris* between the mattress and headboard, put the passport and credit cards in Faith's purse, then stripped down, donned the splint, and crawled into bed.

About an hour later, I was awakened by the sound of a helicopter flying low over the house. The heavy thok-thoking rattled the mirror in its white lacquer frame. I listened to it fade into the distance, already missing the warmth of Tony's body.

How quickly we become spoiled.

In the morning, after I'd done my exercises, showered, and dressed, I went to the dining room for breakfast. Or tried to. Halfway down the stairs, I stopped short. The dog was back.

Zef sat on his haunches on the bottom landing, toy skunk between his lips. The fur of the skunk was matted with slobber. I waffled, then continued. I was not going to let him get between me and a buttered scone, no matter how sharp his teeth were.

As my foot touched the landing, Zef dropped the skunk, then stood and backed away from me, sitting a few feet down the hall. I eyed the dog for a long moment, not wanting to turn my back on him. He lunged forward, snatched the skunk, and shook it just out of reach, taunting me with it. When I didn't respond, he trotted triumphantly down the hall, pausing about three yards away to look back at me.

I followed, figuring it was better to have the damn thing in front than behind. He paused at the foyer and stood stone-still, except for his ears. They cocked front, then back, the dog listening intently.

I took advantage of Zef's distraction to slip down the other hall and into the dining room. A place had been set, a tall glass of orange juice sweating beside the silverware. I sat down and took a swig. Zef reappeared, remaining at the doorway. He eyed me all through the meal, breaking off only to look at the old woman when she came in with a tray of food or coffee. Thinking he might be hungry, I threw a bran muffin at him. He caught it, then spit it out and sniffed it suspiciously. He threw a stare at me like I'd just tried to poison him.

Malincollies were smarter than I thought.

Just as I was finishing up the meal, Zef spun around with a loud bark and disappeared down the hall. A few moments later Mando appeared, dressed like a gangster, his canine admirer bouncing circles around him. He gave the dog a few hearty pats, then regarded me, smiling. "Look at you, sitting at the adult table."

I offered him a croissant. "You want some breakfast?"

He shook his head. "Already ate. Stopped for some steak and eggs on the drive up." He glanced around. "Where's Tony?"

"Gone," I said, a little curt because I was jealous about missing out on red meat.

"Gone?" His eyes bugged out. "Where?"

"Pebble Beach. To deal with his wife."

"Shit." He pulled a chair out, sat slowly in it, rubbing his forehead. "Shit. I hope he listens to Ruiz this time. She's never gonna come back to him, no matter how—" he broke off and grinned at me incredulously. "He told you about Ilsa?"

I nodded. "And Ruiz."

"How'd you take it?"

"I took it."

Mando sighed. "This is the worst timing. We've waited years for conditions like this. Last thing we need is for Tony to be distracted by that vindictive harpy. He'll get us all killed."

Jana sauntered in, wearing a silk kimono and house slippers. She tossed me a haughty stare, then regarded Mando. "Why did you bring her down here to eat?"

"I didn't. She was here when I got here."

Jana stared at me, then looked at Mando, then at me.

"Tony gave me the run of the house," I explained.

"What are you doing here?" she asked Mando.

"Wanted to talk to Tony. Try to convince him to abort."

"He's gone. He took Kam and Glen with him. But we're still moving forward. You need to take her to Gower's studio today. Check into the Bonaventure. You're going to stay in L.A. for a few days, until the Truby's party. Tony will meet you when his business up north is finished."

They locked gazes until he looked away, suddenly tense. He opened his mouth, then paused. His eyes flickered over me, and then darted back to Jana. "What am I supposed to do? Handle this without him?"

"Yes. That's what you're paid for."

"You're sure he wants it this way?"

"We talked about it last night."

"You talked about it, you mean. And he was probably so stressed out, he agreed with you."

She settled in a chair like a cat gloating over a caught bird. "Probably."

"You're a bitch, Jana."

She lifted one shoulder, face demure and businesslike, brows arched with some inner glee. "That's what I'm paid for. Now, take her upstairs and get her ready," She told Mando.

"Ready for what?" I asked.

Mando sighed and poured himself a cup of coffee. "Scotty rejected Tony's offer. You're the only one he'll deal with. Which means another meeting with Seward and Cortelaine."

"But first, she meets with Gower Dillington. Make sure she brings the credit card," Jana told Mando.

"You can talk to me. I'm right here, you know," I told her crossly.

"Tony gave you a credit card?" Mando asked me, brows raising.

"A palladium card," Jana confirmed.

"What good is that going to do?" I asked Jana. "I'm buying a recording studio, not a jet ski."

She sighed, like I was one of the denser people she'd dealt with lately. "Faith steals money from people. If you'd do your homework, you'd know that."

"I do. I mean, I do know that. But who buys a business with a credit card?"

"The card is linked to Faith's private bank account. You'll use it to verify the funds in that account. Once they see the balance, they'll know Faith is hiding Tony's assets for him."

"Only," I said, catching on, "Faith wouldn't follow through. She'd find a way to take off with all of it."

"Precisely." Jana nodded. "You're going to offer Gower ten percent to wash the funds through his production company. He'll turn you down, most likely, but Scotty's got that studio bugged. He'll know Faith is hooked into Tony's finances."

"How is this supposed to get us close to Brighton Leigh?"

"For that kind of green, he'll come out of the woodwork," Mando sighed. "A prize like that will be too enticing for him to pass up."

I shook my head. "It won't work."

They both shot doubtful, slightly annoyed looks at me. "Why do you say that?" Mando asked.

"Because Brighton Leigh's catering to the rich and powerful perverts of the world. Which means he's probably blackmailing half of them. Which means whatever Tony's got is chump change, compared to Brighton staying safe in hiding."

They both stared at me, their lips pursed, brows furrowed. I thought I detected a little flicker of admiration in Mando's face, but Jana's expression turned sour. "Tony has a lot of money."

"He does. But people don't do things for money. They think they do, but they're confusing money with what it can do for them. A guy like Leigh would know that. He'd know that Tony's money won't get him what he wants."

"You're an expert on Brighton Leigh, now?" Jana asked derisively.

"I'm a military brat. I'm an expert on petty, power-hungry sadists who like to throw their weight around. Like you. And Brighton Leigh."

Jana's eyes flashed with anger. She was about to unload on me, but Mando held up a hand to her, and leaned towards me, interested. "What do you think he wants?"

"To be free."

"He's already free. He escaped custody." Jana left the 'you idiot' off, but you could hear it in her tone.

"He's a fugitive. He can't operate in the open. He has to go through people like Scotty. I don't know about you, but every sadistic asshole I've ever known was also a control freak. So, this proxy stuff has got to be killing him. You need to offer him a way to retake control of his life. That's what will flush him out."

Mando studied me with a thoughtful expression, as if he was considering my words.

Jana rolled her eyes, waving me off in a dismissive gesture. "What he wants is to hurt Tony for capturing him. Especially when Faith comes along as a bonus prize."

"For him to torture me, you mean?"

"He'll try," Mando nodded. "But I'll protect you."

"I know you're a badass, but you're just one guy. What if—"

"You're safe," Jana assured me. "Stop thinking you're smarter than all of us. We know what we're doing. The only way they can use you is alive and well and stealing Tony blind."

I thought about this. A tight, burning sensation fizzled slowly down my throat and settled in my gut. "But if you're wrong, and Brighton's more interested in hurting me than he is in the money?"

Jana gave me a saccharine, superior smile. "That's what you're paid for."

***

Since we were going to spend the night in L.A. after the party, Mando insisted I pack two suitcases of Faith crap. She was, apparently, a bit of a clothes horse, and liked to keep her options open. I made sure I left all the purple outfits in the closet and packed the items Mando had chosen in matching designer bags. Mando, coffee mug in hand, stood near the dresser and studied the passport and palladium cards. "He really did it, huh?"

"Passed the prints? I guess so."

"I wonder who he went through?"

I shrugged and lifted the *kris* up from where I'd stashed it. "Should I bring this?"

His brows arched in amazement. "Where did you get that?"

"Tony gave it to me."

"Tony?" Surprise raised his voice an octave. "Gave you his *kris*? When?"

"Last night."

"Oh, God," he laughed so hard he had to sit down. It was nervous at first, but then more relaxed, more bold, as if an outrageous joke had just been played. "Oh, my God." He could barely keep from spilling coffee all over himself.

I glared at him. "What's so funny?"

"Nothing." He shook his head, wiped his eyes, mumbling, "Jana's going to be so pissed."

"Why?"

"You know what that is? You know what a *kris* is?"

I shrugged defensively. "Sort of."

"It's Tony's spiritual proxy."

"His what?"

"Proxy. Where Tony comes from, if a guy can't make it to his wedding, his *kris* stands in his place. It's just as binding."

I held the dagger up, incredulous. "What, like an engagement ring?"

"Yeah," he chuckled again. His dark eyes shone with disbelieving mirth. "The crazy son-of-a-bitch is really in love."

***

The limo whump-whumped across the cobbled courtyard and onto a gravel road that tunneled through a grove of eucalyptus. Sleek, tawny dog shapes skirted the underbrush, running parallel to the road. About five minutes into the green maze, a huge wrought iron gate appeared through the trees, flanked on either side by a twelve foot adobe wall. Razor wire topped both wall and gate like a crown of thorns. Two uniformed, Javanese guards carrying semi-automatic rifles manned the gate. Another guard supervised from a reinforced gatehouse. He waved to Percy, and triggered whatever mechanism was necessary to open the gate.

Once we reached the highway, I opened my cosmetic case and started to apply my make-up. I had tucked the *kris* inside, not wanting to leave it behind after what Mando had told me about it.

Mando watched me for a moment, then tipped the refrigerator door open. He sloshed some orange juice into a glass tumbler, following it up with a shot of vodka. "Screwdriver okay?"

"I, uh—" I broke off, realizing that teetotaling wasn't in the contract. I'd have to drink something. Might as well be vodka. "Just a sec. Let me finish up." I checked my lipstick, my eyeshadow, and then fluffed my hair up.

Mando chunked some ice into the glass, then held the drink out, waiting expectantly for me. When I couldn't postpone the inevitable any longer, I grabbed the vile swill, knocking it back all at once so I wouldn't sour my mouth with the taste.

His eyebrows arched as I handed tumbler back to him. He stared at me for a moment, then set the empty glass down on the bar and pressed the button to raise the thick Plex divider between us and Percy, regarding me intently.

A little unsettled by his odd behavior, I scratched my nose with the splint.

He pressed another button, and a driving, synthesized techno beat boomed from the six speakers, loud enough to blast the bark off a tree. Some breathy female voice started rapping off a string of F-word laced obscenities interspersed with Afrikaans. I winced, physically pained at the noises assaulting me. A similarly accented male voice broke in on the chorus, singing "Baby's on Fire!" along with a string of words that sounded as dirty as what the woman was singing.

"Die Antwoord," Mando grinned and poured me another drink. "Tony's favorite band."

Oh, Hell. I was shagging a philistine.

He chuckled at my consternation, leaning forward to place the re-filled glass in my hand. His voice was low, barely audible over the madness that passed for music: "Still want to stick around?"

I nodded slowly, feeling guilty, for some reason.

Mando's face hardened. That fierce light burned in his black eyes. He pulled a cigar from his pocket and lit it up, taking a few long puffs before asking: "Do you know what'll happen?"

I shrugged. "Scotty is supposed to snatch me, and then you and Tony will follow my implant to Brighton Leigh."

"What's to keep him from killing you along the way?"

"Brighton wants revenge. Kinda hard to torture a corpse."

"I have some D.E.A. friends in Nevada who can hide you out for a while." He reached under his jacket, produced an airplane ticket, and offered it to me. "The flight leaves from Burbank at seven-thirty. You can be in a safe house in Vegas before Tony even knows you're missing. And then he'll have no choice but to abort."

"If I make him abort, he'll come after me. Especially if I take off with this palladium card."

"So leave the card with me. You're an amateur. A wildcard. Nobody expects you to put your life on the line for the organization."

"Tony does. And he'll probably go after you, for letting me disappear. If he can't get Brighton, he's got to get some one. He's that kind of guy."

"He goes through with this, he'll get us all killed, anyway. Either that or arrested. You're no fool. You're a survivor. Take this and get the Hell out of Dodge." He forced the ticket into my hand. "Let me deal with the fallout. I think I can make him see reason."

As I sat staring at him, trying to decide what to do, the limo turned left, heading south along Pacific Coast Highway, thrusting me into a quadrangle of sunlight. My purse was partly open, and the little holograms embossed in the surface of the Passport card caught the light, spraying shards of rainbow across Mando's face, accenting the icy flatness in his gaze.

A sudden dread chilled me, all the hair bristling along my spine. This was no request. It was a demand. And Heaven help me if I didn't follow through. I looked away, biting down hard on the expletives souring my mouth, infuriated that he'd threaten me. For some reason, I thought he'd be above all that.

"No," I told him, handing the ticket back. "I'm playing Faith."

He drew deeply on his cigar and exhaled a jet of smoke against the window glass, where it roiled around in a gray soup before drifting up to hang in a pall from the headliner. "You're in love," he murmured. "He's got you head over heels."

"No. It's just—" I shook my head. How did I explain what I didn't understand myself? "A deal is a deal," I finished lamely. "I made a promise. I have to stick by it."

"Even if that promise might get you killed?"

"So?" I shrugged, feeling more defensive than I wanted to. "If I have to die to get rid of a rat-sack like Brighton Leigh, I'll do it. I'm not running away from this."

"Never pegged you as a martyr."

"Never pegged you as a backstabbing coward."

His cheeks tightened, anger rippling off him like heat from a coal. "Take the flight. Scotty's a cruel son-of-a-bitch. You could be maimed. You could be raped. We might not be able to get there in time to stop it."

"I'm the only one who can do this. I won't let Tony down."

He sighed, and looked down at the ashen ember that tipped his cigar. "All right, then. This is what you need to know when you meet with Gower..."

***

Gower's recording studio was in a seedy section of Hollywood, on a small side street between Sunset and Hollywood boulevards. It was a squat, industrial building with a small parking lot lined by a high chain link fence topped with razor wire. From the outside it looked more like an auto body shop than one of the top recording studios in the city.

I'd been here once before, the week before Christmas when Jim and I had come to cut a demo. Ardis, Jim's mother, had arranged it, and gotten us some free, off-hour studio time through some friend she had remained very close-lipped about. For Ardis, that usually meant a serious romantic involvement. I hoped to be that sexually active when I was her age.

I removed my splint and left it up front with Percy, while Mando escorted me inside. The lobby was just as I remembered it: understated, maroon-colored decor punctuated with potted plants. The lighting was subdued, recessed. The air-conditioning gave the atmosphere a scrubbed, ionized flavor. After suffering three hours of musical assault and battery during the drive down here, the quiet was a blessed relief.

A happily smiling receptionist greeted us, then pointed us down a hallway that led away from the studios. "Mr. Dillington is expecting you. His office is at the end of the hall."

Gower's office was a windowless, pine-paneled football field, with a pair of large, opposing roughcut couches arguing over a woodslab coffee table on the fifty-yard line. There was a matching desk off to one side, and a rustic-looking bar with bark-legged stools beyond that. It was the kind of furniture that must've cost forty grand but looked as if some ranchero with a chainsaw and a mallet made it in his spare time.

Gower, shirtless, was seated cross-legged on a woven reed mat in an alcove across from the bar. His fit torso looked like it had been carved from black walnut wood and burnished to perfection. He was still handsome, even though he looked older than in his movies. Curly grey hairs adorned the taut curves of his chest, like silver trim on a sports car. A hidden, high fidelity sound system played a lone flute's lilting melody. Not an artist I recognized, but the music was arresting nonetheless.

He didn't move a muscle at our approach, following us only with the hazeled wisdom of his eyes. He seemed amused at our presence, at our very existence, a much different person than the tense, troubled man he usually played in the movies. I wondered if this was an act, or the real person.

Mando, playing the paranoid bodyguard, circled the room a few times, examining the layout, fingering a few objects which seemed to attract his attention. When finished, he looked inquiringly at me. I waved him toward the door. "Go ahead and wait outside, hon. We need some privacy."

Mando nodded and stepped out, closing the door.

The music stopped and Gower unfurled himself from the floor, his lithe body seemingly unaffected by his age. He threw a blue cotton sweatshirt on and regarded me. "'Ere without Tony, I see. I'm surprised, I am."

I paused for a moment to adjust to the sheer, rolling sexy of his native Welsh accent. His voice had such depth, such range, and the singsong pattern was so different from the clipped American way he spoke in his films. To cover, I sighed melodramatically and said:

"Don't see why. I'm not known for my lifelong devotion."

He chuckled and moved toward the bar. "That's not exactly what I was referrin' to. What I meant was: I'm surprised to see you so unattended. Especially 'ere in L.A. After what I 'ear 'appened between you and Scotty..." He raised a single brow at me.

I nodded. "A man can't keep secrets from a girl like me."

One corner of his mouth hooked up. He shook his head. "You 'aven't changed a bit." He set two snifters up on the bar and reached into the refrigerator. "'Ow are things with you?"

I shrugged. "Can't complain—although with that detective pesterin' Tony, I'm not so sure. Prison just sends everythin' cattywumpus. A girl needs a man she can depend on. I don't have the patience to wait, if you know what I mean?"

Gower nodded slowly. He tipped the glasses half-full of bottled water and held one out to me. "You look thirsty."

"Not for Perrier. Have any tequila?"

"No." He sipped his own, staring at me over the rim of the glass. "You are wantin' somethin', Faith. What is it?"

"You seriously aimin' to become governor?"

He didn't answer, but his weight shifted subtly, as if I'd sparked his interest.

"Don't be coy, now. I know that's why you decided to divest from Scotty's partnership. You don't want to be dragged through the mud come election time." I smiled. "That's only two years from now, and you're not only a foreigner, you're—"

"I've got dual citizenship. I'm as American as you."

"Of course you are" I smiled and nodded. "But, I imagine you'll need a hefty campaign fund. I'd like to help y'out with that."

"And what do you want from me?"

"I'd like to make a contribution, is all. Just a little helpin' hand. In return for your expertise with a difficult financial situation I'm in right now."

Thoughts, assessments churned in those hazel eyes. He tipped his chin at me, a signal for me to continue.

I hesitated decorously, then gave a little cough. "Well, I'd like to invest in a film being made in Europe right now, but the EEC is so stringent with their banking policies—not to mention the computer tracking the Federal Government is doing with international transfers nowadays. I was wondering if I mightn't invest through your production company—with your firm receiving distribution rights in the U.S., of course. You—"

"Whose money, Faith?"

"Why, mine, of course. It's in my name."

He snickered, like he didn't believe me. "And 'ow much of a 'contribution' did you plan on makin' to my oopcomin' campaign?"

"Oh," I rolled my eyes. "About seven-point-five million."

His brows raised. "Expensive favor."

"Well, you know how time sensitive investments can be. The potential profits from getting in on the ground floor are—"

"Campaign contributions by individuals are limited to twenty-five-hundred by law." He glared pointedly at me.

Uh-oh. Forgot all about that. Why didn't Mando warn me? "Ain't nothin' stoppin' me from makin' some generous donations to a GoFundMe account. Or maybe, bein' from Wales and all, you have an account in Guernsey or Ireland I can wire into?"

"I pay my taxes, I do. All of them. Maybe if people like you and Scotty did the same, this country wouldn't be in the mess we're in."

Sheesh, he was a tough sell, not the rapacious power-hungry politician I'd expected. "Well, that's why I decided to ask you for help. Everybody knows you're a hardworkin', honorable man. You deserve a nest egg for your production company. Put it toward—"

"Faith," he said, sounding irritated. "You're tryin' to bribe me to get this stolen money out of the country."

"I wouldn't call it that, exactly. It's a—"

"A bribe, it is. A payoff." He sniffed with a little grimace, like I'd just passed gas but he was too polite to mention it. I knew by his expression I'd lost him. Probably never had him, but for some strange reason this relieved me. Refreshing to meet a straightforward good guy in this maze of deception.

"I could squeeze eight million out for you," I wheedled, wanting to make things look authentic.

His only response was a dubious frown.

"All right," I conceded, "nine. And I'll have it to you by the end of the week."

Something about my desperation sparked an idea in him. He drummed his fingers on the bar. "This isn't—you're not screwin' Tony out of 'is money, are you? You can't be that stupid, not with Scotty already after you."

"All right, ten. But that's as high as I go."

A guttural sound of disbelief shook him. "Crikey. You won't live to spend it. The only thing keepin' you alive is Tovenaar. Without 'im, you're sharkbait."

"Do you want the ten million or not? You can funnel it into your campaign through a dummy PAC fund. And you keep the interest my money makes while in your accounts. You're bein' a fool to pass this up. Think of all the good you can do once you're elected..."

He stared at the clear liquid in his glass, twirling the stem between his fingers. "How much do you need to 'invest'?"

He was reconsidering. Figures. Nobody could stand being a hero nowadays. I smiled falsely, a smokescreen for the disappointment stabbing at me. "A hundred. Minus the contribution, of course."

"Of course." He drained his glass, planted it on the bar. Tension crept in along his shoulders, showed in tight bunches at his jaws. He picked up the half-full snifter, the one he had poured for me, and drew an idle design in the sweat on the side of the glass. It was a dollar sign.

"What do you say? Are we partners?" I held my hand out.

He regarded me, then thumbed an 'x' through the design on his glass and held it up. "No. You know where the door is."

It was all I could do not to tell him he had my vote.

***

After we left the studio, Percy guided the limo through a maze of back streets. The way he flung the car around made me pine for something more sedate, like a Demolition Derby.

Mando put Die Antwoord back on, and poured me another drink.

I took it, ignoring the way we shot through a yellowing intersection. "Gower turned me down."

"That was expected," Mando nodded. "He's as honest as they come."

"How long before Scotty comes after me, do you think?"

He pursed his lips, then shrugged. "He won't move until he's got verification that you've got Tony's money. So not until after—

" He broke off, grimacing at something he saw through he back window. "Shit! It's Hollis."

I followed his gaze. A familiar tan sedan with a flashing dash cherry sat on our back bumper. Its siren gave an abbreviated bleat, the policeman's equivalent of a throat clearing.

"Want I should lose him?" Percy said over the intercom.

"No," Mando said after thumbing the mic. "He'll just call a bird in. Go ahead and pull over, but keep your hands free."

The limo glided to the curb, the sedan stopping precisely one car-length behind it. Detective Hollis unpacked his big, beefy frame from behind the wheel. He tucked his shirt in and straightened his tie before sauntering over and knocking on the tinted Plex of the window. "C'mon out, Tovenaar," he said pleasantly.

Mando looked at me. "You're going to have to talk to him. As Faith. Don't volunteer anything. About anything."

"No problem," I assured him, my success with Gower having gone to my head.

Hollis knocked again. "Open up, you oily bastard. I want to talk to you."

"He's sharp," Mando warned. "Be careful." I nodded as Mando opened the door. "Good afternoon," he said to Hollis, and stepped out onto the curb. He stood there, glancing around with a preoccupied concentration that put me on edge.

"Yeah." Hollis ducked his head into the limo, frowning when he saw I was the only other occupant. "Where's Tovenaar?"

I shrugged. "He stayed home. Can you imagine? He didn't want to go shoppin'."

Hollis seemed to really notice me for the first time. His eyes canvassed my face, then my body. A single brow lifted when he saw my right hand. I was suddenly glad I'd left the splint with Percy. "Is there a problem, officer?" I gave him my best charming Faith smile, batting my eyes for good measure.

A subtle shifting of thoughts accompanied the hardening of his jaw. "I'm Detective Hollis, LAPD. Who're you?"

"Faith Hopkins. Of the Texas Hopkinses. You've heard of us? My daddy owns half of Austin, along with—"

"Great." He was unimpressed. "Lemme see some I.D."

"Certainly." I fumbled around in the purse and handed over the passport card.

"Wait here." Hollis tromped back towards his car, leaving the limo door open so that the hot August sun made me bake. Mando glanced at me, lips tight, then continued to glance around like a soldier expecting an ambush.

Hollis fiddled around with the computer in his car, then returned to hand me the passport card back. He had a tablet with him, this time, and held it out to me. "If you don't mind, I'd like your fingerprints, to verify your ID?"

"What for? I wasn't even drivin'."

"To be sure you don't have any outstanding warrants."

"I know my rights. Y'all had to have probable cause to run a print search."

"Your limo was exceeding the speed limit and committing numerous moving violations. I'd say that's plenty of cause."

"But I wasn't drivin'," I repeated, like he was an idiot.

"Since you're in a vehicle registered to a suspect in several homicide investigations, I can run a routine check on the occupants of said vehicle." He held the tablet under my nose.

I huffed and crossed my arms, because that's what Faith would have done. "This ain't right," I complained to Mando.

"Just do it, Faith. It won't bite." Mando actually seemed curious as to whether or not it would really work.

I rolled my eyes and placed my right hand on the screen and waited. A few seconds later, the green dot winked and "Hopkins, Faith" lit up the screen.

I coughed to cover my shock. Tony had really done it. Was there anything that man couldn't fix?

Hollis seemed disappointed with the readout that followed. He scraped his massive paw along one florid jowl, deep in thought. Eventually, he looked up at me, scowling.

"What're you doing with him?" He jerked a thumb at Mando, as if anybody who worked for Tony was a lower life form.

"Why, he's my bodyguard. Goober and I have been—"

"Goober?" Hollis interrupted.

"That's a nickname," I explained. "Tony's so sweet and all I just had to name him after my favorite candy. We were made for each other. Like movies and pop—"

"You're Tovenaar's girlfriend?"

"Fiance'," I corrected. "Don't you be surprised to hear weddin' bells, soon."

"Miss Hopkins, if you don't mind, I'd like a word with you. Alone. It's about a murder investigation..."

"Murder? What murder?" I poured a drink and offered it to him, like I couldn't wait to hear the latest gossip.

He looked at the glass, as if tempted, but waved it off. "Take your pick. There have been at least four in the past two months that can be tied to Tovenaar."

I took a gulp from the glass he snubbed. "I'm afraid I don't know a whitlin' about Tony's business practices."

"Well, every little bit helps." Hollis sat down and started to pull the door shut.

"Ah-ah-ah," Mando caught the door, held it open. "Can't do that. Don't want you drilling holes in the woman I'm being paid to protect."

Hollis glared at the smaller man, looking genuinely offended. "I'm a cop. I don't murder people."

"No offense, Detective, but if I trusted in the incorruptibility of law enforcement, I'd be dead by now. Numerous times. Just let me sit in, I won't say a word."

"You sit anywhere, it'll be on a booking bench. You let me talk to her, alone, or I'll pull the lot of you in."

"On what charge?"

Hollis' yellow teeth resembled a row of tombstones under the shadow of his red cauliflower nose. "You think I need one?"

Grumbling, Mando released the door. Hollis slammed it with a smug, victorious look. Mando stood beside the car, watching us through the bulletproofed glass.

Hollis fiddled around with something in his pocket. A muted beeping sounded, repeating every ten seconds. "If you don't mind, I'll be recording this conversation."

"I do mind. I want my lawyer."

He held his hand up. "Before you start screaming for counsel, let me share a little background information about your new boyfriend. First off, he's a crook. But you knew that already, didn't you, sweetheart? The big, dark criminal types are your forte'. Or do I have you confused with another Faith Hopkins? One who skipped off with forty mil of somebody's dirty money, and set her dear friend Omar up to take the fall? Now Omar's on a coroner's slab with every bone in his body in five or six pieces and no *cajones*. With people who'll do that after you, it's no wonder you fell in with Tovenaar. He's probably the only guy in town who can keep your hide intact. That's the good news."

He fished a cigar out of his breast pocket, bit the tip off, and spat the nub onto the carpet between us. "Now, the bad news is, Tovenaar's not going to be around much longer. I know, because for the past three years he's been pouring most of his assets into offshore holdings. The kind of accounts that are easy to access from a country with no extradition agreement with the U.S. He's gonna bolt like a scared rabbit, and when he does, his own people will probably shoot him in the back. His whole organization is rotten."

He paused to light the cigar. It smelled much ranker than Mando's, and I wondered if this was Hollis' way of pissing all over Tony's territory. He sent a puff toward the roof, then continued: "Can't say that I'd miss him. I've been watching his ass ever since the Agency drummed him out."

"Ain't that sexual harassment?"

He scowled at my quip and continued his glowering rant: "That skeevy bastard's into everything from murder to kidnapping to arms trading and counterfeit securities. A simple bullet would be much too good for him. Personally, I'd like to see him tortured to death, like those kids he sold to Brighton Leigh."

"What kids?"

"Didn't he tell you about that?" His eyebrows arched at the distaste on my face. He smiled suddenly. "No, he wouldn't. As a matter of fact, since there wasn't enough evidence to convict, he'd probably get his legal barracuda to sue me for slander if he knew I was talking about it."

It scared me, to think that Hollis might be right, but I knew better than to show fear. There was nothing more dangerous than an overzealous peace officer fishing for a lead. "You have some point to make, Detective? The boutique I'm goin' to closes in fifteen minutes."

He gave a little snort of disgust and leaned closer. "Tovenaar is a slippery bastard. He'll use you, then leave you to the wolves. That's how he gets away with everything. Always casting reasonable doubts, so no jury can convict him. Hell, when internal affairs came after him, he set up his own supervisor up to take the heat. Three good men dead. Three women widowed—two of them had kids—and the worst they could do to Tovenaar was fire his ass. He's not someone you should turn your back on."

"Thanks for the advice, Detective. I'm sure Daddy will be jest tickled to know I've been consortin' with the Bogey man. Now, if you don't mind..." I motioned to the door.

Hollis grabbed my right hand and squeezed, as if checking for himself that it was actual flesh and blood. A frustrated, bewildered expression crossed his face. He pulled me towards him, until he was so close, I heard the air whistling through his flared nostrils.

"Go," he whispered and jerked his chin at the door. "Shop. But when the shit hits the fan, you sing to me if you want to save your skin, because when Tovenaar turns rogue on you, what happened to Omar will look like a week's vacation at Club Med. Tony likes to make people suffer, especially—" He mimicked my Texas accent "'—sweet young thahngs' like you."

He released my hand, spat his cigar on the carpet between us, and ground it out slowly, glaring at me. His suit rustled as he threw the door open and stepped out into the heat. "Stay out of my way, you son-of-a-bitch." He shoved past Mando with a sneer, stalking back to his sedan. He settled his bulk behind the wheel, killed the dash cherry and drove away.

I watched the tan sedan disappear into traffic, wondering how much of what Hollis said was true.

Mando re-entered the limo, ran his little black box routine, then tossed the cigar butt into the gutter before closing the door. He knocked on the partition. The limo pulled out as Mando fixed his gaze on me, probing, intense. The silence was thick, full of questions and half-truths.

I held my breath. Suddenly, Mando's fierce gaze crumbled into a long, low chuckle. "Goober?" he asked.

I laughed, too. Nervously. I wanted to ask him about what Hollis had said, but I knew he'd pooh-pooh the whole thing. Besides, shouldn't I ask Tony? Go to the source?

"Don't be so down," Mando said, misinterpreting my sigh. "You did great."

"Thanks," I said, not really meaning it. I turned the AC up to offset the heat that sitting around in the sun had generated. We drove for a bit, until Percy guided the limo onto Figuroa, slowing as we reached the intersection with Fifth.

I looked out the window at the Bonaventure hotel, wondering why Jana had specified such an iconic place. Maybe Tony owned it. Or maybe Tony owned the company that owned it. The largest hotel in the city, it consisted of four mirrored-glass cylinders surrounding a central cylindrical tower. An icon of futuristic, postmodern style, it looked to me like the architect had drawn his inspiration from four AA batteries stuck to a central tootsie roll.

Percy guided the limo into the underground parking lot, rolling into a parking spot designed specifically for limos.

Mando smiled at me. "Ready to check in?"

CHAPTER TWENTY

From the parking structure, the elevators whisked us up to a huge, multi-storied atrium style lobby that had more water features than an amusement park. I navigated around them, heading for the check-in area, but Mando steered me towards the concierge instead.

The woman at the concierge desk had a wedge haircut, but her eyes were too buggy and her cheekbones too blocky to really pull it off. She looked like a pug wearing a hand broom. Her name tag said Loria.

I put the palladium card on the counter and asked for the biggest suite they had available. Her eyes bugged out even more, and she picked up the card, examining it like it had fallen off a UFO. When she finally got over her shock, she asked for my ID. I handed over the passport card. Mando tensed a bit as we waited for her to swipe the credit card. His eyebrows arched in surprise when the transaction seemed to go through without a hitch.

"How many keys would you like?" the woman asked, laying the simper on pretty heavy.

"Four," Mando said, before I could reply. He took the card keys from her. She pointed us toward the proper elevator, which was one of those exterior glass ones that looked like a birdcage made of gold-tinted glass. It allowed a stunning vista of the city and the curved portions of the hotel as we climbed.

The suite itself was all cream and gold and wood paneling, decorated with modernist furniture and actual topiary plants. Aside from the big flat screen on the wall of the common area, it was such a throwback to the 1980's, I half expected a brick of cocaine to fall out of the couch cushions.

Percy put my luggage in the bedroom, then took a card key from Mando and headed out. I wasn't sure where he was going, but right then, I didn't care, too busy ordering lunch from room service.

"You want anythin'?" I asked Mando, after I put my order in. He shook his head, giving me a dubious look.

After I hung up, Mando said: "Tony won't like that."

"Tony's halfway acrost the state." I shrugged, walking over to the windows to take in the impressive view of the city. "Besides, I need red meat. A girl can only eat landscapin' for so long."

We were twenty-nine floors up and only a half-a-mile from the L.A. Music Center. If those banking hi-rises weren't in the way, I'd be able to see the Disney Concert Hall.

Figures. Stupid money always obscuring art.

After what seemed like forever, but was probably only about thirty minutes, a knock sounded at the door. Gun hidden at his side, Mando checked the peephole, then admitted a waiter pushing a serving cart laden with a silver dome, a yellow rose in a bud vase, a crystal water goblet, a linen napkin, and gold utensils on a cream-colored linen serving mat. The aroma alone induced projectile salivation.

"Finally!" I sat at the table and signed for the meal, adding a hefty tip. When the waiter was gone, Mando told me to wait and did his black box scan. As soon as he gave me the all clear, I lifted the silver dome to reveal twelve ounces of real, honest-to-God, grass-fed organic prime rib, just the perfect shade of deep pink. The blood ran off to form a moat around the loaded baked potato. The only green in sight was a sprinkling of chives.

I carved a slice and shoved it into my mouth with the cultured aplomb of starving lioness. The juices caressed my taste buds, forcing a grin so wide the corners of my lips met at the back of my head. Magnificence in horseradish.

I devoured a goodly portion before becoming suddenly aware that Mando was snickering at me.

"What's so funny?" I asked, wiping a smear of juice off my chin with the back of my knife hand.

"You react to everything on a gut level. Like a little kid."

"What's wrong with that?"

"You give too much away. Like telegraphing punches before you throw them. Your opponents are always ready for you."

"Can't help how I feel."

"No," he agreed. "But you can think before you act, instead of after. Look a little farther down the road than the tip of your nose." He checked his phone, then regarded me hopefully. "It's only three. Still time to make that flight."

I crammed another slice into my mouth and chewed, staring at him until I finally swallowed. "Why do you care so much about what happens to me?"

"I don't want to see you hurt."

"Why are you so sure that's going to happen?"

He pulled the ticket out again, and tucked it into my purse. "I can't tell you everything about this job. But if things go the way I think they're headed, you will get hurt. Not can. Will."

I considered his words as I worked my way through the last bit of perfection on my plate. "I'm okay with that."

"Really?"

I slurped the blood off my lower lip and gave him the same maniac stare that had put the fear of God into Pinky Webster and his frat buddies. "What doesn't kill me had better turn tail and run."

His eyes narrowed. His lips pursed. He studied me, and was about to say something when he paused suddenly and cupped his hand over his ear. He listened for a moment, then rose and moved to the door, slipping his gun out from under his jacket.

"Should I hide in the bedroom?"

He shook his head, checking the peephole, then opening the door. I had expected Percy, or maybe Glen, or Kam. Maybe even Tony. But it was Rossi and Iso Iso who stepped through the door.

They were dressed in Panama shirts, jeans and tennis shoes, not the suits I had come to expect. Each carried a gear bag and had a tactical backpack slung over one shoulder. Iso Iso carried a large gear case of ballistic plastic, the kind DJs use for transporting electronic turntables. He set it down on the coffee table. The marshals looked at the empty, bloodstained plate in front of me, and then at the room service cart.

They shot questioning looks at Mando, who shrugged and said: "Tony's in Pebble Beach."

"Fair enough," Rossi nodded to Mando. He handed her two of the card keys he'd taken from the concierge, keeping the last one for himself.

"You can go," Iso Iso told Mando. "She's our package, now."

"Wait, what?" I said, not liking this turn of events. "I don't want to stay with these deppity dumbshits."

Both marshals shot me a glower. I stuck my tongue out at them and turned to complain to Mando but he was already heading out the door.

"What the Hell?" I muttered.

Rossi made a tour of the suite, then motioned Iso Iso to place the plastic case in the spare bedroom. He moved into that room, deposited all his gear, then came back out for one of the key cards, along with Rossi's gear. When he had collected everything, he disappeared once again into the room and closed the door. Rossi turned and grinned at me, drawing the sidearm she had holstered under her Panama shirt.

"What the Hell?!" I complained again, louder this time.

She sat on the couch, gun resting across her lap. With her free hand, she picked up the remote for the flat screen and turned it on. "Welcome to WitSec, Miss Hopkins."

I gaped at her, feeling betrayed and abandoned.

Why hadn't Mando warned me about this? I never would have agreed to be alone with these slimeball marshals. Then again, maybe that's exactly why he hadn't warned me. I growled and went over to the refrigerator, grabbing the first thing that came to hand. A ginger ale. I slurped it loudly.

Rossi flipped through the schlock that made up day time TV. She finally settled on a home improvement program. I had no desire to see how to properly repair a subfloor, but I felt like retreating to my room would be a mistake. This was my house, and these tin star staph infections had invaded it without my invitation.

I didn't know why I felt territorial about a hotel room that I'd spent less than two hours in, but I did. Maybe it was because I'd finally gotten some red meat. At any rate, I sat down on the couch and started talking some mindless, annoying Faith babble, specifically designed to interrupt the critical points in her show. It took her about fifteen minutes to catch on to what I was doing.

Tony would have picked it up in twenty seconds.

"If you don't like what I'm watching, Miss Hopkins, you can watch whatever you like from your bedroom."

"I could. But why should I have to? This is my suite."

She muted the TV and swiveled her legs around, so that she was sitting crosswise on the couch to face me. "Let's get something straight, Miss *Damiano*." She stressed my name, staring at me like a base commander dressing down a new recruit. "This is my suite. You are here because I want you here. You work for me."

"My contract's with Tony. This suite is being paid for by Tony."

"Who works for me. Ergo. You. Work. For me." She paused to let that sink in, and then continued: "Tovenaar's job was to prep you. To make you into Faith, so that you can properly perform the mission I have in mind for you. I am the leader of this Special Fugitive Task Force. So. Shut the fuck up, unless you've got something relevant to say."

I scowled at her. "You don't have to use the f-word."

She looked puzzled for a moment, as if wondering if I was genuinely offended or just messing with her.

"I don't like the f-word," I insisted. "Don't use it, please?"

"All right," she dipped her head in a brief nod. "Anything else?"

"Why am I here? What's the mission?"

"You are Faith Hopkins. After what happened to Omar, you have turned witness for the prosecution. Hence, you are now in our Witness Security Program." She motioned to the hotel suite.

"Pretty moronic, to check in under my own name if I'm in hiding."

"Yes. It is a mistake we expect Scotty to exploit. Our intelligence indicates he will attempt to snatch you some time in the next forty-eight hours. When he does, we expect he will take you to Brighton Leigh. We will follow your signal to that location, and we will make the arrests. We. The marshals. Neither Tovenaar, or his people are to get anywhere near the fugitive. His organization's part in this mission is over."

"Aside from me."

"Aside from you," she confirmed.

I thought about this, feeling uneasy with the plan. I didn't trust Rossi, or her team. "What if your intelligence blows? What if they don't make an attempt to snatch me?"

"Then I will learn all about how to remodel a bathroom on the government's dime." She unmuted the TV and turned her attention back to the screen.

"Scotty won't try and snatch me from you," I pointed out. "A full frontal assault on law enforcement is not his style."

"I've only spent the last year and four months studying him, his people, his financials, and pretty much everything about him. So, of course, you've met the man once and you're the expert."

I looked down to peer intently at the cushion she was seated on, tilting my head this way and that.

"What are you doing?" She glanced sidelong at me.

"Sarcasm was so thick, I wondered if any had dripped on the couch."

She snorted and shook her head, returning her attention to the TV. "You've got some backbone, I'll give you that."

"Did the marshals pay for my hand to be re-genned?"

"Tovenaar did. We don't have the budget for that sort of thing."

"But you're not above exploiting me after the fact."

"You signed a contract."

"With Tony. Not you. I bet he's bankrolled all of this. But you're keeping him from the prize. Why?"

"We need Foster and Leigh alive."

"And you're sure Tony won't follow through with that?"

She shot me a look that said I couldn't be that gullible.

I tried another tack: "If they're dead, they can't escape custody."

"If they're dead, we can't identify and arrest those who attempt to help them escape custody."

I hadn't thought about that. My brow furrowed as I tried to come up with a rebuttal.

"Someone at a very high level of government was behind Leigh's escape," she continued. "That is the prize we're focused on. That is why we are even willing to deal with Tovenaar and his organization."

"Why does everybody hate him so much? He's been good to me. Honorable, even."

"That's because you're the only person who can get him what he wants. As soon as he's achieved his goal, you'll be out in the cold. If you're lucky."

"What's that supposed to mean?"

"How do you think things are going to end, here? You really think you'll go back to playing the piano as if nothing had ever happened? You do things his way, I'll arrest you as an accessory to murder. You do things my way, he'll take it as a betrayal. You either go into WitSec and leave your old life behind, or you spend it on the run from him and Villalobos. None of those scenarios has you on the stage tickling the ivories."

I huffed and folded my arms across my chest defensively, unhappy that she had voiced the truth that had been sharking around my subconscious ever since I'd freaked out about getting on the helicopter. There was no going back. I should have taken Mando up on his offer.

She sighed, swiveling on the couch to face me again. Her hardened demeanor softened. "Look, I get it. You imprinted on him during stasis, and now you've got that whole misplaced loyalty thing going on. But, trust me, Tovenaar is not the man he has presented to you."

"What do you mean, imprinted?"

"He didn't tell you? Of course. He wouldn't." She made a derisive sound, shaking her head. "He's such a weasel."

"Tell me what?"

"One of the side effects of stasis is that subjects develop strong emotional attachments to the first people they see upon waking. The theory is that it mimics the parental bonding process in infants."

The way she worded it made my brain work at understanding. "You're saying I feel loyal to him because he was there when I woke up from the surgeries?"

She nodded. "Whole conversion and interrogation techniques have been developed to exploit the phenomenon."

"What, like you waterboard people by putting them in stasis?"

"Something like that," she nodded, then shrugged. "I'm not familiar with the details. But, I heard it's something they've been using at the Agency for over a decade."

Was everything between Tony and me just some insidious side effect? I thought back through my experiences, sifting through how I'd felt, and when.

Something resonated between us, forcing vibrations whenever we were close to one another. Maybe it was just hormones, but I had felt it the moment I'd first laid eyes on him at the train station, and again when he chatted me up at the police station. That pull was there long before the nightmares of stasis, or even the truth serum bit. Which, I reminded myself, had been a very dick move. I owed him an ass-kicking.

Despite that, he had kept up his part of the bargain admirably. Without him, I wouldn't have a hand. That was a lot of money and effort he could have avoided spending, simply by tagging me and letting me loose as Rad. Instead, he had put me back together.

But, then, without Mando, I wouldn't have needed Tony's help to keep my digits. Had it really been an accident? Or had Mando deliberately maimed me so that I would have to play Faith? He could have aimed for Sloan's head. He shot for the heart, instead.

I turned that over in my mind. I had forgiven Mando awfully quickly in the hospital. He had destroyed my life, but after a few weeks he's like a father to me? Looking at it in retrospect, that was kind of weird. Especially for me, who still held a grudge against El Pollo Loco for discontinuing their taquitos over a decade ago. So, maybe Rossi's stasis theory held water with Mando, if not Tony.

My burgeoning doubt must have shown on my face, because she made a soft murr, brown eyes brimming with sympathy.

"Believe me, Tovenaar is not your friend. Neither is Villalobos. The only people with your best interests at heart are me and my team."

"That's just bullshit. You guys suck."

"Why would you say that?" She actually looked offended.

"You made the emergency room doctor try to trick me."

"Given your background, I thought it best to try the soft approach."

"More bullshit. You hadn't gotten my background when you came to the hospital. Or you'd have known you couldn't pass my prints. Which you obviously did, or I wouldn't be here, now."

"We didn't pass those prints. Tovenaar did."

"How?"

"No idea. Best guess is, he has an in at the State Department. But even that doesn't really fit, since they don't work that fast. They have more red tape than we do. To make that happen in less than a week, it's a Christmas miracle. In August."

I pursed my lips, quirking my mouth to the side as I recalled the device in Tony's bedroom and the sly, secretive way he acted when taking my prints. "What do you know about him, anyway?"

She shrugged, hand tightening around the grip of the pistol in her lap. "His mother was in Naval Intelligence. As part of her cover, she operated a transportation company based in Indonesia. It allowed her to gather data on movements of ships, materiel, and personnel in and out of all ports of call throughout Southeast Asia. She was so effective, they kept her in place for almost a decade past the initial tour. Tony was born during her second year in country. Grew up in the game, just like his brother. He is eminently capable of convincing you he is on your side, right until he slips the blade between your ribs."

"So you believe what Hollis does?"

She shrugged. "I'm reserving judgement."

"If he's as bad as Hollis says, then how come nobody's been able to convict him?"

"Rumor is that Tovenaar gets away with what he does because his mother's at the Pentagon and his brother still works for the Agency."

"Is his brother older? Like a lot older?"

"By about ten years," she nodded. "How did you know that?"

"Does he have yellow eyes?"

"I don't know. Never met him. Point is, Tovenaar is going to be whatever he thinks you need him to be in order to get what he wants. He was raised with spycraft the way you were raised with karate."

"How do you know what I was raised with?"

"Please. That's all your father talked about. How many karate tournaments you'd won that year. How many more he expected you to win. That's why I went in soft at the hospital. I knew how dangerous you might be if you felt cornered."

"You knew my father?"

"He was one of my favorite instructors at Glynco."

"Really?" She did look old enough to have trained under Papa when we lived in Georgia. Even so, I wasn't sure if she was being truthful, or if this was some sort of calculated manipulation. Probably both.

She nodded. "It was tough, being a female in that environment. The Commander was very supportive. He treated me the way he wanted you to be treated when you were old enough to follow in his footsteps. And now, here we are. Me, looking out for you."

"If deliberately setting me out as bait for the most notoriously sadistic human trafficker in modern history qualifies as 'looking out for me,' then go you."

"Tovenaar's doing the same thing," she pointed out. "In addition to trying to turn you into an accessory to murder."

"Tony asked me. He gave me a choice. You're just ordering me."

"What choice was that? Option A) Fix your hand and let you get captured under a controlled situation, or Option B) Lose your fingers and get captured anyway? Of course you'd choose Option A."

"By that logic, I signed that contract under duress. Which makes it null and void. Which means I don't work for either of you." I stood up and headed for my bedroom.

"That's not what I meant."

"That's my take away. We're done. Null and void. I'm unemployed. Good talk." I shut the door on her reply, and then locked it.

I turned the TV on, making sure it was loud and tuned to an action movie. I pulled the sheathed *kris* out of my cosmetics case and used that to cut the underwires out of a few bras, then cut the straps off, as well. I fashioned a makeshift handcuff key out of one piece of wire and hid it in the waistband of my stretchy black exercise pants, just in case my plan failed miserably.

With the other wires I jury-rigged some lock picks. I tucked them all in the one Faith purse that was satchel styled, rather than clutch. I stuffed the splint, the plane ticket Mando had left, and the passport and palladium cards into the purse, along with two hand towels and some mouthwash from the bathroom.

Then, I used the tip of the *kris* like a screwdriver and removed the ventilation grates. Both intake and exhaust grates were on the top third of the wall behind the bed. Each was larger than a king-sized pillow. My eighteen month stint as a teenaged burglar, combined with an introduction to architecture course I'd taken my freshman year, told me that the intake and exhaust ducts both had to be routed through the hotel's support structure.

Because they'd be surrounded by all that concrete and rebar, they'd hold my weight. Judging from the size of the soffits in the ceiling, they were also likely to be large enough for me to travel through, at least as far as I needed to go.

The exhaust duct made an obliquely angled 'T' to conform with the soffit. When I stuck my head inside, I heard the tapping of computer keys. That must lead to the room that Iso Iso had set up in. I peered into the intake duct and saw a wide, vertical shaft dropping down into darkness. Intake for the win. Rossi was bound to have marshals posted in the hallway outside the suite, but they likely wouldn't be guarding the floor below us.

I tied the sheets to one another, then one end to the base of the rolling chair by the writing desk. Then, I gathered up some long silk scarves and made a makeshift rig to tie the blade to my back with the pommel angled for a left-handed draw.

I put on the exercise pants and a tank top, then the makeshift rig, and then put two other layers of baggy silk Faith clothes on top of that. I wrote a note for Rossi and left it on the dresser.

Purse over my shoulder, I put the chair on the bed, wrapped the free end of the sheet around my leg and left arm, and climbed backwards into the intake shaft to lower myself down. It was a tight fit, one that allowed me to support myself by pressing outward against the duct walls with my knees and thighs while I threaded the sheet down the shaft and pulled the chair up until it stuck in the opening.

I climbed down into darkness, smirking to myself at the three words I had written on the note. If Rossi was telling the truth about Papa, she would know exactly what they meant. They'd been his mantra, the words he used to motivate his SeAL team. The only tattoo on his whole body, he'd had them inked over his heart the day he left his last shitty foster home to join the Navy: *Cape Sors Tuum.*

Seize Your Destiny.

I dropped into the room below my suite after kicking the ventilation grate out. My right hand ached a bit from all the exertion, but clutching the sheet wasn't any different than some of the exercises I'd performed with Dr. Lelani, other than the added weight.

Luckily, it was early in the day as hotels go, and nobody had checked in here, yet. I immediately moved over to the phone and called the concierge desk. Loria was still on duty, and she fawned over me with all the obeisance of a star struck fan.

Amazing, what a palladium card can do.

She helped me arrange everything, from the cash advance she was going to deliver to the rental limo I now had waiting in the parking structure, to booking the flight to Aruba. It only took her about fifteen minutes to accomplish all of it.

I told her to expect a hefty tip.

Now, to see if I could actually make it to the elevator and down to the car without my implant alerting the marshals that I was on the move. I wasn't sure how the device knew where I was, or what kind of range it had. I guessed that it provided a GPS style longitude and latitude, but not elevation. So long as I stayed inside the hotel, I probably wouldn't trigger any alarms.

Even so, my heart was pounding as I eased the door to the room open and peered out into the curving hallway. The coast was clear, so I darted down to the elevator and hit the call button. Thankfully, there was no marshal stationed inside.

The glass elevator, however, didn't provide the type of cover I had been hoping for. The suite was situated on the curve of the building facing me, so that when I looked up through the top of the elevator, I had an unobstructed view of Rossi sitting on the couch in the common area. On the other side of the dividing wall, Iso Iso sat at the desk in the bedroom. They weren't scrambling around, which meant they hadn't heard me climbing down the shaft and kicking out the grate.

Unless the implant alarmed when I reached a certain distance, or someone was actively monitoring it, the marshals may not even discover I was missing until dinner. Maybe even longer, since I'd already ordered room service. I hit the button for the shopping level and quickly turned my back on the suite I'd so recently claimed as my own. As I looked out over the city, I hitched the top layer of Faith silk up over my head and tied the arms into a makeshift burka to hide my hair and face.

As the elevator descended, the old, familiar rush of elation coursed through me. I had felt it every time I had gotten away with burglary. I stepped out onto the shopping level, which was a few stories above the lobby. Curving walkways arched around the space, leading to various stairways that served the multiple levels of the atrium. It was both visually stunning and insanely confusing, like being in a life-sized M.C. Escher drawing.

There were probably folks in the lobby looking out for me. Or looking out for people looking for me. I asked a waitress at one of the restaurants in the food court how to get directly to the parking levels. She kindly pointed me towards a set of stairs that led to the proper elevator.

I shared the ride down with a hipster lesbian couple speaking Korean and giggling to one another between kisses. I feigned ignorance and didn't let them know I could understand all the racy things they were going to do to one another after they got back from dinner. We'd lived in Korea for twenty months after the fiasco in Corpus Christi when Papa found out Chris had been born with the wrong blood type.

The doors opened out into that echoey gloom all underground parking structures seem to have. The bold primary colors painted on the columns and bright lights around the valet station tried to perk things up. A neon Band-Aid on a gray concrete scar.

I looked around before exiting the elevator. A black, tricked-out Mercedes Sprinter van was already waiting for me in front of the limo service that worked out of the hotel. I couldn't spot anyone that screamed Fed or gangster at me, but I did see Loria standing next to the limo. She held a tablet and an envelope, and talked with the chauffeur.

I moved over to them in that drunken Faith shuffle, and gave them a cutesy wave. "Y'all are here for little ole me?"

"Miss Hopkins," Loria gushed, ignoring my strange attire. "So good to see you again." She presented the tablet. "If I can swipe your card, we can proceed with the advance?"

"Shore thing." I handed it over, and signed on the dotted line, and she presented me with my cash advance limit of five grand. I handed her a hundred back. "Thanks, honey. You're a lifesaver. I am so needin' a shoppin' spree right now. I'm hatin' my wardrobe so bad, I can't even show my face."

The chauffeur, a wiry, moon-faced Japanese fellow whose name tag said Bernard, asked for my ID. He inserted the palladium card into his tablet reader and had me sign on the screen. When the transaction cleared, he opened the door. I peered inside before climbing in, just to make sure there were no nasty surprises. Relieved to have the cabin all to myself, I stepped in and took a look around while Bernard shut the door.

Unlike Tony's Mercedes, this Sprinter limo was a cross between a party bus and a rolling office. Tall enough to stand up and walk around in, it boasted four leather reclining seats that faced one another and another bench seat in the back that folded out into a bed. Three refrigerated bins under the bench seat carried bottled water, sodas and mixers, and high end alcohol, respectively. A cabinet held blankets and pillows, and another had crystal highball glasses and packaged snacks. Each of the recliners had a pull out desk, and the entire thing was rigged for wifi. A flat screen with satellite TV and a very high end sound system completed the ride.

I closed all the window shades and then removed the top layer of blousy Faith clothes, having donned them to protect myself from the sharp sheet metal inside the vent shaft, as well as to confuse descriptions of me.

Bernard got behind the wheel and looked at me in the rearview. If he thought it strange I was wearing multiple layers of clashing colors and showed up wearing a blouse wrapped around my face, he didn't say anything. "Where to, Miss Hopkins?"

"The Concerto Club. And step on it. I gotta get my party on."

"It's only 3:30. I don't think they'll be open yet."

I grinned. "I'm countin' on that."

CHAPTER TWENTY-ONE

Since it was the beginning of rush hour, it took an hour to travel the ten miles from the hotel to Beverly Hills. I sweated it out, calming myself with the thought that even if the implant had alerted the marshals I'd left the hotel, they likely couldn't travel any faster than we were going. And they wouldn't call local law enforcement in to head me off, to avoid getting Hollis involved.

When we reached Rodeo Drive, I told Bernard to stop at the Louis Vuitton store. Forty-two thousand dollars, a complimentary red-eye mocha latte, and a half-hour later, I emerged wearing designer sunglasses and a sequined cowboy hat. I rolled along with a new set of luggage and shopping bags filled with a sequined leopard spotted evening dress with matching jewelry and heels; several scarves; assorted jeans, belts, jumpsuits and tops; and a pair of black and gold sneakers with the appropriate name of Runaway.

I wondered how rich people stayed rich. I'd just spent a third of the cost of a house in Georgia when I could have bought similar items at Target for less than a grand.

Bernard loaded all my purchases in the cabin with me, while I enjoyed a mocktail of ginger ale, grenadine and cranberry juice. I swapped the contents of the satchel purse to my new Louis Vuitton backpack and threw the old purse into the gutter before Bernard slid the door shut.

Then, I put the sneakers on as we cruised up Rodeo and turned the corner to park in front of the Concerto. It hadn't meant much to me before, but now that I knew Scotty's association with Leigh, the club's street address on Brighton Way seemed like a sinister coincidence. Or a deliberate 'eff you' to the authorities.

By this time, it was a little after five. The club wouldn't open until after eight tonight, so only the prep cooks, Tina the bartender, and Lonny the manager were likely to be around. Perfect.

"Wait here. It could be a while," I told Bernard, and climbed out of the limo with one of my new, empty, rolling carry-on bags.

I walked around to the back entrance, picked the lock, and eased into the dim quiet of the backstage. I took the sunglasses off and stuck them in the suitcase, then quietly moved through the teasers towards the hallway, carrying the bag so the sound of the rollers wouldn't draw attention.

I suppressed a shudder when I passed the dressing room where I'd been shot. There were stains on the floor that I realized were blood: mine, or Sloan's, no way of knowing.

My goal was to sneak into the men's bathroom, which shared an interior wall with the back room of Scotty's office. The same back room Mando had exited the night I'd been shot. The room where he'd gotten the 5D discs. I was going to break in.

With any luck, I'd be able to find some evidence that I could use as leverage. The kind of evidence Mando wasn't able to hide in a coat pocket. Like, maybe, a private server that utilized those encryption algorithms for streaming that reprehensible kiddie porn.

I eased the backstage door open and peeked through. I didn't see anyone in the hallway, but I heard movement and clinking glass ahead. I crept towards the alcove that housed the entrance to the restrooms, pausing when the wall opened up on one side to reveal the dining area and bar. I slowly eased my head out to see Tina stocking bottles behind the bar. I heard muffled voices in the kitchen, and the sounds of dishes being washed and vegetables being chopped. No Lonny, but his car was parked out in the alley, so he was around here somewhere. I glanced up to see if he was in the lighting booth, but my luck was holding. It was empty. Anybody up there could see the entire house area of the club, including the restroom entrances.

I waited until Tina bent down to open a box and darted for the alcove, freezing behind the sidewall of the arch. I listened to the clink of glass, the rustle of her clothes, the bored exhalation of breath, waiting until the pause told me she was opening another box, because the movement of the door would draw her attention if she'd been standing.

A quick, silent box step into the men's room door, and I was in. I locked the men's room door, and then immediately wedged a wet paper towel over the small wireless camera hidden in the filigreed sconce, since I remembered seeing an image into this room on the wall of monitors in Scotty's office.

I paced the distance along the wall, matching it to the dimensions I remembered from that fateful night. All the plumbing was along the shared wall with the women's room, so once I found my spot, all I had to do was cut through the drywall with the *kris*.

It always cracked me up, how people in apartments would put security gates on their doors, and bars on their windows, completely oblivious to the fact that the only thing between their belongings and the empty apartment next door were two sheets of drywall and some insulation. About ten minutes later, I was through. Would have been quicker, but my right hand was still too weak to be of much use.

I crawled through into a disappointment.

There wasn't any rack of servers, or rat's nest of cables leading to some cool neo-tech contraption, like in the movies. It was a small bedroom, with a single bed, a two leather wingchairs, a low dresser, and forest green wallpaper and mahogany wainscoting that matched the office. There was a humidor and a collection of very top shelf booze on the small mahogany bar. The most neo-tech thing in there was the server for the holographic décor in the main room.

It was fastened to the wall beside the door to the office, with four rows of conduits that stretched up to the ceiling and down to the floor. A stack of square cases were on a shelf beside it, each the size of a compact mirror.

I popped one open, and found it had two 5D discs inside, each etched with the projector company logos, and a small insert with the name and pictures of the interior of the palace it was emulating. The rest of the stack was similar, only the case for discs that were already loaded in the projector was empty. Out of spite, I ejected the discs that were in the machine and slotted in one disc from a Turkish palace and one from the Vatican. As soon as the projector was turned on, the club would become the interior design equivalent of the Crusades.

Let Scotty deal with that PR nightmare.

I put the ejected discs in their case and shoved the whole stack in my bag. Then, I searched the room. What I found was disturbing:

The top drawer of the dresser held two dress shirts, several silk ties, and a pair of pants, along with a matching set of gold cufflinks and a tie tack, but the other three were filled with sex toys. Not the goofy, neon silicone marital-aid vibrator kind, but the evil metal and leather torture kind. There were strange, patterned scuffs on the sides and edges of the dresser. The legs and corners had weird bulges. When I ran my hands over them, little iron loops swiveled out. Tie points. The dresser doubled as a whipping horse.

Now thoroughly creeped out, I searched the rest of the furniture. I found similar tie points on the bar, along with more torture stuff, like nipple clamps, knives, and surgical steel pins. The bed was its own bucket of crazy, since there were hidden tie points all around the solid mahogany base, and when I slid my hand under the mattress to see if anything was hidden there, I triggered a latch that popped the entire mattress platform up to reveal a hidden, coffin-like enclosure built into the base, complete with handcuffs and leg irons bolted into the bedframe. There were stains on the wood floor of the coffin in the shape of a person, made by blood, sweat and body oil. Someone had been imprisoned here for a very long time. Or a parade of someones.

A little bile rose up in my throat. I was suddenly, insanely grateful that Mando had forced me out of the club that night.

Cold fury surged through me. Screw Scott Foster and his skeevy, deevy bullshit. I spit all over one of the ball gags in the dresser, then rolled up my left sleeve. I took a knife from the bar and cut my forearm and painted 'SCOTTY KILLED ME' with my finger on the bottom of the mattress platform. Tony might have changed my looks, but he couldn't have changed my DNA. I dripped more blood on the dresser, the bedframe, the carpet, and the bar. If Hollis wanted to pin my murder on somebody, let it be Scotty.

As I smeared a bloody handprint on the inside of the coffin, I noticed a small night vision camera fixed to the underside of the platform. The cable to it ran towards the head of the bed. I followed it to the baseboard, and from there to one of the conduits leading up to the holo projector box.

I puzzled over that, until I realized that this was just the data engine for the projector. The actual controls for the décor were most likely located in the lighting booth, since that would allow you to see the entire room to adjust the focus, color, and brightness of the holographics. But why put the engine here in this private area, where it would require a server to feed the information to the lighting booth, when it would have been much easier and more efficient to locate everything in the booth?

Because Scotty had been streaming images of the poor unfortunates trapped in the bed. He'd been using the algorithms on the 5D discs in the data engine to encrypt the images, and then sending the encoded stream out via the server.

I rethought my Crusades plan and popped those discs out, placing them back into their cases. Then, I used the *kris* to cut the cables and unscrew the data engine/server from its mounting plates on the wall. It was a tight fit, but I managed to shove it into the rolling carry on. It was heavier than I'd expected, but maybe the lasers needed to read a 5D disc were more robust.

I carefully put everything else back the way I had found it, then eased the carry on back into the men's room and climbed through after it. I grabbed a wad of paper towels to stem the trickle from my forearm, waiting until it had stopped bleeding before rolling my sleeve down over the wound. I shoved the bloody paper towels down the toilet and flushed them, washed my hands, and put the section of drywall back, propping it up with the trash can.

Mission accomplished. Now, all I had to do was get back out to the limo without being seen. Easier said, than done, since as soon as I cracked the men's room door open, I came face to face with Lonny.

"Faith?" His jaw went slack in surprise. "I haven't seen you in over a year."

I stepped out quickly. "I came lookin' for Scotty."

His brow furrowed as he stared at the suitcase, then looked at the door behind me. "In the men's room?"

"I wanted to try out the urinals. See how the other half lives. Tequila doesn't pee itself." I noticed some gypsum dust from the drywall on my sleeve and snorted it like it was a line of coke. "That's better," I grinned to hide the wince from my protesting nasal passages. "Yee-haw!"

It was just Faith enough that he nodded, but he kept looking at the suitcase, as if trying to make sense of it.

"We're gonna be partners, and I wanted to give him a present,"
I explained. "You know, a peace offerin', 'cause things didn't end
well between us." I waggled the handle of the carry on. "I found
this new adult store that has—"

He cut me off with a raised hand, clearly finding that TMI.
"Scotty's not here."

"Okay. I'll just mosey back later tonight."

"He won't be in at all. Scotty's got a fundraiser tonight. A big
gala at that restaurant at Union Station."

"Oh? And he didn't tell me about it?" I slapped my chest as if
stabbed through the heart. "Men are so thoughtless."

"I can call him and ask him to put you on the list," Lonny
offered. "But the tickets are a thousand dollars a plate."

"Aw, that's chicken scratch," I waved my hand dismissively.
"And I'm sure it's for a good cause."

"It's for a nationwide network of shelters for runaway kids."

My stomach churned at the thought of Scotty and Brighton
Leigh having access to such a vulnerable population, but I smiled
and said: "I'll be tickled to attend. And when you call Scotty, tell
him to bring Randall and Dave. We got some documents to get
signed." I waved at him and headed for the backstage.

"Uh, okay. Bye."

I left the air conditioned gloom of the club for the baking heat
of the alley, slipping the sunglasses back on. When I reached the
front of the club, I glanced around, but didn't see any marshals
standing by the limo, so I strolled over and got inside, lugging the
heavy suitcase in and setting it on the floor. "Bernard, honey,
could you loan me your cellphone? I left mine at the hotel."

"Sure," he said, handing it over with a smile. He'd seen the tip
I'd given Loria.

"Thanks, darlin'." I closed the privacy screen and ran a search
for Hollis' precinct, then dialed the number listed for detectives. I
got an answering machine, since apparently detectives only
worked from nine to five. Which made me wonder why Hollis had
shown up at Union Station so close to midnight. Maybe he'd been
following Tony's limo. That guy must really be obsessed.

I left a message as Faith, describing what Scotty had going on
in his secret sex room, and that he'd hinted that he'd killed
Damiano.

"Where to next?" Bernard asked via the intercom.

I toggled the mic. "Burbank Airport. Got a flight to catch."

**

Because it was well and truly rush hour, it took an hour and a
half to travel the fourteen miles to Burbank. I donned the splint,
since my hand was hurting, and used the time to prepare for the
next stage of my plan. I stripped off the gypsum gritty Faith silk,
then removed the makeshift rig for the *kris* and the exercise pants.
I swapped the makeshift handcuff key to the waist band of my

new silk girlboxer style underwear, then fashioned a better rig for the *kris* from the belts and scarves I bought.

I used the *kris* to slice the lining of my second new carry on and slipped the 5D cases inside, then tied the unsheathed *kris* to the metal base of the telescoping mechanism. With any luck, it would hide the shape from the TSA scanner. I then packed my back up clothes and belts on top of the cut, putting the sheath for the *kris* between the curled belts of the rig, and then the splint on top of that. The sequined dress went on top of it all.

The sequins would likely scatter the signals, hiding the blade even more. And even if they saw something funky on the scan and opened the bag, they'd see the dress and the splint and the sheath and think that's what caused the problem. I hoped. Just in case, I put a thousand dollars in one of the little clutch purses I'd bought, and put that on top of the dress.

I'd never bribed anybody, but I'd seen Papa do it quite a few times. The most memorable being the time the cop pulled me over when I was eight. I'd started driving early, since Mother passed out a lot and refrigerators didn't magically grow food.

It was now almost three and a half hours since I'd left the hotel. It was slightly disturbing that nobody had corralled me yet. I'd been sure that they'd have caught up with me in Beverly Hills, but here I was.

Maybe the marshals hadn't bothered to monitor the implant because they believed me to be safely tucked away, sulking in my room. Government types were notorious penny pinchers, so it made sense to avoid paying someone to monitor me without cause. That, or the implant needed a booster, like a cellphone within range, to send a signal back to whomever was monitoring such things. Calling Hollis may have set things in motion, and tipped my hand. They also could be aware I was gone, and just be tracking me from a distance, since my vitals didn't indicate I was in distress. Waiting for someone to snatch me.

Or, the implant didn't exist. Just a bullshit story designed to keep me from running and make me trust they'd recover me before I got seriously hurt.

Regardless of the reasons why, I was still on the loose when the Mercedes pulled up to the curb outside the airport. Determined to make the most of my freedom while I had it, I pulled out two hundred dollar bills and rolled the privacy screen down.

"Thanks for the phone, honey," I dropped it over onto the seat beside him, wrapped in a hundred.

"My pleasure," he said, a happy vibrato in his voice as he saw the money.

"How much longer do I have you for?"

"Standard rental is for six hours, but you can extend to up to twenty hours, total. The hourly rate is $225."

"The full twenty, if you're amenable."

"Aren't you catching a plane?"

"Oh, I sometimes freak out about flyin' and have to go party to forget, so I need you to wait in the cellphone lot for me. I'll call you once I know where I need you next."

"You want to write down my number?"

"Naw, I memorized it. Just add another fourteen hours to my bill."

"You want me to wait in the cellphone lot for fourteen hours?" he asked, plugging a striping device into his tablet.

I handed over the card and then signed the screen after taking the card back. "Well, seventeen, since I've still got three left. But I doubt it'll go that long."

"Okay. It's your money."

"Ain't it, though?" I chuckled and held out the other hundred. "You got anythin' smaller than this?"

"Let me see." He pulled out his wallet and made change for me in tens and twenties.

"Thank you, darlin'." I opened the door and slung the backpack over my shoulder as I scanned the crowd for potential threats. Or deppity dumdums. I didn't spot any, but the sun was bright and it was hard to see who might be inside.

Bernard got my luggage out. I thanked him and headed off towards the skycaps for my flight, a twenty already in my hand for a tip. I handed over my passport card and the ticket Mando had given me and told the skycap to check the bag with the data engine. She tagged the bag and handed me my boarding pass, cordially informing me which gate my flight left from, adding that I'd better hurry, because they were going to start boarding soon.

I thanked her and headed inside, holding my breath as I passed through the automatic doors and into the long, wide terminal building. Burbank was an older, small airport, so there weren't crowds to get lost in, like LAX or Atlanta. If anybody was waiting for me here, I'd have to run hard and fast to get away.

Nobody seemed to take notice of me, which was the good news.

The bad news was the security screening line wasn't very long, so the *kris* was more likely to get noticed. And if the marshals were wanting me, they'd send an air marshal to nab me as soon as my ID was scanned. Even so, I thought it worth the risk. When I got to the front of the line, I handed over my passport card and boarding pass, smiling at the uniformed TSA agent.

He was a bored-looking older Latino with a drooping right eyelid and scar at the corner of his eye that told me he'd been a gangbanger in his youth. "Where you headed?"

"Las Vegas."

He looked at my ID under the ultraviolet light. All the proper things glowed. He looked at my face, read the boarding pass, and said: "You have Pre Check. Go in that line." He pointed out the one on the end with nobody in it and handed back my stuff.

"Thanks," I smiled again and turned towards the screeners, drawing in a deep, steadying breath. My heart beat faster, my throat tightened. This was it. At least they let me keep my shoes on, which would make running easier.

I set my carry on and backpack on the conveyer and went through the body scan, waiting for the telltale finger crook that would mean my bag needed inspection. I didn't see it, but when I went over to grab my things, the amply-endowed, aging Valley Girl behind the conveyor asked: "Is this your bag?"

I nodded, slinging the strap to my backpack over my shoulder and reaching for the carry on, ready to grab and run.

"It is so cute! I love it. How much did it cost?"

"Sixty-nine hundred dollars. Plus tax."

"Oh my god! Really? Too rich for my blood. Have a nice flight!"

"I will, thanks." I took the bag, extended the telescoping handle, and made a beeline for the boarding gate. My ticket was first class and had the super deluxe ultra zoot priority boarding. I looked around at the passengers who were waiting, and spied a woman in marine fatigues who looked to be traveling alone. I sat down next to her with a smile. "Howdy."

She smiled back. "Hi."

"You look like you deserve an upgrade to first class." I held my boarding pass out. "Enjoy."

She looked it over, and then at me. "How will you get on the plane?"

"We'll trade seats. I just wanted to thank you for your service. I know the sacrifices you folks make."

She gave me a shy smile, and handed hers over. Just then, they gave the call for priority boarding. She got up, slung her pack over her shoulder, and got in line. I smiled, watching her board, then got up and found the nearest restroom.

Once inside, I changed into a jumpsuit, donned the sequined cowboy hat, put the sunglasses on, threw a scarf around my neck and part of my face and headed out towards the baggage claim carousel. I glanced around when I moved out onto the street, almost disappointed it had been so easy.

The data engine was on its way to Vegas to linger in unclaimed baggage. Well out of Scotty's immediate reach. Maybe Mando's D.E.A. friends would pick it up when I didn't get off the plane, which would put it even further out of Scotty's reach.

Meanwhile, the coast still seemed clear, which kind of bothered me. I had expected at least the marshals to try and scoop me up the moment I went through TSA. If Faith was such a high priority catch, why wasn't anybody trying to do just that?

Maybe I'd been too smart for my own good. Maybe they just hadn't realized I was missing yet.

I crossed the street to the parking structure and walked on to the Metrolink station at the other side of the airport. I bought a fare to Union Station with cash and sat down to wait.

The train was on time, and it only took a half hour to get back to downtown L.A. Once at Union Station, I called Bernard from a borrowed cellphone, telling him I had freaked out and decided not to fly and instructing him to come here and pick me up at the entrance. He was happy to oblige.

After the call, I moved over to the windows on the south side of the waiting area, to see what was going on with the gala. Even though the sun hadn't set completely, spotlights shone down from the clock tower onto the rows of vintage cars clustered on the south patio and arcade areas. More lights shone down onto a red carpeted walkway leading into the restaurant. Celebrities and bigwigs strolled around the cars, tuxedoed gentlemen and ladies in evening gowns parading with the undeniable air of privilege imparted by bodacious amounts of money. A giant multiscreen in the courtyard area flashed the logo of the charity and images of past events and kids needing help. The press interviewed various celebrities as they arrived.

It looked like a big deal. Good. No way Scotty would try something with all these people around.

Traffic must have eased, because it only took Bernard forty-five minutes to arrive. He didn't have any tail that I could see, and there weren't any marshals inside, so I hopped in with my backpack and carry on. He smiled over his shoulder at me and asked: "Where to?"

"Oh, just drive around for a little bit, then we'll be back. I need to make an entrance."

I closed the privacy screen and stripped down, pouring some of the scotch from the fully stocked bar on me, then steeling myself and taking a few swigs. I transferred the wire handcuff key to the waistband of my new silk panties, just in case. The newer, better rig went on. I sheathed the *kris* in it, making sure it was snug in the small of my back, so that it wouldn't interfere with the lines of the dress. Then, I put on the sequined leopard evening gown and the heels. Even as an Irish shorthair, I looked hot. Like a shimmery, redheaded man-eater.

I had originally bought the dress with the idea of wearing it to one of Scotty's nightclubs tonight, in order to get his attention, but attending his gala was even better. A little thrill ran through me. This was going to be fun. Playing the part, hamming it up. Almost like being on stage, except that here, the biggest critics were packing guns.

I swapped the lock picks, the cash, the passport and palladium cards, and one of the 5D discs into my stylish new chained clutch, and when I gave Bernard the word, he headed back to Union Station. The limo pulled into the lot, the sunset behind us splashing red and gold highlights across the arched windows of the main building. No one else had a limo quite like mine, and a few heads turned as Bernard helped me step out onto the red carpet. I gave them all a coquettish smile, then wobbled a bit drunkenly in the heels as I approached the restaurant entrance, where a tuxedoed doorman asked me: "Invitation, please?"

"On the list. Faith Hopkins."

The doorman smiled, scanned his list, then looked up at me. "Identification, please?"

"Jesus," I exclaimed in a loud Houston drawl. "That's a mite pretentious for a little ol' party, don't you think?"

The doorman shrugged apologetically. "Rich crowd. Security's gotta be tight."

I pulled out the passport card and handed it over. He checked it, looked at me, then handed it back and said: "Welcome, Miss Hopkins. Enjoy your evening."

I tucked the card back into my purse and sauntered into a large, earth-toned room supported by pillared arches and crowded with partygoers. A big, U-shaped bar dominated the center, the drop-down ceiling above it decorated with tile mosaic and hammered brass in the same Southwestern style Art Deco as the main Union Station. Tables covered what looked like a dance floor. Along the right wall, a curving, red tiled stairway led to a mezzanine studded with cozy, slab-sided booths. Jazz piano music filtered from hidden speakers above, loud enough to sound festive, but not deafening. I glanced around, looking for Scotty, but somebody caught my elbow. I turned my head and saw who: "Mando?"

He looked both amazed and angry to see me here. "How did you get here? Thought you boarded the flight."

So, at least Mando had made an effort to keep track of me. "I came to meet with Dave and Randall. About the deal."

"You shouldn't be here without your friends."

I knew by the way he said it that he meant the marshals. He guided me through the crowd, tightening his grip on my arm as we circled the bar and I saw the man sitting in the alcove, fingers deftly carving sweet, smoky Jazz from a baby grand piano: Jim.

The sight of him hit me physically, like a blow to the sternum, but before I could say anything, Mando steered me up to the bar. "What are you drinking, Miss Hopkins?"

"Oh, uh..." I cleared my throat, coming back to myself. I wasn't Rad anymore. I was Faith. And no matter how hard it was to pretend I didn't know Jim, that's exactly what I'd have to do. "I'll have a margarita—strawberry, please, with a little shot of Midori." It was a drink I'd seen Faith order a million times, but one I'd never tasted before. I hoped I could stomach it.

"And give me a single malt whiskey on the rocks," Mando instructed as the bartender dumped various fluids over the ice in the blender. "Glenfiddich, if you have it."

The bartender nodded, continuing with his machinations. I rested an elbow on the bar and scanned the crowd idly, trying to resist looking at Jim again. I saw Jana sitting at one of the booths on the mezzanine, along with Dave Seward and Randall Cortelaine. I waved to them. Jana stared at me, then pulled out her phone and started tapping away, acting as if I didn't exist. Dave gave me a wave. Cortelaine just stared at me. Right about then, my willpower snapped.

My gaze slid surreptitiously back to Jim in his black tux, his fingers dancing over the keys. True to the Jazz image of the evening, he wore dark glasses. He'd cut off his long hair, shaved it down to a severe, skull-hugging style that showcased a widow's peak dipping toward his forehead. He'd lost weight, too. The way his thin pencil neck poked out of the dark jacket made me think of tongue depressor dipped in tar. An unlit cigarette hung from the corner of his mouth. A pack of Marlboros sat on top of the piano, next to a big glass tip goblet. I wanted to go put the rest of my cash in there, but a tap on my forearm made me turn my head.

Scotty stood next to me in a too-tight tux, a cold grin on his lips. "He's not your type, Faith. He's got nothing worth stealing."

"Neither do you," I remarked drily.

His expression hardened. "You'll pay for it, though."

I laughed, high and twittery, Faith's way of telling him he was full of shit. "Scotty, darlin', I'm already payin'. I've got to listen to that." I hooked a thumb at Jim, then turned to snatch up the drink the bartender set down before me.

"You've got a lot of nerve coming here."

I sipped the margarita, surprised at how good it tasted. Didn't think strawberries could kill so much of the alcohol. "Thought you wanted me back."

"Oh, I want you." He pressed against me, hazel eyes sparkling with malice. "I can hear you screaming already."

I laughed again, to hide my discomfort with both his words and his proximity. I wanted to kick his ass so badly. Instead, I leaned in to whisper in Scotty's ear: "I stole your li'l ole data engine. And your server. You better play nice if you want 'em back."

He stared at me, as if he wasn't sure what I'd just said. He glanced furtively toward Mando, who was awaiting his change from the bartender for our drinks.

"You know," I whispered, leaning in so my lips brushed his earlobe. I bit it, hard, but not hard enough to draw blood. "That secret decoder ring on the wall of your sex room? You might wanna text Lonny and see if the décor turns on."

He paled, and then shook his head, stepping away from me to pull his phone from his pocket. He started texting furiously. While Scotty was busy confirming my claim, Mando held his arm out. "Shall we?"

"Now, that's a gentleman." I looped my arm around his.

He escorted me towards the stairs to the upper level. "Where did you get those clothes? That purse?"

"Bought 'em this afternoon."

"You look...amazing."

"Thanks."

"You should have taken the flight," he murmured as we started up the stairs. "We don't have any security in place. Nobody expected you to be here."

"That's all right. Brought my own security."

Mando surveyed the room from the top of the stairs. He frowned, murmuring: "I don't see Rossi."

"I don't trust those marshalmallows," I murmured back. "They don't even know I'm gone."

"How did you find out about this event?"

"Is Tony here? I need to talk to him."

"Still in transit. He hopped a flight as soon as you checked in for yours."

I sighed, disappointed. Even more disappointed when I heard Jana say "Faith," in a voice dripping with disdain.

I turned to face the table, taking a big gulp of the margarita and plopping myself down next to her with the sloppy moves of the well-oiled. Despite the sloshed act, I was careful to sit up very straight, since bending forward would reveal the *kris*. "Fancy meetin' you here. I thought Daenerys had all the dragons chained up."

Mando coughed to cover his chuckle. He remained standing, waiting for Scotty, who was now mounting the stairs like an angry bear. Cortelaine smirked at my joke, but Dave Seward just looked clueless. I nodded to them with that sugary Faith smile. "Let's do this. I got a party to hardy."

Jana's nostrils curled up and she scooched away from me. "Are you drunk already?"

"I dunno."

"How can you not know?"

"Can I help it if my drunk-o-meter's broke?" Brightening, I lifted my glass. "Maybe another one of these will—"

"Don't fuck with me." Scotty stepped up and smacked the glass out of my hand, sending it skittering across the table to shatter on the tiled floor at Mando's feet. A sudden silence enveloped the area as people at nearby tables gaped at us. Scotty seemed to realize he'd gone a bit overboard, and straightened his suit. "Move over," he growled at me.

"Anythin' for you, Scotty, darlin'." I allowed him to shoehorn me into the booth next to Jana. He sat down quickly, as if to prevent my escape. Or maybe it was just so he could knock back the scotch Mando handed to him. He handed the empty glass back to Mando, who turned away wordlessly and headed back toward the bar.

"Bring me another one, too," I shouted after him, then turned to Scotty. I slid my hand down his thigh, and gave him a bit of a grope under the table. He wasn't anywhere near as impressive as Tony. "Hon, you think maybe we could do some dancin'? I love to dance. Of course, we'll need better music—"

"This isn't that kind of function," he warned, but he didn't remove my hand from his privates.

"Let's get this over with," Jana groused.

Dave Seward pulled a tablet from a padded sleeve and held it out to me. "It's all there, waiting for your signature."

Jana pushed a stylus at me.

"Oh," I looked over the contract, then shook my head. "Y'all misunderstand me. I ain't here to sign anythin'. I'm here to renegotiate." I gave Scotty my best shit-eating grin. "Scotty's decided to sign over his half of the studio to me. When that's done, then I'll buy out Gower."

There was a stunned silence while everyone around the table gawked at me like I'd just announced I was screwing the Pope.

Mando arrived with the drinks right about then. He paused, his dark gaze sweeping over them. His brow furrowed with puzzlement as he set the drinks down on the table. "What did I miss?"

I picked up the fresh margarita with my free hand and sipped it, bouncing my head up and down to an imaginary techno beat. "Buh-buh-buh-Baby's on fire..."

"Faith," Scotty began, searching for words. I could feel him vibrating with fury. "You are fucking insane."

"I don't think so." I smiled at him, squeezing his balls painfully through the fabric of his pants. "You owe me. For Omar."

"You're dead," he snarled at me. "You are so dead." He shoved away from the table and stalked down the stairs. Cortelaine nodded to us all and slid out of the booth to follow him.

Dave Seward looked across the table at me as he made his way out of the booth. He tucked the tablet under his arm. "Was that wise?"

"Who needs wise when you got the winnin' hand?"

"Faith, he just threatened to kill you."

I rolled my eyes. "As if. He ain't no threat to me. I got Tony wrapped around my finger."

Jana shot me a scathing glance, then shook her head.

"Well, I hope you know what you're doing," Seward said.

Mando stepped back to allow him to scurry down the stairs, then regarded Jana with a confused expression. "What did I miss?"

"Your fucking wildcard just destroyed two years of work," Jana snarled through gritted teeth. She jabbed me with her elbow a few times, until I got out of the booth so she could exit. She stood up, glowering down at both Mando and me. Like her being taller than us was supposed to scare me or something. "Stay with her," she ordered Mando. "While I go talk to our friends at the hotel and find out how this bitch got off the chain."

Mando stepped up beside me. Together, we stood at the rail, watching as Jana descended the stairs, all grace and malice.

Down below, at the end of the bar near the door, Scotty was in a heated discussion with two men I didn't recognize. He paused to exchange a brief word with Jana before she left, then resumed his conversation.

Mando pulled a cigar out of his pocket and lit it up, ignoring the frowns from people at nearby tables. "What," he took a long puff, then exhaled out over the crowd below, "did you do?

"All y'all's job for you."

"What's that supposed to mean?"

"Can't breach a castle by playin' pattycake with the gatekeeper."

"How else do you get the keys?"

"Screw the keys. And the gatekeeper. Scotty'll be off the board tomorrow, arrested for Damiano's murder as soon as Hollis gets a search warrant."

"You tipped off Hollis?"

I nodded, then took a big sip of my strawberry flavored victory. I was feeling loose, relaxed, in control. Maybe alcohol wasn't so bad, after all.

I could tell from the way his jaw pulsed that Mando was growing more and more upset. "Without keys, how do you get into the castle?"

"The sewer line, silly. Every castle's got a sewer." I opened my purse and produced the 5D disc for the data engine.

"That's just for the holo projector."

"You'd think. But it's really a mainline to the king's most secret chamber." He slanted a bewildered look at me, so I spelled it out: "Scotty's been streamin' a feed, encryptin' it through the algorithms hidden on the 5Ds used for the décor. Sendin' it out via a server hidden inside the same box as the holo projector's data engine. This ain't no industrial production kind of thing. It's intimate. Personal. The kinda thing shared between a twisted lackey and his sick asshole of a boss. My guess is, you examine that server, you'll get every IP address Leigh's ever used to access that feed."

Understanding dawned, and his expression went from angry to calculating. "Maybe. But we'd have to get our hands on both the discs, and the server."

"Already done. The flight shoulda landed by now. Tell your friends to check the baggage carousel for my luggage. It's a Louis Vuitton bag with cartoon cats on it."

He blinked at me, stunned.

I gave him a toothy grin and released the 5D disc into his palm, mic drop style. "You're welcome."

CHAPTER TWENTY-TWO

We sat in the booth while Mando held a text conversation with the folks in Vegas. I bobbed my head up and down between sips of margarita, watching Scotty say his goodbyes and leave, frustrated that I couldn't see Jim from where I was sitting.

Finally, Mando looked up at me from his phone. "You did all this in less than seven hours?"

I nodded, draining my glass. "Woulda been five, but traffic sucked."

"Where are the other discs?"

"Safe in my limo."

"You have a limo? How?"

"Palladium card," I shrugged. "What happens next?"

"We wait until Jana tells me what to do."

"Do I gotta go back to the hotel?"

"Dunno. They may not want you back, considering how badly you've derailed this whole thing."

"Can we go look at the cars while we wait?"

"Don't see why not." He slipped his phone back into his pocket and stood, holding a hand out to me. His expression grew serious. "Things are gonna get really dangerous, now."

"Like they weren't before?"

"Not like this. We're off script. That's when mistakes happen."

I took his hand and stood up, a little wobbly for real this time. The room was a bit swimmy and I couldn't feel my teeth. "Is this what being buzzed feels like?"

"You spent four years at college and you've never been buzzed?"

"Didn't want to wind up like my mother."

"Fair enough." He took my arm and helped me down the stairs and through the crowd, doing his best to block my view of the piano. Some of the partygoers did a double take as I walked past them, registering both recognition and surprise. A few scowled at me, but more waved and nodded.

I guessed Faith had made quite the impression when she had been dating Scotty. The music stopped as we reached the end of the bar, and I glanced over at the piano to see Jim stepping through a side door into the courtyard with the pack of cigarettes. I sighed, pained to see him heading off for a smoke break.

The crowd thinned once we got outside, and my head cleared a bit. The air was summery, with a light breeze that made the palm trees above the cars sigh. The first vehicle we came to was a 1959 Maserati Tipo 61. I had heard about the birdcage Maserati, but had never seen one up close. It was a magnificent blend of red curves and pugnacious promise. I wondered what it'd be like to take such distilled speed for a spin. Probably way more fun than the Formula Ford I used to drive for Uncle Fangio.

As I bent down to look into the open cockpit, I felt a strange, electric heat behind me, like I was standing too close to one of those megawatt spotlights near the multiscreen. I glanced over my shoulder to see Tony reaching out for me.

He wore a black tuxedo with a powder blue bow tie and cummerbund. Star sapphires studded his shirt and cuffs, a larger sapphire replacing the ubiquitous diamond stud in his ear, resonating with the blue of his eyes. Maybe it was the alcohol, but my wariness towards him seemed to have crumbled. I was just plain happy to see him.

I wanted to hug him, but the grim set to his jaw and the abrupt way he grabbed my shoulder made me unsure. And then he bent down to kiss me, sliding his other arm around my back, and my hormones popped off like fireworks at the Hollywood Bowl. His fingers smoothed along the top edge of the *kris* where it was strapped to my back. A warm flush surged through me as I slipped my arms around him. The outline of his shoulder holster pressed against my breast as we embraced.

"I'm glad you're here," he said, after pulling away. He searched my gaze, gratitude and a kind of hungry excitement twinkling in his eyes. "Thought I'd lost you."

What he meant was, he was relieved I hadn't betrayed him. It rankled me, that he thought I was capable of that, so I replied: "Night's still young."

He chuckled and leaned in to nuzzle my ear. "Marshals will be here in ten minutes. If they get ahold of you, they're not gonna let you go. We need to move. Now."

"Won't they just track us?"

"Not with this," he murmured, his hand smoothing along the *kris*.

Understanding flashed, and I snickered. That was why nobody had come after me all afternoon. The *kris* had been jamming the signal from my implant. He took my hand, pulling me towards the curb, where Glen and Kam stood beside Tony's limo. Percy waved from behind the wheel. Mando walked along beside us, still smoking his cigar.

"Shit," I said as the familiar sand colored sedan rolled up to block the limo from the front.

"Hollis." Tony hooked us left, back inside the restaurant.

Mando kept going towards the limo. "I'll delay him."

Tony and I plowed through the crowd, heading around the bar and through the doors on the street side of the building. The mellow looseness of the alcohol evaporated, replaced by a stark, urgent clarity. Amazing how quickly adrenaline sobers a person.

We moved past the restrooms and down a darkened thruway, only to be stopped by a locked door.

"Shit," Tony said, glancing around for other options. I pulled my makeshift lock picks out and went to work.

He grabbed my shoulder and started to pull me away, but the lock clicked, and the door swung wide. We passed through into a dark space that had strange echoes. I relocked the door as Tony fumbled the lights on to reveal an abandoned micro-brewery. Several huge, tarnished stainless steel tanks took up most of the space, but there was a padlocked door was on the far wall.

The concrete floor was riddled with puddles from a leaking pipe overhead. To the left, a side door was propped open to allow several power cables to snake through into the main patio area. More cables threaded through a maintenance panel in the conduit of a hooded ceiling fan overhead. As we cleared the row of tanks, I noticed all the cables terminated at a portable light board set up on rollers between the last two tanks. A cable as thick as my wrist left the back of the box, patched into a fuse panel on the wall.

None of it looked to code.

"Tony, give me your phone. We can use my limo."

"You have a limo?"

"For another thirteen hours or so," I nodded.

"How much is that costing me?"

"You don't want to know."

He snickered and handed me his phone. While I told Bernard to drive to the south side of the building and wait, Tony tested the chained door. "Shit," he muttered, cupping his hand over the sapphire in his ear for a moment before heading towards me, drawing his gun. "Hollis is getting the door unlocked, and there are two uniforms coming around towards the side door."

"You're going to shoot them?"

"No." He pressed his gun in my hand, then reached into a holster at the small of his back and pulled out another pistol. "Can't be found with weapons on me. Still under suspicion for murder." I shoved the two guns in my purse, then gave his phone back. My purse was full, now, and I needed both hands for the two guns he slipped out of ankle holsters, along with four spare clips and a wicked-looking titanium folding knife. "We gotta hide you."

He put his phone in his pocket and searched the room with his gaze. He followed the cables to the maintenance panel in the ceiling and pulled it open, revealing a small ladder-stair to a catwalk which ran parallel to the venting conduit. "Get in here. If he arrests me, head out to your limo and go back to the Ranch."

He lifted me into the space, and I shoved the weapons onto the catwalk before clambering up, ignoring the sharp, painful twinge in my right hand and wrist. It was getting quite a workout today.

As Tony shut the panel, I peered around the catwalk, surprised to find that the ceiling, although appearing solid from below, was just a series of see-through, perforated panels hung from the catwalk superstructure. Intrigued, I crawled along the catwalk around the ventilation shaft, holding the weapons against my belly with my right arm as I scoped out the room below.

An Amtrak cop unlocked the door and Hollis bulled in through from the restaurant, accompanied by a uniform. The hinges on the side door squealed, and two more uniformed cops burst into the room, guns drawn. "Don't move!" Hollis shouted. "Hands where we can see them."

"Hello, Wanker."   Tony raised his hands with a bored expression. "What brings you here tonight?"

Hollis didn't answer, motioning for one of the uniforms to pat Tony down. The other two glanced warily along the row of tanks.

"Where is she?" Hollis demanded.

"Who?"

"Your fiancé. Faith Hopkins. The woman you're leaving the country with tomorrow. I just saw you with her."

"Don't know what you're talking about."

Oops. I had forgotten to mention to him that I'd bought tickets to Aruba for us. I'd meant them to be another misdirection, if I managed to evade capture for that long.

"He's clean," announced the man who patted Tony down.

Hollis scowled and waved the other two cops towards the door. "Search his men, and the limo, too. If you find any weapon that's not on their permits to carry, throw the cuffs on them."   He turned to the first cop. "You go out, find that girl. And make sure none of the vehicles associated with Tovenaar have left the site. There are marshals en route."   The uniforms nodded and scurried into the thruway toward the main dining room.

"Don't bother looking, Wanker. Faith left without me."

Hollis circled the stove toward him, a slow grin spreading under his pink cauliflower nose. "This is the end of the line for you. I am not gonna let that poor girl wind up another one of your mysterious 'statistics,' like that Damiano woman."

"I didn't kill Damiano."

"Of course you didn't. Not that I can prove in a court of law, anyway. But I know what you did to her. I know what you're planning to do to Miss Hopkins."

"You know you can't touch me. Why waste my time?"

"I didn't used to be able to touch you. But you're drawing outside the lines on this one, aren't you Tovenaar? And now, all those little Company dweebs you've been hiding behind have yanked your raincoat. They don't care if somebody gets you wet. So, turn around. Face the tank. Put your hands on your head."

Tony rolled his eyes and assumed the position, which just so happened to be in the center of a puddle. Tony made a face.

Hollis grabbed the back of his collar, shoving him face first into the tank. He slapped a handcuff on Tony's right wrist, ratcheting the other cuff to the metal pipe running vertically up the tank.

"What the fuck?" Tony protested. "You've got nothing on me."

"I don't need anything, anymore." Hollis searched Tony himself, brows raised in discovery as his hand hit something hard in Tony's pocket. He drew it out, disappointment plain on his face when he saw it was the phone.

"I know you're obsessed with me, Wanker. But shouldn't you kiss me before feeling me up like this?"

"Fuck you." Hollis slammed the phone into Tony's nose, then tossed it away. It skittered off across the wet floor to rest in a puddle near the side door. "Don't call me Wanker. Now where's the gun? Where's the girl?"

Blood spurted from Tony's nostrils, pouring down across his lips and chin. "This is harassment. It's against the law to handcuff a prisoner to an immovable object. My lawyer will—"

"I don't give a fuck about your lawyer." Hollis peered through the small, dusty window into a now defunct walk-in fridge. "Where'd you put her, Tovenaar? Poor girl's probably scared out of her wits." He continued searching the room, checking between the tanks and under the counters. When he reached my access panel, he popped it open and peeked inside, shining a flashlight up the stairs.

The ventilation shaft shielded me from his gaze, so I was safe as long as I kept still and quiet. Stymied, Hollis circled the room again, checking everything, even the padlocked exterior door. The radio clipped to his pocket crackled, and a male voice announced: "Uh, the girl isn't here, Detective. Nobody's seen her since she left the room with Tovenaar."

Hollis toggled the mic: "And what about his people? They all present and accounted for?"

"Yes, sir. Saraskoss, Mitchell, and Villalobos. Got 'em right in front of me. And the marshals just arrived with Slager."

"Any unauthorized weapons?"

"No, sir. They're clean. Campos is searching the limo right now, but, so far it looks like that's clean, too."

"Did you check the driver?"

"Yes, sir. Nothing on him, either."

Hollis frowned, cursing softly to himself.

"See?" Tony looked up at him smugly. "She's not here. And I'm not packing. So, why don't you let me go, and I won't press charges and get your ass thrown off the force?"

The detective glanced around the room again, unwilling to admit defeat. His gaze lingered on the lighting board for a moment, an idea seeming to spark in the dark reaches of his mind.

"You sold her, didn't you?" Hollis stalked back to stand above Tony. "To Foster, to get on his good side before you shoved the knife in his back. Or were you gonna keep her for yourself? Make a snuff film with her, like you did to those kids in Borneo?"

All the color drained out of Tony's face. He shook his head, his eyes wide, focused on some inner demon. "I didn't—"

"Of course you did, you sick fuck. I saw the footage at the debriefing in Jakarta." Hollis spat at Tony's feet, revulsion twisting his features. "No wonder your wife left you. She figured out what happened to your son. You report him kidnapped, let your corrupt little Indonesian police officials pretend to look for him while you string your own flesh and blood up. Did you get your rocks off watching Scotty work him over? I know you keep a video of it."

"No." Tony shook his head. A dark heat crackled within him, that black kernel of rage coming to life as he pushed off his knees onto his feet. He lunged. His ankle flashed out in a sweeping kick, but the water on the floor made his footing slick, and his cuffed hand yanked him off balance. He went sprawling to the concrete.

Hollis chuckled and drove a vicious foot into Tony's kidney. I gasped, but the sound was lost in Tony's agonized yelp, and in the scuffling as Hollis kicked again and again. Tony scrambled to protect himself. And then, suddenly, Hollis grabbed Tony by the hair, forced him to lock gazes.

"You're not leaving here tonight, Tovenaar," he vowed, voice ringing with hate. "A Hollis helped bring Dillinger down. I'll be damned if I let you flee the country tomorrow." He turned his back to Tony and walked around the stove, so that his back was to me. He pulled something from his pocket that I couldn't see from my vantage.

His radio crackled: "Uh, Detective? The limo's clean. So are the other vehicles. No sign of the woman, but the marshals want to speak with you."

"Okay," Hollis replied. "Looks like we struck out. I'll be right out." But he didn't move, fiddling around with something on the counter near the fuse panel.

Tony glared at his back, panting, then pulled against the cuffs to wipe away the blood streaming from his nose. "You can't leave me like this, Wanker."

"You're right." He turned around, an open fold out knife in one hand, and a stripped length of cable in the other.

"Shit," Tony whispered, eyes going wide. He scrambled to get to his feet as Hollis rested the bare wires on the pipe Tony was cuffed to and reached for a switch on the lighting board.

Oh, dear God. *No.*

Hollis threw the switch. Sparks flew from the cuff on the rail and Tony's entire body lifted in a grotesque, pain-wracked spasm. After an endless second or two, the lights dimmed, a fuse blew in the panel, and Tony slumped down, body jerking in haphazard spasms.

Hollis flipped the switch off, and then stepped over to Tony and felt for a pulse. Ten seconds later, he smiled and stood up, straightening his jacket. "About fuckin' time somebody took you out, Tovenaar." He unlocked the cuffs, wedged Tony's scorched wrist between the pipe and the tank, and then strolled whistling back into the thruway, locking the door behind him.

I crouched, frozen, paralyzed by disbelief. And then I was scrambling along the cat walk, weapons falling like rain as I dropped through the access panel to the floor. I kicked the cable away and jammed my fingers into the soft flesh of Tony's neck, searching for a pulse amid the random spasms rocking his body.

Nothing. And he wasn't breathing.

CHAPTER TWENTY-THREE

Trembling with adrenaline, my own heart pumping enough for us both, I tugged Tony's wrist free and straightened him out, tilting his head back and sweeping his mouth to clear it, coming back with bloody fingers. To make sure his airway was clear, I emptied my lungs into his, and pulled away, frantic at the way the air rushed so uncontrollably out of his flaccid body.

My hands felt through his shirt to locate his xiphoid, and I started the compressions. One hundred beats per minute, like a metronome. After that, I paused for a pulse check.

Damn.

Another hundred, and still no pulse. Sweat streamed from my temples, heart thrumming like a jackhammer. I smelled urine. The shock had done that to him, right? Right? I didn't know. Tears of frustration welled up in my eyes.

His ribs cracked under my palms as I worked through another hundred. And another. Four minutes, not counting the time it took me to crawl down here. Still no pulse. And his skin was so clammy...

My right arm started cramping halfway through the next set, but I powered through, anyway. "Don't die, Tony. Don't you dare die on me, you inconsiderate bastard."

I checked his pulse again, to rest my hand a moment, and felt a steady fluttering in the hollow beneath his jaw. I pressed harder, afraid I was fooling myself, sensing my own heartbeat in place of his.

Yes. He was alive. But still not breathing. I leaned over and set my lips against his, forcing my breath into his.

Suddenly his entire body arched, racked by a wheezing, lung-deep breath. His eyes shot open, and he gawked at me, his expression half fear, half wonder. "Man'o," he slurred, "'m dreamin' 'gain."

Then he vomited, a dark stream of blood and scotch spewing onto my nine thousand dollar dress and splashing down across his white tuxedo shirt. The tang of blood was on my lips, as well.

Oh, crap. Had I pressed too hard and punctured a lung with one of his ribs? I had no idea.

I wiped the red stringers off his lips and chin, preparing to breathe for him again, but he continued to gasp and cough, rolling onto his side and drawing his knees towards his chest. His legs and arms twitched and jerked with convulsive spasms. As the tremors died down, he groaned, coughed, and spat more blood on the floor.

His breathing settled into a shallow, steady rhythm. Little red bubbles appeared in his nostrils, and I realized with relief that he wasn't hemorrhaging, after all. The blood from his nose had collected in the back of his throat.

He gave a high, quavery moan and grimaced. "*Wat de fok...?*"

"You've been electrocuted. I gave you CPR."

He blinked at me several times, as if he wasn't sure who I was. "Rad? Why're you Irish? Am I dreamin'?"

Oh, boy. "I'm Faith, Tony. Remember? Faith?"

He stared at me for a few seconds, uncomprehending, and then it clicked. "Ohhh. Right." He nodded. "Faith. You're Faith." He rolled over onto his hands and knees and grabbed the tank upright with his uninjured hand. His right wrist was red and blistered where the handcuff rested against his skin.

I put a hand on his shoulder. "Don't get up. You've been seriously hurt. I'll call 911." I ran over and picked up his phone, then squatted beside him.

He grabbed my wrist. "No ambulance. No hospitals. Help me up."

"Tony, you need medical attention. You *died*."

"Not the first time." He made a guttural cry, half moan, half roar as he forced himself to his feet. "Won't be the last." His voice was clipped, breathy. "Gotta get to the safe house."

I rose to steady him as he staggered away from the stove towards the wall beside the side door. He was determined, and I couldn't force him to seek treatment. I wondered why nobody had shown up looking for us, yet, then realized that Hollis would have gone out of his way to keep anybody from visiting this area to make sure Tony was good and dead before someone found the body.

Tony favored his right leg as we moved, keeping it more extended. His foot kicked a magazine, and he stopped and stared down at it, then glanced around us. "Why are my weapons on the floor?" He tried to bend down to pick the magazine up.

I prodded him towards the wall. "You'll fall. I'll get them." We tottered him over, and he leaned his cheek against the peeling paint beside the door, panting. I collected everything I could find, tucking each item back in its appropriate place on Tony's person, wincing as I saw the red exit burn on the side of Tony's right calf when I snugged the gun into his ankle holster.

Footfalls approached from outside in the courtyard. I lunged and grabbed for the handle to hold the door shut. Too late.

It swung wide and Jim, of all people, stepped through, a half-smoked cigarette in his hand. I'd forgotten he was on his break.

He froze in surprise when he saw us. His mellow, soulful features contorted with a hateful fury I had never seen in him before. His cigarette dropped, fizzling out in a puddle. "Tovenaar," he growled, lunging for Tony with a cocked fist.

"Jim, no!" I hip checked him as he threw the punch, knocking him back just far enough that he barely tapped Tony's shoulder.

He had no idea how to fight, or even make a fist. If he actually managed to connect, he was bound to hurt his hands. I used several parrying blocks, making sure he kept his distance, until I could trap one of his arms under mine.

"Who the fuck are you?" Tony asked, bewildered.

"You killed my best friend!" Jim wrestled to resume his attack. "Kidnapped her right out of the police station!"

"Jim. I'm alive," I told him. "It's me. I'm right here!"

He kept fighting, and managed to get his hand free. I drove my left shoulder into his solar plexus and knocked him back against the open door. It swung away from our combined weight, and we tumbled to the wet concrete. The door slammed against the wall and bounced back. The edge smacked hard into the knuckles of my right hand. Pain from the impact jolted up to my shoulder, but at least Jim broke my fall.

I straddled him and pressed down on his collarbones with my left forearm to keep him down. "Relax, relax, I'm alive. Tovenaar didn't kill me."

He glared up at me, his ribcage pumping like a bony bellows. "Rad?" The fight drained out of him as comprehension seeped past his fury. "Rad? No way. Is that really you?"

"Yeah. It's me, Jim."

"Rad..." His gaze searched mine, as if he was seeing God in my face. His hand reached up to caress my cheek. "You don't look like you."

"I know. Tovenaar faked my death. So he could fix my hand." I slid back off of him and showed him how my fingers curled and extended, wincing at the sudden pain. "See?"

"Holy crap, it is you!" He sat up and threw his arms wrapped around me in an embrace so tight, I thought his bony stick arms might splinter. I hugged him back, nuzzling my face against his neck, the way I had always dreamed of doing. He smelled like cigarettes and empanadas.

It seemed so unfair. I'd fantasized about being in just such a position with Jim for the past four years. Now that I finally had him in my arms, all I wanted to do was get the Hell out of there before Tony collapsed. I swallowed hard and scrambled up to prop Tony up. "Gotta go. He's hurt bad."

Jim clambered to his feet, looking at the blood on my dress, and the mess on Tony's tuxedo shirt. "You're leaving? But you've been gone so long. You have to tell me what happened."

"No." I draped Tony's good arm across my shoulders and gave Jim a guilty look. "Can't tell you anything. Go back to the piano."

"Fuck that! I'm not letting you just disappear again!"

I shook my head, limping Tony over to the door. "Just go."

"I'll help you. Let me help you."

He stepped up on the other side of Tony, and we sandwiched the big guy between us, easing him through into the same unlit colonnade that Fox-face and Doughboy had forced me along. It shielded us from the glaring lights of the patio.

We trudged along in the gloom, unnoticed by the partygoers strolling around the patio behind us. Random tremors vibrated through Tony's limbs as we moved. His breathing was labored. The smoking area in front of the Water District building was about fifty yards away, but it seemed like a mile.

"Where you been all this time, Rad? What the hell happened to you? Why do you look so different?"

"Witness protection." It wounded me to lie to him, but it wasn't that far from the truth. "My name is Faith, now. And you can't tell anybody you saw us."

"Not even Richie?"

"Anybody. Unless you wanna wind up disappeared, like me."

"Will I ever see you again?"

"Not until it's safe."

A long sigh left him. We staggered along in silence for the last few paces to the end of the building. We rounded the corner and were greeted by the gleaming chrome of the Mercedes logo centered between the red glow of taillights.

"Nice limo," Jim said, impressed.

Tony hawked a gob of blood and spat it into the gutter.

Bernard stood beside the sliding side door, his brows arching when we emerged from the shadow of the building into the bar of light from the limo interior. "Wow. You guys are fighty drunks."

"You should see the other fellers," I told him, slipping back into my Faith skin.

Jim remained on the sidewalk while Bernard helped me maneuver Tony into the vehicle. Tony made a loud, buzzing groan as he settled into one of the recliners. I made sure it tilted back all the way, so his feet were elevated. I wasn't sure if his disorientation was due to shock, or was a side effect of the electrocution, but I was sure he needed a doctor.

Jim started to climb inside, but I blocked him. "You gotta go back. You gotta act like you never saw us."

He squinted at me, like he wasn't sure why I was suddenly Texan. "But, I want to help."

"That's the best damn help you can give. Trust me."

He stared at me, then looked past me at Tony, at the limo, and at Bernard. A long sigh escaped him. "Guess this is it."

"Guess so." I climbed back down to the sidewalk to meet his gaze, grateful to have had a chance to see him one last time.

"Take care of yourself." His voice was thick.

"You, too. Go be famous. Don't hold back."

He nodded and threw his arms around me. I hugged him back. When he drew away, he kissed me. It was a chaste, bittersweet kiss, closed mouthed and tender. But it flooded me with a fire that I hadn't felt since Chris was alive.

"Bye." He cleared his throat and wiped his eyes as he stepped away.

"Bye," I echoed, my voice rough. I gave him a wave, and watched as he headed back along the colonnade. Bernard gave me a curious look as I climbed back into the limo. I said nothing, so he slid the door shut.

I grabbed a blanket and laid it on Tony. His eyes opened. His face was drawn with pain, but he forced a smile. "I miss you, Rad. Wish I could see you again."

"I'm Faith. And I'm right here, Tony."

"Right. Faith." He snickered, then winced at the effort. "That's good. We got a long way to go, yet."

The limo shuddered as Bernard climbed behind the wheel. The front door slammed. "Where to, now?"

Tony rattled off an address I didn't recognize.

"What city is that in?"

"Yogyakarta."

"We're in Los Angeles, hon," I reminded him.

He grunted, and went quiet for about fifteen seconds before giving an address in Echo Park.

"I'll give you five hunnert bucks if you get us there in five minutes or less," I told Bernard.

"Sounds good," he replied, putting the Mercedes in gear.

I closed the privacy screen, disturbed by Tony's confusion, and worried he might say something else that shouldn't be heard by folks like Bernard. Or me, for that matter.

Thankfully, he remained quiet for a time, until suddenly he grunted, and sat up, hissing as another spasm racked him. When it passed, he panted and lay back, closing his eyes. "I'm sorry, Rad," he murmured. "He shouldn't have died."

"Who?"

"I know you loved him."

"Who?"

"It was bad luck. I did what I could."

"We're almost there," Bernard said over the intercom.

I lifted the screen to glance out the window, surprised to find that "there" was an industrial compound surrounded by a chain link fence topped with concertina wire. Not a hospital in sight. Spooky. "You sure this is the right address, Tony?"

His head rolled to the side and he looked out the window with one eye open. It took him several long seconds before he pulled out his phone and keyed something into it. "Yah."

The gate opened. Bernard guided the limo up the driveway between two concrete and glass buildings. We emerged in a parking area surrounded by more chain link. To the left was another structure that looked like a warehouse, with a roll-top door already raising at our approach, revealing a cavernous space lined with pallets of industrial equipment.

"Stop there," I told Bernard over the intercom.

The limo screeched to a halt next to the open roll-top.

"Keep this. Don't let anyone know you have it. Even Mando." Tony handed me his phone, then forced himself to his feet. He gripped the bulkhead unsteadily. Bernard opened the side door, and together we helped Tony down onto the asphalt.

"Wait here," Tony instructed, "It could be a while."

Thinking he was talking to Bernard, I stepped up to assist him, but he shook his head and pointed me into the vehicle. "Wait."

"But, you're—"

"That's an order." There was an implacability to him, a formidable air of command that made me realize I would never change his mind. I nodded with a sigh and climbed back into the limo, slipping his phone into my purse.

"And clean yourself off," he added as he turned and hobbled through the roll-top, which began to close as soon as he was inside. "You look like a goddamned vampire."

I stared after him, dread snaking up my spine like a spiteful boa constrictor. If he died all alone in there, I was going to kick his ass so hard, every donkey in the world would feel it.

When I felt calm enough to play Faith again, I turned to Bernard and handed him his cash. "Good drivin'."

"Thanks." He pocketed the money and helped me back into the limo. I could tell he wanted to ask questions, but knew better. I guessed discretion is in the job description for limo drivers.

He closed the door without another word. I made sure all the shades were down, then took Tony's phone from my purse. I sat in the recliner, looking to see what he had done to get the roll top door to open, but the screen was locked and I couldn't get past it.

As I fiddled with it, a searing tension cramped my right wrist and forearm. My fingers were swollen and a bruise was forming across my knuckles where the door had slammed into it during the scuffle with Jim. It made things difficult as I stripped out of my blood and vomit spattered dress and scuffed up heels.

By the time I'd strapped the kris to my left calf and donned a blouse, jeans and sneakers, the pain had become a constant, jangly shout. I shoved Tony's phone in the back pocket of my jeans, opened a bottle of water and used one of the cloth napkins from the cabinet to clear the blood from my face and hands. I kept moving my hand and arm around, trying to find a comfortable position, but it hurt no matter what I did. Time for the splint.

I pulled it out and fiddled with it, trying to work my hand inside. My knuckles were so swollen, I couldn't work the sheaths for the splines down my fingers. Frustrated, I tried to force it, dropping the splint as the pain exploded up my arm.

"Waugh!" I leapt to my feet, sticking my arm out instinctively, as if the further my hand was from my body, the less it would hurt. My arm was on fire from fingers to shoulder. Extension wasn't working, so I cradled my forearm against my midriff and folded my body over it. There was no position I could find to get away from the agony.

After a while, the spasm quieted, the pain dulling down to a bearable ache. I grabbed the ice bucket and dunked my hand inside its half melted contents, hoping to reduce the swelling enough to allow me to don the splint.

Since it was both boring and depressing to sit there in the dark, I turned the TV on, not even caring what show was on, but wanting the company of humans, regardless. I raised the shades so that I could see what was going on inside the building, but all I could see was lights illuminating various windows.

The ice hadn't quite melted completely when Tony's limo and that blue BMW M5 pulled up and parked, flanking my Sprinter. Mando emerged from the BMW, and Kam and Glen from the limo. They looked at me as they walked past on their way to the building. I scowled to myself as they entered the warehouse through a pass-through door beside the roll-top.

About a half hour later, they emerged from the warehouse and climbed into the cabin of my limo. Kam plopped down in the recliner to my right and offered me a stick of gum. I waved him off. Glen sat in the recliner across from Kam, arms folded across his chest. He seemed annoyed at Tony's plight, and annoyed with me for somehow causing it.

Mando shut the door, then went through the cabin with his little black box before sitting down in the recliner across from me with a grim, serious expression.

"What's goin' on?" I asked, turning the TV off. "What is this place?"

"Safe house," Mando explained.

"How come I can't I go inside? I wanna be safe."

"You don't have the clearance."

"So, what's goin' on in there?"

"We set up a trauma team and the requisite equipment here, in case somebody gets injured when Foster snatches you."

"In case I get injured, you mean."

"You, me, Kam, Glen. Never expected it to be Tony." His jaw tightened, his knuckles going white as he gripped the arm of his recliner. "How'd he get hurt? He doesn't remember."

"Hollis stomped him into a mud hole, then walked him dry."

"He what?" Kam was apparently unfamiliar with Texas vernacular.

"Beat the shit out of him," I clarified. "Then electrocuted him."

"He *what*?!" Mando and Glen roared in unison, outraged.

"Electrocuted him. Made sure he was dead, then moseyed on away."

"But he's not dead," Kam pointed out.

"I resuscitated him."

"You?" Glen gave me a dubious look. "Performed CPR?"

My initial reaction was to take offense, but then I realized he thought I was Faith, who was, as a general rule, entirely useless. So, I made up a plausible story: "Had a girlfriend who OD'd on fentanyl. Ruined my entire party. So, I learned CPR. Figgered that—"

"Can you excuse us?" Mando looked at Glen and then Kam. They exchanged glances, then rose in unison and exited the limo.

"Tell me," Mando said, after they'd closed the door, "exactly what happened. I need to know everything. What was said. What was done. Every detail you can remember."

I recounted the night's events starting from when we ran back into the restaurant, but I left out the entire Jim incident, figuring he didn't need to know.

Mando let me go without interruption, then asked me to repeat the story. This time, he asked me questions, probes to jog my memory. A troubled look tightened his cheeks when I came to what happened between Hollis and Tony. "Hollis took Tony's phone?"

"No. He smashed him in the nose with it, then tossed it away."

"So it's still in the old brewery?"

I shrugged, not wanting to lie, but not wanting Mando to ask me to turn it over, either.

"You're sure he said that the Company dweebs have yanked Tony's raincoat?"

I nodded. "What does that mean? Have they sanctioned him?"

"Not yet. But that's the first step."

"How did Hollis know?"

"Back in the day, he was with the Agency. Still has friends there."

"Hollis was C.I.A.?"

He nodded. "Scotty was, too. He funded black-ops through the Asian Development Bank before he fell in with Brighton Leigh."

"What about Tony? Who'd he work for?"

"Ask him," Mando suggested, with a look that said not to press the issue.

"Tony didn't really kill those kids, right? Make snuff films with them? Hollis was just saying that to get back at him for the Wanker stuff."

Mando didn't answer immediately, guilt and indignation swimming in the dark echoes behind his eyes. All at once his expression blanked. "I wasn't in Kalimantan. I can't tell you."

"But you wouldn't be here if you thought he did. You wouldn't work for someone who raped and murdered little kids. Right?"

His cheeks tightened with an emotion that looked suspiciously like shame. "Things happen during deep cover operations. Especially when you're surrounded by people like Brighton Leigh."

"You're saying he did do it?"

"I'm saying now is not a good time to talk about it."

I recoiled from him, skin crawling at the mere idea that what Hollis had said might be true.

Mando's phone buzzed. He checked it, then sighed. He remained silent for several seconds, the liquid intelligence of his eyes clouded with worry. "They're going to begin re-gen soon."

"Re-gen? Tony's going into re-gen?" I was both horrified and relieved. Horrified at the idea that Tony would have to undergo stasis. Relieved that the damage Hollis caused could be reversed.

"Electrical burns create internal injuries along the path of the current. If you re-gen quickly enough, you can reprogram the damaged cells into thinking they were never injured. Good job, getting him here this fast."

"Does he really have to do the stasis thing?" I didn't wish that experience on a scumbag like Scotty, let alone on Tony. Although with Mando being so evasive, maybe Tony was a scumbag, too.

"If he doesn't re-gen now, he's going to have serious long term complications. The surgery shouldn't last long. A few hours at the most. The biggest concern is that the electrocution might have caused some short-term memory loss. He might not remember anything that's happened today."

"Is that so bad?" I asked, nervous at his grim expression.

"He changes the codes each time he taps his accounts," Mando explained. "And he transferred the bulk of the money out of Faith's J.P Morgan account this afternoon."

"Why?"

"You were in the wind. Until you checked in at Burbank, we thought you were fleeing the country."

"Oh. Because of the Aruba tickets?"

He nodded. "He doesn't record the codes anywhere. Just memorizes them."

"Crap." once again, I'd been too smart for my own good, and totally screwed everything up in the process. "Was he able to see his little girls? It'd suck if he forgot being able to see them after three years."

"Dunno. We didn't get a chance to discuss that."

I sighed and pulled my hand out of the ice bucket, to see how much the swelling had gone down. I winced. Not enough.

Mando read my face, his lips hardening as the full impact of what had just happened finally sunk in. Our gazes locked; mine searching and bewildered; his full of tenderness and sorrow and a pride so fierce, I knew he, at least, understood how much I had risked. How much I might have lost.

"You okay?" he asked softly.

"Fine." My voice sounded small and far away. I eased my hand back into the bucket.

He sighed, tapping his fingers on the arm of the chair. "I get the clothes. And the limo. But why buy the Aruba tickets?"

"Because Jana's plan was stupid. Brighton Leigh was never going to come out of hiding to capture Faith. Or to snag Tony's fortune. And I was tired of sitting around being bait for a snatch that was never gonna happen."

"So, what was your plan?"

"Basic military strategy. Cut off the communications and supply lines, then set an irresistible lure to get the besieged to leave the castle, and make them think they have a short window of opportunity to seize the advantage, so they can't fully prepare. The Aruba tickets were the short window."

"And the communication and supply lines?"

"Getting Scotty arrested for Damiano's murder. Which was also the lure."

"How do you figure?"

"When I broke in and stole the holo projector, I planted lots of DNA evidence in Scotty's back room."

"What kind of evidence?"

I showed him the cut on my forearm. "Blood. Spit. Also, I wrote on his coffin bed that Foster killed me, in my own blood, and left a big bloody handprint there."

His eyebrows arched. "Holy shit. Scotty's gonna have a tough time wriggling out of that."

I grinned, proud of myself. It had been rather satisfying to frame that scumbag for something that I was sure he had done to lots of poor unfortunates. "Especially since I called Hollis' precinct as Faith, and left a message that Scotty had confessed to me that he'd kidnapped Damiano and held her prisoner there."

"So, Hollis is gonna get a search warrant and shut the Concerto down as soon as he gets into the office this morning. And then he'll be arresting Scotty."

I nodded. "And if your D.E.A. friends turn over the server and data engine to the marshals, they can get search warrants and shut down all of Scotty's other clubs in order to see if those holo projector boxes have secret servers. Since Scotty is running Brighton Leigh's business, using his clubs to hide and launder Leigh's illegal revenues, getting Scotty arrested and the clubs shut down will cut off Leigh's communication and supply lines."

"But Scotty knows he didn't kill you."

"Right. That's the lure, see? After last night, Scotty knows I, Faith, was at the Concerto, stealing his server and data engine. Which means I, Faith, must be the one who planted Damiano's DNA in Scotty's skeevy sex room. Which means I'm Damiano. But, I checked into both the Bonaventure and my flight as Faith, using an official U.S. Passport card. And I dropped forty-two grand of Tony's money at Louis Vuitton with a palladium card in Faith's name. So, even though Damiano had an arrest record, and the marshals couldn't pass my prints, Tony somehow managed to officially turn her into Faith."

Mando nodded, catching on: "Which means that whatever Tony managed to do to pass your prints is legit enough to give Brighton Leigh an entirely new identity."

"If he can get Tony to do the same for him, he won't be a fugitive anymore. But, because we're set to fly to Aruba tonight, he'll have to move fast, with very little time to plan and execute."

"Because if Tony leaves the country, he'll miss his window."

"Exactly. See? Basic military strategy."

Mando stared at me, a new respect dawning in his eyes. He looked at the warehouse Tony had disappeared into, then back at me. "You are one Hell of an amateur."

"I am my father's daughter," I shrugged.

"If the marshals find out Tony's this injured, they'll abort the mission."

"Thought you wanted it to abort."

"That was before you put all these balls in the air. Now we're in the game. There's too much at stake to fold up and go home. Besides, losing out on his last chance to get Brighton, on top of stasis and everything going on with Ilsa, is going to destroy Tony."

I thought about that, trying to reach past the brooding fire in my chest to find some compassion, but Mando's words felt like a manipulation. It angered me. "Did Tony kill those kids, Mando? Rape them, the way Hollis said he did?"

"I told you, I wasn't—"

"But you saw the snuff films Hollis was talking about. You know about that thing Tony carries around with him."

He opened his mouth to speak. Closed it tightly, jaw muscles pulsing, eyes growing cold. Menacing. "This conversation is over." He stood, and reaching for the door handle.

"If I find out that Tony's a murdering pedophile, I will—"

"Enough!" He whirled around and loomed over me. Ferocity glistened in the hard black stones of his eyes. "That man," he pointed in the direction of the warehouse. "Is a good man. An honorable man. He's brought more assholes to justice in the past seven years than Hollis has in his entire career."

I leaned back and away, drawing my ice bucket with me, surprised at his rabid, balls-to-the-wall defense of Tony after all the dissembling he'd done earlier.

But he wasn't finished: "The next time you talk shit about him, you and I are going to mix it up, and only one of us will walk away. Is that understood?"

I nodded, reassured by his vehemence. By the fire of commitment in his eyes. "Why didn't you just say he's innocent? Why do you guys always have to keep me in the dark? String me along?"

He drew in a deep breath, a great weariness settling over him. "There's a rule in this business: If you're not cleared, don't ask. Don't even wonder."

"I'm not in this business."

He grinned, cheeks taut with a sad, knowing look. "That's what Tony thought when he first started out."

CHAPTER TWENTY-FOUR

After Mando went inside the building, Kam came out, carrying a cloth shopping bag loaded with chemical ice packs, elastic bandages, and a jar of some kind of salve. He dumped the melted ice out of the bucket and returned it to its cubby, and then pulled the table top out and instructed me to rest my arm across it.

"What's that?" I asked, as he snapped some nitrile gloves on and unscrewed the top of the jar.

"Should help with the pain. You can ice it afterwards."

I nodded and let him massage the pungent salve into my arm. It smelled like citrus, pepper, and diesel oil. He started just above the elbow, working his way down with gentle, swirling strokes. For a man of his bulk, he had surprisingly fine fingered hands. His gum snapped at the side of his mouth while he worked. His brown eyes had a little dusting of amber in the center of the irises. His mouth pursed with sympathy when I groaned as he reached my knuckles. "Sorry."

"It's okay. Can't be helped."

When finished, he snapped two of the chemical packs, sandwiched my hand between them, and wrapped the bandage around them to keep them in place. "Better?"

I nodded. It was, actually. "Thanks."

"Don't mention it. You hungry? I'll send Percy out."

"What kind of food?"

"Whatever you want."

"Korean BBQ?"

He considered that for a long moment. "So long as it's chicken, it should be ok. And I'll tell Percy to put it in the trunk."

That seemed like a fair compromise with Tony's delicate sensibilities. Kam withdrew a phone and made a text. A minute or two later, Tony's limo fired up and drove off.

Kam pushed his recliner back and reached for the remote. "Might as well settle in. Gonna be a while."

I followed his lead, kicking back and propping my hand up so that it was above my heart. He flipped through the channels, finally settling on an animated show about an eccentric family running a burger joint. I glanced sidelong at him, raising a brow. In the hospital, he'd watched Inspector Gadget and Sponge Bob non-stop.

"What?" he said defensively. "It's a good show."

"All you watch is cartoons."

"I wanted to be an animator in high school."

I smirked and shook my head, closing my eyes. It had been a long, stressful day. Whatever Kam had put on my arm had made the pain tolerable. I dozed until the food came, devoured it, and found the swelling had gone down enough that I could actually put the splint on.

With the pain dampened even further, I fell into a deep sleep. Aside from Tony's phone digging into my ass, this had to be the most comfortable emergency waiting room on the planet.

I was awakened a few hours later by the door opening, and the movement of the suspension as Kam stepped out and Mando stepped in, carrying a small gear bag. He looked me over. "How you doing?"

"Okay." I hit the button to raise the recliner up, blinking the sleep out of my eyes. The sky was light outside, but the sun hadn't crested the horizon yet. Judging from that, I had a few more hours left on the limo rental.

Mando snapped some nitrile gloves on and pulled a plastic garbage bag from his pocket. He gathered up Kam's used gloves, the remains of our meals, the empty bottles of water, soda cans, and every other little bit of evidence of our presence in the cabin. When finished, he set the trash bag aside and sat down in the recliner opposite mine.

His serious expression alarmed me. "Everything all right?"

"Surgery went well. He's almost as good as new."

"So, what's the problem."

He drew in a deep breath, gathering his thoughts for a moment before revealing: "Tony's going to be coming out of stasis in a few minutes. He'll be FUBAR for the following twenty-four to forty-eight hours. Confused. Disoriented. He'll need someone. I can't do it. I have to run interference with the marshals. And he doesn't trust anybody else to stay with him. Except you."

I wasn't thrilled with the idea. Considering what I'd experienced, I didn't really want to be around Tony when he was in stasis lag. Aside from the chance of him getting physically violent during a hallucination, there was also the risk of that weird resonance between us getting out of hand. It'd be like babysitting an uncaged, acid-trip inducing tiger. "Can't Jana do it?"

"You've had stasis. You really think Jana's the right person to help him through this?"

He had a point. "How can I be with him if I don't have clearance to get inside?"

"He'll be coming out. You'll take this limo to this hotel," he handed me a piece of paper, "Where you'll say good bye to your driver and give him this," he handed me a wad of cash. "To keep his mouth shut about all of this, and then to use hydrogen peroxide on the bloodstains, thoroughly vacuum the limo, then steam clean the interior. After he drives away, you'll take the elevator to level three of the parking structure and take this vehicle from the nearby handicapped slot," he handed me a fob.

"Take it where?"

"To the location Tony tells you."

"What if he's not functional enough to tell me anything?"

"Then you pick somewhere. I can't know where you've gone. None of us can. That way we can't perjure ourselves if the marshals decide we're breaking covenants with them. You need to stay under the radar until Tony's got his head on straight. Or as straight as it can be, with the divorce." He handed me another wad of cash. "For expenses."

I nodded, memorizing the hotel address. I handed the paper back and put the key fob and cash in my purse.

"Where are the discs? For the holo projector?"

I pointed at my carry on. "Inside the lining."

He moved over to the suitcase and removed the clothes I had packed inside, frowning at the blood all over the dress. He worked the cases out of their hiding place and pocketed them, then repacked the suitcase. "I'll get all this cleaned for you."

"Okay."

He motioned to the gear bag. "That should be enough for a few days."

"Enough what?"

"Clothes. Scotch. Food. Burner phones."

"Ah. The essentials."

He smirked, then grew serious again, his gaze locking with mine. "Take care of him."

I nodded. "I will."

"And never, ever, repeat anything he says while hallucinating. To anyone. That stays between you."

"You think he's going to hallucinate?"

"I don't know what he's going to do. He's never had stasis lag after being electrocuted before. This is unchartered territory."

"Do you think he'll get violent?"

"He hasn't in the past. But the temporal shifts may be more pronounced. They seem to be influenced by biomagnetic fields and electrical activity in the brain. Because of the electrocution, his are more erratic than normal."

I was still having trouble wrapping my head around this whole temporal shift thing. "Mando, you're a grown ass man. How can you actually believe Tony's time traveling while in stasis lag?"

"I don't. I believe his consciousness is time traveling."

"You can't be that stupid. First off, people's minds don't go wandering around on their own. That's moronic. Secondly, he's not going into the past, any more than I did. It's just memories. Horrible, repressed memories."

"What about the future? Didn't you experience something that you know is going to occur, but hasn't happened yet?"

"Are you even listening to yourself? How can I verify what I experienced if it hasn't happened yet? Those are dreams. Fears. Projections of the subconscious. They're not glimpses of the future. They're just the brain making sense of the crap swirling around in my head."

"There's no time to explain quantum holographic consciousness or bioelectromagnetic transpermanence. You're not cleared for most of it, anyway. So let's just drop it."

"Using bigger words doesn't make it any less stupid. People do not mentally time travel just because they undergo stasis."

He gave me a stern look that said the conversation was over, then turned towards the door. "Tony does."

***

Tony did, indeed walk out of the warehouse, but he needed help from both Kam and Glen. His right leg kept buckling under him.

He was dressed in a clean black T-shirt and jeans, and leather moccasin style shoes. His right wrist had a gauze bandage wrapped around it. His nostrils had cotton plugs stuffed up them, and he had those raccoon bruises that usually result from a broken nose.

Somebody must have poured scotch on him, because he smelled like a distillery when they lowered him into the recliner beside me. Before they left, Kam gave me a look that said 'good luck', while Glen gave me a look that made it clear he thought this was a terrible idea and he blamed me for it.

I smiled back like clueless Faith, not wanting to let him know how much I shared that opinion. They shut the doors and then walked over to Tony's limo and drove off.

"Hey babe," Tony smiled at me, reaching across the space between the recliners. There was an odd light in his eyes, like he was privy to some immensely important secret that both amused and terrified him.

"Hey. How you doing?"

"I'm very..." He trailed off, as if just noticing where he was. "This is a nice limo."

"It is," I agreed. "You need to stay quiet until we're in the other car, okay?"

He nodded, bobbing his head up and down way more times than necessary. I wasn't sure if he could actually keep silent, so I blasted pop songs on the sound system and stowed the splint in the gear bag before rolling down the privacy screen.

Bernard had been dozing on the front seat, but he sat up when he heard the screen motor buzzing. "Ready to go?"

"Sure am." I told him the address of the hotel, which was in nearby Glendale, about five miles away. We were there in a few minutes.

Elated at his very generous cash bonus, Bernard promised to clean the limo thoroughly, inside and out, and then helped me load Tony into the elevator and position him in the corner for support. I waited until he drove off before pressing the button for the third level of the parking structure.

The car turned out to be a black Cadillac Escalade with tinted windows. I'd had a lot of experience maneuvering drunks around throughout my childhood, so despite Tony being a head taller than me, I got him safely into the car. He petted my hair and murmured in Dutch as I leaned across him to buckle him in. When I looked up at him, he kissed me. On the lips.

That strange, electric tingle pulsed between us, and I drew back in surprise. "Wait. You have to wait."

"Don't wanna wait." He gave me a lovesick, sappy smile. "It's been so long. I've missed you so much, Rad."

Oh, boy. "Just a little longer. We have to get somewhere safe."

"Right." He made that head bobbing nod again. "Safe." He tore the gauze off his wrist to reveal a white band of fresh, new skin, like a tan line left by a wrist watch. I wondered why they had bandaged it at all, then realized they'd wanted Bernard to believe he was still injured, so as not to raise questions.

I got behind the wheel and we left the hotel parking structure with the prepaid card key that was on the dash for that purpose. Once out on the street, I asked: "Do you know where we're going?"

"To the house."

"Which house? The Ranch?"

He snorted, shaking his head. "Got rid of that years ago."

"What year do you think it is, Tony?"

He squinted at me, brow furrowing. He seemed to be sorting through possibilities, until something seemed to click for him. "You're Faith."

"Yeah."

He reached out and ran his index finger lightly along my bruised knuckles, my swollen fingers. "What happened to your hand?"

I realized that I should put the splint back on, so I pulled into a grocery store parking lot and rummaged around in the gear bag for it.

He watched me as I put it on, confusion clouding the strange light in his eyes. "Did someone kill me last night?"

"Tried to."

"That's why I talked to the Commander." He nodded, then scowled. "You're father's not a very nice man, Rad."

"He was to me." I got back behind the wheel and started the Escalade up. I decided to take the 134 freeway heading west, just to put distance between us and the hotel where Bernard had dropped us off. "How did you know him?"

"Mnnnnh," he blinked a few times. "He's always there. In the dead place."

"Purgatory? With the frozen grass? And the river?"

He nodded. "Technically, that's not really the dead place. It's just dead place adjacent. The actual dead place is across the river."

I shuddered, considering that, and how Papa had insisted I not come any closer to the river. "Have you been there? Across the river?"

"A few times." He grimaced and shuddered. "I never stay long. Mostly I'm on the frozen grass. Where the Commander is."

I didn't like where this was going, but some part of me wanted to go there, just the same. I was burning to ask if Tony had, indeed killed Papa, the way my dream had indicated. At the same time, I felt like asking him about it while he was in such a vulnerable, disordered state would be a violation, a sort of mental date rape. So, I just let him talk, and resolved to ask innocuous questions.

"He's always there," Tony continued. "On the grass. Every time I've been there."

"How many times is that?"

"Not sure. You counting now me, or future me?"

This again. I rolled my eyes and cursed at the car ahead of me, pretending it had cut me off. I didn't want him to see how annoyed the whole ESP thing made me. "I guess it doesn't matter. He's dead."

"Maybe. But he's still an asshole. But I don't think he is."

"An asshole?"

"Dead."

I didn't know what to say to that. I wanted Papa alive. Fervently. Desperately. But I didn't think I could handle finding out that he was. I'd had so little love in my life, I didn't want to wind up hating him for leaving Chris and I alone all this time. Nor did I want to kill the hope that my stasis dream had sparked up in me. "What did he say to you?"

"All sorts of shit. Made me want to kick his ass."

"Like what?"

"He was angry at me. For getting you involved."

"Involved in what?"

"The dead place. He knew you'd been there, and he knew I'd brought you there. He made it very clear how he felt about that."

"If he's not dead, why is he appearing in the dead place?"

"I dunno." He thought about that. "Maybe he's in a coma. He can't be in stasis all this time. Can he?"

"You tell me." I slanted a glance at him. "He's been dead for nine years. Stasis hasn't been around that long, has it?"

"Dunno. Probably. They had it working well enough when I first had it seven years ago. But to keep someone in stasis for all that time," He shook his head. "That's insanely expensive. And difficult."

"Why would anyone want to?"

"Mnnnhhh," he sighed, closing his eyes and slumping back in his seat. "You're Faith, now. Don't think you have clearance, yet."

I was both relieved and resentful that he had terminated this subject. We were in Toluca Lake, now, coming up on the transition to the 101 and 170 freeways, so I asked: "Where to, Tony? Give me a place. An address."

"Go to the Ranch. Well, near the Ranch. The coast road on the back side of the Ranch."

"We're supposed to lay low. The Ranch is the first place the marshals will look."

"They can look all they want." His lips twisted into a mischievous grin. He reached over and put his hand on my arm. My hormones burst loose like wild mustangs escaping a corral. "They just won't find us."

I smirked and headed north on the 101.

***

Tony dozed most of the way, interspersed with occasional bouts of angry or fearful sleep talking. About sixty percent was in languages I recognized but didn't understand: Russian, French, Dutch, Malay, Javanese, and Spanish. The remainder was sometimes heated, sometimes mournful, sometimes urgent discussions with people in English.

He argued with Mando about a man named Pete. He broke the news to his little girls about their brother's death. He warned somebody about something called Emerald Dream and urged them to evacuate a facility. I was grateful he hadn't dreamed about the torture. I don't think I could have dealt with him screaming in anguish during that long drive.

I pulled off the freeway and found a gas station in Gaviota. Once parked, I woke Tony up. I hadn't wanted to wake him while I was driving, in case he freaked out or had a medical emergency, but I wasn't sure which particular road he wanted me to take from here to reach the Ranch.

He started awake with a protesting groan when I gently prodded his shoulder. His unfocused eyes held a luminous spark, and when they turned towards me, I felt a sudden wave of crackling, jangly energy wash over me. If it had been lust, I wouldn't have minded, but this heavy dissonance awakened a black snake of doom in my gut. "You okay?"

"Jesus, Rad. I can't believe you lost your client."

He said it with such anger and disdain, I felt compelled to defend myself. "I didn't lose anybody, Tony. I'm playing Faith."

"No, you're not. You're..." He blinked, and looked around us. At the road, at the gas station, at the freeway in the distance. "I think we're late for the funeral."

I wanted to ask him whose funeral, but decided against it. "We're going to the Ranch. I'm Faith. You're in stasis lag and we are hiding out from the marshals." He kept regarding me dubiously, so I pulled on my short red hair. "See? Faith."

"Faith..." He nodded. Understanding slowly filled up his eyes like sand in an hourglass. "You're Faith."

"Good. Yeah. So, what road do I take, now?"

He directed me through town, past a campground, and then up to a narrow, winding back road that would have been immensely fun to drive if that strange energy hadn't been filling up the car like floodwater leaking through the vents.

After several miles, we crested a hill and I caught a glimpse of fuzzy ultramarine dusted with fog through the canyon to the left, and the Spanish revival style perimeter wall of the Ranch stretched across the hillside in the distance to the right. A few minutes later, Tony told me to pull off the road into a grove of cottonwood trees. There was barely enough room to park between them, but once we were clear of the asphalt I could see a barranca dead ahead.

I regarded the steep, rocky sides, and the wash of sand and rock in the dry, sinuous gully ahead. "Tony, this is an Escalade. We'll get stuck."

He reached over and turned a knob on the dashboard I hadn't noticed before, and the heads up display showed me I was now in 4W low. "Go ahead."

I gave him a dubious look, but moved ahead into the barranca. I really didn't trust the sand with tires designed for the highway, so I tried to keep the speed up while navigating the ragged gully and low hanging tree branches. After a quarter mile, we reached the Ranch's perimeter wall, which was crowned with concertina wire. I didn't see a gate, but there looked to be a concrete drainage opening with a metal grate at the base of the wall where the barranca terminated.

"Now what?" I turned to Tony.

He patted his pockets, then frowned. "Where's my phone?"

I slipped it out of my pants pocket and handed it over.

He frowned at it. "How'd the screen get cracked?"

"Hollis smashed it into your nose."

"Huh." He looked surprised at that, then unlocked the screen and keyed something in. A length of the wall disappeared, revealing a dull, Mylar-coated panel that telescoped into itself, allowing us access to a tamarisk-and-brush-lined concrete wash barely wide enough to fit the Escalade.

A holographically disguised access gate. Tricksey.

He motioned me to keep driving. "Usually I'd walk from here but, I'm not really up to going that far on foot."

"Why didn't we just take the tunnel in from the yacht?"

"How do you know about that?"

"You told me about it. That you had a bolt hole to the ocean, if you needed it."

The road—for lack of a better word—ran under cover of tamarisk and cottonwood. Thickets of wild bamboo grew along both sides of the wash. After about five minutes of this, the bamboo was so overgrown that it squealed against the front fenders.

Tony told me to stop. I did.

He opened his door, and slowly climbed out, propping himself up by holding on to the car. I turned the Escalade off, grabbed the gear bag and stepped out of air-conditioned comfort into the hot, dusty August day. The sweet, earthy tang of summer was heavy in the air. Insects buzzed in the bamboo. A breeze rustled the upper branches of the cottonwoods, but didn't penetrate to where we stood.

Tony took a deep breath, bracing himself, and then started up the small embankment at the side of the wash where there was a break in the bamboo, following a deer trail into the brush. I caught up with him, worried his leg would buckle and he'd fall flat on his face. The heavy vegetation and open air made me feel both claustrophobic and uncomfortably vulnerable. At least that sense of impending doom I'd had at the gas station had dissipated once we'd left the road.

"We're just gonna leave the car there?"

"Nobody will see it down here." He turned left, down another trail running parallel to the wash. His gait was evening out, becoming more confident, but he was still moving at half his usual pace. I could tell he was weak on the one side.

I slung the strap for the gear bag over my head, wincing as the edge of the bag caught on the splint. I shook it free and followed him, concentrating on the delicious interplay of his butt muscles as he walked. All this moving around was making my hand throb, but I found lust a good distraction.

We hobbled along this way for about a half hour. The trail wound away from the shady lushness of the streambed and cut upwards through chaparral and sage towards a small plateau. From this higher elevation, I made out the tiled roof of the main house about a quarter mile to the north, although the rest of the mansion was hidden by trees and the shade-screened fence surrounding the pool.

We were on a low ridge, situated behind and below the house. To the south, I saw the blocky tip of the shooting range set halfway up another ridge. The far edge of our own plateau was ringed by a thick copse of eucalyptus. In the center of that stood a twelve-by-twelve foot structure of weathered adobe on a concrete slab. A clamorous mechanical hum emanated from the building.

"Stay close to me," Tony warned, and walked towards the building. Something—five somethings, actually—rustled in the deep shade of the trees opposite us. The telltale chuff of panting grew louder. I swallowed hard and pressed up against Tony, twining my left hand in his waistband.

I'd forgotten about the dogs.

And these weren't even decently sized fawn-colored Malincollies like Zef, but big, black, intense looking animals, with shortish fur striped with faint hints of rust and tan, and a rusty half moon under their chins. They crashed toward us, pointy ears up, long, feathered tails curved slighty over their backs, slobbery tongues hanging from between rows of white, white teeth. I could feel their footfalls through the soles of my feet as they drew close.

"What kind of dogs are those?"

"Groenendals mixed with Dutch Shepard and Beauceron."

"So...Groucherons?"

"I call them Groenies."

"Because that's so much more elegant."

He slanted an annoyed glance at my sarcasm, and then turned to the dogs and slapped his hand on his thigh. "Hi, guys," Tony said brightly "How're my little soldiers today, huh?"

They ran up, bouncing against each other as each fought to be the closest to Tony, but none of them actually jumped on him. They all half-reared in a begging posture, making little grunts and whimpers of pleasure. They must have weighed eighty to a hundred pounds each.

"Good puppies." Tony squatted down and petted them all. The biggest one backed up and came around to the end of the line to get another turn. "Yeah," Tony thumped its side energetically. "Missed you too, Liv." He started nonsense talking, hugging the animal, letting the damn thing lick his face. The others pressed in, trying to get their licks in, too.

I watched all this with cool detachment. How could a grown man baby-talk a dog? And how could these big, black nasties eat it up? It was crazy. Not knowing whether to feel nausea or envy, I looked disgustedly into the distance and whistled the theme song to "Lassie."

Tony skewed a glare at me, mouth tightening into an unappreciative smirk. He stood, waved his hand, and said some more mumbo-jumbo, but in a commanding tone.

The pack split up and scampered away, disappearing into the brush. Tony watched them go, an odd wistfulness in his eyes, then turned to me and scowled. "Such a smart-ass, aren't you?"

I whistled louder.

We launched into a glorious, mutual glower of nuclear proportions. Neither of us blinked. Neither wavered. We just stood there in the hot sun, sweat dribbling off our chins, jaws set in mirrored outrage. He stepped into me. The heat from his body, and the smell of him made my lips twist into a smile. He tried to keep his glower going, but it disintegrated into a chuckle, drawing an answering snicker from me.

He snaked his arms around me, and pulled me into an embrace. "God, I missed you."

I wanted to tell him I hadn't gone anywhere, but his proximity shut down my mental circuits, flooding them with such an unexplained sense of relief that I had to swallow hard and clear my throat before I could speak. I wasn't sure why I was so relieved, but it made me a little giddy. Despite his weakened state, and my fear of canine witnesses, I had a sudden urge to rip his clothes off and shag him right there in the dirt. The rise in his pants when he cleared his throat and turned his back on me told me he'd felt it, too.

He hobbled to the weathered looking door of the pump house. Despite looking utterly neglected, when we were up close, I saw both door and jamb were steel, and the decrepit weathering was a paint job. Tony punched some numbers into his phone, then held it to a biometric lock set flush into the doorjamb. When it beeped three times, he thumb printed the readout screen.

The door opened. A grinding noise spilled across the plateau, the steady thrum-thrum-thrum of some kind of pump or generator. Tony grabbed me by the shoulder, steered me into the building, and shut us in with the racket. The pump was to our right, a large, transformer-like thing to our left.

Tony threaded his way past the transformer, slid a memory card out of a compartment on his phone, and slotted it into a controller box on the far wall. "Stand over there," he shouted, pointing through the maze of machinery toward a concrete slab outlined in scuffed red paint. I complied.

He stabbed a code into the controller, withdrew the chip, and joined me. The slab lurched, and then sank slowly into a concrete shaft. We came to rest about twenty feet below the pump room, in front of another steel door. It clicked open to reveal a large, well-lit tunnel, complete with golf cart. Pipes and conduits ran overhead. There was a stale, musty flavor to the air.

Tony grinned. "Welcome to Oz."

I smirked and whistled 'Down Under' while he climbed behind the wheel of the cart. He threw me a mock angry glare as I sat beside him.

"You gonna be okay driving this thing?" I asked.

"You don't know which way to go."

"You could tell me."

He smirked and pressed the accelerator. "Where's the fun in that?"

CHAPTER TWENTY-FIVE

From what I could tell, our route followed the spine of the ridge, arcing back toward the house when the plateau was high enough for the tunnel to burrow under it.   Three other tunnels branched off from this one, all big enough to accommodate an electric cart. Tony pointed out the one that led to the yacht. I only saw one other door, which Tony said led to the helipad.

We soon reached a low-ceilinged charging bay where the tunnel terminated.   The bay housed two other electric carts. Tony parked in an empty charging slot, and then led me to another steel door at the end of the bay. He slotted the memory card into the lock and keyed a number. We passed into a stairwell.

I helped him up the stairs, steadying him when it seemed his right leg was close to giving way. Halfway up the next flight, at the landing, he stopped and opened an access door to reveal the switch room. We passed into the small space, Tony slotted his chip, and we were in his secret suite.

I helped him over to the couch and half lowered, half dropped him into it as his right leg turned to rope. He was making a series of ragged huffs and hisses, his lips pulled back with what looked like a mixture of exhaustion and anguish. I dropped the gear bag off my shoulder and squatted down in front of him, looking him over. "Does it hurt that bad?"

He opened his mouth to reply, but was interrupted by a muffled bark. The door to the bedroom burst open and Zef sailed through, launching himself at Tony with wild abandon. Tony caught the beast, holding him on his lap while Zef wriggled and licked and whined with happy enthusiasm. "I'm here," he assured the dog. "I'm here, I'm okay, don't worry."

Not satisfied with slobbering all over Tony, the dog turned to me. He got a few good licks on my lips and cheek before I recoiled and stood up. I was grateful my mouth had been closed or the damn thing would have Frenched me. He went back to snuggling up against Tony, laying his head on Tony's shoulder. Tony's arms slid around him and hugged him close.

I turned away, feeling suddenly unwanted and uninvited. And maybe a little bit jealous. Why the dogs seemed to spark that emotion in me, and not Jana, I wasn't sure. To keep myself busy, and cover for my pique, I went to the kitchenette and grabbed a bottle of water out of the fridge. I cracked it and took a swig, then grabbed a second one for him. "You thirsty, Tony?"

He didn't reply, but I heard an odd choking sound, and turned to find him with his shoulders hunched, face buried in Zef's fur, entire body rocking with the force of his silent, strangled sobs.

I stared at him, disbelieving. I had never seen a man cry like that. In the movies, or on TV, yes. But not a real man. Not a guy like Tony. To comfort him was to acknowledge his weakness, but how could I deny his pain?

Men were such delicate creatures.

I set the water bottles down, moved over to him, and put a hand on his shoulder, careful not to disturb the dog, who seemed just as worried as I was.

Tony was so lost, so wounded and full of despair, I had to wrap my arms around his head, cradle him close. The dog wriggled out from between us, and Tony's arms enveloped my hips, hugged me so tight that the hard line of his cheekbone dug into my belly. I was almost embarrassed for him, but he was Tony. There was eloquence to his weakness, nobility even in his need.

We stayed that way for a long time, until he pulled away and touched his lips to my navel through the fabric of my shirt. "It's all such a mess. I'm sorry," he said in a hoarse whisper. "I'm so sorry I dragged you into this madness. I just—" His mouth moved, but the words had stopped coming. He looked away, sighing. "Have to bury him."

"It's okay," I soothed, smoothing his long black hair from his temple the way I'd done with Chris when he used to cry. "I know you loved him."

"Please don't leave. I know things are screwed up. I know. I'm sorry it played out this way. It was never my intention."

"I'm right here. I'm not going anywhere, Tony."

He pulled me down atop him on the couch, hugging me so fiercely I wondered if he had some grizzly bear in his DNA. "I love you, Rad."

Panic rose up in me at those words. At how true I suspected they might be, and how incapable I was of mustering any coherent response to them. I tamped the fear down, trying to stay strong, and in control. Tony needed me. "You need to drink some water and go to bed, Tony. The stasis lag is messing with you."

"Stasis?" he looked bewildered, but he took the bottle of water I handed to him and drank it obediently.

"Hollis electrocuted you. You've been in stasis most of last night."

He stared at me for several seconds before nodding. "Right. Right. You're Faith, now."

I tugged on his hand until he stood up. Together, we shuffled into the bedroom. Diffused lighting turned on when we stepped inside, and I got a clear view of the whole shebang for the first time. The place had the smoky, bittersweet tang of burned sage.

During my last visit, I had already glimpsed the bed, the armoire and other furniture, and the doors to the bathroom and closet. What I hadn't noticed before was that the ceiling was coated in Mylar baffles, like the walls at the Concerto. The bed frame was clear, solid Plexiglass, including a neo-tech headboard with embedded gold circuitry deliberately forming a sort of abstract fusion of what looked like Polynesian designs. In contrast, the linens were simple cream-colored fabric with a slight sheen.

The wall that was shared between the bedroom and the kitchenette was nothing but interlocking ultra hi-def flat screens, but the really odd thing about the room, aside from the clear Plexiglas neo-tech headboard, was the wall opposite the foot of the bed:

It was paneled in split bamboo and decorated with row upon row of masks. Some masks were gold, filigreed with intricate designs, some were simple wood carvings or woven palm fronds. All looked ancient; museum quality pieces fit to represent various long gone tribal cultures. Beneath each was a weapon which matched the culture of its accompanying mask. A knife, an arrow, a saber, nunchakus, a sword, a bo stick, a club; all sorts of things. Each held a perimeter glow of a light pastel blue, which was where the diffused light was coming from.

They looked expensive. Seemed odd Tony would have them in his bedroom and not on display in a more public part of the house. Maybe they were here to remind him to look for himself amid all the roles he played. I'd ask him when he was less loopy.

Zef followed us, trotting over to another dog bed between the armoire and one of the chairs, and snatching up his skunk. He brought it over, tail wagging hopefully, as I lowered Tony onto the bed.

"Nay," Tony told him, and pointed him back to the dog bed. His ears went back, and he trotted back, head lowered, hopes crushed.

I eased Tony's shoes off and set them aside. As I helped him remove his T-shirt, my fingers brushed along the rippled muscle of his torso. His breath caught sharply, and I froze, worried I'd hit a sore spot. But the look in his eyes wasn't pain, or even fatigue, but a burning flame of desire, an echo of what I'd been repressing during our hike here.

The hunger, the supplication in his eyes struck a note in me. It resounded, set my whole body singing. The next thing I knew, I was kissing him, my tongue searching deep and passionate as his hands caressed my breasts. I tugged his zipper down, freed the hard eagerness beneath his fly. I stroked and caressed him as he fumbled my designer jeans down, pausing as he saw the *kris* strapped to my calf. He grinned, removing it reverently. He set it carefully atop the small table beside the bed, and then he was on top of me, panting in my ear as he sheathed himself between my legs.

Despite the suddenness of it all, I had been ready for him. The wetness between us perfumed the air, slicked our bodies with the sweltering heat of our need. We built the fire hotter, hotter, until our bodies disintegrated, brought us crashing down into exhausted ecstasy. I cried out first, my fingers clawing his back, my legs locked around his hips.

He shuddered, gasped, and collapsed to the side of me, his arm draped across my bare chest. "God," he murmured, his voice husky, and a bit muffled by the swelling in his nose, "please don't leave me, Rad. You're all I've got."

I wrapped my arms around him and kissed him again because my throat was too tight to tell him I understood. Words seemed treacherous to me, too fickle to hold any real weight.

A slow grin of comprehension came over him. He kissed me back. "I'm yours. You're mine. Forever. Understand?"

I nodded and stiffened in his embrace, tired and relieved and just a little afraid of what trick Fate was playing on me. He wasn't in control of his faculties, so I couldn't expect him to follow through with those promises, nor hope he'd even recall saying them. I'd learned, at a very early age, to never trust someone under the influence.

Yet, here we were, and for this moment, this one moment, it was almost as if Papa and Chris were still alive and Beethoven still coursed through my veins.

He stroked my hair and kissed me softly on the top of the head. "Welcome back, Rad."

"Sure," I said, wondering why he kept coming back to my leaving, or having left, or being gone.

He hugged me so hard I thought my spine would break. "Don' leave me," he mumbled again.

When he finally released me, I finished taking his pants off, and then I wriggled out of the remnants of my clothes. He was subdued, almost dazed, as I crawled in beside him. In the darkness he lay nestled under my arm, his head on my breast, his sinewy forearm squeezing my torso with such quiet tenacity I felt supercharged, as if the force of his need was filling up some long empty reserve inside me. The stillness pressed in and brought a comforting obscurity to our silence. He relaxed. His breathing grew slow, steady.

Sleep wouldn't come to me. I lay immobile for a long while, feeling that strange energy charge me, until I was bursting with a fullness, a contentment at being needed. At being wanted.

If I slept it would all be over too soon...

***

"Tole you, I dunno," Tony mumbled. "Don't know." He moaned, stiffened in the bedsheets next to me, his skin clammy with sweat.

I'd been awake for a few hours, trying to coax the throbbing in my hand to a semblance of quiet. Even with the splint, it ached. Tony had been sleeping fitfully, tossing, murmuring. This was the first time I'd actually understood what he was saying.

"Motherfuckers. Fuck you." His whole body arched and twisted as if he was trying to get away from some unbearable pain.

He cried out—louder, this time—in a ragged voice thick with fear: "Fuck you!"

His eyes shot open. He stared at the ceiling, breath coming in quick, shallow puffs, his expression a mixture of distilled hatred and bone-deep agony. He looked gray, ashen in the diffused light emanating from the masks. His raccoon bruises had darkened further.

"You okay?" I smoothed my fingertips along the taut edge of his chin, up his jawbone, then pushed his hair out of his face gently. He must have been sweating a lot, because my hand came back wet.

His eyes flickered over me, narrowing as the reality of my presence chased the last of the demons away. He seemed both surprised and relieved to find me there. "Yeah," he managed roughly. "I am now."

It felt like he was lying, but I let it slide. "What was that all about? Bad dream?"

His face blanked. He rolled away, onto his side, and leveraged himself up on his elbow, growling with the effort. "What time is it?"

I waved my splint at the clockless room around us. "No clue."

"Shit. My arm is like spaghetti. The fuck happened to me?"

"Tony, don't use the f-word."

"Oh. Right. Sorry." He swung his legs over, sat on the edge of the mattress with his back to me. "Lights on."

The Mylar baffles overhead transformed into a drop ceiling embedded with several banks of warm yellow LED lights, illuminating us in a golden wash. I gawked at them for a moment, wondering why anybody would go to the trouble of encoding such an ugly holographic ceiling, but Tony's groan reminded me that my attention was needed elsewhere.

"Holy shit." I gaped at his back, and ribs. Blood streamed from countless crescent-shaped wounds dotting his torso. He held himself like a boxer the day after a particularly brutal bout. His thighs and buttocks were a mass of bloody welts. "What happened to you?"

"Huh?" He glanced over his shoulder at me, then down at his torso. "Oh. Abreaction. Happens sometimes. They should go away, now that I'm awake."

"You randomly break out in bloody wounds?"

He nodded. "When the dreams are intense enough."

"What kind of dream causes *that*?"

"Warehouse. Mineshaft," he replied simply, and forced himself to his feet. "I'll shower it off." He tried to take a step, then sagged back onto the bed again, his breathing shallow and pained. "Shit," he groaned. The muscles of his back were taut. "What's wrong with my leg? My arm? They're so weak."

"You got electrocuted. The tissue was re-genned."

"Huh," he said, as if that was news to him, but not particularly disturbing news. Which I found a little disturbing, myself.

He waited as I got out of bed and helped him up. His thighs and groin were dripping with blood. Zef blinked sleepily at us from his dog bed as we left a trail across the jute floor on our way to the bathroom. The shower was about half the size of the one Faith had upstairs, but still big enough for us both. I propped him up in the corner and turned the water on, letting it warm up while I removed the splint and set it on the vanity.

The shower head was one of those removable ones, so I gently soaped him up and sprayed him down, surprised to find that the wounds were, indeed, healing up rapidly, becoming pink half-moons rather than open sores. I was especially relieved that the blood from his groin washed away to reveal no real injuries. The amount of blood from there had been frightening. "That is so weird," I muttered, shaking my head

"Psychosomatic," he explained. "Like stigmata."

I glanced up at his face, expecting him to be on the verge of a complete psychological breakdown, but instead he watched me with a sappy, lovesick expression. Or maybe the bruises on his face just made it seem that way. His black hair hung down across his face in heavy strands, too sodden to be from the steam. I held the spray over his head, and saw a flush of red spill down across his shoulders.

Of course. The scar.

I carefully reached up and parted his hair to see that the waxy white was now an angry pink. At least it wasn't bleeding any more. "Does this hurt?"

"Not any more than usual when this happens." He lowered his head to make it easier for me to shampoo and rinse the blood away.

"How often is that?"

"Oh, whenever when I'm around people in stasis."

"How often is that?"

"What happened to your hand?" He caught my right arm and looked closely at my knuckles, frowning deeply at the swelling and bruise.

"I hurt it resuscitating you." And protecting him from Jim, but if he didn't remember Jim being there, I wasn't going to remind him.

His fingers rubbed my knuckles as if soothing a frightened bird. "We should talk about the future."

"My future's shot until this heals. Literally."

"Make a new one." He smiled at me, water dribbling off his chin. "There's a lot more to you than a pair of hands."

"Like what?"

"Like, I want you to come work for me."

"Thought I already was."

"Not as Faith. For real. A fully trained operative."

I studied his gaze as the fear swelled up in me. He was playing, dangling hopes in front of my eyes, a little boy getting ready to yank a string away from a kitten. It pissed me off. "You don't have to hire me just because I saved your life."

He stepped into me, his right hand moving over to rest on my hip. "I mean it. I want you on the team."

"What if that's not what I want?"

"What do you want?"

"Right now, I want to get you clean, so we can go back to bed."

He pursed his lips, and reached past me to turn the water off. "I'm clean. What do you want?"

"What does it matter? I won't get it anyway."

My anger disturbed him. His gaze disengaged from mine. "You won't get anything you don't ask for."

I snorted and rolled my eyes. "I wish."

"What's that supposed to mean?"

"I didn't ask for any of this. Didn't ask for my hand to be shot or my car to be stolen or my eyes to turn green, but I got it. Why bother asking when nobody gives a damn what you want anyway?"

"Why can't you just say it? Say what you want?"

I shook my head and grabbed a towel from the rack, swiping it down across his body, too annoyed to let that familiar tingle run away with me, this time. How did I know what I wanted from life?

Ever since I could remember I hadn't lived any one place for more than two consecutive years. What's the sense in planning for a future if you don't know what continent you'll be on when summer rolls around? It's a wonder I made it through—well, almost through—college. The future was easy for guys like Tony. They had homes, friends, family, money. All sorts of yardsticks, measures of security. All I had was me, and how do you build anything on a foundation of quicksand?

"Can you stand on your own?" I asked him. "I need to change the sheets."

He squinted at me, mouth quirking up at one corner. Something swam behind that blue gaze that I wasn't sure about. Because of the swelling around his eyes and nose, his face was more leonine than normal, and the grey-purple of the bruises made him look as if he was turning into a gargoyle.

"Tony." I repeated more slowly: "Can you stand on your own?"

"I can handle myself." He pointed at a long vertical cupboard beside the sink. "Sheets are in there."

More relieved than I should have been that he had stopped pressing the issue, I grabbed another towel and quickly dried off. I gathered a fresh set of sheets and moved back into the bedroom.

Zef had disappeared somewhere, perhaps into the room with the kitchenette to sleep undisturbed. Behind me, I heard Tony shuffling around. The bathroom door shut, followed a few seconds later by the muffled but distinct sound of a man relieving himself in the toilet.

I got to work, stripping off the bloody sheets and tossing them into a wicker hamper, then fitting the new set. As I was smoothing out the last few wrinkles before putting the pillows back, I accidentally bumped the strange, neo-tech headboard with my elbow. The room went instantly pitch dark, even the glow around the masks cutting out. I heard a hum above my head, and a clicking sound from two separate corners.

Instinct drove me to the floor, the rough weave of the mat skinning a few layers from my knee. I rolled behind the headboard and came up in a defensive crouch, looking for the source of the sound.

I saw stars.

Not smack-on-the-skull, tweeting-bird stars, but real ones, patterns stretched over a night sky, like colored gems on black velvet. The entire ceiling was covered with them, tiny pinpricks moving slowly across the eternal path of the earth's rotation. I realized after a moment that the constellations—mostly unrecognizable at first—were from the Southern Hemisphere.

Tony had a planetarium in his bedroom.

More sounds started up, an entire symphony of nature. Frogs, insects, birds. The low, distant cough of a tiger. The steady shushing of a nearby stream. The air grew heavy, humid, filled with the sweet odor of wild orchids, the rich smell of loam, the delicate, slightly bitter scent of rain-soaked banyans. The walls themselves became shadowy outlines of tree trunks and rainforest plants, while the green ready lights on the locks glowed like the eyes of wild beasts.

Hell, he had a whole jungle in his bedroom.

The bathroom door swung open, with Tony silhouetted against the harsh bright light inside. His head tilted up, glancing from side to side. He stepped into the room and shut the door, plunging us into the night again. Purple-green splotches popped across my vision, imprinted with the dark, stylized outline of his masculine nakedness. He seemed a spirit—no, a God—in this artificial world.

"You found Gunung Mulu." He ambled toward the bed. He sounded pleased with himself.

I glanced around warily, waiting for my eyes to re-adjust to the soft glow of starlight. The smell of rain made me uneasy. I stood up, moving towards the shape of him. "What's that?"

"It's a national park. In Sarawak."

"How is it here?"

"Holographic environmental sense recording. This is a prototype one of my companies has been working on. It'll be ready for market in about seven months. The Trubys and I are partners in the R&D."

"But why is it in your bedroom?"

"For me. For when I get homesick. Helps me relax."

It made me chuckle. "You relax with all that noise?"

"Sure." He reached out and took my hand, and then sat on the bed, pulling me down to sit beside him. "As long as the jungle's singing, you're safe. It's when things get quiet, you know the predators are on the move."

"What predators?"

"Leopards. Tigers. Crocs. Men. Depending on where you are, of course."

"Of course."

He chuckled at my sarcasm. His breath warmed my cheek as he reached across me and fiddled with the headboard.

The stars changed, rearranged themselves, the pole star shining brightly, too high overhead for California. The sounds became riddled with crickets, the sighing of wind through trees. A wolf howled. The air became colder, tinged by the clean, acid scent of pine and a sweet tang of huckleberry.

"British Columbia." Tony explained. "The Rockies."

He cycled through a few more faraway place: The South African bushveld, the Australian outback, the Amazon. He turned the lights on. There was a childlike glee to him. "Pretty cool, huh?"

"Yeah," I agreed, smiling along with him. It was cool, especially seeing him so happy, so unguarded. His hand was still in mine, so I climbed up on the bed, ignoring the sharp twinge when I put weight on my right hand. I tugged him after me until we were stretched out on our sides, facing one another. I snatched up the pillows from the floor and snugged them into place.

He watched me, still smiling. "You really hurt your hand resuscitating me?"

I nodded, and his smile widened. His reaction bothered me. I wasn't sure what I'd expected, but this was not how I wanted this to go, especially when his follow up question was:

"Why did Hollis electrocute me?"

"Because he said the CIA had yanked your raincoat and he wanted to make sure you didn't leave the country."

"Why did he think I was leaving the country?"

I chewed my lip, sensing this was a bad subject, at a bad time. "What's the last thing you remember before waking up from stasis?"

His lips pursed, his gaze going faraway as he tried to recall. Then a slow, secret grin crept over his face. "Kissing you."

"Where?"

"On the lips."

"No, I mean what location were we in?"

His eyes narrowed as he searched his scrambled memory. "We were outside. Standing next to a birdcage Maserati." His eyes lit up, mouth stretching wide as his big palm reached over and slid across my hip, moving over to the small of my back. He drew me against him. "That was a Helluva kiss."

"It was," I agreed, reliving that glorious burst of awesome in my head.

"I wanted to kill you."

I blinked, pulling my head back to regard him quizzically.

He kept on grinning. "After all this bullshit with Ilsa and her lawyers, I found out that you'd taken off. With the *kris* and the palladium card. Jana said you were heading to Aruba."

"With you. I bought tickets for Faith, and for you. So you'd know we were in this together."

"That's why Hollis thought I was fleeing the country?"

I nodded, giving him an apologetic shrug. "Sorry."

He made a knowing murr. "I underestimated you. You faked us all out. We were all so sure you were running. But there you were, at Union Station, with Mando. You'd never planned to leave, at all. I was so happy to see that. To see you." His hand snugged against the small of my back, where the *kris* had been. "To know you were keeping the blade safe for me."

He pulled me in for a kiss. As our lips touched, I felt him stir against my leg, his heat stoking my own fire. That current surged between us, sweeping away my good sense. Once I let him in I couldn't—wouldn't—survive losing him.

I knew it, as sure as I knew gravity existed, but as our lips fused together, and we alchemized the way Jim's music had once melded with mine, I found myself murmuring against his lips:

"This. I want this."

He pulled back to meet my gaze. "You're sure?"

I nodded. "This. Every day." My voice was rushed, breathy. My hands had already started roaming into those intimate places that make men shiver and moan. Swept away in that irresistible torrent, we crashed together again, and again. It was a hot, sweaty blur of desire and need, but there was also a tenderness, an intimacy that broke open something inside me.

As I lay there in the afterglow, passing out with joyous, exhausted contentment, I wondered if this was how a butterfly feels when it breaks free of the cocoon.

Nah. Butterflies don't have multiple orgasms.

***

It was one of those long, lazy awakenings, the kind where awareness dawns in gentle, sweeping stages; a feather-fall into cozy reality. Eyes still closed, I reached out for Tony. My hand brushed his naked chest. He murmured and rolled toward me, his arm draping across my torso. A perfection of bodies and bedsheets.

And then somebody held an ice cube against my spine.

"Waugh," I arched my back, away from the sensation, realizing as the bed shuddered with sudden weight that Zef's nose had moved from my back to my neck. Face licking was imminent. "Bleah!"

I tried to fend him off, but he just hopped over us both and began licking Tony, instead. A deep chuckle escaped Tony and he trapped the dog in a one-armed hug, murmuring what sounded like endearments in Dutch.

I took advantage of their mutual admiration moment to scurry into the bathroom. The room smelled of sex, and I was pretty sure so did I. Not that that was necessarily bad, but my hand was hurting and I needed to get showered so I could put the splint back on.

Unfortunately, after all that prep work, my knuckles were too swollen, and the bruised area too tender to get the splines to fit again. I sat naked on the toilet to struggle with it, my arm outstretched on the vanity.

The door creaked open. Tony stepped in and moved to the sink, wearing blue silk boxer briefs. I groaned in appreciation. He glanced down at me with a frown as he turned the water on. "You need to see a doctor? I can call Lelani."

"That's probably a bad idea. We're supposed to be in hiding."

He looked surprised at that, regarding me in the mirror as he began shaving with a lather that smelled like sandalwood. "From who?"

"Hollis. The marshals. Scotty. Everybody."

"Why?"

"You had stasis. Mando said to keep you on the down low until your head was on straight. Said Rossi would abort if she knew you were as messed up as you were."

"She would." He pursed his lips at that and examined himself in the mirror, tilting his head this way and that. He set the razor down and gently worked the packing out of his nose. "Man, Hollis did a number on me, this time."

"You remember?"

"Not the incident itself. But, I recall you told me about it."

"What else do you remember? About yesterday? The night before?"

He gave me a brief rundown of his leaving Ilsa's lawyer's offices after finding out about my imminent flight to Aruba. Hoping to track me down before I could flee the country, he had chartered a flight from Monterey to Van Nuys. While he was in the air, he found out I had checked into and boarded the flight to Vegas. His charter was refueling in Van Nuys, so he could follow me to Vegas, when he got a text from Jana that I had appeared at Union Station. He had Percy pick him up and drive him there.

He sounded quite focused and coherent, so I became reasonably sure he was out of the stasis lag. "Did you get to see your little girls?"

He scowled. "No. Ilsa pulled a bait and switch."

I sighed, and put my hand on his hip in sympathy. "Sorry."

He gave me a look of wan gratitude before returning to his shaving. "I remember kissing you." A genuine smile broke across his face at the memory. I smiled, too, our gazes meeting in the mirror for a moment before his brows furrowed in thought. "I remember we were in a really nice limo. But it wasn't mine. And then we were in an Escalade. At the gas station near the highway, on our way to..." he grimaced and shook his head. "No, that hasn't happened yet. We drove to the secret gate. We argued about the Groenies. Then we were here."

"Nobody wants a dog breed that sounds like a pot scrubber."

"What would you call them?"

"I dunno. Something with panache. Something punchy. Like Col Pugnos or something." I held up my fist. "It means 'with fists'."

He rinsed his face off and wiped it with a hand towel, tilting his head from side to side to make sure he'd gotten everything. "Maybe. So, what made you decide to flee protective custody?"

I shrugged. *"Cape Sors Tuum."*

He did a double take, looking at me with alarm. The mood in the room flipped from pleasant and relaxed to intense and dangerous. Like he thought I'd suddenly transformed into a werewolf or something. "Where did you hear that?"

"Papa used to say it all the time. Seize your destiny."

"That's right. Your father." He relaxed slightly, nodding as he put his shaving kit away. But his jaw pulsed, and a strange dark energy seemed to radiate from him.

It unsettled me. "Why? What's the big deal?"

"What made you decide to seize your destiny?"

"Rossi kept talking smack about you. Saying I couldn't trust you. But I didn't trust her, either. And Jana's plan was just plain moronic. So, I decided I should stop being a football."

"And become a quarterback, instead?"

"Something like that." I laid out my plan to him, detailing what I'd accomplished during the seven hours I'd been in the wind.

After Mando's reaction, I'd been feeling rather proud of myself, but the longer Tony listened, the more claustrophobic the room became. His expression never wavered, but a roiling distress seemed to bubble up beneath his surface calm, making the air thick and hard to breathe. By the time I finished, his hands gripped either side of the vanity, and his eyes bored straight down at the drain. His breathing was slow and controlled, but there was ice in his voice when he spoke:

"Get dressed." He left the bathroom without another word.

I followed him, a cold sensation in my gut. "Tony, what's—"

"Get. Dressed." He scooped my clothes up off the chair, hooking them in my direction. I caught the jeans, but the underwear and blouse were too light and fluttered down onto the bed. He limped over to the other side of the bed and picked the *kris* up off the end table.

"What are you doing?" I asked, feeling betrayed.

He didn't reply, just left the room and slammed the door.

As I put my clothes on, I wondered at how quickly the storm clouds had moved in, and what, exactly, had set him to thundering. Zef was nowhere to be found, which made sense. Animals seem to sense impending disaster.

I tied my new sneakers, then gathered up his clothing from last night and carried it to the hamper in the bathroom. His phone slipped out of his pants pocket, so I set that on the vanity, next to the splint. I stayed there, in the bathroom, with one hand on each, because it felt safer, somehow.

Like, as long as I could see Faith in the mirror, it would be her he was angry with, and not Rad. Although, truth be told, I was angry with myself. I should have known better than to think what happened last night would survive the light of day.

Never trust a drunk.

About ten minutes later, I heard the bedroom door open. "Where's the card?" Tony demanded, his footfalls heavy and uneven as he closed the distance to the bathroom door.

"In my purse."

I watched through the open door as he diverted to the chair, where my purse was hanging. He opened it, withdrew the palladium card, and glowered at me. "And my phone?"

I took it and my splint off the vanity and trudged towards him, holding the phone out.

He scowled at the screen, then looked at me accusingly. "It's cracked."

"That's not the only thing," I muttered, unable to resist a little passive aggression.

He glowered at me, then spun on his heel and headed back out to the outer room. "Come," he said curtly.

"I'm not a dog, you know." I followed him into the other room, but only after stringing my purse over my shoulder.

When I got there, I saw one of the burner phones from the gear bag was plugged into the console, next to an open bottle of scotch and a half-empty highball glass. The *kris* rested beside it. He pointed me towards one of the swivel chairs. "Sit."

"Tony, why are you—?"

"*Sit.*"

"—being such an asshole?"

"Why do you think?" He raised the *kris*. "You knew what I needed to do. You knew I needed to get close to Brighton. You fucked me out of my only chance to put my son to rest."

"What are you talking about? I got you closer to Brighton than Jana or the marshals ever would."

"How, exactly, was your plan supposed to work, now that we have missed the flight to Aruba, and, therefore, Brighton has missed his shot at us?"

"We'll just book new flights to somewhere else."

"Because the marshals won't put us on a no fly list, now that you've embarrassed the Hell out of them by escaping their custody." His sarcasm burned like acid.

"It's not my fault Hollis tried to kill you!"

"You fucked me, Rad. You handed Foster to Hollis on a silver platter, and you gave the marshals probable cause to seize all the data engines and servers from his other clubs. You gave them everything they need to run Brighton down. Without me."

The pain in my chest rivaled the worst my hand had ever been. He was right. I sank slowly into the chair, knowing there was no way to make this right short of stabbing Brighton Leigh with the *kris* myself. "I was trying to help."

"That's the only reason you're still alive, right now."

"Oh, like you could really kill me?"

"You think I can't?"

"You just got re-genned, dumbass. Your whole right side has the muscle tone of a dead eel. I'd wipe the floor with you."

"Don't call me a dumbass."

"Then don't let wankers like Hollis electrocute you! My plan was perfect until *you* screwed it up. Or would you rather I not resuscitate you and rush you to a safe house the next time you're dead? Or look after you when you're tripping balls from stasis?"

He grabbed the *kris* and brandished it at me. "I had a plan. It was my only chance to put Stefan to rest. All you fucking had to do was get on that flight to Vegas. But you fucked it all up with your *Cape Sors Tuum* bullshit. Fucking contrary piece of shit."

"If I'd known the plan, I'd have gone to Vegas. But I didn't get on that flight because I refused to betray you! And stop using the f-word!"

He raised the blade, taking a step towards me. His bulk loomed ominously over me. "Fucking make me stop."

I snorted. "You wanna match crazy with me? Fine." I spread my arms wide and leaned back in the chair, giving him a clean shot to my chest and throat. "Go ahead. Kill me. That'll make this right."

He growled, but took a step back and lowered the dagger. "I'm not going to kill you."

"Why not? That'll free your kid's soul, right? And ooh, added bonus, it'll trap me inside the opal. You can keep me with you forever, that way. None of my contrary bullshit, plus the security of knowing nobody can kill you. Win-win for you."

"Stop making fun of me."

"Stop being a shithead. Things went sideways. We'll rally. We'll figure it out."

He glowered at me, then turned away with a sigh. He set the *kris* back on the console and moved over to the open gear bag, rummaging around inside. "I'll rally. I'll figure it out. You," He pulled out a stack of cash and set it on the console in front of me. "Will be gone."

I stared at the cash for about half a minute, until I realized what was happening, here. The money was my severance pay. I was being fired. "Tony, I—"

"You told the marshals you signed the contract under duress. That you considered it null and void. They're holding me to that." He pulled some alcohol swabs and a drug patch from the gear bag, then removed a shrink-wrapped device that looked a nerf pistol mated with an electronic hole punch. "Bend your head down. Rest your forehead on the console."

"What for?"

"So I can remove your implant." He cut the shrink wrap with the tip of the *kris* and peeled it away from the device.

I stared at him, beseeching, but he radiated that same commanding implacability he'd had outside the warehouse. I rubbed my face, took a deep sigh, and then assumed the position.

The alcohol swab cooled the skin on the back of my neck. I felt the device moving up and down until it beeped. Tony pulled the trigger, and a sharp, shooting pain went into my skull and down to my shoulder, accompanied by a very disconcerting crunching sensation. He withdrew the device. Felt like he was pulling a wire out of the neck muscle, and then all that was left was an ache and the warm trickle of blood down my spine.

I heard him toss the device into the kitchenette sink. He stepped behind me again. He wiped my neck with another swab, then placed the drug patch over the wound. The swivel chair beside me creaked as he lowered himself into it. Ice tinkled as scotch poured. I heard him swallow a few times.

"You can leave, now," his voice was thick and bitter.

I couldn't. I was having trouble moving. It felt like my blood had drained out my feet, leaving me cold and lifeless and alone. With great effort, I lifted my head and gave him an imploring look, but he just tapped away at his keyboard. His right hand moved a bit slower than his left.

"Because you saved my life, I'll arrange for Balcour to see you this evening. After that, we're square."

"But, how will I—?"

"Take the Escalade. I'll remotely open the locks and signal the dogs to head to the kennel. You have forty minutes to reach the gate." The room grew still. Light from the screens danced across his face and thrust his swollen nose and battered chin and cheekbones into sharp relief. The only sounds were our breathing and the humming of the monitors. "Clock's ticking."

I swallowed the pin cushion in my throat and got to my feet, realizing belatedly that the splint was still in my hand. "I don't want your cash."

"Take it anyway. You're going to need it."

He was right. I shoved it into the purse next to the Escalade fob and headed for the door. The handle turned smoothly.

"It would have been nice," he said to my back.

"Yeah." I stepped into the switch room and out of his life.

CHAPTER TWENTY-SIX

I guided the Escalade through early evening traffic, moving through the chromed heat towards Vic's office in NoHo. I'd received a text to the nav display that my appointment was at 1900 hours.

The sun was low in the west, but wouldn't set for at least another hour. Everything gleamed in a golden, syrupy light that hurt my eyes. I'd had a headache since Tony had removed the implant, but that didn't compare to what was going on in my hand. Or my heart.

Rossi had been right, all along. I didn't mean anything to Tony. I had never meant anything to him. I was just a hired hand. Somebody to use and abuse and throw away. Someone to manipulate, like all the other people in his life. Nothing had substance to him beyond his own dark and mysterious goals.

It was all so easy to see in the baked plastic density of Southern California. The sun burned away the shadows, exposed every secret to the ruthless light of day. What was he, really? Behind the facades, the endless series of masks, was there anything human? Or was he just a phantom, a spirit feeding off the havoc of long ago traumas?

I didn't know. Didn't think I'd ever know.

I'd almost bought into it. Almost conned myself into becoming the same formless enigma that Tony was. Playing one role after another, telling lies until nothing seemed real. The freedom, the irresponsibility of it beckoned me, even now.

But who was I kidding? I couldn't trust Tony. Couldn't trust anybody who worked for him. Couldn't trust the marshals, couldn't trust the cops. The only people I could trust were Vic and Jim, and they were in danger simply knowing about me, so long as Foster and Brighton Leigh were on the loose. I should take what I could and get out. Make sure my hand was okay and walk away, before the quicksand of this lifestyle swallowed me alive.

The parking lot to Vic's building was almost empty, so it was no problem docking the Escalade in two spaces. At least it was an automatic, so I could prop my hand on the passenger headrest during the long drive. Keeping it elevated had reduced the swelling, so maybe Vic wouldn't blow his top when he saw it.

The building was deserted when Vic buzzed me in. Even the security guard at the lobby desk was gone. Vic met me at the door to his offices, an idiotic grin on his distinguished black face. "Good to see you, Miss Hopkins."

"Right nice seeing you again, too, Doctor. Although," I held up my right arm, "Kinda wish the circumstances were a mite different."

His smile decayed, his bushy white brows falling into deep thought. "You're not wearing the splint?"

"Tight here." I produced the splint from my backpack purse. "Cain't get my fingers in. They're all swole up."

He made an unhappy noise and gave me his angry school marm glower as he escorted me back to the exam room. He kept the look up as he prepped his equipment, then took my hand gently. He cradled my elbow in the palm of his other hand. He extended my fingers, frowning at my wince, and examined the bruise across my knuckles. "I told you not to hit anything."

"I didn't. It up and hit me."

"You've been doing the exercises?"

"From day one."

He switched the overhead monitor on, unclipped a broad imaging stylus from the CPU and stretched my arm out prone. I winced, but managed not to jerk away from him. He poked the stylus along the meaty section of my forearm from elbow to wrist.

I almost clocked him from instinct alone. God, that hurt.

His jaw tightened as the readout crawled up on the monitor. I wasn't sure what exactly was on the screen, but I could tell he was worried about it. "Your flexor tendons aren't moving through the metacarpal tunnels smoothly. The blockage is occurring right here," he indicated the back of my hand just above the wrist. Right where the door had smacked me.

"In English, Doc."

"The tendons can't slide effectively along your arm and the back of your hand because the regenerated bones are slightly out of alignment. If this had happened a month from now, it wouldn't be an issue, but your muscles haven't built up enough strength to keep the joints properly aligned after a blow like this." "

I nodded understanding. "How do we fix it?"

He sighed, turned the monitor off, and drew two plastic baggies with drug samples out. He placed them on the counter next to my elbow. "Muscle relaxants and analgesics should relieve the spasms and most of the swelling. Alternate ice and heat."

I nodded and watched him retrofit the splint with larger sheaths around the splines. He gently eased my fingers into the new configuration and turned the splint on. I sighed with relief.

"You need to wear that a minimum of eight hours a day. Nothing but gentle stretching exercises for the next week, or you'll just aggravate the sheaths and cause even more scarring." He took my good hand and held it, face solemn. "I'm sorry."

"Not your fault." I shrugged. "Just a minor setback. I'll be good as new afore you know it."

His lips pinched together. He shook his head. "As long as the misalignment is there, you'll be building up scar tissue. Which will lead to chronic pain and stiffness."

"How do we realign them?"

"Surgery. But that'll likely leave more scarring than simply working the muscles to the point they pull it all back into place. I don't suppose your boyfriend will spring for more re-gen?"

"No. Ain't no way I'm ever doin' stasis again."

He sighed. "I'm sorry, then."

"You mean I won't be able to—?"

"Yes," he cut me off before I could drop completely out of character. "Without another bout of re-gen, your fingers will never be as quick as they were. Not concert quality, anyway."

I stared at him, wondering how many times I had to hit ground before I stopped bouncing and died already. Ironic, that it was Jim who put the final nail in the coffin.

"Thanks," I finally said, scraping the drugs into my purse before shuffling out of his office like a zombie.

***

When I reached the parking lot, I saw a familiar blue BMW parked beside the Escalade. Mando stepped out at my approach, a look of somber sympathy on his face. His hair was uncombed. He wore jeans and a faded green T-shirt with a logo from Phillipe's the Original. There were random splotches of bright, primary colors on his clothes. He noticed me looking at them and explained: "Finger painting."

That's right. He had kids. A family. A life.

I sniffed and walked around his car, but he moved to block me, holding a hand up. "I'm here to take you back to the Ranch. Tony has an obligation to look after you until you're back to your old self."

"That's not gonna happen."

"It's not safe for you. Not looking like that."

"He doesn't want to see me again."

"He has other houses he can stay at, if that's the case. But you need to be protected until the effects of the implant wear off."

"I'll dye my hair. Use contacts. I'll be fine."

He sighed and ran his hand along the gray streak in his hair. "You should have gone to Vegas. I knew you'd get hurt."

"I thought you meant physically. Not like this. Besides, people in Nevada think Beethoven is something you do at a craps table."

He gave me a puzzled look.

"Beethoven. Bet often?" I shrugged. "Not my best..."

"Just get in the car, please? He's angry now, but he'll get over it. What you did saved all our asses. Especially his. Eventually, he'll see that."

"What about the Escalade?"

"I don't think Dr. Balcour will mind if you leave it here over night. I'll have Percy move it to the long term storage lot at the Van Nuys Flyaway bus station tomorrow, so you can get it whenever you need it."

"Rather have my Mazda back."

"You know where it is. I'll take you to it."

I heaved a deep sigh and moved over to climb into the passenger side of the Beemer. "Only if we get a steak along the way. I need to fortify myself for another three weeks of vegetables."

He grinned and got behind the wheel. "Deal."

***

We stopped at a steakhouse on the pier in the seaside town of Ventura. Dinner was glorious.

Prime rib with horseradish, a baked potato oozing sour cream and chives, and no vegetables or tofu in sight. Mando watched me eat, amused, and put away a couple of crab legs and a virgin Mary. He asked me about myself, and I told him how the story of how I wound up driving my uncle Fangio's Formula Ford car after he broke his leg falling off a ladder taking the Christmas lights down. We talked about Mando's kids in general, and his new baby daughter in particular. For a while there, I actually felt like I belonged. It was strange, that sense of acceptance. Except for the concert hall, I hadn't belonged anywhere since Chris died.

When we left the restaurant, the sun was down and the sky was fading from electric blue to navy. Mando flung the car around a maze of back streets in the ubiquitous ritual for losing tails. His almost religious fervor made me pine for Percy's sedate driving habits.

"So, tell me about the library," he said, when we pulled onto a main street that paralleled the highway.

I told him about Jim and Webster and how I'd thrashed that bully so hard I'd put him in the hospital. He laughed and asked me more about Jim. I babbled on about how I'd met him in my freshman year and how we'd become fast friends. Mando hooked a left down a trashy alley and turned into a gated warehouse compound, and I interrupted myself to ask, "what are we doing here?"

"Tony liked that Sprinter you rented so much, he wants me to check in with his customizer about getting one bulletproofed."

"It's almost nine. Will they even be open?"

"Chuy's expecting me. It won't take very long. C'mon inside and meet him. He's a car guy. You'll like him."

"All right," I crawled out of the car, eager to do something normal for a change. I was so done with all the cloak and dagger crap.

We walked across asphalt that still radiated the day's heat and up some concrete steps, stopping on top of a loading dock beside a normal-sized swing door. Even with the sun down, the heat radiating off the dark paint hit me like a two-by-four. I wiped a trickle of sweat from my temple as Mando turned the handle and waved me inside.

A blast of cool air hit my face. I closed my eyes and I stepped into the room, enjoying the relief. A noise sounded to my right, the sound of cloth rustling against a vinyl chair. I looked over.

Behind a battered desk was a grinning blonde man wearing a suit so tight it groaned at the seams.

Scott Foster.

I shouted a warning to Mando, then whirled a sweeping kick at two black-clad figures who flanked me from nowhere. I hit one in the midriff, jumped away from the other. Mando lunged into the room, something black and deadly in his hand.

And then he pointed it at me and pulled the trigger.

Two pinpricks hit me and the seconds stretched into one long eternity as my whole body lifted in a wracking, thrashing arch, every muscle strung to breaking—and then I was falling, a buzzing, heavy sensation in my limbs. I smelled the biting scent of ozone.

"Don't move." Mando stood over me with the Taser gun in his hand, two thin wires snaking to my ribcage. "You piss me off, you get another jolt. *Comprendes?*"

I blinked, too dazed to do anything but remember how to breathe.

"Good." He stripped my purse away and looked at the men in black. "Tie her up."

They left the Taser wires in me. One of them zipped a thick plastic tie around my ankles, the kind riot police use for emergency handcuffs. The other hitched my left hand behind my back to a cord looped around my neck. Together they muscled me into a wooden chair near the desk and zipped my already bound hand to a back rung.

My splinted right hand dangled freely. I tried to use it to pull the wires out, but my arm spasmed in mid-strike, my whole body jolted by another 50,000 volts.

"Thought you knew better," Mando grabbed my wrist as I recovered from the blast. He sat on the edge of the desk facing me, and pinned my forearm under his leg.

I gulped some air and blinked again. My head was clearing, but I couldn't believe this was happening. Couldn't believe Mando was doing this. I'd been so sure he was on my side.

"You sumbitch," I hissed at him. "I oughta—"

"Temper, temper," Scotty admonished from the other side of the desk. He removed the splint from my hand and traced his finger over the new pink skin where the gunshot had been. "You wouldn't want to go through this again, would you?"

I swallowed hard.

He waved at the two suited gangsters. "Wait outside."

They moved to the door, and I prayed they'd drop dead from the heat. Dressed as they were, it wasn't impossible. Scotty watched them go, but Mando's Hell-black eyes remained focused on me.

When they were gone, Scotty dumped my purse out and pawed through the contents. "You've caused me a great deal of trouble, Rad. Snitching me out to Hollis."

Rad. Not Faith. He knew.

Of course he knew. Mando had probably told him everything. Scotty enjoyed my reaction. "But it's nothing I can't get past. Who do you think was waiting for you in Vegas? My people. I have the data engine. And the holo discs. The marshals aren't going to be able to do shit without them."

I grimaced, seething as it all became clear: Mando had never been looking out for me. He'd been trying to get Tony to pass my prints, so that he could get the technology for Scotty and Brighton Leigh.

Scotty circumnavigated the desk and squatted next to me. His hands dropped to my thighs, and he yanked me forward, so that I was perched on the edge of the chair.

He pushed my blouse up and hooked his fingers around the waistband of my pants. He pulled them down my thighs slowly, savoring the way my body tensed to deny him. His eyebrows raised when he saw my red-blonde pubic hair. His hand cupped my bare buttock, palm moving in slow, sensuous circles. Without warning, he drew his arm back and slapped my butt cheek, leaving a blazing five-fingered print. "If Tovenaar wasn't such a eunuch, he'd know Faith has a birthmark there." He stood, leaving my blouse up, my panties down. An erection strained at his pants.

He noticed me staring at his crotch and smiled. "Maybe later, if we have time." He took the Taser from Mando, examined it nonchalantly. "This may take a while." He fixed his eyes on me. "Did Tony ever tell you about how I had him begging for mercy, screaming out every wretched little secret?"

I glanced nervously at Mando. He showed no emotion, just a seriousness which frightened me more than Scotty's perversions. Panic surged up within me. "What do you want from me?"

Scotty frowned, like I'd taken all his fun away. "I want you to shoot Tovenaar in the back."

I jerked my chin at Mando. "Have him do it."

"You misunderstand me. I don't want Tovenaar dead. I want him owned. Or, more accurately, I want to own what he owns. And I need him alive to hand me the reins. That's where you come in, my dear. You're my Trojan horse." His eyes crawled over me. He dropped his hand, dragged his knuckles across the exposed part of my cleavage. "You're going to keep that lusty bastard occupied while I get into position."

"And if I say no?"

His brow wrinkled. He held the Taser a few inches from my nose and moved his thumb over the trigger switch, lowering it slowly, slowly, so I couldn't miss what was coming next. A helpless rage washed over me, the same bone-deep fury I'd had when my mother's cigarettes charred holes in my back. I snapped my head forward, sunk my teeth into his wrist just as the electric shock seized me.

Scotty yelped and swiped at me, trying to dislodge me, but all my muscles were locked up from the current. As long as the buzzing monster possessed my body, there was no way I could let go, even if I wanted to. I tasted blood before Mando knocked the Taser out of Scotty's hand.

Relief swamped me with the warm knowledge my body was my own again. I sagged down, head resting on my outstretched arm, breath labored. My right hand was ablaze, the fragile new muscles and tendons screaming from the spastic overload.

Scotty whipped out a handkerchief and wrapped it around his bloody wrist, then cradled his hand close to his chest. His erection was gone. I allowed myself the merest hint of a smile, and then Mando grabbed a handful of hair and held my head up, his eyes glittering with menace. "Do that again, you're dead. Understand?"

"Yeh."

He threw my head away, then stood and picked up the Taser. By the time I realized my right hand was free, Scotty held it pinned. He stared at me, a snarl curling his upper lip. "You really should help me, Rad. Really. I'm not asking much. Just a few bits of information."

"Like what?"

"Like where are the tunnels?"

"What tunnels?"

"The tunnels you used to get into the Ranch yesterday," Mando said. He handed the Taser back to Scotty, who held his bloody thumb over the switch.

My mouth dried up. I tensed, bracing for the charge. "I don't know about any tunne—" My denial ended in a shriek as the shock hit me again. The pain in my arm overwhelmed me. When it subsided, my voice was hoarse from the screams.

Scotty tilted his head, amused. The bulge in his pants was back. "I can listen to that all night, if you want." His expression hardened. "But the more I wait, the more I'll want to take it out on your ass."

I weighed my options and decided that the only way out of this was to lead them on. I mustered an equally hard stare. "You need me, pay me. One million dollars in a Swiss numbered account. You give me the access information when I give you the chip."

"What chip?"

"The one you need to travel underground. All the locks use this special chip Tony's got hidden in his phone."

They pondered this.

"Where's the card?" Scotty demanded.

"What card?"

"Faith's palladium card," Mando replied. "The one you had at Union Station."

"Tony took it back. He wasn't very happy with me, remember?"

They exchanged calculating glances.

"He did give her the *kris*," Mando pointed out.

Scotty nodded. "And Tovenaar thinks with his cock."

They smiled, big Cheshire grins, and nodded in unison. "You make him happy, again. You get Mando that card and that chip by tomorrow night," Scotty said, "and I'll give you your one million dollars."

"Sure," I agreed, wondering if Faust felt this cornered when he made his deal with the devil. "Piece of cake."

***

"Here," I said dully. "To the left."

Mando looked over at me, dubious. The turn indicator clicked ominously in the quiet. "There's nothing there."

"There is. In that open spot under the trees."

He assessed me with that mortician's smile. "You better not be shitting me." He gassed the car, swung it over the double yellow lines of the highway into the moonlit gloom of cottonwoods. The headlights illuminated the barranca ahead, and the faint yellow smear of adobe that made up the wall.

"Well I'll be damned," Mando exclaimed. He stepped out of the car, and walked forward, squinting at it.

I watched, throat tight with guilt. Less than twenty-four hours after I'd promised Tony, and here I was rolling over on him. But what else could I do? Let Scotty fry my nerve endings all night while he waved an erection in my face?

All that would have gotten me was dead, or worse. Playing the compliant stooge was the only way to find out what double cross Benedict Mando had planned. The only hard part was acting scared and deferential when what I really wanted to do was tear his kneecaps off and feed them to him through his nose.

Mando turned grimly away from the gate and crunched across the dried leaves to the car.

"Why you doing this?" I asked as he settled behind the wheel and killed the headlights. "You have kids. A family. Why risk them?"

He shrugged. "More of a risk working for Tony. He used to have the knack, but he's lost heart. Man drinks like a fish, breaches his own security over a wildcard like you. He's bound to make a mistake, take the whole team down with him."

"Thought Tony went through Hell to save your ass. Doesn't that count?"

"That was a long time ago. Things are different now. Tony's different now."

"He's still your friend. It doesn't make sense."

"Makes perfect sense. Only friends can get close enough to stab you in the back."

I stared at him for a long time, at the tight way he gripped the steering wheel, the way his sad-fierce eyes reflected the dappled moonlight filtering through the trees. "And I'm the knife?"

He held his breath and ran his tongue along his upper teeth, lips pulled back in a pained grimace. "Yeah," he said gruffly. "You're the knife."

He backed carefully out, then drove a little farther up the road with the headlights still out. He turned onto a dirt track on the opposite side of the highway from the estate. We bumped and bottomed our way up a number of switchbacks, until we cruised to a stop at a turnout that commanded a broad panorama of Tony's holdings.

"Once we get through the gate," Mando asked as I took in the view, "where do we go?"

I pointed out the streambed, described the trail we had taken from the gate. I told him about the pump house, and what to expect underground, but left out any mention of the side tunnels and Tony's hidey hole. Instinct told me those were as important to Tony as his *kris*. As I spoke, a pack of Groenies appeared from the underbrush inside the adobe fence and barked at us.

"Fuck," Mando said, scowling.

"What?"

He waved at the dogs. "You don't see any Mals, do you? Tony's on high alert. The Groenies will attack anything outside a vehicle. And they only answer to Tony."

"What about the handlers? Somebody feeds them, don't they?"

"From the cart." Mando shrugged. "Anyone on foot is dead meat. One of Tony's insurance policies against intruders."

"You could shoot them. The dogs, I mean."

He shook his head. "They've got monitor implants and transmitters in their collars. Any severe change in body function—like death or tranquilization—and that damn smartphone tips Tony off. That paranoid bastard can tell when and where any dog in the pack is taking a shit."

"So why not just drive through the gate, park in the garage and wait for Tony to show?"

Mando shook his head. "He won't come in if he thinks anything might be wrong. Why do you think I'm talking to you out here? Everything's surveilled. Every inch of that driveway, every nook of that house. I couldn't bring a gnat in without Tony knowing two seconds after I cleared the gate."

"Well, then, you can forget about the tunnel. There's no access to it without vid coverage."

"That's where you come in. Tony's camera shy. My guess is that chip reprograms the surveillance systems to dummy coverage. It would explain why he never appears in any recordings of the house or gates."

"How you gonna get his print? You need his print for all the locks underground."

Mando sniggered. "I've worked with the man for seven years. You think I don't have his print?"

"It still won't help you. The tunnel's a half hour's walk from the gate. The dogs would probably get you before you reached the pump house—if you could find the trail in the dark."

"What makes you think we're coming in at night?"

I shrugged. "I dunno. I just sort of assumed."

He stared at me like he was trying to see into my skull. "You get that chip and that card for me by the time I take you to the doctor tomorrow afternoon."

"What about my money?"

"We'll make the trade after you see Balcour. You'll get your cut out of the palladium card."

"Sounds good." I nodded, smiling like I was happy with the deal. "When are you making the hit?"

His mouth drew into a taut line. "You don't need to know."

"Then how can I distract him for you? Scotty said he thinks with his cock."

He started the car up, pointed it down the road. "With this divorce he'll be plenty distracted, no matter what you do."

"What makes you so sure?"

He didn't respond immediately, his eyes fixed on the rutted track ahead. After a few minutes he glanced over, his expression oddly soft, almost gentle. "It's his weakest spot."

"What?"

"His heart." He looked back at the road. "When Ilsa left, he was worthless for months. Stefan almost killed him."

"Who's Stefan?"

His jaw tightened. A faint snarl edged his lips. "You should know. Tony gave you his *kris*." He stopped the car and looked at me. "Or are you just trying to protect him?"

My throat tightened. I didn't say anything.

He took it as an admission. He sucked his teeth and started the car up again. "A million dollars is a lot of money," he said as we wound our way toward the house. "Be a shame if you let a monomaniacal bastard like Tony keep you from spending it."

CHAPTER TWENTY-SEVEN

Jana and two armed Javanese guards greeted us when Mando walked me into the house. "What's she doing here?"

"We have to protect her until the implant wears off," Mando replied, walking me past her towards the stairs. "Read the contract."

Jana huffed. Her heels clacked on the tiles as she caught up with us. "What if the marshals find her here?"

"They've already searched the place. So has Hollis. Unless you text them a selfie with her, how are they gonna know?"

"Tony's not going to like it."

"Where is he, anyway?"

"Not sure. Haven't heard from him since that phone conference with Rossi this morning."

"How'd that go?"

She shrugged. "They have opted to pursue Leigh without our services."

"That's expected. What'd they say about her?" Mando hooked a thumb at me as we started up the broad staircase.

"In light of what's going on with Hollis's case against Foster, they're denying any prior knowledge of Damiano's impersonation of Faith Hopkins."

"They're pinning it all on us?"

"No. Rossi said our contract with her was invalid, since it was signed under duress. And her escape proves she has refused to cooperate with law enforcement and rejected protective custody."

Mando glanced sidelong at me.

I shrugged. "She pissed me off."

He looked across me at Jana. "That means Damiano acted as an independent, with no State affiliation. Whatever evidence she's turned up will be totally admissible. That's a good thing, right?"

Jana nodded. "Makes both the marshals' and Hollis' cases that much stronger."

"Makes her that much more of a target." Mando indicated me.

"Pretty much," Jana gave me an evil, told-you-so grin.

I accidentally-on-purpose tripped on the stairs and jabbed an elbow into her boob as I fell against her. She cried out and swept a forearm at me, but I'd been expecting it and easily dodged down, pretending to recover my balance. She hissed and shot a glower at me. I gave her an innocent look, but didn't apologize.

"If the marshals find you," Jana said to me, "you'll go to jail."

"For what?"

"Burglary. False police report. Planting evidence."

I rolled my eyes. "Big whoop. That's like, a year. Maybe six months, if the jails are full. I'll be out on time served. If they can even prove I did it, since Lonny saw Faith, not me."

"If Scotty finds you," Mando added as we turned down the corridor leading to my old room, "you'll be looking at a lot worse." He gave me a warning look, then regarded Jana. "Which is why we need to keep her here until that whole thing plays out."

Jana made a frustrated growl. "You are such a choirboy. You explain to Tony why she's here, when he specifically told her to get the Hell out."

Mando watched as she stormed off, then escorted me to the bedroom door. The latches clicked free at our approach, and he opened the door, but didn't let me through. He regarded me with that flat black gaze.

I didn't blink or look away. It seemed to bother him.

While we were engaged in this staredown, Zef romped up the hallway towards us, claws clicking on the polished tile. He wagged his tail, licking Mando's hand, then mine. I curled my fingers into his fur, but didn't drop my gaze.

It was Mando who finally looked away. "Tomorrow," he murmured. "I'll find Tony and send him up."

"Whatever," I said, and stepped past him into the room. I half expected Mando to follow me and try more intimidation tactics, but it was the dog who bounded in, wagging his feathery whip of a tail. I pointed to the door, about to order him out, but Mando had already shut me in with the beast, who swiveled his head to see what I was pointing at, and then sat down with a quizzical look.

"Bah!" I turned away from him, slinging my purse off my shoulder and fishing the splint out. It fit, but wouldn't turn on, since the multiple Taser shots had fried the circuits. I had to resort to the pills Vic had given me to take the edge off the pain, which made me sleepy. I stripped my clothes off.

When I got under the covers, Zef threw one paw on the bedspread, and whined. I pulled away, wondering what the animal wanted. "What?"

He must have been waiting for me to say something, because he leapt up on the bed and hunkered down next to me, eyes bright, tongue lolling. I patted him gingerly.

He wriggled around, like his whole body was a wagging tail. I sighed, stared at the ceiling, and continued stroking him. It surprised me that the idle movement somehow brought me comfort. Zef was an enigma, something I couldn't fully comprehend. Did he really like me, or was he just lonely?

Just before I fell asleep, I realized it didn't matter.

***

The bed shuddered and jostled violently, jarring me from the oblivion of sleep. I rubbed my eyes, trying to figure out what had just happened. An earthquake?

No. Must've been Zef jumping off the bed. I looked around in the dim light and saw the dog over by the door, dancing around in little half-hops. He yipped at me, then raised himself up on the wall and pawed at the lock. A stab of sympathy ran through me. He was trapped by what he was, same as me. I got up and tried to open the door, but it wouldn't budge. Without my implant, I couldn't go anywhere in the house unescorted.

"Sorry," I told him. "You're stuck with me, for now."

He whined more loudly, and scratched the door, then barked and looked up at me impatiently.

I sighed and crawled back into bed, ignoring him. He barked again, then paced around, whining.

I stared at the eerie way the pool lights bounced across the ceiling. My head and hand ached too much to sleep, so I pulled the keyboard out from under the bed and rested it across my lap. I ran my fingers over it, not bothering to turn the light on. The dark seemed safer, because I wouldn't have to see how much I'd lost. I'd been avoiding it, knowing that I'd never see the stage again, not wanting to face the loss, but now that I was bound to lose Tony, too, the music had a kind of narcotic draw.

I limbered up my left hand, then settled into a string of Godowsky's left-handed pieces, one after another, just losing myself in the illusion of being whole, the pretense of the moment. As long as the music echoed against the walls, I was still breathing. Still fighting.

The door opened just as I finished the *Impromptu in E flat minor*, and Zef launched himself at Tony's silhouette in a happy, bouncing frenzy.

The distinct, triangular Glenfiddich bottle was in Tony's hand, the light from the hallway making a star in the green glass.

I regarded him, trying to gauge his mood. Not good, I decided, when he stepped into the room without even a word to Zef, who slunk into the hall with his ears back as if he'd been chastised. Tony closed the door and stalked over to one of the wingchairs near the window. I swallowed and turned the keyboard off, stowing it under the bed.

Tony made a breathy, growling exhalation as he collapsed into the chair. "Mando said you were back."

"I want my car."

He snorted. I heard the swish of liquid, the sound of a messy swallow. "What is it with you and that piece of shit?"

"It's my piece of shit. Just like you and your *kris*."

"Stefan's *kris*," he corrected.

"Stefan's *kris*," I agreed.

Neither of us said anything for a while, long enough for me to count two more swigs.

"I'm sorry," I said, breaking the silence. "About how things played out. Truly sorry."

"Sorry doesn't fix anything."

"I know. Neither does alcohol."

There was a long silence, and then the noise of a cork being tapped into the bottle. "You're right."

That surprised me. My mother would have smacked me for being insolent.

"What did the doctor say? About your hand?"

"Splint's broken. Have to go back tomorrow. See if he can fix it."

"How'd that happen?"

"Can we go somewhere else? Somewhere safe?"

"This is my house. You don't think you're safe here?"

"Not in this room. Not anywhere Mando has access to."

The silence stretched into a minute or two. Liquid sloshed in the bottle as Tony got to his feet and moved over to slot his chip in the lock. "Let's go."

I grabbed a robe and followed him out into the hall, surprised to find Zef sitting there. He padded a precise distance from Tony's left side and sat patiently whenever we stopped to open a door. Every once in a while, he licked Tony's hand.

Soon enough, we were in Tony's secret suite.

A half-eaten microwave pasta dish sat on the console next to the *kris*. Ice melted in a bucket next to an empty Glenfiddich bottle on the kitchenette counter. The monitors were all on. One showed Jana asleep in her bed, a few others showed various guards on post, watching their own monitors. One showed my room, with me sleeping soundly. Tony fed the pasta to the dog, then sat in one of the swivel chairs and stared at the wall of flat screens. "I'm listening."

I drew in a deep breath and broke the news:

"Mando's working for Scotty. That's how the splint got broken. Mando Tasered me. More than once." I showed him the vampire punctures left by the Taser as proof I wasn't lying. "So did Scotty."

He didn't flinch, didn't react at all to my words, just stared silently at the monitors for so long I wondered if he'd passed out with his eyes open. I glanced uneasily at the dog, who had finished the pasta and was now studying me, licking his chops.

"Tell me," Tony said in a dead monotone, "exactly what happened."

Starting from the parking lot at Vic's, I ran through the evening's events, all the way to the point Mando left me in the room. As I spoke, the room filled with a dark, heated energy. When I finished, Tony uncorked the bottle and took a long swig, then grimaced. "Seventy-eight hours."

"What?"

"That's how long it took Foster to break me. Seventy-eight hours. Made me watch Eddie die. Strung me up. Broke my bones. Cut me. Brighton watched it all, laughing. Cackling like a cockatoo. But Mando was depending on me. Had to give him enough time to get out."

My stomach lurched at his description, and then a fiery, crackling rage built up inside me. "And now he betrays you."

He tore his gaze from the screen. "And so do you."

"Me?"

"Five minutes? Is that all I meant to you? Five fucking minutes with a Taser and you're licking Scotty's boots?"

It was like a fist to the gut, but I didn't let it show. "What else was I supposed to do? At least this way I'm alive to warn you."

"Alive to spend your million dollars, you mean."

"Tony, get your head out of the bottle! I don't give a shit about the money. I did that for you."

He scoffed, shaking his head. "I'm not drunk enough to swallow that level of bullshit."

I resisted the urge to throat punch him and picked up the *kris*, instead. I brandished it at him. "Think about it. What jury in the world would convict a man for stabbing the people who broke into his house and threatened to torture him if he didn't falsify their identities? Even the marshals couldn't make that stick. Especially if you have all this video evidence." I waved at the wall of screens.

He looked at the monitors, blinking slowly, then regarded me. "You want them to come here? To the house?"

"Duh. That's where your machine is, right?" I pointed at the cubby that held the device that had given me the Passport card. "I bring them here. And you," I raised the *kris*, "Do the rest."

His gaze fell to the blade in my hand. I offered it to him, pommel first. He took it, cradling it against his chest as if it was the most precious thing in the world. "That's not a bad plan..."

He took several deep breaths, then murmured something in Javanese to the opal and kissed it. He looked up at me, his voice hoarse when he said: "Thank you."

I nodded, feeling my anger drain away.

His eyes held a stark clarity that punched through the dulling layers of alcohol. He set the *kris* down and pulled a touch board out of the console. "I'll dummy a chip for you. And encode a trojan into the palladium card, to back trace all the accounts Foster transfers the money into."

His fingers flew over the touch board, his attention fully mired in the gibberish on the screen. Curious, I peered over his shoulder. Somehow the symbols there made sense to him, but all I could read were squiggles, codes, and nonsense words. "Didn't know you were a computer nerd."

"There's a lot you don't know."

"Why don't you enlighten me?"

He shot me a devilish smirk. "It would take too long."

I snickered and sat down on the couch. Zef took that as his cue to trot over and press his slobber-encrusted toy skunk in my lap. I picked it up, thinking to toss it away, but he kept hold and tugged.

I let go, and he ran away, then circled back and pressed the toy into my lap again. I got the idea and held on, this time. We battled over it, with him making happy growls and wagging his tail. Slobber aside, it was actually more fun than I expected it to be.

We played, while Tony did his computer thing. Soon enough, Tony held the chip and palladium card out to me. "All set."

I didn't take them. "To really sell this, we need to go back to my room. Mando might check the security recordings, so I need to steal them from you."

His mouth quirked to the side. "Like I'd ever let that happen."

"Scotty said you think with your dick. Hate to disappoint him." I waggled my eyebrows lasciviously.

He snickered. "You're insatiable."

"And you're a lush. We all have our vices."

"Fair enough." He rose and held a hand out to me. "Let's go put on a show."

It was the best show I'd ever been in, one that left us both exhausted and sated amid the happy ruins of Faith's bedsheets. While Tony pretended to doze, I eased the chip out of his phone and the card out of the wallet I found in his pants, and hid them under the control board of the splint. Even broken, it provided support that eased some of the pain.

I took another round of drugs, climbed into bed, and feigned passing out beside him. Then, of course, Tony doctored the feed and we snuck back to the secret suite, programed a virtual image of Tony sneaking out of my room and me sleeping through the night.

Then, we went into Tony's bedroom and had sex all over again.

***

Tony tightened the Velcro strap around my calf, adjusted the sheath, and looked up at me. "That okay?"

I turned my ankle from side to side, scrutinizing, making sure the *kris* wasn't distorting the baggy fabric of my Faith pants. "It'll do." Tony had insisted I carry it, pointing out that it would cement both Mando and Scotty's beliefs that Tony was crazy about me. Or maybe that he was just plain crazy.

As he stood, his hands glided up the warm silk covering my torso. He pulled me out of the swivel chair and drew me close. I hugged him back, his suit rough against my cheek. He kissed me on the top of the head. "You remember everything I told you. No telegraphing. You're Mando's insider, his mole to gather information on me. You do exactly what he says, and you act like a scared rabbit."

I nodded. Squeezed him tighter.

"You ready?"

I nodded again, lifting my chin to meet his gaze. "I was born ready," I told him confidently, repeating a line Papa used to say.

"It'll be dangerous."

"I know." A little chill ran through me as I realized the moment of truth was rapidly approaching.

"You'll need a few bruises on your face. Do you want to do it, or should I?"

"Why? I mean what do you have to hit me for?"

"Insurance. Brighton's got his kinks. He insists that his 'subjects' faces are entirely uninjured. Swelling or discoloration ruins his enjoyment, so if we bruise you now, he and Scotty will likely wait until your injuries clear to seriously torture you."

His words were like cold water. I mean, Brighton Leigh. This was real. This was really real.

"You'd better do it," I conceded, holding my right hand up. "I don't want to take a chance with this."

He took a deep breath, preparing himself. A guilty look crossed his face, and then he brought his fist down across my cheek, crossing another lightning quick into the ridge over my eye. It didn't hurt me too badly, but I knew it had really pained him.

"Hey," I tried to brighten the mood. "We can be twinsies."

He gave me a confused look, and I pointed to his raccoon bruises, which had developed into a spectrum of yellow, green, blue and purple. "Hollis did you a favor. You look like a Technicolor bandit."

He smirked and eased out of the embrace, nudging me toward the door. "Go get some breakfast. He's waiting for you."

As I crossed over to the door to the switch room, I glanced idly at the row of vid monitors displaying scenes from every room in the house. In the dining room, Jana sat at the head of the table, perusing her tablet while eating some kind of omlette. Mando sat across from her, his plate already empty. He sipped coffee from a steaming mug. I pointed. "He's mine, you know."

Tony studied Mando's image, then shook his head. "Not if I get to him first."

***

"What the Hell happened to you?" Mando asked as I sat down across from him. Jana looked up, her brows arching with elegant surprise as she studied my face.

"Payback," I shrugged, sitting down and waiting for the kitchen lady to pour me some coffee. "Tony's not a forgiving man."

They exchanged glances, then looked back at me. Jana seemed pleased with this development.

"He can be a real shit, sometimes." Mando gave me a sympathetic look that seemed so sincere, I wanted to punch his two-faced teeth down his devious throat. His black eyes glistened with concern. "How is he?"

I moaned and stretched in that 'we totally had sex' way. "Awesome. But I don't think he swings your way."

He snorted.

Jana scowled, going back to her tablet. "He always did like picking through the trash."

"No wonder your face is so pinched," I told her. "Your omelette's totally jelly."

Mando snorted again.

Jana turned her icy, pond scum gaze on me. "Don't you have somewhere to be?"

"We should get going," Mando agreed, rising to his feet and circling the table to pull my chair out. "It's a long drive." We headed out to the foyer, and he opened the door to reveal his BMW under the portico. "How's the hand?"

"It hurts," I admitted. "But I'll live."

He turned that predatory gaze on me. His compact body demanded the space of a much larger man. "Here's hoping."

***

"Did you get them?" Mando said over the soft purr of the Beemer's engine. We were coming up the grade into Calabasas, eastbound on the 101.

"Get what?" I asked, although I knew exactly what he'd meant.

"The chip," he said through his teeth. "And the card. You better have them, or I'll put that quack Balcour to rest the minute he steps in the examining room." The savage glint in his eyes killed the comeback in my throat.

I swallowed hard. "I got them. I'll give 'em to you when we park the car."

He held his hand out. "Give me the chip now."

"But you said we'd trade after I saw the doctor."

"You're not going to the doctor. You've got an appointment with somebody else."

"Who?"

"Scotty."

Damn. I removed the control board from the splint and dutifully handed the chip over.

He pocketed it, held his hand out again. "And the card?"

"What about my million?"

"You get it when you access the card. Now, give it to me."

I did, and resealed the splint. He smiled, triumphant, and turned his attention back to the road. We topped the grade and descended into the San Fernando Valley.

I closed my eyes, leaned against the window, and tried not to think about how far my head was sticking into the lion's mouth. A few miles passed and the car slowed. I opened my eyes as we rolled to a stop at the Winnetka off-ramp.

Didn't think Scotty lived in Tarzana. Mando made a left onto Ventura Boulevard and pulled to the curb across the street from the parking lot of a coffee shop. The same coffee shop across the alley from where Jim lived.

Oh, Hell.

Mando noticed my expression and chuckled. "Just wanted to make sure you gave me the right stuff."

"I said I would—"

"Sure. But I believe in hedging my bets." He pointed down the alley behind Jim's house, where a dark haired man sat behind the wheel of an ivory-colored sports car. "That's Nelson. Over there is Sebastian." He gestured toward a pickup truck parked around the corner, about twenty yards from the driveway where Jim's old Dodge rested. The driver there was tall and blond. "And here," he pointed at the Range Rover parked ahead of us, "is Monica."

A middle-aged, dark-complexioned woman in a brown dress smiled and waved at us from behind the wheel of the Rover.

"They've been staking out your friend here. Making sure we know where he is at all times, in case we need him for something. Like now." Mando waved at Monica. She nodded and stepped out of the car, heading for the crosswalk. As she crossed the street both the man in the pickup and the one in the sports car sat up taller, heads following her.

Mando twisted around to face me. The hand he rested on the top of the seat held a silenced automatic. "This is to convince you I mean business. Nothing personal."

"What? What are you going to do?"

He tipped his head toward Jim's house. "Watch."

Monica had crossed the street and was stepping across the broken sidewalk. Her dress was plain but good quality, the kind Jehovah's Witnesses approved of for canvassing neighborhoods. One hand rested inside an oversize leather handbag. With her free hand she hoisted the strap further up on her shoulder and mounted the stairs.

"She's the best." Mando smiled that mortician smile. "She can ice a man on his doorstep in broad daylight and walk off, squeaky clean."

Ice? As in kill? No. I shook my head, disbelieving. "Why take Jim out? He's not hurting anyone."

"Don't worry. She's a pro. He won't know what hit him."

She was crossing the porch, lifting her left hand to knock on the door, her right still sunk into the depths of the handbag.

Mando smirked as my eyes widened. He didn't move, just held the gun leveled at my head.

"Call her off."

Monica waited on the porch, looking for all the world like a grandmother on an innocent visit. I prayed that Jim wasn't home, that he was asleep, that he was drunk or in the shower, or even shagging Richie. Anything that would keep him from opening the door.

"Mando, I swear the stuff is good. I'm not double-crossing you. Don't let this happen. Please?"

He didn't even blink.

Shit. I swiveled to my right, like I was reaching for the door, then snapped my left forearm back to pin his gun against the passenger headrest. He leaned into me and I slammed the back of the splint into his nose and snatched the gun away with my left hand. I pointed the gun right between his Hell–black eyes. "Call her off."

"That was a mistake." He leaned back, blinking the tears away from the shot to his nose. Behind him, I could see Jim's front door crack open....

"Call her off!"

Halfway open...

"Now!" I shouted, my voice high and frantic.

He rested his hand on the steering wheel with a sullen look and honked the horn. Monica glanced toward us, hand still in the bag. Mando waved her back.

Right then, Jim appeared in the doorway, looked questioningly at her. Monica gave him a flustered smile and asked him something. He smiled back and stepped out on the porch to point down the street, talking with that save–the–world expression on his face.

I groaned inwardly. Only bleeding heart Jim would give directions to his own murderer. Monica nodded thanks and started down the porch steps. When she reached the crosswalk, all the air left me in one big whoosh of relief.

All at once the car doors flew open and Nelson and Sebastian sandwiched me between the barrels of their two small but deadly looking automatics. Mando grinned and held his hand out, palm up. I sweated for a few moments, then gave him his pistol back. Nelson and Sebastian waited for him to holster it, then eased quietly out of the car.

"I suppose we have an understanding," Mando said as he fired the ignition and slipped the M5 into gear. "Fuck with me, say goodbye to your buddy Jim."

CHAPTER TWENTY-EIGHT

"What in the Hell is this shit?" Scotty snarled into my ear. "What the fuck is wrong with you?" His voice echoed ominously off the bleak warehouse office walls.

I sucked in a quick breath and held it, my fingers twitching nervously as I waited for the readout to appear. I'd already tried to access the palladium card's brokerage account three times, and no luck. Scotty was becoming suspicious, the bloodthirsty gleam in his eye shining brighter with each failure.

Even my tonsils were sweating.

"Maybe the system's down," Mando offered.

"And maybe this bitch is trying to set us up." Scotty dug his index finger into the motor point of my shoulder.

"It's my million, too," I said, wincing. "Right? My money's coming out of this."

"Then get it out," Scotty jabbed his finger deeper for emphasis. "Quit fucking around."

A prompt popped up on the screen, asking for the access code. My breath tumbled out in relief. I keyed the number in and waited the endless twenty seconds for the screen to prompt for my print. I pressed my left thumb on the pad, praying this would work, hoping it didn't, because I didn't want these assholes getting their paws on Tony's cash.

"Son-of-a-bitch," Mando exclaimed, when the actual money screen appeared. My face—my Irish face—glowed on the monitor, along with Faith's name and birthdate, but all the other info normally called up was blanked out with bold red letters spelling out "BLOCKED."

"'Blocked,'" Scotty said contemptuously, grabbing the back of my neck. "What the fuck is your account blocked for?"

"Ow," I protested. "I don't even know what it means."

Had Tony screwed up? Never trust a drunk, especially in matters of life and death. I had a sinking feeling I was dead.

"It means we can't access the money from the internet, you little cunt." He yanked me from the chair. "We have to go to the brokerage office in person."

"Tony did it when Faith was in the wind," Mando said. "He thought she was stealing from him."

A growl escaped Scotty, and he slammed a fist into my ribcage. "Worthless piece of shit." He followed up with a blow to my solar plexus. I teetered on my feet, steeped in pain, unable to breathe for almost half a minute.

Scotty snickered and stepped closer. He pinned my arms against the wall above my head, shoved one of his legs between mine to keep me off balance. I moved my legs even wider, afraid he might feel the sheath strapped to the inside of my calf. The hardness in his groin pressed against my thigh. His leer devoured my terror, my anguish. "Bitches like you are only good for one thing."

"Mando," I groaned, beseeching. "If the account is blocked, isn't that a good thing? It means he hasn't transferred the money out. Just kept me from getting it without showing up in person."

Mando grabbed Scotty's fist as it cocked back to strike me again. "She's right."

Scotty eyed him, miffed at the interruption.

Mando threw his head back and laughed. "Mother of God, you know how much that's worth?"

"What?" Scotty gruffed, wary, intrigued.

"Tony's divorce," Mando explained. "Ilsa's sharp enough to know Tony owns a lot more than he's ever told her about. She's hired some investigators to track his stash down. The way those sharks work, they'll find every penny, even in the numbered, offshore accounts. Ruiz has finally convinced Tony she won't reconcile, so he needs that money where her lawyers can't access it." He indicated the brokerage account on the computer. "Like Faith's account."

Scotty loosened his grip on me, but didn't let go completely. "How much we talking?"

"Six, maybe seven hundred."

"Million?" I feigned amazement, knowing it was even more. "Dollars? In one account?"

"That's a lot of money to trust to a wildcard," Scotty said, still unconvinced. "Even if he is in love with her."

Mando nodded. "Probably why he blocked the key. So she couldn't access it unless she showed up in person—hard for her to do without my knowledge. And I'm the most loyal fuck on his payroll. He knows I'd never let her stab him in the back."

"Shoulda asked for five million," I muttered under my breath.

Scotty grunted, the sick light in his eyes glazing over with greed. Relief flooded through me. It was all I could do not to smile.

Scotty scooped up the palladium card and tossed it to Mando. "Get her to the broker," Scotty said. "Get past that block, and make sure she wires everything into a single cash account."

Mando raised his brows. "You're not coming?"

"Can't be seen. Seward might give Hollis a call."

"How are we making the transfer, then?"

Scotty scowled at him like he was an idiot. "We're not taking the money until we've got our accounts set up under our new identities."

"Oh. Right."

"And you—" Scotty jerked me away from the wall, twisting my good wrist behind me. His suited arm looped around my neck and wrenched me backwards into him. His chin rested on my er, dug into the same motor point he'd drilled on before. 1ake sure no questions get asked. Any more inconveniences come out of your hide. Literally."

I tried not to react, not to give him any more of what he wanted, but I couldn't help shuddering when he palmed my breast as he let me go.

It was like being fondled by a corpse.

***

Eight hundred ninety-three million, five hundred seventy-one thousand, two hundred and six dollars. And forty-two cents.

It was scattered across twelve different corporate accounts, according to the acronymical mumbo-jumbo on the large screen behind Dave Seward's nervously bobbing head. "Don't believe what you see," he warned. "All you've got access to right now is a hundred million."

"That can't be right." I gave him a dubious look.

He pointed to the monitor, to a small string of code at the bottom of the main screen. "See this here? It means the transaction hasn't cleared yet. These," he circled the bulk of the information with a bony index finger, "are all international accounts. The funds won't clear for withdrawal until Monday afternoon."

"You mean I can't touch my own assets? What kind of malarkey is that? I want it all in a cash account, pronto. Except for a million wired into a numbered account in the Caymans. For mad money."

"We can put the request in, and it will go through on Monday. As soon as the prior transaction clears. But I really advise you against consolidating it into a single account. It's much better to remain conservative, and spread out your risk."

"I'm only conservative when the tequila's running low."

He chewed the thin pink line of his upper lip. "You're sure this is what you want?"

"Absolutely." I smiled at him, acutely aware of Mando behind me, staring implacably over my shoulder. "As soon as possible, hon."

Seward began gathering the paperwork. "You are aware, of course, that there's an extra handling fee for this type of transaction?"

"Of course. Y'all need to make some money, too."

"All right, then. You need to fill these out." He lined the desk with a never-ending stream of forms, none of which I could make much sense out of. Rather than broadcast my ignorance, I delegated.

"Mando," I said, batting my eyes. "Be a gentlemen, and fill all these boring papers out for me. I'd be so much obliged."

Dave cleared his throat. "Uh, Faith, you shouldn't let people know the details of your account information."

"Nonsense. Who says I can't trust him? He's my bodyguard."
I shoved the pen in Mando's hand and stood up, feigning interest
in the abstract holo-sculpture set in the center of the office.
"Why, I don't remember this. Is it new? It's beautif—"

"No. It's not. You say that every time you come here, Faith. If
you didn't drink so much—"

"You're such a sweetheart. I'll have a strawberry margarita."

"This is a brokerage firm. Not a bar."

"Oh. Right. Just a scotch, then."

He sighed, looked wistfully out the window at the Century City
traffic clogging the streets twenty floors below, and trudged off to
beg a bottle of scotch from one of the senior partners.

I watched Mando with the forms, feeling a strange sense of
elation at how easy it had been to set the hook. Dave brought me
the drink. I sipped it, reveling in how much fun it was to really
play Faith. As the alcohol went down, vengeance was all I tasted.

***

The BMW crunched toward the hidden gate, sequestered from
the highway by the cottonwood trees. Mando parked, then eyed
me over the seat. "Get out," he commanded.

"What for?"

"Get out," he said again, voice soft and deadly. He watched as I
eased the door open and stepped onto the dusty, brush-bordered
track. "Close your door. Come around to my side."

I did. He rolled his window down, staring at me for what
seemed like forever. The sun was below the horizon, but the sky
was lit with brilliant oranges and magentas. The moon was just
peeking over the eastern ridge. I heard crickets in the dry
streambed on the other side of the gate. He handed me the chip.

"What's this for?"

"I watched the security vids. Never saw Tony hit you."

A cold ghost hand clawed down my spine. "He's not stupid
enough to leave evidence of a battery on his own security
recordings."

"You've got forty-five minutes to be in the house, or your
buddy Jim is dead." He started the car up. "I'll meet you inside."

"Wait," I lunged for his door, hanging onto the sideview mirror
as he backed away. "Wait! You want me to break in?"

He braked, glared at me. "I think you snitched."

"I didn't! I swear, Mando, I didn't."

"If I'm right and you hit those locks, all Hell is going to break
loose. It breaks on you, fine. I'm out of here."

Oh, Hell. He knew. *He knew.*

"I can't get in this way, Mando. I don't have Tony's
thumbprint."

He snorted, reached into his breast pocket, and handed me
another chip. "Try that."

"But the dogs," I countered. "I can't get past the dogs. And
it's an hour walk just to the pump house."

gunned the car backwards, yanking the mirror out of my
    As the car swerved backwards onto the highway, he leaned
his head out the window, smile gleaming in the fading light. "So
run."

I watched his dust for a moment, cursing him. When I was
sure he was gone, I bolted, grateful for my Louis Vuitton sneakers
instead of those moronic Faith heels. I followed the Escalade's
fading tire tracks along the sandy barranca to the wall, where I
searched for a good spot to climb. Found a place near an
overhanging tree branch where I could reach the motion sensor to
glitch it, and use the branch to get over the concertina wire.

I hit the sandy ground running, the soles of my feet stinging
from the ten-foot drop. Hopefully, I'd glitched the sensor long
enough for me to pass over unnoticed. Last thing I needed was a
jeepful of transplanted Indonesian security guards waving assault
pistols at me and jabbering instructions I couldn't understand.

The brush was thicker inside of the wall. The chaparral clawed
at me, picked little holes in my silk outfit. I angled south, toward
the concrete channel which led to the pump house, then cast about
for the break in the bamboo that led to the bank.

The sky had inked over, turning purple and electric blue, and
everything looked strange in the shadows. The air was still warm
from the day. The crickets had stopped, their silence more
ominous with the rustling of leaves in the slight breeze off the
ocean.

I was breathing hard, my heart beating faster and faster. I was
positive, positive, the trail was here, but I couldn't find it. The
longer I searched, the less chance I had of making it to the house
in time. Not that I had any idea of how I was going to get in
without setting off all the bells, whistles, and lights this side of
Santa Barbara. I couldn't use the chip, because Tony had tagged it
to shut down all ingress and egress to the tunnels once the first
underground motion sensor was tripped, in order to trap any
intruders underground in the dark.

But without the chip, I couldn't access the tunnels, and without
the tunnels, I was basically canine steak tartare. Or target
practice. But I had to try. For Jim's sake.

An engine rumbled off to my left, approaching slowly. I heard
voices, saw a spotlight crawl up the adobe wall near the place
where I'd hopped the fence.

I ran up the channel, my sneakers making swishing noises
against the concrete. Dogs barked in the distance to my left,
higher up the hill. There was a single, answering bark to my
right, but that sounded farther away. I ran faster, following the
silver path of moonlight through the looming shadows of tamarisk
and bamboo, trying not to stub my toes on the stones and small
boulders littering the concrete.

The boulders grew larger, more frequent, and then I had to
climb a small cliff out of the trees to where the channel became a

flume. The brush grew chest high on either side, providing adequate cover, so I jogged up the flume. It was steeper than the channel, but easier to follow. I just hoped I didn't step on a rattlesnake soaking up the heat radiating from the concrete.

I stopped to grab a few quick breaths and catch my bearings. I was at a junction where the flume switched back to climb higher up the hill towards what looked like a water treatment facility. Below me, to the right, I could see the pump house through the trees. Behind me, headlights crawled along the channel, spotlights and flashlights strobing through the brush. Murky forms moved around the jeep, large, four-footed Groenie shapes. An occasional bout of barking punctuated the excited shouts of the Jeep's operators.

I was dead.

The barking to my right sounded closer. Snaps and popping brush sent me winging it up the switchback, until I reached the spine of the hill, where a fire road cut a rutted swath through the sage and chaparral to a large, cylindrical structure crowning the hill. A water tower. As I cleared the crest, I saw the yellow gleam of headlights flashing along the hill beyond. Another jeep was crawling up the saddleback, heading straight for my tower. I had about two minutes to disappear before—

Oh, Hell. The dog. It panted not twenty yards behind me, its claws scuffling rapidly through the rocky dirt. I bolted for the tower, for the ladder marching up its side. Three strides later my shoe caught on a rock and I went tumbling, hugging my splint against me, turning my shoulder under the way Papa had taught me to fall. If I hit just right, my momentum would carry me to my feet before the animal was on me.

The shredding of silk and the sudden pain of skin being sandpapered off my back told me I'd missed horribly. And no matter how much my heart screamed and pumped adrenaline, I wasn't going anywhere until my lungs got back on the job and stopped whining about having the wind knocked out of them. I forced air in and out, and swung my arms and legs up to protect my vitals from the slavering beast barreling toward me.

The dog ran past—or jumped over me, I wasn't sure. It spun around, kicking stones across the path, and lunged toward me, only to feint away in a see-sawing hop that brought it closer to my head. I ducked my chin into my chest, bringing the splint up to cover my ear even as the hot stench of canine breath hit my face. I was too late.

A hot line of liquid painted my cheek, and fangs pressed against my jawline. I hammered a fist at a furred shoulder blade, but the dog was already dancing away, making little whining yippy noises and spinning itself in tight little circles. I blinked at it, wondering why there was no pain with the bite. Why the dog seemed so much smaller than I'd expected.

then it hit me. I blinked into the gloom, wiping the dog ny face. "Zef?"

He yipped and dove toward me, plastering a series of wet, sloppy kisses across my nose and mouth.

"Zef," I whispered, smoothing my hand along his tawny flank. Definitely not a Groenie. "What're you doing here?"

The dog didn't answer, of course, and I immediately berated myself for talking to him in the first place. I'd just been so surprised. Only place I'd ever seen him was around the house.

Or in Tony's hidden suite. So how did he get out?

The way Tony felt about dogs, he wouldn't leave Zef locked up in the house. Or in the tunnels, for that matter. There had to be another way in. A doggie door, or something. I scrambled to my feet, sifting desperately through my memory for the commands Tony had used. "Zef," I said, pointing toward the house. "Nar Yah..." What was it? Kah-something. "Naryah Ka!" I tried, hoping it would be enough.

The dog sat down and looked at me like I was crazy.

"New!" I said, remembering that much.

Still nothing, and the headlights of the approaching Jeep were flashing across the top of the tower. At least we were on the shadow side. "Find Tony," I babbled. "Go find Tony, Zef."

I heard an engine hum. Behind me, tires crunched through brush. Shit.

"Slop Karma!" I suddenly remembered, knowing that it was ludicrous to put my faith in a dog. "New!"

The damn thing trotted off toward the water tower, wagging his tail. He stopped by the ladder, nosed the bottom corner of a riveted metal panel that looked like all the other panels, and disappeared into a square of darkness.

I grinned. Son-of-a-bitch.

I pushed through myself and scuffled downward on my hands and knees in coffin-black darkness for a few minutes, until the pipe-filled conduit intersected the lighted tunnel below. There were no electric carts here, so I repeated the command "Slop Karma!" and jogged off after Zef, hoping the command didn't mean "yacht" in Dutch.

Zef's claws clicked along ahead of me, echoing off the curved walls. I jogged after him. After a few minutes of running, the tunnel grew narrower. The roof dipped, so that I had to duck my head. The string of lights overhead terminated and the concrete underfoot gave way to a soft, powdery silt. The tunnel walls became jagged, natural rock. About ten feet in, the darkness seemed to suck the breath out of me. The path began to wind, twisting and folding in on itself like a length of intestine.

The change spooked me, because I didn't remember anything like this. I felt blindly along the rough walls, finding comfort in Zef's steady panting ahead.

The rock passage forked, splitting itself on the corner of a cinderblock foundation. The dog padded off toward the left. I followed, forced to crawl as the tunnel shrank down to the diameter of a barrel. Zef barked. He was answered by a series of electronic peeps and the soft slither of a sliding panel. A voiceprint doggie door. Leave it to Tony.

I scrabbled forward toward a grey patch in the darkness, but the dog was through and the panel shut before I could reach it. A howl of frustration left me, a release for my mounting panic. I banged on the panel, shouting "Zef! Here, Zef!"

No response. I patted the cinderblock, searching for a lock, a control bus, anything I could try Tony's print on. Found nothing but a ridge, just a lip of mortar left by a sloppy bricklayer. A lip with four distinct bumps, and a gap the size of a coin slot.

Worth a try.

I removed the chips from the liner of the splint, where I'd put them for safe keeping, pretty sure that the one on the right was the one with Tony's print. If I was wrong, all Hell would break lose, but since the control panel on the splint was fried, I didn't have any light to compare. I slotted the right chip quickly, afraid to waste time second-guessing myself.

A series of peeps sounded, but the panel didn't move. I pressed the bumps on the wall one at a time. On the second, a mechanical hum started up, then stopped. The rest were dead. I tried them all again, and this time the panel slid up.

I belly-crawled through, smack into a sheet metal barrier. I was in a space the size of an airfreight dog kennel. The panel closed before I could back out. The floor lurched, moved upward. The space moved with it, and a minute later, I was lined up with another panel. Light leaked in around it. I pushed, testing, and found my head sticking out of a ventilation panel into a closet full of hanging jackets.

An exuberant Malincollie licked my face.

I batted Zef away and crawled out to find myself in the closet under the stairs. Twenty yards down was the dining room, beyond that, a landing. I bolted for the stairs, and rabbited up to my room, Zef bounding at my heels.

I used the print chip to open the lock and found Mando stretched out on my bed, smoking a cigar. Another cigar was in his hands, the one with the pink band that he'd given me after his daughter's birth. I'd left it on the dresser. I panted for breath while Zef hopped up on the bed to lick Mando's face.

Rotten fickle beast.

Mando petted the dog a few times, then pushed him away. Zef returned to me, shoving his head and shoulder against the outside of my thigh until I gave him a few absent pats. Most of my attention was divided between getting enough air to my lungs and eyeing the phone couched on a pillow beside Mando's elbow. He looked at me without sitting up, then motioned me inside. "Close the door."

I complied.

He checked his phone. "You're late." He drew on his cigar and exhaled slowly. "Three minutes." He watched the smoke rise slowly to the ceiling. "And you set off an alarm climbing over the wall. Climbing." He shook his head.

"Had to climb," I said between gasps. "The dogs. Had to draw the dogs away. Make 'em chase something that wasn't there."

"I watched the security feed. You didn't enter through the pump house. You didn't use the chips."

"The chips dummy the feed!" I argued, frantic. "You wouldn't see anything."

He swung his feet over the edge of the bed and regarded me, that black, dispassionate gaze crawling over my face, my tattered clothing. He looked at the dog still pressed against my thigh and drew another puff from his cigar. An idea sparked in his eyes. "The dog..." A calculating grin widened his mouth. "Zef got you in, didn't he?"

"No," I shook my head, still playing the game even though I could see in his face he had decided it was over. "I came in through the pump house."

"The goddamn dog." He laughed. "Should've thought of that ages ago." He picked his phone up, slid it inside his jacket, and headed for the door, tapping his thigh and clucking to Zef. Stupid thing ran out into the hall as soon as Mando opened the door.

"Wait," I called. "What about Jim?"

He paused, turned diffidently toward me. "You were late."

"You already told her to—?"

"I know you snitched." He showed me the cigar with the pink band and snapped it in half. Metal gleamed inside, the components of a listening device. "Your buddy pays the price."

I lunged forward, to shred him into human taco meat, but he slammed the door shut in my face before I could reach him.

Oh, Hell.

CHAPTER TWENTY-NINE

I rocked the handle, but the door wouldn't open. I clawed at the jamb, pounded the electronic panel, but the damn thing held fast. I was trapped, caged in my room while Mando had Jim executed and then prepared to ambush Tony. After a few frantic paces, I calmed down enough to realize I should use the chip with Tony's print. I felt around under the splint but could only produce the chip that Tony had doctored. The one that would sound the alarm and shut the power down. My blood turned to ice. I'd left the one with Tony's print in the tunnel downstairs.

Panicked, I grabbed the *kris* and tried to slip the latch, but a guard plate welded to the door kept me from getting access. I brought the heavy stone lid from the toilet tank out and smashed the lock casing off, hoping to hotwire my way to freedom. All the lock internals except the slot driver and keypad were covered by a thick sheet of steel. I punched holes in the dry wall with the corner of the tank lid, hoping to dig through the wall, but the whole thing was lined with rebar. This room was harder to break out of than some jails I'd been locked up in.

Sweating, winded, and terrified, I sat on the bed and took several deep breaths, forcing myself to calm down.

"Once fear drives you, you're bound to crash," Uncle Fangio used to say when we were at the race track. "Take control of the wheel and put fear in the back seat."

Right. Right. The threat to Tony, on top of the one to Jim, had unbalanced me. Now that I was thinking straight, I realized it was Friday. Jim probably had a gig tonight, so he wouldn't be home for Monica to do her dirty work. And they probably wouldn't try anything at a public venue. There was still time. Still hope.

I just had to get word to Jim to stay at a hotel. Or better yet, fly to New York and stay with his mom for a while. I could ask Tony to send the marshals to protect him. And Vic, too, for good measure. I just had to get word to Tony.

I glanced up at the ceiling towards where I guessed the security camera was hidden, and began blinking a message in Morse code. Rossi had said Tony was trained in spycraft at an early age. I knew from Papa that Morse was the fall back protocol for field ops in remote and rural areas where sat phones often failed. Since Tony had grown up in Indonesia, I figured it was a safe bet.

Papa had made a game of teaching Morse to me when I was little. I had loved it. The rhythms and tempos of that particular form of nonverbal communication spoke to some borderline Asperger's part of me. It had been our secret, hide-in-plain-sight language, a way to talk and joke without Mother interjecting her sour opinions.

Maybe that's why I had taken to tapping keyboards at such an early age.

If Tony had been watching the feeds from his secret suite, he would already know that Mando had locked me in. Which meant he would have witnessed my panicked destruction of large parts of the wall and door jamb.

Oops. He could take the damage out of my pay. If we survived this. But it would be his fault, anyway, since he could have remotely freed me. Unless Mando was with him, already.

I finished blinking out the message, then repeated it, but this time by tapping my palm on the dresser, in case the blinking had been too subtle. As soon as I finished with that, the ready lights on the lock keypad flickered through a pattern which I translated as: *10-4. Jim safe. CM.*

CM. Charlie Mike. Shorthand for 'Continue Mission.'

How? I tapped back.

Wait.

I sighed and signaled to the camera: *10-4.*

We had hoped to trap them in the tunnels with the phony chip, but with Mando so suspicious, there's no way that Scotty or Brighton Leigh would enter the premises without the entire place being secured. Mando had sent me over the wall to distract the guards and keep them and the dogs busy looking for an intruder that wasn't there.

He probably hadn't planned on me even reaching the house, but had expected me to be captured and detained until Tony intervened. Mando knew Tony had given me the *kris*. He knew Tony wouldn't let anything happen to me. If Tony didn't blunder into whatever trap they had planned, Mando would just leverage him in. Use me as a hostage until Tony surrendered.

Even drunk off his ass, Tony wasn't the type to blunder. So, I was back to my original role as bait, but for Tony, this time. Mando knew how dangerous I was, but I could tell from the way Scotty had treated me this afternoon that in his mind, I was still Faith. Useless, drunk, conniving Faith. I'd use that misapprehension to bury him.

I took the *kris* into the closet, and used it to pry the dowels off some of the pants hangars. Faith's stupid silk belts finally came in handy, since I used them to bind the dowels to my forearms and shins, and some of her bra tape to make sure they stayed in place. The dowels stuck out at the elbows and knees two inches. Used in the right way, those two inches could be devastating.

I took another fabric belt and weighted the ends with the 5D discs that held the sheet music for the keyboard, then used the wire from a hangar to make a few handcuff keys. I hid one in my mouth, having mastered the art of cheeking small objects during an eight-month stint in Juvey when I was fifteen. I folded the second key into the weighted belt and tied it around my waist, then replaced my torn, sweaty blouse for a fresh one of dark forest green.

As I worked, my fear evaporated completely, subsumed by a bloodhound anticipation. Jim was safe. Tony must have some plan in mind. Whatever happened, I would be ready for it. When I finished, I sheathed the *kris*, stood behind a curtain of clothing just inside the closet door, and waited.

About twenty minutes later, the lock chirped. The door crashed open and whumped into its stop. "Jesus," Jana exclaimed. I heard her stepping into the room. She must have seen all the holes in the wall and the chunks of drywall scattered on the carpet. "Look at this! All this bitch does is cost us money!"

I hadn't expected her. Mando, yes. Or some of Scotty's flunky gangsters. But not the Ice-Queen of Snoot and the Vomit Isles.

"Miss Hopkins?" she called out. There was an edge to her voice that went beyond the pique of her reaction to the destruction I'd caused. I didn't know her all that well, but from the timbre, it sounded anxious, almost fearful. A familiar wooden squeak accompanied her footfalls, one I recognized as the mahogany serving cart. The smell of coconut curry and lemongrass wafted in through the open closet door.

Jana had brought me dinner.

I wondered if Tony had enlisted her help with the Mando situation, or kept her in the dark because she didn't need to know. I had reasons to dislike either scenario. I had planned to remain hidden and attack whoever came looking for me, but I really didn't know if she was friend or foe. Well, not a friend to me, but at least loyal to Tony.

"Miss Hopkins? Please come out. Tony sent me to bring you dinner." Her tone had a quaver to it that made worry someone was holding a gun to her head, so I carefully peeked around the door jamb, relieved to find her alone.

She spotted me immediately, looking just as relieved as I felt. "Thank God. Thought I was too late."

"Too late for what?" I asked, walking out of the closet.

"Just come on. There's not much time. Mando's working for Scotty. Tony sent me to get you out." She opened the side panel to the serving cart and motioned to the space inside, which was just big enough to hide someone my size.

Something about this just didn't seem right. Tony had told me to sit tight. To be the bait. Now, he wanted me to leave? "Where's the kitchen lady? Tony's step-grandma?"

"He sent Gwenda to L.A.. He sent all the house staff to L.A. this morning. To help with the Trubys' party ."

That made sense. We hadn't discussed it as part of the plan, but Tony wouldn't want any of his domestic staff getting caught in the crossfire. "Who made the food, then?"

"I did. There's this new invention called a microwave."

"Oh, you mean a science oven?"

"Just get in the cart," she huffed, exasperated. "I'm supposed to smuggle you down to my car before Foster sends his men to get you."

"Where is he?"

"Foster? En route. We only have a fifteen minute window before he arrives and your release is off the table, so stop asking questions and put your ass in gear."

"I meant where is Mando?"

"In the dojo with Tony. Tony agreed to give Mando what he wants, but only if you and I are safely off the premises."

"But, I'm supposed to help. I'm supposed to be there when Tony faces Scotty and Brighton Leigh."

"You're a civilian. You can't be involved in any of this. Especially after you told Rossi that the contract was null and void, because you signed it under duress."

"No. I have to be there. I have Tony's *kris.*"

She froze, her pond-scum eyes flashing with alarm. "That's not possible. He'd never give that to you."

I pulled up my pant leg and twisted my ankle so she could see the opal on the pommel sticking out of the sheath.

She stared at it. Her hands slowly curled into fists. Her cheeks flickered with a pained disbelief before she heaved a deep sigh, lowering her head to her chin. I almost felt sorry for her, but then she kicked the cart onto its side and stormed out into the hallway. "Fuck this shit. You're on your own. The both of you. I'm done."

I followed after her, wincing at the sharp reports her heels made on the tiles. Why would anybody wear shoes that noisy when you could have sneakers? When we reached the bottom of the stairs, two men wearing all black converged towards us from either side of the archway leading to the foyer. At first I thought they might be some of the Javanese security guards but when they moved out into the light, I realized they were too tall, too dour, and wore black leather jackets and ugly silk ties.

Jana breezed past them, radiating a monumental resentment bordering on hatred. "She's all yours."

She threw open the door to the cobbled courtyard and stalked towards a Mustang parked beside Mando's blue Beemer. The thugs shot surprised glances at her, and then turned their attention towards me. I stood there like a deer in headlights with a petrified look on my face, but inside I wasn't afraid at all. They sauntered towards me, all cruel smiles and confident brutality.

I waited until they were almost an arm's length away, then turned and rabbited up the stairs. I went just far enough for them to get up to running speed, then went down on one knee. I ducked my head to catch a targeting glimpse behind me, and drove my weaponized elbows into their groins.

A dowel to the junk at full speed stopped them both in their tracks, especially when their forward motion lodged my fists in the crook between two steps, turning the dowels into unforgiving pikes that impaled their genitals with the full force of their momentum. Their instinctive response to this assault was to thrust their bodies violently away from the pain and grab at the injury with both hands. This meant that as their heels kicked up, their faces slammed down into the top edge of the stairs, effectively curb stomping them with their own mass. I heard the squelch of flesh, the crack of bone, and shuddered.

Hadn't expected that tactic to be quite so effective.

They weren't moving, so I took their guns. I tucked one under my blouse, in the small of my back, secured by the hidden, weighted belt. The other I carried in my left hand, down at my side, the way Papa had taught me to carry the revolvers we practiced with at the shooting range.

I knew that they were likely sadistic rapists and had planned to be if not my executioners, at least accessories to it, but it still bothered me to think I was capable of causing so much damage in three short seconds. One of them moaned and rolled around in dazed agony, coughing blood and spitting teeth out onto the polished mahogany stairs. The other just lay there staring sightlessly, mouth open, jaw broken. I pulled him into a recovery position, so he didn't drown on his own blood, and realized with horror that I recognized this one. He had been one of the men in my stasis dream. One of the men I knew I would kill.

Spooked by the coincidence, I ran back up the stairs. As I headed down the corridor towards the elevator, I heard the growl of a Ford V8 accelerating away. I looked through the window to see Jana speeding down the drive towards the main gate. I think she smoked the tires.

I hit the call button for the elevator in the hallway near my room, the one that went down to the basement where the dojo was. Only, it wouldn't open for me. Without an implant, this house sucked. Even Zef had more access. Mando had probably locked the poor little guy away somewhere, another hostage to bend Tony to his will.

I went back down the stairs, picking my way carefully around the injured thugs. I ran down past the dining room to the elevator again, hoping it might open to this floor, but no luck. Moonlight spilled in through the ornate, arched windows lining the corridor, and when I glanced up at the luminous disk, I noticed a set of large green and red lights zooming through the sky. They were too large and low to be a commercial jet. Curious, I stepped up to the window. As I watched, they grew bigger, brighter. A searing white spotlight popped on, illuminating the chaparral, and then zeroing in on the helipad. Somebody was coming in on a bird, and from the shape, it didn't look like Tony's Jet Ranger. Since it came in from the south, I guessed it was Scotty. With any luck, he'd have Brighton Leigh with him.

I heard the slight click of the elevator doors opening behind me, and spun around to see Tony, shirtless and shoeless. He held the terminal from the hidden cubby in his secret suite with both hands, still favoring his right side.

Behind him, Mando held a gun to the back of his head. I brought my own gun up, but Tony's bulk obscured most of Mando, who ducked further behind Tony when he saw me, muttering: "What the Hell? She's supposed to be with Jana."

Tony grinned at me, a little pride flaring up in his eyes as his gaze focused on the gun in my hand. I smiled back, feeling that irresistible pull his presence exerted on me.

"Put the gun down," Mando growled as he prodded Tony out of the elevator. "On the floor. Slide it over. Then put your hands on top of your head. Fingers interlaced."

I looked a question at Tony. He nodded.

I frowned, uncomfortable with giving up the weapon, but I followed Mando's directions. He picked up the weapon, and used it to point me ahead of them both, down the hall towards the dining room. "That way. Keep your hands on your head. Don't try anything, or I shoot Tony."

"That's a stupid threat," I countered, while complying with his orders. "You shoot Tony, you can't get him to change Brighton Leigh's identity."

"He doesn't need his kneecap for that."

He had a point. I walked ahead of them, glancing in the windows at our reflections so I could get a better idea of Mando's positioning. He held himself with that relaxed, alert readiness that was the hallmark of someone who had complete command of the situation. Tony's body language, on the other hand, was one of pained resignation. Mando's attention, however, was focused on my and Tony's backs, which meant he missed Tony meeting my gaze in the window and blinking: *CM. Wait.*

10-4, I blinked back, anxious about Mando having the upper hand. I did not relish the idea of being at Scotty's mercy, let along Brighton Leigh's, but I trusted Tony to know what to do in this situation.

When we reached the dining room, Mando instructed me to face the window and keep my hands on my head, while he had Tony set the terminal down on the table, jack a landline cable into it, and sit down in one of the ladder-backed chairs. I watched their reflections as Mando cuffed Tony's hands behind his back, looping the chain around one of the rungs. He then forced Tony's legs back, so that his ankles were aligned with the back legs of the chair, and duct taped them there.

With Tony secured, Mando holstered his own gun, then came over to me and patted me down. He ignored the belt under my shirt, and didn't pat down my shins and forearms, so missed the dowels there, but he did collect the second gun, as well as the *kris*. He tucked the *kris* into his waistband. "Thought you said she was unarmed."

"She was supposed to be." Tony shrugged as much as his cuffed hands would allow.

"She was supposed to be gone with Jana," Mando groused as he spun me around and cuffed my hands in front. "Supposed to be on the plane to Vegas, too." He scowled at me, as if trying to flay me with those obsidian eyes. "Don't move."

I stared back at him, unable to keep my fury at his betrayal from leaking through. I was allergic to restraint, so that spot between my shoulder blades started to itch. So did the tip of my nose. I scratched it.

"I said, 'don't move!'." He slammed the muzzle of his gun against my solar plexus, hard enough to really hurt, but not hard enough to knock the wind out of me. I oofed and bent forward with a grimace. He yanked my hands above my head, looping the cuffs around one of the scrolls in a wrought iron wall sconce. It wasn't impossible to escape, but it would take time, which I suppose was all that Mando wanted.

He backed away, threw my guns into a locking china cabinet, and secured them inside. He turned to Tony. "Wait here. Don't move. If you move, I shoot her. *Comprendes?*"

Tony nodded. Mando unhooked my hands from the sconce and pushed me ahead of him towards the foyer. He paused for a moment, as if expecting to be joined by others, but then his gaze fell on the two figures on the stairs. Mr. No Teeth was moaning softly and bleeding profusely from his nose and mouth. Broken Jaw wasn't moving at all. Mando stared at them for a few seconds, long enough for me to make a move on him, but because Tony had told me to wait, I just stood there patiently. "*Madre de Dios.* Both of them?"

"Where do you think I got two guns?"

Mando growled and shoved me ahead of him. We moved out into the courtyard to the covered, upscale golf cart. "Drive."

"Where?"

"Helipad."

That explained why the cuffs were in the front. I got behind the wheel. Mando sat beside me, keeping the gun on his opposite side, but trained on my midsection. I turned the key and guided the cart out along the paved pathway towards the helipad, squinting against the harsh white light of the spot trained on us. The cart jostled as the rotor wash hit us.

I slowed to a stop, closing my eyes against the light and to keep the stinging dust out. The turbulence ruffled my short hair. A disorienting, jangly sensation washed over me, carrying with it a strange sense of portent. I felt dizzy. Spun, as if I'd been swallowed by a whitewater river current made of tiny electrical impulses. I gripped the wheel tightly, afraid if I didn't, I'd be swept away.

What was it with me and helicopters, all the sudden? When I was a kid, I flew in birds all the time. Well, not all the time, but I'd never gotten freaked out by them, not like this.

The shocks of the cart adjusted as people climbed into the back. That weird current surged into a crackling, claustrophobic sense of urgency. I felt like I was back in a stasis dream, being chased by that anthropomorphic dodo bird. Through my eyelids, I could see a luminous, gossamer thread tied around my wrists, stretching out to tie me to Broken Jaw, who stood a few feet away, staring at me with a sour, accusatory look. I began to tremble.

"Drive," Mando growled beside me. "To the house."

I opened my eyes, relieved to see nothing but lawn and pavers and helicopter in the glow of the cart's headlights.

Broken Jaw and that luminous thread were gone, although that eerie current still seemed to be flowing around me. My skin was all goose-pimpled as I pressed the accelerator and guided the cart around to point it back at the house. I'd hoped that some distance between me and the aircraft would dull that electric sensation, but instead it brought it into sharper focus, like I was an iron filing caught between the poles of a magnetic field.

I stopped the cart under the portico. It shook as the occupants behind me exited, and then Mando grabbed my right bicep and pulled me along to exit on the right. Scotty stepped up to leer at me, wearing the same too-tight suit he'd had on earlier in the day. He carried a black briefcase of ballistic plastic.

Scotty's companion, an older man, stepped up to examine me in the lights of the portico. His presence thickened the air with a brisk, lime-scented cologne. His bald, bulbous head perched atop a whipcord neck, nose sticking out like a flamingo's beak. He had pinkish, leathery skin and thin, pipestem arms attached to a beachball torso. He looked like dodo bird in an expensive worsted suit. All except for the eyes: a ruddy brown, with a soulless bloodlust in their depths.

I sucked in a deep breath through my nose, fighting the panic as that electric current crackled again, and a flood of hospital dreams echoed in my head. This was the sinister dodo bird, the one that cackled with glee as I was tied up and beaten. It was Brighton Leigh.

The Brighton Leigh. Wrinkled and hairless, but the same monster I'd seen being arrested on the vid years ago, while newscasters recounted a litany of his crimes.

"She's wonderful," he said to Mando. His voice was a cultured tenor, with an Australian inflection, slick as blood on a razor blade. "Wonderful." He smiled at me, anticipation bright on his weathered face. "I'm looking forward to taking you apart."

"Likewise," I thought to myself. Then, I heard the echo off the portico ceiling and realized I'd used my out loud voice. This bizarre disorientation was messing with my perceptions, giving me that sense of dual worlds, one superimposed on the other.

I wondered if Mando had drugged me, or if Broken Jaw had put some kind of ghost curse on me. Or maybe it was just my own crazy finally surfacing under the pressure of the situation. I could feel the whirlwind of stasis dreams battering at the door to my subconscious, trying to burst free.

Leigh's eyes narrowed, a thin smile stretching his lips as he ran his hand along my jawline. "Defiance. Especially fun. Pity about the bruises." He traced the edge of the swelling on my cheek with his manicured finger. "We'll have to wait a few days to really enjoy ourselves."

Scotty regarded me from over Leigh's shoulder, amused speculation swimming in his hazel eyes. "Can't wait."

Sadism glowed in their eyes like birthday candles, and I was suddenly glad for all the things my mother had inflicted on me. The molten, seething rage she had forged in me was quenched in the cold reality of Brighton's presence. I became a weapon. All the duality burned away into a sharp, steel-edged resolution: I would kill him. Kill them both. Send them back to the planes of Hell, where they belonged.

Fear wasn't in me, nor pain, nor any other feeling save a singular sense of certainty that I had finally found a purpose that didn't rest on anything or anyone outside of me. I felt free. Clear-headed. Passionless. Absolute. I couldn't be wounded, any more than a sword was wounded clashing against another in battle. Scarred, maybe. Broken. But not hurt.

Mando must have seen the cold light of insanity flare up inside me, because he gripped my bicep tight enough to bruise and shoved me into the foyer. Leigh and Scotty followed us.

"Son of a bitch!" Scotty exclaimed in his gravelly baritone.

From this angle, the blood spatters and broken teeth on the tile and the two bodies sprawled halfway up the stairs were far more noticeable. One was still moaning. The other, I knew, was dead. Mando kept me moving, steering me into the dining room.

"Fucking Tovenaar," Scotty muttered as he and Leigh entered behind us, apparently assuming Tony had been responsible for the wreckage on the stairs.

Still tied to his chair, Tony glanced up at his name. He and Scotty stared at one another. Suddenly, Scotty rushed past Mando and me to grab Tony by the hair.

"Did I say you could look at me, you piece of shit?" Scotty cranked Tony's head back, so that his shoulders and neck were taut with the strain. "You forget your place? You forget how long I made you scream?" Without waiting for an answer, he snapped the back of his hand into Tony's balls, eliciting a sharp, hissing exhalation from Tony, who writhed against his restraints, lungs working in short, spastic bursts. It wasn't a solid punch, but clearly it's been hard enough to get Scotty's point across.

Scotty smiled, stroked his knuckles along Tony's cheek. "Tell me how much you want to go through that again."

Tony's mouth labored noiselessly. He shook his head, averting his gaze.

Leigh cackled, clapping his hands together. "I've missed you, Pete." Enthralled, he drank in every twitch, every nuance of Tony's pain. "I see someone put you back together. Too bad about your face. We'll have to take you apart again when that's all cleared up." He patted Tony on the shoulder. "You'll look so good on the feed."

I understood, now, why Scotty did the dirty work. Brighton enjoyed the spectacle far too much to distract himself by active participation. It disgusted me, filled me with such outrage to know a human being could be so thoroughly evil. That they planned to direct that evil against Tony made my entire body hum with vengeful, righteous fury.

"You've been a very bad boy." Scotty told Tony. "You're going to pay for what you've done to my men. But first," He back handed him in the groin again. "You're going to give us new identities."

Tony moaned, his body straining to fold in on itself. "Yes, sir."

"Good boy." Scotty chuckled and released his grip on Tony's hair, letting his head fall so that his chin rested on his chest. As Tony alternated between gut deep groans and labored hissing noises, Mando hooked my cuffs on the wall sconce again and moved over behind Tony's chair. He released one of Tony's hands but kept the other cuffed to the back rung of the chair.

When Tony recovered enough, he turned the terminal on and pecked away at the touch board rigged to it. As he worked, Scotty sat on the table and examined the device. "This is an older model. I recognize the serial number. This is the one we used to have in Sumatra. How'd you get it?"

"Stole it."

"How? Equipment like this goes missing, all sorts of shit hits the fan."

"Missing, yes. Destroyed, no. Stole it during evacuation. Right before the tsunami hit."

Leigh cackled, sitting down beside Tony. "You always were a clever boy, Petey."

"Need a chip. From my phone. Right front pocket."

Mando slipped his hand into Tony's front pocket and removed the phone. He blinked and examined the cracked screen with momentary surprise, then shot me an angry glower. I stared back at him with an innocent look. I'd told him Hollis had tossed the phone away after smashing Tony with it, but omitted the fact I'd recovered the damn thing.

Mando handed it to Brighton, who fumbled with it until he found the hidden compartment in the case that held a row of micro cards. He looked a question at Tony, who muttered: "The center one."

Leigh removed the chip and delicately placed it in Tony's palm. At his touch, Tony froze for an instant, the howling frustration at having his tormentor so close, yet so inaccessible, plain on his face. Leigh noted it. Reveled in it. He put his knobby hand on Tony's shoulder. "Go on, now."

Tony keyed in a series of instructions and slotted the chip. He shoved the touch board at Leigh. "Enter the data for your new identity."

Leigh typed it in.

"You need a photo."

Scotty stepped up with a chip.

Tony slotted it into the touch board and pecked out more data. "Right hand on the glow pad," he told Leigh, who complied. There was a delay, then: "Left hand."

Leigh switched, his arm crossed awkwardly across his potbellied torso.

"Stay there for a sec." Tony keyed one last instruction into the board, and then a U.S. Passport card hummed out of the terminal with that chemical smell of hot plastic.

"Son-of-a-bitch," Mando said, leaning in. "He's done it."

"He has." Leigh looked the card over with delight.

He handed it to Scotty, who seemed surprised at first, then impressed. "Now me."

While they were distracted passing Scotty's prints, I spit the makeshift key into my palm and released the tension on my wrists, backing the cuffs off so they were loose bracelets I could strip off at will. I twisted my body so that my right arm obscured my left, and eased the left one down to untie the weighted silk belt hidden around my midriff. I gathered it up in my left hand, eased my hand back into the cuff, and waited for Tony to give me the signal.

Once Scotty had his new identity, he opened that black briefcase to reveal some sort of portable sat-link computer. He fired it up while Mando re-cuffed Tony's hand through the back rung of the chair.

"The card." Scotty held his hand out to Mando, who produced Faith's palladium card and handed it over. Leigh and Scotty turned their attention to creating new accounts under their new identities, so they could siphon off the millions Tony had hidden in Faith's name. They sat side by side, peering at the computer. The glow of the screen reflected off their faces. Between Leigh's birdlike features and Scotty's yacht-tan skin and flat-top blondeness, it wasn't hard to imagine a vulture and a news anchor trying to figure out an ATM.

"What the shit?" Scotty growled and scowled at Mando. "Told you to transfer it all into one account."

"I put the order in, but the international transfers are still in process. Won't clear until Monday. There's still a hundred mil you can play with until then."

Unhappy, but resigned, Scotty went back to work. He and Leigh spoke to one another in French. Since they didn't use any musical terms, I didn't understand what they said.

The minutes stretched into an hour, and beyond. Mando sat on the table, splitting his attention between me and whatever Scotty and Leigh were doing. I shifted my weight often, doing heel raises to keep my blood moving, and my body limber. At least my hand was above my heart. Tony sat with his chin on his chest, utterly still, aside from his slow, measured breathing. I wondered how he could possibly fall asleep under these conditions. Didn't he feel that driving, relentless current sweeping around us?

As soon as that question crossed my mind, he smiled, a peculiar serenity to his features. He lifted his head, and met my gaze, the current fountaining out of him, rushing into me, like a breaker crashing into the shore. I gasped, swept up in it. For a moment, I was convinced he had been meditating, focusing that energy, and with that single look, he had somehow thrown it into me. A hyper awareness, as if time had slowed, parceled out in tiny, easily digestible chunks for my own personal consumption.

A second later, the logical part of my brain considered that glance a coincidence, and the feeling of temporal retardation a result of the adrenaline surge created by the shifting, triumphant timbre of Scotty and Leigh's voices. My gaze was still locked with Tony's, and he blinked out a short, simple: *CM.*

I gave him a little nod, feeling floaty. Invulnerable. Swept up in that stark clarity and the whirling, invisible current washing through me. I was a subtle, recurrent melody hidden beneath a sinister tempo.

Leigh pushed his chair back from the table and stretched, turning his dead gaze on me. "Time to get to know my new pet. Bring her over," he instructed Mando. "I want to get a closer look at the merchandise."

I cowered, feigning a fear I didn't feel as Mando slid his butt off the table and glided towards me in that jaguar way of his. I tightened my fist to hide the silk in my hand and tilted my arms so that the cuffs would stay on while he unhooked them from the sconce. He dragged me over to the table, to stand between Leigh and Scotty's chairs.

This close, I could smell Leigh's limey cologne. Mando backed away to stand behind Leigh's chair. To remind me to behave, he trained his laser sight on Tony's forehead.

Scotty turned the computer off, shut the briefcase, and grinned. His moist hand palmed my left breast through the silk of my shirt. He teased my nipple with fat, stubby fingers. "This is going to be such fun."

I shuddered, ducking my head and hunching my shoulders as if terrified, lowering my center of gravity and causing Brighton to lean in closer to get a better view of my face in the process. Scotty's grip on my nipple tightened. I whimpered and bent my knees, sinking down further as if trying to get away from the pain, but in reality I was coiling the spring, ready to strike. Just as I was about to attack, Leigh said something that froze me solid:

"You look just like your father."

My breath caught. I met his gaze, feeling the energy churn and roil inside me, as if a cross current had been introduced. Polluted sewage mixing with the clear, swirling current. I recoiled. All the hair on my body raised up. Was this what evil felt like? Was it a palpable force that could infect people?

He made a high-pitched chortle at my reaction. "Just like him. I mean, if you take away the Faith disguise. And the obvious..." He twirled his fingers at what Scotty was touching. "You're a spittin' image of him." He chortled again. "This whole thing has been about you."

"Me?"

"The money, the new identities, they're perks, to be sure. But you...you..." His wide, froggy mouth spreading to reveal blocky, uneven, cigarette-yellowed teeth. "You're going to come work for me. Just like your father."

"He'd never work for you."

Leigh cackled. "He did. He does. And so will you."

I knew it was a ploy. Knew he was just messing with my head, torturing me with lies. But some part of me wanted so desperately to believe that Papa was still alive that I completely lost focus on the mission and gave Leigh my full attention. "Prove it."

"You know it, already. You're a sharp girl. Your father's daughter. Somewhere, in the back of your mind, you *know*. How else did more than a million dollars wind up scattered across your family's trusts? SGLI only pays out $450,00 for members who die in the line of duty. And then, there's the matter of that South Dakota account in your name. The one you never opened, in a state you've never been to. Ever checked the balance on that?"

I swallowed hard, feeling that black, oily effluent seeping through me, settling in my bones as the truth of what he said revealed itself. "Why would he work for a pustule like you?"

"Things went pear-shaped after Petey stabbed him in the eye. He needed somewhere to go. To hide."

I glanced at Tony, looking for...what? Confirmation? Salvation?

He raised his head, his eyes locking with mine. The world spun, shifted, and I could see the young Tony sitting there, with his yellow eyes, his brown hair cut in a high and tight. There was a tattoo on his left pec that wasn't there in the now. In his hand was a small blade with a U-shaped handle. It was spattered with blood, and a clear, gooey gel. There was a faint, dark thread tied to that blade, stretching off into the shadows. Without thinking, I threw my mind—my soul?—after that thread.

It was like swimming up a firehose of the worst humanity had to offer. The images, the sensations passed by in tiny fractions of a second, but weight of the pain, the suffering, the insanity and the pure, unadulterated evil clung to me like mud, and suddenly I was standing back on that featureless plain of dead, frozen grass, next to a figure so familiar, I knew it better than my own. "Papa!"

"Radiana!" He regarded me with alarm, and I once again felt that repulsive force as I tried to approach him, as if he could will me away. "Go back. You can't be here."

"Papa, where are you? I'll come save you."

"There's no saving me. Go back." He made some strange, ripping gesture with his fists and I snapped back into myself.

My body was cold, trembling. There were tears streaming down my face, but I didn't know how they'd gotten there. Since my limbs had gone slack, the cuffs had slipped off and caught in the fabric of my blouse. One end of the weighted belt in my hand had unspooled, as well, but Leigh didn't notice, since he was focused on my anguished face.

Scotty's fingers were still pinching and pulling on my nipple. I felt exhausted, but at the same time, charged, animated by this strange mix of dark and light that I didn't understand.

I wasn't sure how much time had passed, but my gaze was still locked with Tony's. Blue-eyed, black-maned Tony.

He blinked out: *CM.*

Scotty pushed me away and rose to his feet. The laser dot from Mando's gun glided across the tight, dark fabric covering his back as his fist hammered Tony in the gut. "Did I say you could look up?"

At Tony's pained grunt, the rage flared up within me. I slammed an elbow dowel into Scotty's kidney. He roared in pain and arched back to clutch the area with one hand. Leigh lunged for me, but I side stepped and swung the weighted end of the silk belt in my hand at his ugly dodo face. It cracked against his cheekbone and he recoiled, throwing his hand up in a belated attempt to block.

I knew the real danger was the gun, so I roundhouse kicked Leigh across the ear with my doweled shin, driving him backwards into the chair with enough force to knock it over into Mando's gun hand. I heard the weapon clatter to the tile as I stomped Leigh's groin on my way to snatch the *kris* from Mando's waistband.

I could hear Scotty move towards me, so I slammed him up the side of the head with a reverse crescent kick. He fell against the table and then down over Leigh's thrashing form. While they struggled to untangle their limbs from one another, I sprang up and slammed my elbow dowels into his rib and temple. At the same time, I drove the dowel on my right knee into the soft flesh at the side of his throat with an awful, hollow crunch.

When I drew my leg back, Scotty's blood fountained over Leigh. He was scrambling on all fours to get away from Scotty and the downed chair. And me, of course. I snapped the weighted belt out, looping it around Brighton's throat and yanking him back into range.

Mando recovered his gun, but before he brought it up, I slashed Brighton with the *kris* across the flank. Brighton screamed, high and frantic. I drew the blade up across his body, then stabbed down into the triangle at the left side of his neck, between the collarbone and the scapula. A pulsing spray painted me with red. I had pierced a major artery.

He clawed at me, begging for pity through the red froth on his lips. I stabbed again, aiming for the heart but the blade deflected downward off his ribs and sliced deep across his midsection, slicing open his abdominal wall. My face and chest were hot with blood as his guts spilled out and soaked my shoes.

Tony glanced up at me in bloodthirsty wonder, gaze transfixed by the gore dripping from the blade in my hand. Mando, too, seemed mesmerized by the carnage, his pistol hanging limply by his side, his black eyes full of revulsion and wonder. I dove at him, hoping to take him out him before he came to his senses.

"Rad, no!" Tony threw his head and shoulders forward, crashing his chair into me before falling onto his side on the floor. It gave Mando enough time to put the table between us. He pointed his gun at me.

Right about then, a woman shouted from the archway: "FREEZE, U.S. MARSHALS! DROP YOUR WEAPONS!"

Mando froze and put his hands up. I lunged for him again, but a crushing weight tackled me from behind. Red lights pinged on inside my skull as my chin hit the tabletop, my vision fading momentarily as a large man pinned me and wrestled me into a full nelson. Somehow, I kept hold of the *kris*.

Hands still up, Mando squatted down and slowly set his gun on the floor. His obsidian gaze met Tony's sapphire one in a look of mutual triumph as Rossi moved quickly into the room to kick his gun away. She bent down to check Brighton's pulse just as his final, rattling breath spattered blood all over her wrist and forearm.

Even dying, he cackled.

Iso Iso pulled me up to a standing position, my arms still interlocked with his. The bloody *kris* was still in my hand, a loop of intestine tying it to the corpse at my feet. On the ground, still bound to the chair, Tony regarded me with a gratitude so intense, there were tears in his eyes. "Soul for a soul," he murmured.

Rossi scowled and prized the *kris* from my grasp. She put it into an evidence bag. Two other men holding guns and wearing vests emblazoned with U.S. MARSHALS entered the dining room.

Jana watched all this from the doorway, a deep frown on her face. "We got here too late," she sighed.

Hands still up, Mando rose to his feet when Rossi motioned him to leave with them. He stood in front of me, blocking my view of Tony, his expression loaded with somber intensity. "Rad, you have the right to remain silent. Don't talk to anybody without Jana present." His dark gaze searched mine. "*Comprendes?*"

I shook my head, wondering how I could project so much calm with so much fury sandblasting my insides. How I could feel this betrayed and not kill anyone.

Mando and Tony had set me up. They'd put me in mortal danger, and let me believe if I didn't come out of this alive, Tony was as good as dead. And so was Jim.

"Rad," Mando repeated, waving his hand in front of my face. I focused on him, then glanced over to where the *kris* was in its evidence bag, calculating whether or not I could wriggle out of Iso Iso's hold and plant it in Mando's eye before the others stopped me. "You have the right to remain silent. Understand?"

I nodded, but something in my expression turned his into one of concern. He backed out of the room, watching me with a sad, guilty look.

Iso Iso forced my left arm down and slapped a handcuff on my wrist, then repeated the process with the right. "Radiana Damiano, you are under arrest for the murders of Scott Foster and Brighton Leigh."

CHAPTER THIRTY

The marshals took us to the nearest Federal court building, which was in Lompoc. They searched me, removed the bloody clothes and the equally bloody dowels bound to my forearms and shins, and took them as evidence, providing me with clothing that Jana had sourced from Faith's room. They even took my Louis Vuitton sneakers, so I was back to the Faith heels.

As part of the search, they had me open my mouth, but they still didn't find my makeshift handcuff key. They brought me into an interrogation room with cinderblock walls painted an annoying yellow that was a shade too neon for cream. It lacked the typical two-way mirror, but had two cameras set in opposite walls and a wire-reinforced vertical window running the length of the door. They sat me at a metal table bolted to the floor, cuffed me to one of the loops welded to the edge of the table, and read me my Miranda rights. Rossi left.

Iso Iso sat across from me, trying to look like he really cared what happened to me. "Homicide is a serious charge. Three counts is even worse. You want to claim self-defense, you need to get out ahead of this. Tell us your side of the story."

I stared back. Silent.

What did it matter? I had become a willing catspaw to tease out Brighton Leigh. Tony had expertly manipulated me into killing the man, exactly as Rossi had predicted. Meanwhile, Tony had been restrained the entire time. A passive observer, incapable of lifting so much as a finger against Scotty or Leigh. As much as they wanted to pin those deaths on him, there was no way they could do so without outright lying about what they had witnessed. The security feed would show the truth in all of its Technicolor glory: I had been swept up in whatever insanity that weird stasis flashback had caused, and become everything my father had hoped for. Everything my mother always said I would be.

Regardless of whether or not Brighton Leigh had been baiting me, or telling the truth about Papa still being alive, I'd been an idiot. Love was just an empty word. Why had I believed it when Tony had said it?

Rossi had warned me. She'd said that Tony would see the pain, loss and loneliness in me, and then craft a persona to exploit that. He'd told me what I wanted to hear. Been who I needed him to be. He had gotten exactly what he wanted, and I was taking the fall. No statement I made would exonerate me from my own blind, hopeful stupidity.

Iso Iso laid out all the reasons I should share my side of events.

I said nothing.

He wheedled, cajoled, threatened, and pleaded.

I said nothing.

After an hour of my silence, he left me alone.

I spit out my makeshift key, unlocked myself, relocked the handcuffs around the table leg and the arm of the chair, and laid down under the table to take a nap, since I'd been up all last night, and most of the night before.

Being arrested made me passive aggressive, and handcuffs always made me itchy.

I dreamed I was sitting on the sofa in the living room of in our house in Georgia, staring at a blank TV screen. In that weird dream logic, I was somehow both thirteen, and twenty-eight. I wore a leather Ducati motorcycle jacket, soaked entirely through with rain. Blood from a bullet wound in my shoulder oozed out onto the leather. There was another wound in my thigh, and arterial blood had colored the gold fabric of the sofa a wine red. I felt the icy lassitude of impending death.

Papa sat beside me, simultaneously the young, virile superman I remembered from Glynco, and the older, grizzled one from my stasis dreams. He wore a faded Navy blue T-shirt with a twisted triangle shaped logo I didn't recognize, also soaked with blood. His right eye had a gauze patch over it, with a gauze headband keeping it in place. His single good eye focused intently on the blank TV screen, as if he was watching the final, heated lap of a Grand Prix. Instead of the usual Georgia pines, the windows outside looked out onto eerie, disjointed images of blood and death that left me strangely unmoved. People I didn't know, doing violent things to corrupt monsters who clearly deserved some sort of punishment.

Papa took a long swig of his beer, then sighed. "You're in it now, Radiana."

"In what?"

He put his hand over mine and squeezed. "I did my best to prepare you."

I felt the warm, calloused strength of his grip. Tender. Comforting. And then his index finger swiped out a message in Morse code across my knuckles: *Don't ever come looking for me again.*

I swiveled my head to regard him with alarm, signaling back: *Why not?*

He pointed the remote at the TV and switched it on. The image transported me to a place that took my breath away, but before I could make sense of it, the metal chair screeched on the concrete floor beside my head and I started awake.

"No!" I groaned, trying to scrape together the gossamer threads of that last image before they drifted beyond memory, but it was no use. I looked down at my hand. I could still feel the lingering warmth of his touch. "No..."

"Care to join us?" Rossi asked, motioning me out from under the table.

I turned away from her and cheeked the key that still rested in my palm. Reluctant, I crawled out, steeling myself for her to put the cuffs on me again. Instead, she helped me to my feet and walked me to the door. The dream had left me with a deep sense of foreboding, as well as a perverse sense of hope:

Nobody rides motorcycles in prison.

Rossi escorted me down the hall, and into a well-used conference room with décor that was equal parts Antique Cinderblock and Bureaucracy Modern. Jana sat at the far end of an oblong conference table of fake cherry wood. A flat screen on the wall behind her showed an a security feed image of me on the stairs with the two thugs, who were frozen post genital impalement, but pre-curb stomp.

Iso Iso sat to Jana's left, next to an open chair. Opposite him sat Tony and Mando. They were in mid-discussion, but paused when we entered. Rossi pointed me to the empty chair at the end of the table opposite Jana, and took her own seat beside the Samoan. Rossi pointed at Jana. "Your lawyer is now present."

Iso Iso turned back to Tony and Mando, motioning to the image on the screen. "You really want me to believe you did not instruct Ms. Damiano to attack those men?"

Tony nodded. "Never said a word to her about any such thing."

"I tried to get her captured by the exterior security teams. But that didn't work, so we sent Jana to escort her to the car and get her off site," Mando added.

"Is this true?" Rossi asked me.

My lip curled in disdain at how they'd duped me, but I nodded.

"You were given an opportunity to flee the situation, but you chose not to?"

I nodded again.

"Why?"

I looked at Jana, not sure if I should answer that. She pursed her lips, but dipped her head affirmatively. I glanced back at Rossi. "Because I thought Tony was in mortal danger, and I didn't want to abandon him to face Scotty and Leigh alone."

"So you chose to stick around and ambush them?"

"No, I chose to stick around and complete the mission."

"What mission was that?"

"To trick Scott Foster and Brighton Leigh into stealing part of Tony's fortune, so that a program could be planted that would back trace through their digital financial transactions and report back on where and how their money was moving globally, regardless if it was fiat or cryptocurrency."

"Report back to who?"

"You. The marshals. You said you wanted to find out who Leigh was cozy with. What better way to figure out who helped him escape than to follow the money?"

"So, you had no intention of killing either of them?"

"I never had any intention of killing anybody."

"Then why were they dead before we could arrest them?"

"I feared for my life. For Tony's life. Scotty had struck me several times earlier in the day, and threatened to rape me. Leigh threatened worse. And those guys," I pointed at the thugs on the stairs. "Were chasing after me with guns drawn."

Iso Iso waved a hand at the image on the screen, then turned to Tony. "If you haven't trained and briefed her on these tactics and on the men you've been targeting and eliminating for the past three years, how do you explain a hundred-and-thirty pound woman taking out two armed men twice her size?"

Tony shrugged. "Can I help it if she's an idiot savant at this shit?"

"I know, right?" Mando chimed in. "Freakin' Spec Op Rain Man."

I swept them both with a glower scathing enough to rival a flame thrower.

The marshals exchanged glances. They'd seen me dispatch Scotty and Brighton Leigh with their own eyes. Plus, I'd escaped their protective custody within the first two hours.

"She is the Demon's daughter," Rossi sighed, using the nickname Papa had earned while with the TURTLs. She turned to me. "I told you if Leigh wound up dead, you'd be going to jail."

"You did," I agreed.

"But you didn't consider that worthy advice."

"You didn't consider my history of ignoring worthy advice with astonishing frequency."

Iso Iso looked at Rossi. She sniffed, drumming her fingers on the table top with a sour look. I listened. It wasn't Morse. It was simple, focused frustration.

"Do you really want this going to trial?" Jana interjected. "I mean, look at how that will play in the media: Gold Star daughter of a decorated Navy man gets kidnapped and tortured by the most notorious human traffickers since the Triangle Trade. Now, the U.S. Government wants to charge her with murder because she fought for her life in self-defense."

"Neither Leigh nor Foster were sanctioned. Nor were any of the others she killed."

"If she'd been on the payroll when those deaths occurred, then you'd have a case for an internal investigation and reprimand. But Gomez and Maitlin died before she ever signed on. And you yourself dissolved that contract before Leigh and the others died, since she claimed it was signed under duress."

"She fled custody," Rossi pointed out. As if that made a difference somehow. "To rejoin you." She shot a meaningful glance at Tony. "Why was that?"

He shrugged. "Ask her."

Rossi turned her gaze on me. "Why did you return to Tovenaar, if you believed the contract null and void?"

I looked at Jana, realizing it was a bad idea to tell the marshals my opinion on how stupid their plan had been. She considered the question, then nodded slowly.

I quirked my mouth to the side. I didn't want to lie, but the other side of the truth (that I had really really liked shagging Tony) was going to get Jana mad at me. Who was it better to piss off? My lawyer, or the folks arresting me? It was a conundrum.

Surprisingly, Jana came to my rescue: "Trying to charge her with any of this is a waste of time and taxpayer money. How can you possibly get a jury past reasonable doubt? Several witnesses will testify Damiano had a severe gunshot wound, one that would make it impossible for her to perform the actions you're accusing her of a mere month and a half later. Your video evidence shows Faith Hopkins, but you can't prove she was impersonating Faith, since those procedures are still Top Secret. With her implant removed, she'll revert to Damiano by the time this goes to trial."

In that moment, I actually almost understood why Tony kept her around.

Rossi's sour look intensified into one of bitterness, then mellowed into resignation. She pushed away from the table, standing up. The sag to her shoulders conceded defeat, but the look she gave Tony was one of grudging respect. "Take her home. We're done here."

***

"Two hundred and fifty thousand," I insisted, following Jana as she walked through the mansion towards her bedroom. Mando flanked me, his body language loose and relaxed, cheeks tense, eyes moving constantly, as if he expected I'd grow violent at any moment.

Smart man.

It had not amused Jana that I'd demanded payment for services rendered the moment she, Mando and I had stepped into the foyer. It had amused me even less when she told me that since the contract had been cancelled at the marshals behest, I was due absolutely nothing.

She shook her head. "Not a dime. You declared the contract null and void. As a matter of fact, you owe us about eight-hundred, seventy-eight thousand."

"For what?!"

"The medical bills to repair your hand. "

"But you were the assholes who shot me!"

She shrugged, stopping to open a door. I caught a glimpse into an ordered, opulent suite as she stepped inside. "So, we're even."

"What about my car?"

"You'll have to ask Tony about that," she said, knowing full well that Tony had remained in Lompoc with the marshals, to brief them on the backtrace into Scotty and Leigh's accounts.

"He's not here."

"Not my problem." She gave me a cool, measured smile that only served to highlight the gloat in her eyes, then shut the door in my face.

I growled at the door. At her. At Mando standing beside me. He seemed so harmless now, his face smooth and peaceful, his shoulders deflated by fatigue. He sighed. Opened his mouth to speak. Closed it again, glancing down at my feet.

"What do you want?" I snapped at him.

"Don't go," he said without looking up.

It was almost too much for me. "What, are you stupid? You think I'll stick around after what you and Tony put me through?"

"Tony didn't set you up. I did. You derailed the whole plan by not boarding that plane to Vegas."

"You thought I was a coward? That I was gonna run?"

"No. We thought you were a pragmatist. We had it set up for Scotty to snatch you in Vegas. From there, he would use you to leverage Tony into passing Brighton's prints. But, then you faked us all out, and figured out that whole data engine thing. And then you snitched Scotty out to Hollis. Scotty's arrest would have put Brighton in the wind and screwed everything up. Between that, and Hollis electrocuting Tony, we would have lost our only chance to end this. I had to do something to pick up the pieces, so that Scotty would continue to believe I was moling Tony."

He sounded so sincere I almost believed him. Then I remembered who I was dealing with and the rage surged up, hot and molten. "You let me think I'd gotten Jim killed."

"You're too green. No field training. No deep cover experience. And you're such a smart ass when you get cocky. Keeping you blind was the safest thing to do. I've spent the past two years gaining Scotty's confidence. I've been wearing a wire for him every time I came to work. I had to play the bad guy. It wasn't Tony's fault."

I turned my back on him and stormed down the hall toward the elevator. Hell, I'd hotwire my damn car to get out of here.

"Rad," he called after me. "Rad, wait. I understand you hating me. I totally get that. But don't blame Tony for this. He didn't know about it until it was too late to go back."

"Like Hell," I said, thinking about the *kris* and the keyboard and the sob story about Tony's son. As I stabbed the elevator button, I heard Mando come up behind me.

"Your implant is gone." His voice was soft, apologetic. "Aside from the stairs and corridors, you can't go anywhere unescorted."

I snatched one of the bronze sculptures from its niche opposite the elevator doors and headed for the stairs. "You don't know me very well." I ran down the stairs to the door to the garage and smashed the casing off the lock.

Mando followed and watched me try to jimmy the door open. He seemed intent, apprehensive, like I was a shark he was studying through a weakened observation cage.

"It would be better," he said after a while, "if you just waited for Tony to get here."

I ignored him, not wanting to admit defeat.

"You can't go back, you know. You're not the same person you were before."

I swallowed hard, wondering if he knew how true those words really were. Would those weird stasis dreams plague me forever or would they taper off, so long as I avoided Tony? "I'll dye my hair. Wear contacts until my eyes turn brown in a couple weeks."

"That's not what I mean."

The way he said it made me look at him. Our gazes locked: mine smoldering, his sorrowful. Something inside him seemed to crumble. "All right," he sighed and began to climb the stairs. "I won't stop you. Do what you want to do."

"If I did that," I hollered after him, "you'd all be dead."

He said something just before the upstairs door latched shut. It echoed down, lingering in the stuffy, suffocating air of the stairwell: "*Cape Sors Tuum.*"

***

After a few hours of sweating in the air-conditionless stairwell, I finally got past the lock and into the cavernous, climate controlled garage. I stalked by the Lamborghini four-by-four with the gold-plated cheetah hood-ornament and the 1973 twelve-cylinder Jaguar E-type, and stood rooted to the empty spot where my 2008 two-door Mazda coupe had been.

My car. Son-of-a-bitch. They'd taken my car.

It stunned me. I had seen it. Right here. I had hugged Tony because I knew it was here, safe and sound. Now, it was gone. Everything I owned, everything that made me Rad, *poof!*

I leaned against the fender of the Jag and slid slowly to the ground, unable to stand any more. For the first time in this whole sordid mess, I thought I was going to cry.

It was unreasonable, I knew, to expect anything to last. Delusional to expect even the slightest amount of stability from life. But once, just once, I'd like to hang onto something with meaning, some little bubble of warmth and comfort that made the brutal reality of life recede for a while. They were the only ones who ever really loved me. Was it too much to ask?

"Rad?" Tony's voice filtered through the silence.

I drew in several deep, long breaths, fighting to keep myself under control. Whether I fell to rage, or loss, he'd find a way to use it against me. That was who he was. What he was.

Tony's footfalls approached, accompanied by the clicking of dog claws on the concrete.

He'd brought Zef. I covered my face with my hands and drew my knees up to make myself smaller, trying to convince myself I didn't care, any more.

Tony's clothes rustled nearby. "Rad? You okay?"

The hot steam of dog breath puffed against my ear, followed by a cold, wet nose pressed against my cheek. I shoved the dog away and glanced up at Tony. His hair was wet, and he'd changed into shorts, a Panama shirt, and sandals. He smelled clean, with a lingering hint of lavender and hyacinth.

I sighed and rose slowly to my feet. "What did you do to my car, Tony?"

"Nothing."

"Making it disappear into thin air is nothing?"

"I sent it out to get upgraded, that's all." He shrugged. "Bulletproofed, new suspension package, new paint. Pump up the engine. Run-flat tires. You wanted to keep that piece of shit. I couldn't let you drive around unprotected." He smiled and reached into his pocket. "Not when you're wearing this." He produced a ring, an emerald-cut diamond flanked by two teardrops of black opal. "We can announce the engagement at the Trubys' party tonight."

He was as delusional as I was.

"You're married," I reminded him.

"Not for much longer. Besides, it's you I want."

I knocked the ring out of his hand and sent it tumbling across the floor. "I am not marrying you. I am *never* marrying you. I want my stuff. I want my car. And I never want to lay eyes on you ever again."

Zef trotted off to retrieve the velvet case, setting it in Tony's palm with only a slight coating of slobber. Tony turned it over in his hands, regarding it. His face slowly registered pain, like a toddler touching a hot stove for the first time. "What are you so angry about?"

"You lied to me."

"Never. I never lied to you."

"Really? What about my car? You promised me I'd get it—"

"You will, once it's finished. I just—"

"—with everything I'd left inside. *Everything*, you swindling sonuvabitch!"

"It's only stuff. What we have between us is—"

"Nothing! There is nothing between us!"

"Then why did you stab Brighton with Stefan's *kris*? If you don't care about me, then why did you help me avenge my son?"

"Because I thought it was real! But it's not. It was all one big set up. One giant misdirection after the other. You don't care about me. If you did, you never would have let me believe Jim was gonna be killed!"

"You knew there'd be things I can't tell you. I warned that you'd get hurt. You said you didn't care. You wanted it."

"I wanted to get Brighton Leigh and Scotty. There wasn't anything in there about me getting kidnapped by my own bodyguard."

"It was the only way Mando could get us close enough to use the *kris*."

"The only way you could manipulate me into committing murder, you mean."

His hands twitched, palms upward in a gesture of supplication. "I was living in a world full of ghosts. I had to free him. End his song, so he could rest. So I could rest," his voice became husky, tears welling up in his eyes. "How else could I make room for you?"

I almost fell for it. Almost got sucked in by his wounded sincerity, his crocodile tears. Even now, that weird energy was pulsing between us, pulling on me like gravity.

Damn stasis imprinting.

I tore my gaze away from his and shook my head, running my hand through my stupid, short, Irish hair. "I. Want. My. Stuff."

He stood there for several seconds, then sighed and walked across the garage to a series of cabinets. He pulled the handle, and it clicked open the way the automatic locks did. He pulled out a cardboard box the size of a bread loaf, and brought it over to me. His body language was tense, his brow furrowed. He couldn't meet my gaze.

The box was far too small to hold all the stuff I'd kept in that car, and for one horrible moment, I thought he was handing me a box of ashes. But then, I took it and looked, and saw the stuffed baby grand Chris had given me, and the ancient portable DVD player, with the CD from Papa still inside.

That was it. That was all.

I held the box to my chest, stunned with relief that at least that much had survived. Some part of my brain was processing how much was missing, but that hadn't hit me, yet. I had this much. This little bit. Tony might not have loved me, but Chris and Papa did.

He cleared his throat, his rich baritone muted with guilt. "We had already staged the crime scene before I made the agreement with you. Some of your clothing was destroyed in the fire. The other items were scattered around the shell of the car, to make it appear Damiano's murderer had been searching for something."

"You trashed it all?"

"No. It was part of the crime scene. Collected by the LAPD as evidence."

"All my stuff is in an evidence locker somewhere?"

"It was. But the marshals knew you hadn't been murdered. Or kidnapped. They reached out to the FBI, and they made Hollis drop your murder case against me. It wasn't reopened until your stunt with Scotty."

"So, where is it now?"

His lips pressed into a thin line. He swallowed hard, his hand reaching down to touch Zef's head again. "I didn't know," he pleaded with me. "Not until you came to the house. By then, it was too late."

"Didn't know what, Tony?"

"Who gave you those scars on your back."

I scowled. "What does that have to do with my stuff?"

"They sent it to your next of kin."

That marble pachinkoed down from peg to peg, until I realized that, while I considered my Aunt Rosa my next of kin, that's not the person the authorities would have chosen:

"My mother? It all went to my mother?!" A cascade of explosions poured through me. The rage built and built, until my vision dimmed, and all I could hear was a low, humming whine.

I had a vague sense of the world around me. I knew that I had dropped the box. That my hands were now fists, my limbs were trembling, and that my legs stalked towards Tony of their own accord. I knew, in a very detached, analytical way, that I had lost control of that dark, consuming fireball I'd spent my entire adult life trying to contain.

"Rad." He kept me at arm's length. "Calm down."

His touch unhinged me completely. I became all fluid motion and deadly intent. My left fist hit his jaw and knocked him against the cupboards. My right foot snap-kicked into his gut. He oofed, and blocked my next blow, and my next, and then suddenly we were dancing through a lethal strike-parry-strike series of katas.

"Relax! Relax!" he urged me. "Calm down!"

My attacks were furious and unremitting. His blocks and parries were designed to maneuver me into a hold, but his right side was too weak to keep this up for long, and he fell onto the Jaguar E-type, covering his head with his left arm as I moved in to strike again.

Zef snarled and lunged, jaws closing on the splint. The dog's momentum swung me partway around, and Tony's leg shot out to trip me up. I fell atop them both, continuing to pummel and kick whatever was closest.

There was a sssnap! and Zef gave a loud, squealing howl. I twisted, trying to get out of the tangle of me and dog and Tony, but his forearm slammed my head into the side of the Jag and knocked a few grains of sense into me.

I paused. This was not how I had wanted any of this to go. He seized his chance and knocked me on my butt, flinging his body atop mine. He whipped a gun out and held it to my temple.

"Stop! You move," he panted above the pitiful sound of Zef's yelping, "and you're dead."

I thought about moving. Decided against it when Kam and Mando spilled into the room, pistols in hand.

"Hey, Boss," Kam called out, when they'd assessed the fact that Tony had me under control. "You okay?"

"Fine," Tony said. "Just fuckin' fine." He staggered off of me, blood pouring from a welt over his eyebrow. At least I hadn't broken his nose again.

Kam and Mando flanked me. I held my hands up, feeling sick to my bones about what had just happened.

"Crap," I whispered between panting breaths. I put my hands over my head and went fetal, watching them through the triangle of my forearms.

Tony moved over to poor Zef, mumbling words in a soothing tone to quiet the animal. "I think Zef's hip is broken. Get the vet up here."

"Right." Kam holstered his gun, whipped his phone out, and tapped the screen.

"What happened?" Mando moved over to Tony, handing him a garage rag for the blood.

"That," Tony tipped his chin at me, lip curled with such disdain, I knew there could be no forgiveness. No redemption. "Get her out. Get her gone. If I ever see her ass again, I'll kick it so hard, they'll feel it in Siberia."

Before I could grab my stuff, they bustled me into the stairwell, the door slamming behind us with the terminal clang of a prison gate. Even two flights of stairs and four inches of steel couldn't muffle Zef's howls.

***

"Here." My voice sounded too loud after a hundred-and-fifty miles of silence. "Just drop me off here." I gestured toward the Tampa off-ramp. "I'll be all right."

Mando sighed, deep in thought. "You've got to stay out of sight, you know." He gestured toward the little gear bag on the seat beside the Louis Vuitton roll away packed with the clothes I had bought on the palladium card. "Use the dye. Get those contacts in ASAP. And stay away from cops. It'll take a week or two to clear your prints."

"Why doesn't Tony use his terminal?"

"That was an elaborate ruse. Bait to lure Brighton in. We've got to go through the marshals to clear you. Just like we did to make you into Faith."

"Everything you people do is a lie."

"Faith is still a target. That's why we were going to keep you at the estate."

"I can handle myself."

He didn't reply, just peeked over his shoulder and changed lanes. "I'll talk to Tony. He'll listen, after he cools down a bit. He'll take you back."

I snickered without meaning to. "He won't. Not even if I wanted him to, which I don't."

The sedan glided down the ramp and stopped at the light. I reached for the door handle.

"Wait. I'll buy you breakfast."

"It's mid-afternoon."

"So, I'll buy you lunch. Be nice to get a steak under my belt before going back up. And I don't like to eat alone."

"Whatever. Might as well start this homeless thing out on a full stomach."

"Homeless?" He frowned, puzzled, and then the light went on. "That's right. Jana didn't give you any money."

"Nope."

"That conniving bitch," he muttered under his breath.

He made a right, headed for Ventura Boulevard, made another right, and parked in the lot of the coffee shop across the alley from Jim's house. After a moment, I realized the beige sports car was still parked down the alley, the dark-haired Nelson sitting patiently behind the wheel. Sebastian, too, was in position.

"You bastard." I pointed to the cars. "What are they doing here?"

"They work for Tony."

"And Monica, the hit-woman from Hell?"

He shook his head, sheepishness pulling the corners of his mouth. "Her real name is Ruby. She's my housekeeper." He shifted, guilty. "I had to make it look real. Scotty had me—"

"Yeah. Wired." I sighed, disgust flaring up like a bad case of heartburn.

At my expression, his twisted into a guilty look. "Nelson and Sebastian are protecting your friend until this dust up dies down."

Dust up. My killing Brighton Leigh and Scott Foster was a 'dust up.' Everything that had happened to me since that night at the Concerto was a 'dust up.' Papa might still be alive. Tony had stabbed him in the eye. Mando knew about it, and about lots of other things that could help me put Papa to rest, or save him if he was trapped somewhere, but this had all been a 'dust up,' so I didn't need to know.

I wondered if I could ever become jaded enough to treat these types of things so cavalierly. To treat someone's heart like it was a dossier. Decided I was glad things had turned out this way, so Tony couldn't turn me into someone like Mando.

I reached for the door. All I wanted was to get as far away as I could from all this cloak-and-dagger shit. "Hollis was right. Tony's an oily, two-faced son-of-a—"

"Tony's Tony, that's all. He's been through a lot, but he keeps fighting. If you knew how much he's sacrificed to keep the scum from rising to the top, you'd understand."

"Don't tell me he's Mr. Clean, because it still comes down to you guys using me as a murder weapon."

"You could have left with Jana," he pointed out. "You could have disabled them. You didn't have to stab Brighton. Or sever Scotty's jugular."

"I was fighting for my life. Unlike you all, I didn't know the marshals were on their way. That Jana had gone to get them."

Mando closed his eyes and touched his forehead to the top of the steering wheel. Air escaped him in a long sigh. When he looked up, his expression was contrite, beseeching. "I'm sorry. Truly sorry. But don't blame Tony. He never wanted to put you at risk."

"Right." I opened the door, suddenly itching to get away from him. "Thanks for the ride. It was better than a stateside leave."

"Rad, wait." He caught my elbow as I stepped out onto the hot pavement. "Wait." He reached into his pocket, withdrew a billfold, and offered me a wad of hundreds. "I know that's not enough, but it'll keep you off the streets for a while. And here." He handed me the fob for the Escalade. "It's still at the lot in Van Nuys. Keep it until your Mazda is ready."

My first impulse was to scorn his dirty money, but the pragmatist in me won out. I refused to play the prodigal with Jim, and sleeping on the streets wearing clothes that cost thousands of dollars was just asking for trouble. I tucked the bills and key fob away in my pocket, while he got out and opened the back door to grab the gear bag and rollaway. He brought them around the car to me. I took hold of them, and his black eyes searched mine.

"I'd die for him," he said softly.

"Tony?"

He nodded. "I was going to stab Brighton with that *kris*. Before you went all John Wick on everybody."

"Why? You have a family. You knew they'd arrest you for murder if Brighton died."

"Tony's my best friend. And you're the first woman he's taken to his bedroom since Ilsa left."

"Oh, like he hasn't slept with anybody for three years?"

"Not his bed. His *bedroom*. His sanctuary."

"What about Jana? I'm sure she's—"

"Jana wanted to be. You...are."

I froze, wanting to disbelieve him, but knowing it had been too plainly stated to be a lie:

It hadn't been an act. Tony did love me, after all.

Without a word, I turned and walked toward the coffee shop. Halfway across the lot, I heard the Beemer start up, and saw it slink around the restaurant. Mando pulled out onto the Boulevard, heading for the freeway. As I watched his car disappear up the on-ramp, an epic dread sank its icy teeth into my bones.

I'd done it again. Shredded the parachute and gone back to free-fall.

All because I couldn't grasp one four-letter word.

CHAPTER THIRTY-ONE

Once inside the coffee shop, I locked myself in the bathroom and unzipped the gear bag, surprised to find the DVD player and the baby grand inside, along with the note from Jim I'd hidden in the control panel of the toilet.

I was pretty sure that Tony had been busy with Zef, and Jana would never think to bother, so this was yet another kindness, another apology by Mando. I didn't know how to feel about it, so I tucked them away in the gear bag and grabbed the things I needed to dye my hair brown again.

When I was younger, I had often been recruited to apply color to Mother's hair, especially when she was too drunk to manage on her own. She liked to change things up when she knew Papa was due home. Go from brunette to redhead, or blonde to brunette.

When I was little, I thought that it was because she was trying to primp for him. When I grew older, and more cynical, I realized that she wanted to make it harder for people to identify her as the person who'd been seen with other men while he was away.

This was the first time I had attempted to change my own hair color, but because Faith's was so short, it didn't take too long. After I had the contacts in, I almost looked like me again. The hair color was too light brown, too brassy. The brown contacts were darker than my usual toasted brown, without gold accents. My skin was far too pale, with a light dusting of freckles. But, it was a Hell of a lot better than being Irish.

As I washed the dye off my hands, I realized I still had blood crusted under my fingernails, and in the creases of my elbows. I checked myself all over, then, finding some in my belly button. I located spots here and there where blood had seeped through my clothing. I washed them all off, and put on a new set of clothes, tossing the Faith ones Jana had supplied to me at Lompoc into the trash. When I finished in the bathroom, I went up front and sat in a booth with my luggage. I ordered a burger and some coffee, and thought about what to do now that I was not quite Rad, and not quite Faith. I wasn't sure how I felt about myself, or about what had happened. Or about Tony. Or Mando.

The most messed up thing was that part of me had enjoyed playing Faith. Not the gunshot, or the stasis, of course. But crashing the golf cart in front of the Trubys had been a blast. So had escaping the marshals, sneaking into Scotty's office, and stealing his data engine. Even the financial stuff had been fun. Not just setting the hook for Mando, but getting a private meeting with Gower Dillington. And shagging Tony had been the highlight of my sexual experiences, even with both of us injured. How awesome would it have been with both of us at a hundred percent?

In some ways, I'd been born for that job. That life.

In other ways, the whole thing made my skin crawl. Especially when I thought about that weird sense of dual worlds and the freaky way I had hallucinated my way to Papa. I must have some serious emotional monsters lurking around in my unconscious to come up with all of that crap in the middle of a conversation with Brighton Leigh. Not to mention losing control with Tony. I was still angry with him, even now.

But I also felt guilty. And lost.

I hated feeling any of it. Hated, too, that I felt absolutely no remorse about what I'd done to Brighton Leigh and Scott Foster. I'd disabled both of them. If Jana had shown up with the marshals a few minutes earlier, both of them would still be alive. I should feel terrible about finishing them off. The way I felt terrible about killing Mike, and Fox-face and Doughboy and Broken Jaw. But, after all the misery they had caused to so many innocent people, killing Scotty and Brighton Leigh felt like the right thing to do.

Maybe that's why I'd never seen them in my stasis dreams, other than being chased by that dodo bird. Maybe those luminous threads tying me to those ghosts were about things I regretted.

Regardless of what Mando said about Tony's mental time traveling, or the weird way I'd seen what Tony looked like in the past, I didn't really believe that I had dreamed about things I couldn't know about. I must have seen the young Tony with Papa in the past, probably at Glynco when he was training people. Must have picked up some tidbits of information about Papa's eye, overhead things that my subconscious filed away and put together during the stasis. Seeing Broken Jaw in my dreams was probably just a coincidence, a retrofit of my guilt onto the memory of the faceless ghosts I'd seen in the hospital.

I drank a few more cups of coffee, sorting through my options. The music wasn't quite dead, but after what Vic had said about my hand, I doubted that I would ever recover enough to be a world class pianist. I'd probably be a nomad for a while, and that didn't lend itself to the constant practice, let alone the physical therapy and rehab I'd need to reach that level again. To be brutally honest, I'd only wanted it so badly because I knew it's what Jim had wanted. And it wasn't fair to ask him to wait for me.

After a while, I realized there was nothing here for me. When I got my equilibrium back, I'd settle down in another city. Teach karate or become a limo driver or get a job doing repo work. Anything to forget the keyboards. Anything to forget that bastard Tovenaar.

I got up and left the money for my meal and a tip at the table, grabbed the gear bag and rollaway, and started walking. I needed a ride to the Flyaway, where the Escalade was parked. And I needed to say my goodbyes.

I walked down around the corner and climbed the steps onto Jim's porch. Both his car, and Richie's motorcycle were in the

320

driveway. I sighed at that, and knocked on the door. Not only did Richie ride a Ducati, but he was a genuinely nice guy. Smart. Funny. Like his taste in most things, Jim had good taste in men. But I had wanted to do this without an audience.

As I stood on Jim's porch, I heard the sound of water running in the bathroom through an open window, along with muted classical music. Someone was in the shower. I knocked on the door, and waited. When the water sounds stopped, I knocked again. Loud.

I gave it a few more minutes, shifting my weight from foot to foot as I rehearsed what to say. It all flew out of my head when Richie answered the door. His feet were bare and he had a towel around his waist. Water droplets dotted his pale, wiry torso, and his black hair hung in wet straggles over his eyes. He was about my height, and was the only person I knew of Japanese ancestry who had freckles. He squinted, tilting his head. "Do I know you?"

"Yeah. It's me. Rad. Is Jim here?"

"Holy shit. Rad? You're supposed to be dead." He stepped away from the door and shouted towards the back bedroom: "Jim! You gotta see this! It's Rad! She's alive!" He turned back to me and waved me inside. "Come in, come in. You want a beer?"

"Don't drink."

"Oh yeah, that's right. Wow, you look so different..."

I stepped inside and set my luggage near the door, surprised that things had changed so much since Richie had moved in. The furniture, drapes, rugs and lamps were all done in a whimsical, neon post-modern style. Looked like a unicorn had eaten a cubist's lunchbox and sharted all over the room. There was a new, bigger flat screen on the wall. "So does this place."

"Yeah, yeah," Richie chuckled. "Been a while since you were over. Have a seat."

I would have, but the couch was purple. "I'm good. Not staying long."

"Rad?" Jim stepped into the living room. His hair was wet, and his T-shirt was angled, not quite fitting his shoulders, as if he had put it on in a rush. Before the Concerto, I would have felt jealous and betrayed that he and Richie had just come out of the shower together. I would have acted all petty and passive aggressive, and gotten Jim so annoyed, he would have kicked me out. Now, I was just happy to see them both alive and unharmed.

Jim must have felt the same way, because he rushed up and threw his arms around me. He hugged me the way Chris had done when Mother had finally agreed to let me come back from the foster home. "God, it's good to see you."

I hugged him back, fierce with emotion. So fierce, in fact, that when we finally broke the embrace and he pulled back to put his hands on my shoulders, he took one look at my face and asked: "What's wrong?"

His hands slid down my arm, his long, fine fingers cradling my right hand. He stared at it, gently palpating the knuckles, frowning at the last smudges of the bruise there. Seeing it was all there, and not even very swollen, he studied my face, sensing this was about something that went far deeper. "What happened? Did your friend die? The one at the train station?"

"Can't talk about it." I wondered if Tony and Mando felt the same burning sensation in the backs of their throats when they said those words to their loved ones. I offered Jim a rueful half smile. "Just came to tell you not to worry. Everything's worked out. And to say goodbye."

"You can't do that," Richie interjected. "You've been gone for so long. At least have dinner with us. Where you been? Why did the cops say you were dead?"

"Can't talk about it."

Richie was about to press further, but Jim shot him a stern headshake. "Why don't you go put some clothes on, Rich?"

He sighed, but was intuitive enough to realize the gravity of the situation. He nodded and walked down the hall into the bedroom. Jim watched him go, then turned his soulful Jesus expression on me. "You gonna be okay?"

I shrugged. "Dunno. I need to get out of town, for a while. Could give me a ride over to the Flyaway?"

"Sure." He grabbed his keys and put his sandals on and shouted out to Richie he was heading out for a bit. I grabbed my luggage and followed him to the Dodge. He glanced over at my rollaway, then looked me up and down. "Pretty pricey wardrobe."

"You have no idea."

I threw my things on the back seat, and took shotgun. Jim fired up the Dodge and pulled out of the driveway. He didn't speak again until we were turning off Ventura Boulevard onto Balboa: "So, everything's really okay?"

"You're safe. Scotty Foster's dead." When I said it, I felt a little flame of pride spark up, just like I used to get at the shooting range with Papa. It bothered me. But not all that much.

"He's *what*?!" Jim swerved a bit as he shot me an incredulous look.

I pointed him back at the road. "You'll hear about it in the news. Or not. The important thing is, you're safe. Vic's safe. I'm alive. I have my hand back. I'm calling it a win."

He remained quiet, digesting this.

"How've you been? Get any good gigs?"

He smiled, sad, wistful. "I have a concert tour lined up for the fall. And I got approached to do some movie work. We're in negotiations, right now."

"That's awesome."

"Be more awesome with you."

I sighed. He sighed. We didn't say anything for a while, until he pulled into the drive for the parking lot at the Flyaway. "Are you ever coming back?"

"Dunno. Dunno what I'm gonna do. Just need to...go."

"Where?"

"Dunno. Guess I'll know it when I find it."

He pulled to a stop in the loading zone, and got out of the car to hug me again after I got my luggage out. "Stay in touch. Email me, or something. Okay?"

I nodded, but we both knew I wouldn't do it. I was notoriously bad at that sort of thing. Almost as bad as I was about goodbyes. I pulled a hundred out of my pocket and handed it to him. "Thanks. For everything."

"I don't want your money, Rad."

"I know. Buy something nice for Richie."

He met my gaze, fingers crinkling the bill as a slow smile spread across his face. His eyes warmed with a quiet fire. "All right."

He waved to me as I walked away. For some reason, I thought of Zef wagging his tail.

***

I drove south, until I reached the Mexican border and realized without a valid passport card, I wouldn't be able to leave the country. So I turned east, and drove across the desert into the Arizona night. Somewhere in the high starry nothing of New Mexico, I realized that I was almost to Texas, so when I reached Las Cruces, I turned left and headed north on I-25.

By the time I reached Truth or Consequences, I was too exhausted to continue. I bought an air mattress, a blanket and some pillows at Walmart and slept in the back of the Escalade right there in the parking lot. Mando had given me thirteen hundred dollars, and there was another five thousand in cash that Tony had given me the day he removed the implant, but even all that that wouldn't last long if I stayed at motels.

Besides, without ID, I couldn't check in, anyway.

I slept until the Escalade began roasting under the sun, and then started driving again. I hung a left at Albuquerque, preferring the dry painted desert to the capricious thunderstorms that so often plagued the mountains. The Escalade ate up the miles, hour upon hour of droning solitude as I crisscrossed the vast sculpted landscapes of the West. I didn't have a phone to stream my kind of music, and I didn't dare turn on the radio, because the media had been frothing at the mouth about the double homicide of Scott Foster and Brighton Leigh.

I took cat-naps at the side of the road, sleeping only when I knew I was too exhausted to think. To dream. I didn't want to take the chance of seeing Tony again. Of dreaming about him, and Papa. I didn't want to awaken questions I knew could never be answered. And then, somewhere in the cedar-scented wasteland of western Utah, as I stretched under a deep blanket of stars, I figured it all out:

I had to say goodbye to Chris. I had to bury him. And Papa, too.

So, I headed north, to Seattle. I spent the nights sleeping on Aunt Rosa's couch, and the days parked down the street from my mother's house, trying to work up the courage to knock on the door. I wanted my stuff back.

I knew talking to her was a bad idea. The superstitious part of me worried that I would lose control again, and that the dream I'd had in the hospital would come true. I would snap, and her blood would be all over that house, and I'd go to jail for killing her. But I wanted my stuff back. I wanted to take all of those things with me to the cemetery, and finally put the ghosts to rest. Even if Papa was alive somewhere, he'd made it clear he was dead to me.

So, day after day, week after week, I sat there, behind the wheel of the Escalade, or walking around her neighborhood, waiting for her to leave long enough for me to break in and steal my stuff. Hoping she hadn't tossed it into the trash or donated it to the Salvation Army. But the only places she went were the store and to church. Neither gave me a big enough window to ensure I wouldn't run into her face to face.

Eventually, sitting there alone, staring at the flowerbed where Chris had died, watching the dreary Seattle rain fall on Mother's damned purple irises, it all got to be too much for me.

The next morning, the sun made an appearance. I took it as a sign, and this time, I parked the Escalade across the street and walked up to the porch, intending to knock.

But I couldn't do it.

Quiet pooled in the dew-laden grass, so solemn it frightened me. I had come here to say goodbye, but how do you speak when the language of death is silence?

Without thinking, I sang. A soft song. A mournful one. A song of ending, of loss and loneliness and grief that somehow, some way, also spoke of beginning. Of idealism and commitment and stubborn, blind perseverance. All those things life had tried to kill in me, but Tony had somehow kept alive.

I still saw him, sometimes.

In my dreams. In the flickering hope that worried my beaten psyche like a loyal dog snuffling it's master's face. A hope that should have died by now, four weeks after news of Brighton Leighs's death hit the media outlets.

Sometimes, when the hurt went too deep to block completely, I wondered what Tony thought about me. Wondered if he reached out in the night like I did, only to find an anonymous pillow. Wondered if he slogged through the streets just to be moving, because to stand still would be to realize there was nowhere to go.

Tony knew I'd been staying at Aunt Rosa's place. He had to know. I'd seen the spotters in their nondescript vehicles parked along the street, caught the ghosts at the fast food joints that I patronized for lunch. If Tony intended to forgive me, I'd be back at the Ranch.

The morning sun climbed high on my back as my voice fell flat against the vinyl siding. It was, I knew, an imperfect instrument, cracked and ragged from the carrying so much loss. I hid my inadequacies in the lyrics of Chris' favorite rock song. When the words ran out, I sat down on the steps and stared at the spot where he had bled out into my lap.

I knew. At last, I knew, that I didn't have to say good bye to him at all. I would always carry him with me. Him and Papa, both. The one who was truly dead was my mother. Her heart had stopped beating long ago.

It saddened me more than I expected. Surprised me that I actually grieved for her. For a drunken, selfish, crazy bitch, too screwed in the head to even know if she loved me, or to see that the child I'd been had once loved her.

A car whispered up the street and broke the stillness. I looked up, saw a grey Toyota SUV pull up a few feet short of the Escalade. I scrambled to my feet, embarrassed. Strangers didn't need to see my grief. Hard enough to reveal it to myself.

I hurried toward my car, suddenly more eager to leave this state than I could ever remember. Didn't want to chance seeing my mother again. Now that I'd buried her, there was no reason to stay. Just as I rounded the hood of the Escalade, the SUV's door opened. My back itched, that weird current tickling at me.

I didn't look up, afraid I might be wrong about who that was. Afraid I might be right. I fumbled with the door handle through blurry sight.

"Rad."

No. Not now. Not after all this time. Damn him. *Damn him.*

I slammed the door and glared. "What do you want, Tony? Payback for your dog?"

He quirked a look at me, as if the taunt bewildered him. "Zef's fine. He had re-gen." He turned to survey the house, the garage, the flowerbed. "Why'd you come here?"

"Thought you never wanted to see me again."

He shrugged, walking up to stand beside me. "Changed my mind."

"Why?"

"Thought you didn't like your mother."

"I don't."

"Then why do you keep coming back here?"

"Why did you come, you two-faced bastard?"

He nodded, like I'd just answered a test question correctly. "Good. Closure's good."

He snatched the key fob for the Escalade out of my hand. I growled at him, but it was his vehicle, after all. If he wanted it back, he could report it stolen. Not like I had a registration, or even ID to prove it was mine. He turned away, but instead of walking back to his Toyota, he headed up to the porch and knocked on the door.

I climbed into the Escalade and hid, peering over the window sill to watch. Nothing happened, so he knocked again.

Eventually, Mother opened the door. I watched, hearing the muted voices of their conversation, watching Tony offer her an envelope. After a few more minutes of conversation, she opened the door wide, and he disappeared inside with her.

My imagination ran away with me for a moment as the panicky idea lodged in my brain that he was going to murder her, and there's where the dream had come from, but then the door opened, and he walked outside carrying a large cardboard box, with Mother behind him wishing him well in that high, musical voice she reserved for men she wanted to date.

Tony walked across the street and around the Escalade to the shotgun side. He opened the door, and placed the box with all my stuff on the passenger seat. I stared at it, swallowing hard. My hands began to tremble. I felt tears welling up.

He smiled at me, a twinge of sadness and regret in his eyes. He held the fob for the Escalade out. "A deal is a deal."

I took the fob, in shock. He pulled out an envelope and tossed it in my lap. "There's your new I.D. New driver's license. A new palladium card. I can't cut you a check as an employee, because the marshals will be auditing for that. But you can charge up to two hundred and fifty thousand on that card, and I'll pay off the balance. If you still want your Mazda, you can call Mando and tell him where to ship it. The number's on the envelope."

I gaped at him, unsure what to say. He turned around without a word and walked back towards his Toyota. His head was bowed, his proud shoulders sagging with despair.

He was leaving? Without a fight? Without any strings, or manipulations? Without even saying goodbye? I got out and followed him, not sure what I wanted or expected. "Tony."

He turned, hope tightening his cheeks. We stood for a long moment, each gauging the other, looking for the telltale signs of weakness. Of need.

"Why now?" I asked him finally. "After all this time? My car should have been done weeks ago. Why are you doing this now?"

He took a deep breath. Held it. Let it out in a long, measured sigh. His face was a mask of pride and arrogance, but his voice cracked. "Thought I should wait until the divorce was final."

I stared at his clean, chiseled lines, searching for the lie in his straightforward truth. Found nothing but an echo of my sleepless nights in his pale blue gaze.

And then we were all over each other, hands and lips moving in a symphony of forgiveness.

Some music never dies.

ABOUT THE AUTHOR:

P.E. YoungLibby has traveled the world in the pursuit of compelling, insightful, and entertaining stories. When not crashing weddings in Borneo, motorcycles in British Columbia, parties in the cannabis industry, or computers in South Africa, this former law enforcement officer and award-winning author and screenwriter is crafting fantasy, steampunk, speculative and paranormal romance fiction.

OTHER WORKS BY P.E. YOUNGLIBBY:

Feedback, A short story. On Amazon Kindle now!

UPCOMING BOOKS IN THE DAMIANO SERIES:

FLIPPING COIN (Opus 2)   Due Fall 2019

DISSING HARMONY (Opus 3)   Due Summer 2020

DYING GROUND (Opus 4)   Due Fall 2020

CAGING LIGHTNING (Opus 5) Due Spring 2021

KILLING TIME (Opus 6) Due Winter 2021

SOLO IN B MINOR (Prequel) Due Summer 2019

NOVISODES IN THE MUTE PRINCE SAGA:

JAGLANDOR Due Spring 2019
THE GREAT RAX Due Winter 2019

Available at Amazon soon!

If you enjoyed this book, please give it a good review!

Made in the USA
San Bernardino, CA
18 April 2019